Praise f

Casting ...

"*Casting Off* is a beautiful novel of letting go, healing, and redemption. Setting her story in the west of Ireland, Nicole Dickson draws the reader deeply into the magic of a mystical land. A stunning debut."

    —Susan Wiggs, *New York Times* bestselling author of *Just Breathe*

"A remarkable novel about finding your true home, and of holding on and letting go. With lilting and lyrical language, Dickson immerses the reader into the lives and histories of a cluster of tightly knit families on an island off the coast of Ireland. I could hear the soft Irish voices and taste the salty spray of the ocean as Dickson worked her storytelling magic, creating characters as complex and beautiful as the Irish sweaters at the heart of the story. This was a hard-to-put-down book, and I'm already anticipating the next offering from this wonderful author."   —Karen White, author of *The Lost Hours*

continued . . .

Written by today's freshest new talents and selected by New American Library, NAL Accent novels touch on subjects close to a woman's heart, from friendship to family to finding our place in the world. The Conversation Guides included in each book are intended to enrich the individual reading experience, as well as encourage us to explore these topics together—because books, and life, are meant for sharing.

Visit us online at www.penguin.com.

"*Casting Off* weaves a lyrical, emotional, and sometimes ghostly tale of love and loss, and of finding love again. Determined to escape the past, Rebecca arrives on a tiny island in Ireland with her young daughter to study the lore and tradition of its renowned sweaters. There, the two are gathered into the folds of a small old-world community, where their lives intersect and entwine with the colorful locals, and with mysteries as deep as the blue sea that surrounds them. Nicole R. Dickson never drops a stitch as she reveals ever-deepening twists in this lovely yarn of surrender, forgiveness, and redemption."

—Jennie Shortridge, author of *Love and Biology at the Center of the Universe*

"With a pattern as intricate as the sweaters knit in the novel, Nicole Dickson weaves her words into a powerful story of redeeming love and forgiveness. *Casting Off* grabbed my heart on page one and didn't let go until the last breathtaking sentence."

—Patti Callahan Henry, author of *Driftwood Summer*

Casting Off

NICOLE R. DICKSON

NAL Accent
Published by New American Library,
a division of Penguin Group (USA) Inc.,
375 Hudson Street, New York, New York 10014, USA
Penguin Group (Canada), 90 Eglinton Avenue East, Suite 700, Toronto,
Ontario M4P 2Y3, Canada (a division of Pearson Penguin Canada Inc.)
Penguin Books Ltd., 80 Strand, London WC2R 0RL, England
Penguin Ireland, 25 St. Stephen's Green, Dublin 2,
Ireland (a division of Penguin Books Ltd.)
Penguin Group (Australia), 250 Camberwell Road, Camberwell,
Victoria 3124, Australia (a division of Pearson Australia Group Pty. Ltd.)
Penguin Books India Pvt. Ltd., 11 Community Centre,
Panchsheel Park, New Delhi - 110 017, India
Penguin Group (NZ), 67 Apollo Drive, Rosedale, North Shore 0632,
New Zealand (a division of Pearson New Zealand Ltd.)
Penguin Books (South Africa) (Pty.) Ltd., 24 Sturdee Avenue,
Rosebank, Johannesburg 2196, South Africa

Penguin Books Ltd., Registered Offices:
80 Strand, London WC2R 0RL, England

First published by NAL Accent, an imprint of New American Library,
a division of Penguin Group (USA) Inc.

First Printing, August 2009
5   7   9   10   8   6

 REGISTERED TRADEMARK—MARCA REGISTRADA

LIBRARY OF CONGRESS CATALOGING-IN-PUBLICATION DATA:

Dickson, Nicole R.
Casting off/Nicole R. Dickson.
p. cm.
ISBN 978-0-451-22699-0
1. Americans—Ireland—Fiction. 2. Islands—Ireland—Fiction. 3. Fishers—Ireland—Fiction
4. Knitting—Ireland—Fiction. 5. Ireland—Fiction. I. Title.
PS3604.I328C37 2009
813'.6—dc22   2009014754

Set in Garamond Three with Phyllis Display
Designed by Elke Sigal

Printed in the United States of America

For my mother,
Barbara Jean Claudette Beebe Dickson.
For your art and science
For your love and lessons

Acknowledgments

The fabric of story is only as good as the strengths of the tiny threads from which it is woven. For *Casting Off*, I'd like to acknowledge the work of others that made this novel what it is. So, starting with its inception, the woman at Weaving Works Seattle for helping me remember how to knit, Rebecca Nelson for typing the very first draft of the story from my steno pads, Laurie Collins for sitting hours on the phone as I read it to her and also for introducing me to Erin, who taught me how to keep individual characters in the right voice. I thank Orla Korten for correcting my Irish-English. I thank Suzie, my train partner on the Tacoma–Seattle line of Sounder for the editing help. To Mya Herbst for helping with the Conversation Guide. Thank you Amazon/Penguin Inc./Hewlett-Packard for creating the ABNA Contest. I thank Gulru Hakdiyen-Baykal for my beautiful picture. A special thank-you to my agent, Alexandra Machinist, at the Linda Chester Literary Agency, for finding my story in the top 100. And last but certainly not least, a very humble and warm thank-you to Claire Zion of NAL, editor, who taught me so many things but mostly that a small story needs to stay small. Many threads make a beautiful work.

I also wish to, with reference to *Casting Off*, acknowledge all those who entered the crossroad with me in 1995 and walked the road beyond. Each of these people held me in their own way and helped me on my path to this most wondrous place: Anita Galang, Luz Borromeo, Debra Hager, Dean Gomez, Marilyn Capel, Sandy Ward, Robin Lamb, Maureen French, Leigh Massenburg, Jennifer Walker, Imelda Enos, Marc Gordon, Jill Mondry, Genore Schaaf, Mary and Bob Mitchell, Doris Whitaker, Elaine Legg, Christine Schrader, the women of Monday Night meeting San Mateo, California, and the women of Monday Night meeting, Bellevue, Washington, Sherri, Marcy, Kris, Donna Rae Roundtree, Michelle Ransom, Gabriela Young-Trujillo, Pam Stroud, Charles P. Cavanaugh, Quoc Nguyen, Tiffany Howard-Davis, Susan Coulter, Shana Wiesner, Rick Adams, and Gail Savage. For those at work with whom I rode the ABNA wild ride and they lived to tell the tale—Denise Robinson, Terrie Parrish, Katrina Neely, Mary Hanes (thanks for the tissue), Charlene Goolsby, and Carol McDowell.

I'd like to thank my sisters—Laurel Dickson and Rachel Dickson—for their care and love. For my brother, Andrew Dickson, for helping me see the center of most things and to his wife, my sister-friend, Amy Dickson, for rowing the boat when I just couldn't. Thanks to my nieces Erin and Kate Lydin for their enthusiasm for my work and their father, Ralph Lydin, for general support and DIY around the house when needed. Thanks to my nieces Emily Dickson and Arden Dickson, who keep my eyes at the level of the child and remind me of the wonder I can still find there. And to my daughter, Elspeth Rowan Dickson Bartlett. I wouldn't be who I am without her.

Finally, in writing this book, a very quiet man kept coming into my mind. He held his hand out to me at every major crossroad of my life as I grew into adulthood and I saw him there but didn't really "see" him. He came to my surgery even though when asked "Religious Affiliation" on the hospital paperwork, I checked, "None." He was there at my prewedding counseling and the day I got married. He was there when the marriage blew apart and arrived at the first court hearing. I found him standing, holding my newborn baby in the hospital and later at her baptism. He helped lay my mother to rest. I only recall asking for him twice, but all these moments, he was there. Now I don't know if it was my mother who called him or if he just dropped by. Perhaps it was both. Perhaps that is his nature or maybe the nature of his job, but I cannot remember ever thanking him. And as I stand here, at the most amazing crossroad yet, I half expect him to show up, but so far, he hasn't. So I just want him to know that this time, it is my hand that is out, sharing this place with him and though he is not physically here, I hold him in my heart. A most sincere and warm appreciation and gratitude to Reverend Richard B. Leslie.

Casting Off

CHAPTER 1

Casting On

Casting On. 1. Tying a specific number of stitches onto a needle as the first row of a knitted work. The first stitch is a slipknot and then one of the three following methods may be employed for binding on the balance of the stitches: the English method, the Continental method, or Mrs. Blake's method. The first two require the use of two needles; the third requires one needle and a free hand. 2. A beginning.

—R. Dirane, *A Binding Love*

ebecca stood with her six-year-old daughter at the end of the pier, watching the crowd of tourists who had crossed with them on the ferry from Doolin make their way into town. With backpacks, strollers, and children on the shoulders or in the hand, the tourists laughed excitedly and called out to one another in various languages as they shuffled up the road. One- and two-storied buildings lined the street where the crowd meandered up to the bend. Upon reaching the curve, they disappeared with the road. It was then, after the crowd vanished, that Rebecca glanced up to the church's spire, which peeped over the rooftops before her. Its shiny cross winked at her brightly, reflecting the last of the day's sun. She breathed in the sea-salt air, holding on to this moment—her arrival on the island.

Sixteen years ago Rebecca had first met her best friend, Sharon. From the day they started UC-Berkeley together, Sharon had told her tales and histories of her island home and Rebecca had listened and dreamed of Ireland and of this tiny island off the west coast. There were fishing stories and tales of ancient forts, of families pulling seaweed from the ocean to make soil. Then, from the great slabs of stone of which the island was made, smaller rocks were hewn and stacked one atop another as walls to keep the hard-won dirt from blowing back into the sea when the southern gales howled across the island. In that precious, salty soil grew crops to feed the people and grasses to feed the sheep that provided the wool from which they spun yarn. And it was from that yarn that the famous fisherman sweaters were knitted.

Rebecca was an archaeologist. Sharon's stories of the island sweaters had inspired her to specialize in textiles. When they finished their undergraduate degrees, Sharon left for home and Rebecca headed south to Los Angeles for five more years of school as she worked on her master's and then her doctorate. After achieving both, she began to teach, but always the island called to her; the beautiful sweaters and all the legends about them beckoned her. She wanted to record in pictures and in words the living history of the fisherfolk and their sweaters. As Rebecca saw it, the result would be more than an academic paper; it would be a book with photos and biographies of the women from the island. Three years of developing her proposal finally paid off. After receiving her small grant, Rebecca took the summer off to do the project, and now she stood on Sharon's island.

Lavender light sifted gently through the soft mist. Rebecca sighed, glancing once more up the street with hope. She and her daughter had begun this day in California, flying through connections in New York to Shannon, then on a bus to Doolin, and finally across Galway Bay on a ferry to the island. Having been in transit for twenty-two hours, they were unspeakably tired. Here they finally were, with mounds of luggage but no one to greet them.

"Where is that car?" Rebecca muttered.

"I have to go to the bathroom, Mama," Rowan said, sitting on the big black duffel bag and kicking her feet absently.

"I'm not sure where a bathroom is, sweetie. Can you hold it?" Rebecca replied, dialing Sharon on her cell phone. Sharon had arranged for Rebecca to spend the summer in a cottage that belonged to the parents of one of her best childhood friends.

Near the end of a difficult pregnancy, Sharon had had to stay home in Dublin rather than come to the island herself to greet Rebecca. She had, however, promised to send someone to pick Rebecca and Rowan up.

A voice answered on the crackling line. "Hello?"

"Sharon? Sharon, can you hear me?"

"Becky? Is that you?"

"Sharon, we've arrived and there's no car."

"No car?"

"No, no car."

"Huh. Wonder what happened to him. Why don't you go down to the pub—"

"Go to the pub? Sharon, I'm going to start crying. I've been in transit for twenty-two hours. I'm standing on an empty pier, with a six-year-old child who has to go potty. I've got a large duffel, five suitcases, two backpacks, a laptop, and a tripod. How am I supposed to go to the pub?"

"Now, let's not have one of your moments, Becky."

"I'm not having a moment. I—"

"Mama, I gotta go."

"Just a minute, Rowan."

"Go to the pub, Becky."

"What do I do with all my baggage?"

"Mama!"

"Leave it there," Sharon said.

"What?" Rebecca yelled.

"It's an island, Becky."

"I know it's an island, Sharon. What if someone takes my stuff? Then where will I be?"

"No one's gonna take your stuff. Where would they go? It's an island," Sharon repeated.

Rebecca froze, gritting her teeth as air hissed through them.

"Go to the pub and ask Tom for the keys to the house. He'll probably have the car, too."

"Who's Tom?" Rebecca asked in exasperation.

"Tom, Tom. You know Tom. He's the one I told you about who owns the pub."

"Right."

"Becky?"

"What?"

"It'll all be fine—"

"Okay, okay. I know. Thanks," Rebecca said and hung up.

Though it was a dream for Rebecca to come to the island and study the textile art of its people, she still faced the coming months with trepidation. She knew this summer would lead to a book that would bolster her professional résumé and allow her to be more selective when choosing her teaching opportunities. That was why she had come to the island. That was what she had told herself anyway.

But truly she had a deeper motivation—a certain dark crevice—a wound inflicted six years before. From that blackness—the tragedy of her relationship with Rowan's father, Dennis—she had run, driven from place to place, devoid of any contentment or peace she might have built. Though she had never married him, Rebecca had spent the two years before Rowan's birth endeavoring to free herself from his hold on her. She finally succeeded when Rowan was just a month old.

But the abrupt end of their relationship had left Rebecca bound to him in a different way—with memories that haunted her and left her feeling as unsteady as she'd been when she lived with him. In some ways, she felt even more frightened than she'd been before leaving him. The end of that relationship had left her with a restless nervousness that kept her running, moving constantly, from one promising university appointment to another. With each move, Rebecca told herself the opportunity for professional growth was better in her new position. But it wasn't truly her career that drove her. It was fear.

Six years trapped in that odd prison of freedom and flight and insecurity wore away at Rebecca until Christmas Day last. On that day, Rowan had wept when her mother told her about yet another move, crying at the thought of leaving another very-best-friend. Rowan was finally old enough to show Rebecca what their nomadic life was doing to her. Rebecca had quieted long enough to hear her child's tears fall hollowly into the her wounded heart. And she knew she had to find a way to stop. To make it stop. To hold still.

The news of the grant had followed soon after, and Rebecca realized the moment had come to make her dream come true. To stop running from her demons and face them. Sharon's stories told of a place of rock and sea and a people who held on to one another—where no one was blowing away on the wind like Rebecca had done these six years. As an only child whose parents were ten years dead, Rebecca had no one holding on to her but Sharon. Rowan needed the security of a home, but Rebecca had no idea how to make one. Thus, she made her way to the only place she knew home to be—Sharon's island home.

The ferry's engine engaged, startling Rebecca.

"Is the car coming, Mama? I have to go really bad."

"No, Rowan, the car will not be coming. But it'll be fine." Rebecca mimicked Sharon's accent.

"You sounded just like Sharon," Rowan said with a giggle.

"Come on." Rebecca grinned, offering her hand to her little girl. "We need to find Tom."

"Tom? The pub owner?" Rowan asked, reaching for her mother's hand. Gently, Rowan's small palm enveloped Rebecca's first finger.

"How do you know Tom?"

"Sharon told me about him."

Rowan's hair was disheveled and the straps of her overalls were twisted and crossed in the back. Though the shadows grew longer around the two of them, Rebecca knew the deep circles beneath her daughter's eyes had nothing to do with the failing light, for Rowan was slowly rubbing the edge of her mother's finger with her thumb like she always did when she was worried. Rebecca remembered that when she was a child herself, she'd found the same security in the satin binding of her favorite blanket. For Rowan, that comfort came from Rebecca's hands. The thought made her smile.

"I was just thinking, Rowan, how lucky I am to be your blanket."

"What's that mean, Mama?"

Rebecca glanced back over her shoulder at her baggage sitting on the end of the dock. "That I will always keep you warm and safe," she whispered.

Like the tourists, Rebecca and Rowan made their way up the road. As the street curved, dappled light from the stained-glass side windows of the church brushed color onto the sidewalk on the left. Across the street, houses one and two stories high were painted brightly as if to reflect back on the worn brown stone of the church the light from its windows. Here and there, a house was painted white, yet still the door was red or blue or green or yellow, cheerfully greeting all who came up the road from the pier.

The street on which Rebecca and Rowan walked was intersected on the left by another road. They stopped at the corner, shivering in a breeze that blew through the intersection and was cold even though it was mid-June. Kitty-corner from where they stood Rebecca spied the sign for O'Flaherty's Pub.

Before she stepped off the sidewalk, three cyclists sped past the pub, racing around the corner in front of her. They slowed down and came to a stop in front of a line of parked bicycles on the opposite side of the street, where, apparently, there was a shop that rented bikes to tourists. Gazing farther up the road, Rebecca saw the church's front steps. The dusk had deepened to purple, darkening the mist that softened the village. The road continued ahead, veering around a corner to the right.

Unless she was mistaken, that road would lead a mile and a half north out of town to the cottage she was renting and to the island's small fort. The larger fort would be to the south, its ancient walls worn away by sand and wind and gale. Between these two legendary points were three miles of land and rock, north to south. East to west, the island was two miles wide, and most of its one hundred year-round inhabitants lived close to the water on its circumference.

With the road now clear of cyclists, Rebecca took Rowan by the hand and trotted diagonally across the intersection, heading for the pub. She stopped and looked at the brown door of the place, noting the chipped paint and scratches from use and weather. Gazing through the window, she saw the pub was full—packed, actually. A young man with black hair, brown eyes, and a white island sweater leaned against the window at the far right, holding his pint to his chest. Rebecca peered at the patterns of his sweater and then up at his face. Startled, she found that he was looking at her with great interest. He smiled broadly. Rebecca frowned.

"I'm cold, Mama. And I still have to go," Rowan said, her teeth chattering.

"Don't let go of my hand, Rowan. It's very busy in there and I don't want to lose you."

"Okay."

Grasping the brass handle, Rebecca opened the door and shimmied inside. Around the fireplace to her left, people sat at a smattering of tables, eating, while a guitar player in the corner plucked out a tune that sounded very much like horses' hooves. She squeezed past a German couple who were drinking gin and tonics and bumped into an American woman with a Southern accent who was talking to a group of young Spanish men. Slipping around them, Rebecca pulled Rowan in front of her and moved next to a man in a deep blue sweater who was leaning on the bar. He smiled at her, his blue eyes sparkling beneath the pub's dim light.

The bartender glanced over as he topped off a foamy pint of ale.

Rebecca looked at his red hair, then was distracted by his green eyes. She had never seen eyes as bright green as his. They were the color of the new-growth jasmine in the backyard of her childhood home. With that thought, a wave of homesickness rolled through her.

"You all right there?"

"Uh—yes, thank you."

"What can I get you?"

"I'm looking for a key."

"To my heart?" He grinned as he slid the pint to the man in the blue sweater. Feeling the blood rush to her cheeks, Rebecca scowled, glancing away from his eyes and down to Rowan.

"No. To a house. Sharon—"

"Becky?" The bartender smiled wider.

Rebecca blinked.

"Are you Becky? Sharon's friend from the States?" the man in the blue sweater asked.

"Yes," she murmured. "Do—do I know you?"

"Maggie!" the bartender called over his shoulder. "Becky's here! Where's Rowan?"

"Becks?" There, hiding at the end of the bar, was Maggie, Sharon's sister, whom Rebecca had seen only in pictures. But Rebecca would have known this woman was related to Sharon even if she hadn't spoken up. Her dark brown hair was cut to shoulder length and she had no freckles—not like Sharon. It was Maggie's eyes that gave her away. They were as black and bright as Sharon's. As Maggie and Rebecca had spoken over the phone for as long as Rebecca and Sharon had been friends, the sight of her brought a relieved grin to Rebecca's face.

"Hey, Mags. Row—"

"Becks! Look at you! You're finally here!" Moving down the bar, Maggie pulled Rebecca into a hug.

"Rowan has to go to the bathroom," Rebecca whispered in her ear.

"Rowan!" Maggie said, letting go of Rebecca and picking Rowan up. "Rowan, you are so big!"

"I have to go potty," Rowan said.

"Come on, then," Maggie replied, setting Rowan back on the floor.

"I'll take—" Rebecca protested.

"Becky?" The dark-haired man who had smiled through the window stepped past the Spanish men. "I'm Eoman. Eoman O'Connelly. You've come to talk to my grandmother, Liz O'Connelly."

"Oh!" Rebecca smiled, taking his offered hand. As she did so, Rowan followed Maggie down to the end of the bar. "Wait! Mag—"

"This is Paddy," Eoman said, motioning to the man in the blue sweater. "Paddy's mum sent us over here to see if you needed a hand."

"Paddy?"

"Aye," Paddy said, taking Rebecca's hand and shaking it. "My mum is Rose Blake. You've come to speak with her, too."

"Yes! Yes, Liz and Rose," she said as she turned to look at her daughter's small form disappearing into the crowd. "I—uh—Rowan—"

"You want a beer?" Tom asked.

"No. Thanks. Actually I need the car."

"She doesn't drink beer, Tom. Remember?" Eoman said. "Sharon says Becky likes wine and cider."

"Ahhh, that's right, that's right. Cider for you." He trotted down the bar to fetch it.

"Uh, Paddy, my luggage is at the dock and—"

"Sit. Sit. You hungry?" Eoman asked.

As Tom returned and set the cider on the bar in front of her, Rebecca peered into the eyes of blue and brown and green. She realized that each of these men was the subject of at least one of Sharon's stories. Paddy was the farmer with seven kids—or was he the fisherman with one kid? And what had Sharon told her about Eoman? Suddenly

Rebecca couldn't remember. She should know all these people, but she didn't. All this along with the day's travel weighing on her made her feel completely overwhelmed.

"Uh. Actually my stuff's at the dock and I—"

"That can wait," Paddy replied, gently pushing Rebecca onto a stool. "Have some supper. Tell us a story."

"A story?" Rebecca's eyes widened.

"Paddy," Maggie said, returning to the bar. "Your wife just came through the door with Siobhan. They're by the fire."

"Ah!" He smiled and went off to find them.

"Where's Rowan?" Rebecca asked Maggie as she stood up.

"With Paddy's wife and his daughter, Siobhan. I left her by the fire. She said she was cold."

"Becky was going to tell us a story. Tell the one about Steep Ravine and the goat," Eoman said.

"No," said Tom. "The one about Alcatraz."

"Aye, Alcatraz," Eoman replied. "That's a better one. I love that story."

"How do you all know about those stories?" Rebecca asked, bewildered.

"Sharon told us," Eoman replied.

The fact that all these people knew so many stories of her past was very disconcerting. "I need Rowan and the car, Maggie," Rebecca mumbled.

"What car?" Tom asked.

"John has the car," Maggie explained.

"John?" Rebecca asked.

"You know, Sharon's husband," Maggie said.

"He's here?" Rebecca frowned. Sharon hadn't mentioned that.

"Sharon sent him home from Dublin to settle you in."

"He went to Fitzgibbons'," Eoman piped up.

"What happened there?" Tom inquired.

"Bees and Trace," Eoman replied.

They all burst into laughter. Rebecca just stared at them. She was beginning to think either they were crazy or she was.

"Tell us the Alcatraz story, Becky. John may be a while," Tom said with a chuckle.

Rebecca sighed. "I'm sorry. I'm just so—so tired."

"Everything's fine now," Maggie said softly, slipping her arm around Rebecca's shoulders. "Rowan's with Siobhan."

"Who's Chiffon?"

"Not Chiffon, Siobhan. Paddy's six-year-old daughter. Maybe she and Rowan will be friends."

Rebecca stared into Maggie's black eyes. They were solid and sure, just like her sister's.

"Very best friends?" Rebecca whispered, swallowing the lump in her throat.

"Could be. Anyway, Paddy and Annie, his wife, will keep them both safe. And this is a tiny island, Becky. No one can get on or off of it without someone else knowing. No safer place in the world than an island like this."

"No safer place," Tom affirmed.

"No place safer," Eoman said quietly.

Slowly, Rebecca looked from Eoman to Tom to Maggie. If they knew of Alcatraz and Steep Ravine, then it followed that Sharon had told them many stories about Rebecca. And the fact that they were all telling her how safe the island was meant they must also know of her deep insecurity and fear for Rowan. They must know she'd been blowing in the wind. For a moment, Rebecca was overwhelmed by the idea that Sharon had told them so much about her, and fearful that she might have shared with these people the stories of Dennis, but then she remembered why she had come to the island in the first place.

"Trust us, Becky. Okay?" Maggie asked.

Rebecca nodded slowly, promising herself she would try. She had to—she needed to learn to make a home for Rowan and herself.

"Good. Have some cider. John will be back with the car as soon as he's done at the Fitzgibbons'."

"Tell us about Alcatraz," Eoman repeated.

Rebecca leaned back on the stool. Raising her glass to her lips, she swallowed several gulps of cider.

"Maybe later, Eoman," Maggie said, patting the young man on his shoulder. "Let her rest a while."

CHAPTER 2

Mistle Thrush

Mistle Thrush (aka Storm Thrush or Stormcock. Latin: *Turdus viscivorus*). 1. A songbird with gray-feathered wings and a black-and-white-spotted breast. Builds small round nests that can hold a large number of eggs. Though not usually aggressive, it is a ferocious protector of home and offspring and is known to battle birds of prey. Unlike other birds, which fall silent as storms approach, the mistle thrush has a peculiar habit of singing. Its solitary call can be heard through the worst of gales as it faces the fury and sings boldly. 2. An Irishman.

—R. Dirane, A Binding Love

Sean leaned back in his chair, watching the fire and endeavoring to ignore the noise around him. Not often did he come to O'Flaherty's anymore. There were too many ferries bringing too many tourists to the island now, so the pub was always filled with foreigners. He didn't like foreigners. They came here seeking something, and Sean was convinced that whatever it was they sought left the island upon their arrival, packing its bags hurriedly to spare itself the constant din of bicycles, chatter, screaming children, and unreasonably loud laughter.

For Sean, what the tourists came to find on the island was apparent only in solitude. He liked to be alone, difficult as that was to do on the island, where everyone knew everyone else and had done so for more years than anyone could remember. Nevertheless, he had successfully scared off all of the town's children for three generations now. Most of the adults left him alone and kept their children away from him. But Sean always made time for Paddy and Eoman, as they were fishermen, like he had been in days past, and so he was kind enough to Siobhan, Paddy's daughter, though the little girl rarely said more than two words to him.

Shifting in his seat, the old man felt his spine crackle as he moved. He sat before the fireplace, staring at the lapping flames, focusing on a certain hue of yellow that flickered blue and orange. He looked at it, thinking of his youngest's first step. It had happened as Sean had shuffled through his door on that cold autumn morning. There had been no catch that day and the worry of feeding his family weighed heavily upon him.

"God bless all here," he said as he dipped his fingers in the little shell of water by the door and crossed himself. There, upon the floor, sat baby Brendan, just a year old, and peering over his shoulder at his father, he grinned a near-toothless grin. Then, as if he'd been doing it for years, the little boy tucked his heels beneath his bottom, straightened his legs, tottered to his feet, and stumbled toward Sean, arms wide open. Bursting from beneath the clouds at that very moment, the sun poured through the window above his little boy. The light danced upon Brendan's blond head, creating a flickering golden halo.

Sean blinked. So lost in his memory had he been that he hadn't noticed a little girl standing now between the fire and his chair. Her straight brown hair tumbled in tangles about the shoulder straps of her patchwork overalls. Crossing her arms before her, she shivered with chattering teeth as she gazed at Sean's hands. He looked down and realized he was moving his hands together as if he held needles and was knitting. He dropped his palms on his knees and frowned.

"What are you lookin' at?" he barked.

Startled, the little girl stepped back, flicking her mahogany eyes up to meet his eyes. She was too dark to be Irish.

"Your parents don't teach you manners."

"It's all right, Sean," Annie said. He glanced over and found Paddy's wife seated at the table behind him.

"She's no manners."

"I do so," the girl murmured, backing farther away.

"And a Yank. No wonder," Sean scoffed.

"It's all right, Rowan," Paddy soothed as he made his way to them through the tangle of tables. He was followed by Siobhan, who held two glasses of milk.

"Here, Rowan," Siobhan said shyly, handing Rowan one of the glasses and glancing sideways in Sean's direction.

"Rowan," Sean repeated with a sneer. "What kind of given name is Rowan for a little girl? It's a family name, not a first name."

The little girl's brow furrowed. Quietly she said, "It is a tree—a strong, magical tree."

"'Tis an Irish surname. It's for a family, not a little girl," Sean insisted.

"Sean," Paddy said, "she's just a kid. Leave her be."

Before Paddy could stop her, the little girl stomped forward to Sean's knee, placing her face not one foot from the old man's nose; her defiant brown eyes bore down on him. The old man shuddered and slid quickly away from her.

"Rowan is a good name! It's *my* name," she said. "And you—you are not nice!"

Sean sat there for a second, gaping into those piercing mahogany eyes, mouthing a retort that was stuck between his teeth. As he tottered to his feet, Paddy pulled Rowan back into his arms. Sean pursed his lips and silently walked past people sitting at the tables, who were now watching him with great interest. The old man opened the pub door, but before he stepped out into the night, he turned back to the nasty little Yank.

"Rowan is no name for you!" he spat and then tottered outside.

"Yes, it is! It's witchwood. Strong and magical!" The little girl's reply was cut short by the slamming door.

Sean stood in the clear, cold air of early evening, flustered. There had been several townspeople seated at the tables, watching him argue with the little girl. They had even seen him slide away from her accusatory gaze. The episode would be all over town in ten minutes.

"Bloody Yank," he breathed and pulled his old woolen coat tighter around his crooked shoulders, feeling the eighty-three years of his life pressing down on his crackling spine a little more. Glancing up, he watched a mistle thrush flitter in the twilight, racing the night. Indeed, it was late upon its wings. It spiraled twice before disappearing behind the church's spire.

The sky was clear and the evening star was bright above him in the deep lavender heaven. Though the soft wind was scented of salt and seaweed, the quiet belied a brewing storm to the south. Sean smelled it as a certain earthy scent—a fragrance of plowed fields upon an ocean breeze was not a good thing.

"How long?" he whispered, tasting the wind. "Tomorrow. No, the day after. Two nights you'll be before you blow in. I'll tell Paddy tomorrow."

As he headed home, Sean thought of the nasty little Yank and her defiant eyes. He skipped through all the things he should have said to her as he made his way out of town, but soon it was that his mind filled once again with the gold of the fire, the burst of the sun through his little window, and halos.

"Brendan."

CHAPTER 3

Garter

Garter. 1. The simplest pattern, created by knitting or purling every row, never mixing the two. 2. Doing the same thing over and over again, making progress in time, but never moving forward in spirit.

—R. Dirane, *A Binding Love*

Holding the glass before her, Rebecca noted the golden color of the liquid in the dim light. It was fuzzy, and she couldn't tell if it was her weariness or the cider in her empty stomach that made it so. As she turned to ask Maggie where supper was, she noticed a man to her left who, she was certain, had not been there before. He seemed to be in his late thirties and wore a dark leather coat and a white T-shirt, and his eyes were so black she couldn't see his pupils. But mostly she looked at his hair. It was for that reason that her mouth was open but nothing came out.

His hair color was neither the deep red-brown of auburn nor the bright orange of a true carrottop; rather it was a rich, velvety red with golden highlights. The loose curls spiraled off his head, twisting below his ears, both of which were pierced. Upon his face was a neatly kept matching moustache and beard that had a very thin stripe of gray to the right of his lips caused by a scar, the tip-top of which Rebecca could see peeping out from beneath his whiskers.

"Becky, this is Fionn." Rebecca heard Maggie's voice in the distance.

"Fin?" Rebecca repeated softy.

"Yes, Fionn," she explained. "You know—Sharon, John, Fionn."

"Oh!" Rebecca exclaimed as she shook herself from her stupor. "Fionn!"

Fionn was Sharon's childhood friend—the one she didn't marry. John was the one she did. Smiling, Rebecca held out her hand. Fionn did not smile. He glanced at her open palm and Rebecca believed she saw his lip curl slightly. Peering down to his left hand, she found that he held something very important to her—namely Rowan.

"One of Sharon's best friends and all I'm offered is a handshake?" he mumbled, his black eyes staring at her. His expression reminded Rebecca very much of the look in Sharon's eyes when she was wholly disappointed. Quickly, Rebecca withdrew her hand and glanced over to Maggie.

But it was Rowan who said, "Mama, it's Fionn."

"Y-yes, Rowan. Maggie said that," Rebecca replied, a frown deepening on her face. "You know Fionn?"

"Sharon told me about him. Like she told me about Tom," Rowan replied.

"What are you doin' in here?" Fionn asked.

"I beg your pardon?" Rebecca asked.

"You don't have time to be sittin' around a pub and drinkin'. You have work to do. Two months of summer you have and a small grant. So small you couldn't even stop over in Dublin to see your best friend who's about to pop out her first."

"Now wait a min—"

"Time to go. The wee one's tired," Fionn stated, and, turning around, he deftly moved through the crowd, Rowan in tow.

"That's my daughter!" Rebecca protested, following Fionn through the pub. She bumped the Southern woman and two of the Spanish men.

"Bye, Becks," Maggie called after her. "See ya later."

Rebecca waved as she passed the German couple. By the time

Fionn stepped out of the pub, she was on his heels, reaching for Rowan's free hand. Just when she was closing her palm, a tall man with a brown ponytail walked up to her.

"Becks!" John said with a broad smile, taking Rebecca by both of her hands and kissing her right cheek.

"Hi, John," Rebecca said, her eyes watching Fionn lead Rowan over to a motorcycle.

"Good to finally see ya in person," John added. "Got your luggage all packed. Ready to go home?"

Turning toward a very small car parked in front of the pub, John opened the passenger-side door. With a bark, a large brown Labrador retriever barreled out, flying toward Rebecca, who jumped in surprise.

"Trace!" Fionn commanded.

The dog froze.

"Sit."

The dog sat, its tail wagging furiously as it gazed at Rebecca in warm welcome.

"The dog is Trace," Fionn said by way of introduction. "John, you take Becky and Trace. Rowan can go with me."

"No, I'd rather Rowan stayed with me," Rebecca countered, taking a step in Fionn's direction.

"With the dog and the luggage, she'll never fit. Best if she goes with me," Fionn replied, straddling a large motorcycle and engaging its engine.

"On a motorcycle!" Rebecca exclaimed. Her father had been a fireman and he'd told her so many stories of motorcycle accidents, that he'd left her with a lifelong terror of them.

"Oh, please, Mama!" Rowan pleaded, jumping up and down.

"She'll never fit in the car," John confirmed.

"She doesn't have a helmet," Rebecca said, the pitch of her voice rising.

Fionn plopped a helmet on Rowan's head. The little girl giggled.

"I'll drive slowly," he said.

"I don't like motorcycles," Rebecca said. "They're not safe."

"There's one car on the island, Becky, and that's it." Fionn pointed to the small vehicle. "The sky's as clear as your smile and there's not a drop falling from it."

Rebecca scowled.

Fionn cocked his head as he looked at her. "Well, as clear as your smile is in all your pictures with Sharon, anyway. Trust me. Nothin' bad's gonna happen."

"Please, Mama?" Rowan pleaded, the helmet tottering on her head as if she were a bobble-headed doll.

Rebecca sighed. "You'll drive slow?"

"Like I was pedalin' on a Sunday afternoon."

Reluctantly Rebecca nodded.

Fionn slid Rowan into the saddle behind him. "See you at the house," he called as he pulled away from the curb.

Rowan turned around and waved at her mother. At the end of the street Fionn revved the engine and sped around the corner with a little screech, the tiny red taillight disappearing in a flash.

Rebecca gasped. "He said he'd go slow!" she yelled, her heart speeding up and pounding against her ribs. Suddenly it was all just too much for her—the long day of travel, the whirl of new people, everything going as fast as that motorcycle racing out of sight with her daughter.

"Ah, he's just playin'."

"Not with my daughter, he's not!" Rebecca declared, ready to scream in frustration.

"It'll be fine," John said. "It'll only take a couple of minutes to get you home."

"It'll be fine!" Rebecca repeated. "That's all you people say."

"Which people?"

"I'm sorry. Sorry. Never mind," Rebecca said, shaking her head. "I'm just tired." She peered through the open car door. Her luggage was packed in the backseat, ceiling high.

"Where's the dog sit?"

"Between us?" John offered with a grin.

Smiling stiffly, Rebecca lowered herself into the car. As soon as she had, Trace jumped in after her, crawling across her knees. She gritted her teeth.

"Come here, Trace," John called as he slid into the driver's seat. With effort, he shut the door as the dog wiggled between them.

Rebecca took a deep breath. "Whose dog is it anyway?"

"Fionn's. He stays with Fionn's parents—when he stays home at all. Mostly he runs about the island. Usually on the west side."

Rebecca stared over at the big dog filling the small space between them. "How are you going to shift?" she asked.

"It's a small island. We don't go too fast around here. If we did we'd end up in the ocean."

Panting, Trace turned his wet nose toward Rebecca and licked her cheek. She rolled her eyes and pushed the dog's muzzle toward John. He just laughed.

As the car pulled away from the curb, Rebecca glanced up to the silhouette of the church's spire against the night sky. Her mind raced with pictures of Rowan lying in the dark, smeared across a narrow Irish road, the motorcycle's wheels spinning with a squeak over the crash of waves. As they drove along, she saw low stone walls lining the road like ancient, craggy monuments. They looked sharp and irregular, casting deep crevices of shadow across the fields as the headlights passed.

"What if he has an accident?" she whispered to her reflection on the glass.

"He's not going to have an accident, Becky. He grew up here with me and Sharon. We skipped school together, missed Mass, got in trouble. We know every rock and blade of grass on this island. Nothing's going to happen. Look, we're here."

A two-story cottage sat to the left, white as a lighthouse. It had a green door and a slate roof and five small green-paned windows that reflected the headlights when John slowed down, turning off the main road with a bump. Rebecca remembered that Sharon had said her rented cottage was adjacent to the owner's own residence. As the car passed, the little garden of roses near the green door swayed. Slowly, they crept down a gravel lane. Rebecca could see far at the end of the drive a second small white house illuminated by the car's headlights. Fionn's motorcycle stood lonely near the blue door, and a thin wisp of smoke flowed from the chimney.

"There's your house, Becky," John said.

The car's wheels ground to a halt on the gravel. Rebecca flung open her door. She was sure she heard Rowan calling desperately from the house. Trace barked, crawling over Rebecca's lap and tumbling from the car.

"Damn dog," she hissed, rolling out of her seat. Leaving the car door open, she raced through the dust that hung in the air in the car's wake, certain that Rowan was calling to her. She burst through the front door.

"Rowan?" she called in panic as she flew through the tiny front room. "Rowan!"

Rounding a corner into the kitchen, she skidded to a stop. Fionn stood frozen by an open oven with a casserole dish in his hands, staring at her. Rowan sat at the kitchen table, eating a cookie and coloring on a blue sheet of paper. Rebecca blinked and cocked her head. Hadn't she heard Rowan calling for her? Rowan glanced over at her mother.

"Hi, Mama," she said, taking a bite of the cookie.

"Hi, Rowan," Rebecca replied quietly, her heart still drumming against her ribs.

"Can she have biscuits before supper? She looked a wee bit hungry, and my mum's supper here won't be ready for a couple of minutes."

"That's fine," Rebecca whispered.

Fionn slid the casserole into the oven.

"Becky needs a beer, Fionn," John suggested as he passed the kitchen, his arms laden with luggage. Behind him, Trace came barreling in.

"Trace," Fionn said.

The dog stopped in its tracks.

"Sit."

He did.

"A beer," John repeated, heading back out the door.

"Becky doesn't like beer, John," Fionn said. "Remember? That's what Sharon says. But Becky's in Ireland now and Ireland is part of the EU just like France and France has the best wine in the world. Look. Here's a glass of Bordeaux that's been breathing on the counter, waiting for Becky to arrive."

Lifting the glass, Fionn walked across the small kitchen. His black eyes reflected the red sparkle of the wine he held out to her. Rebecca gazed from the wine to Fionn to Rowan.

"You sped off—"

"She arrived here safely without you, didn't she, Becky?"

Fionn's eyes were like the night sky—black and steady and clear.

"W-well, y-yes," Rebecca stammered.

"Then no need for a moment, huh? Supper's in the oven, the fire's burning, and your covers are turned down. You're home now, on a small island in the middle of the ocean where everybody knows everybody. No safer place than here."

"No safer place," John echoed as he passed the kitchen again, this time with Rebecca's large black duffel.

"Drink the wine, Becky," Fionn whispered, placing the glass in her right hand and taking her handbag from her left shoulder.

Slowly Rebecca lifted the glass.

"Relax," Fionn said as he brushed past her toward the door.

"Mama?"

Rebecca looked over to Rowan.

"I don't understand him."

"His accent is very thick. You can ask him to slow down if you can't—"

"It's not that. He asked me if I liked biscuits and I told him I don't, but he was talking about these," Rowan said quietly, holding up a cookie.

"Oh. Yeah. There are different words for things here. If you don't understand, just ask."

"But I did understand and I don't like biscuits, but he was talking about cookies. How was I supposed to know I didn't understand?"

"Where you want this?" John asked, holding out a DVD camera and tripod.

"By the sofa's okay," she said, turning to look at him. "And thank you, John, for bringing my stuff in."

"Hey, Trace," Rowan called. "Want a biscuit?"

The dog stood, trotted to the table, and grabbed the cookie from Rowan's hand.

"You want a pint, John?" Fionn called.

"That'll be fine."

"Beer?" Rebecca asked. "Don't you have to go back to town?"

"You need somethin'?" John asked.

"Well—no. You—you aren't staying in town?"

"We'll stay here tonight," said John.

"Here?" Rebecca asked, glancing over to the small living room couch.

"This one," Fionn said, pointing to Rowan as he handed John the beer from the fridge, "put old Sean Morahan in his place. Didn't ya now?"

"No!" John exclaimed incredulously.

"Who's Sean Morahan?" Rebecca asked.

"The meanest man on earth, Mama."

"Didn't she just say so, to his face, in front of the entire pub?"

"No!"

"Aye!" Fionn's eyes gleamed.

"What did he do to you, Rowan?" Rebecca asked.

"He made fun of my name. So I told him he wasn't nice."

"Oh, Sean's harmless. Rowan shot back at him and he didn't know what to do with himself," Fionn explained.

John burst out laughing.

"Good for you, standing up for yourself, Rowan," Rebecca said, brushing her daughter's cheek. "But I don't see what's so funny."

"Oh, sorry. It's just that I was terrified of the man when I was small," John explained.

"If Sean talks to you again, you let me know," Rebecca said, opening a cupboard, searching for plates.

"He's harmless, Becky," Fionn repeated.

"If Sean Morahan didn't know what to do with himself when he met my daughter," Rebecca said, glaring at Fionn, "he'll never know what hit him if he crosses me. Rowan, go wash up, honey. It'll be time for dinner soon."

Rowan slipped from her seat and was gone. As Rebecca set the table and silence filled the kitchen, her mind filled with the sight of the red taillight of the motorcycle racing away as Fionn drove off with her daughter. If there was a human trait Rebecca disliked, it was a person saying one thing, then doing another. And as she lifted the silverware from the drawer and set it out on the table with a loud thump, she thought about how that was precisely what Mr. Fionn had just done to her.

CHAPTER 4

Stocking

Stocking. 1. The pattern made by knitting one row, then purling the next, alternating between the two with each new row. The garment then has a "wrong" side and a "right" side. The "right" side has a herringbone-like appearance and the "wrong" side has a bumpy texture. 2. The dust of the past.

—R. Dirane, *A Binding Love*

Sean did not require any light to find his way home. All he needed was the sound of the sea. As the town fell away behind him, the ocean called from the west. Galway Bay and the mainland were to his left and east and he could hear them easily enough. But he was a man of this island. He was as old and as west as west could be.

Even now, the lavender light faded to gray, and though he could have stepped onto the road, Sean was not one to walk upon asphalt. It was new and covered the memory of the path he used to take home as a child. He didn't like new. He didn't like asphalt. So always he made his way to his house by walking just off the road, his footsteps leaving a dark, winding ribbon of dirt to follow in the growing night. It was the path he had worn through the years and he knew its every dip, rock, and root. It was the way home—the way west.

The ocean roared, coming closer, and when it was at its loudest, Sean looked to the western horizon. As he stepped off the ribbon of dirt onto the gravel of his walkway, the old man watched the waves rolling in beyond the dark and solitary shadow of his house. Late spring should have had the sea coming in from the northwest; but the waves were hitting his little beach from the southwest, confirming what he was already smelling on the breeze. Two days hence, that surf would push his sand north, crashing in from the south. Heavy southern tides coming in the beginning of June were queersome. The thought sent a bubbling shiver skipping up his spine.

With a sigh, Sean shuffled up to his front door, the sea and sand disappearing behind his house. He turned the knob and stepped into his front room.

"God bless all here," he announced to the darkness of the empty house. Dipping his fingers into the shell of water that sat in its tiny nook in the wall to his right, he brought his hand to his forehead but stopped before crossing himself. He watched the drop of water cling to his finger in the shadows.

"Da?" Matthew, at fourteen years Sean's eldest, called from outside.

"Claire! Look!" Sean squatted down, watching Brendan totter on his feet. "Come here, Brendan. Come here, my boy."

"Looks like he'll be in the curragh faster than us all," Sean's second son, twelve-year-old Joe, said as he followed his father through the door, dipping his own fingers in the shell of water.

"Aye." Matthew chuckled from behind. "Me and you against Da, Liam, and Brendan." And then he dipped his own fingers. "God bless all here."

"You two'd beat us," Sean conceded. "You have Joe and that pipe."

"You're getting better, Da," Joe replied.

Brendan fell into Sean's embrace as Claire came into the room from the kitchen with three-year-old Liam by the hand. Standing up, Sean met Claire's blue-green eyes. He saw her pride in Brendan's achievement. But he also saw they were wide and moist. The small but ever-present furrow upon her brow deepened as she gazed about the floor, seeking that which Sean was unable to bring in from the sea. He hadn't had a decent catch in three weeks.

The older boys must have seen it, too. "I'll just have tea and bread," Matthew announced, skipping past his father. "I'm tired and feeling poorly."

"Me, too," Joe added, following his older brother across the living room.

Sean watched Matthew walk past his mother and disappear into the kitchen. Joe peered back over his shoulder, meeting his father's eyes. He gave a little nod. Sean nodded in return. Though Joe was not yet a teenager, Sean could see the man in him already. Joe vanished into the kitchen.

Sean gazed back to Claire, who stood silent as she wrestled with a squirming Liam.

"I suppose these wee ones are hungry. They'll want stew," Claire whispered.

"Aye. I'll just have tea and bread."

"Me, too," she said and turned back to the kitchen.

Sean looked down at Brendan in his arms, the reflected halo glittering still above his head. With a prayer on his lips, Sean kissed his son's cheek.

⁓

"God bless all here," he repeated, his voice still a whisper. There was no answer, just the sound of his own breath and the light wind blowing through the thatch above his head. Absently, he crossed himself and shut the door.

For a moment Sean thought he should light the fireplace, but then the memory of Brendan and halos and tiny toes taking on the weight of what would one day be a man passed again across his mind. He knew he had work to do, so he left his front room to the darkness, heading instead into the kitchen. There he turned the knob of his gas cooker as he reached for his matches. With a flick of his wrist, the little piece of wood burst into flame, warming the kitchen with its golden halo. The old man set the match to the stove, which glowed blue as it came to life. Placing the kettle on the burner, he took a small round teapot from the shelf above his cooker, dropped in three tablespoons of tea, and set the sugar and his cup on the table. With his matches in hand, he walked around the counter and stepped through the door to his boys' room.

In the darkness, the old man lit a match and set the flame upon the wick that floated freely in the small pool of oil in a seashell that sat on the worktable. He watched the flickering wick, seeking the yellow he had seen in the fire at the pub. It wasn't there. Striking another match, he lit another shell candle, his memory floating like the lighted wick within the oil, drifting back to his boyhood, when the only light his family had was the driftwood fire upon the hearth and these little shell candles. The old man shook his head.

"No. Not that memory. Brendan." He closed his eyes tightly, willing himself to see only yellow—yellow with a certain iridescence.

"It had blue," he whispered to the wick. The shade of yellow in the pub's fire had a blue tone, reflecting the blue flame below. Sean searched his memory for what was blue in the moment Brendan took his first step. The sun burst through the clouds and with it, the blue sky beyond drifted in the window with the light. Sean chuckled, elated to have so easily found what was making the color.

Tottering back to his worktable, Sean pulled from beneath it a box of yellow dye and a box of blue. From a pail on the table, the old man poured water into a large shell and was about to sprinkle the dye into it when he stopped and glanced into the shell. The candles cast a mahogany hue on its shadowy interior. Sean gasped, bolting upright.

"Rowan," he whispered. He could hear her voice. She was new, and he didn't like new things.

"It's witchwood—strong and magical," Sean said, staring into the shell, and as the words came out of his mouth he could see the pain in her eyes. A pain he had put there.

How long had it been since a child had spoken to him—even in anger? They usually skipped away from him like leaves rolling away from a cold autumn wind. But Rowan did not cower. She did not run. Rowan held her ground. And now she was here—her pain, her eyes, and her voice had followed him home.

"Magic," he breathed, her words repeating in his mind. He shook his head sharply. "No—Brendan."

He closed his eyes tightly again. Yellow with blue. He needed swatches.

My name is Rowan. You are not nice.

"What the hell do you know of me? Go away!" he commanded.

The cold hollowness of Rowan's angry eyes poured into Sean. That unfathomable emptiness had once tried to pull him down into the depths of the ocean, and now it grasped his heart, sending it strumming like horses' hooves across his rib cage. Sean grabbed his chest.

"Rowan is no given name," the old man gasped, seeking old memories of windows and halos and bread with tea for supper. The teapot whistled hoarsely in the kitchen. Stumbling out of his sons' room, Sean went back into the kitchen. He balanced his weight upon one hand placed flat on the counter while he poured the water into the pot and put the lid on. Breathing deeply, Sean pulled the milk from his refrigerator and poured some into the bottom of his empty cup. He brought the teapot to the table and sat down to wait for the tea to steep and his heart to slow.

"Bloody Yank," he said with a cough.

As he rested, Sean watched the steam float from the teapot's spout. It drifted in the light from the boys' room and disappeared into the darkness of the front room. Upon the drifting cloud, Sean watched fourteen-year-old Matthew and twelve-year-old Joe eat their bread and drink their tea as Claire fed Liam and Brendan. They were all hungry and cold, but they were together then. Now they were all gone and Sean was alone. He scowled as he poured the tea into his cup, its color mahogany as it hit the milk.

"Witchwood," he hissed. Picking up his spoon, the old man stirred the tea. It turned a milky tan as he did so.

"You—have no manners," he whispered to his cup.

CHAPTER 5

Ribbing

Ribbing. 1. Knitting one stitch, then purling one stitch, creating a pattern that looks like the furrows of waves upon the ocean. This stitch is used widely on the wrists, neck, and bottom of the sweater, for it is elastic in nature and gives easily. 2. A riddle.

—R. Dirane, *A Binding Love*

$\mathcal{R}$ebecca sat sipping the last quarter of the glass of Bordeaux. Dinner was still warm in her belly as she listened to John and Fionn educate Rowan on the finer points of island play. They recommended climbing on the rocks south of town to search for sea anemones in the many tidal pools there. If poked quickly and the finger is removed, John explained, the anemone would spit water. Wagering on who could elicit the highest spit was a favorite game. Then there was the old mare belonging to Fionn's father. Great freedom was to be had riding it on the small ribbon of dirt just off the road that led south, past Sean Morahan's beach and toward the big fort. This was particularly memorable if you went near sunset. No one had a finer sunset on the island than Sean Morahan, for his was the only house that sat on a true beach.

Prowling around town playing scavenger hunt was fun. Inevitably, someone would put "raspberry-colored rose petals" on the list and there was only one place to find those—Father Michael's rose garden. No one voluntarily went in there unless they were playing scavenger hunt, and if the priest caught you, it was conversation regarding mortal sin for tea.

To this, Rowan asked what mortal sin was, causing both Fionn and John to glance over with wide eyes to Rebecca. With an irreverent shrug, she reached down and scratched Trace's head.

As she listened, Rebecca was keenly aware that it sounded like to do anything on the island required other people. All these games could only be played with a friend. Shifting in her seat, she thought of Rowan's life—the constant movement from one university or college to another, losing her childhood on the road between towns. That was what Sharon said anyway, and as Rebecca watched Fionn and John, Sharon's best childhood friends, explain to Rowan how to be a child of the island, the deep hollowness in her heart echoed, causing her to touch her chest to still the emptiness.

It had taken Rebecca two years to get free of Dennis. For those two years he was always there. He would time her trip home; she had to call home when she left work and arrive exactly thirty-five minutes later or he would throw a fit. He would call and leave messages all day on the telephone in her office. As she taught, Rebecca could hear the telephone ringing constantly down the hall. If she went to the store, Dennis would go with her. If she went to the movies, Dennis would go along. Rebecca had not one moment to herself for two years, except her solitary study in the library, and Dennis gave her only three hours a week to do that or he'd lose his temper. There was no time to think, no time to be with herself, no time to center.

When Rebecca finally gained her freedom, she didn't want to report to anyone. She needed to move, to go where she liked, when she liked, compulsively uprooting Rowan and herself to reassure herself that she was still free. But in that freedom there was no peace and very little childhood for Rowan.

"Someone looks sleepy," Fionn noted.

Rebecca started, peering over at Rowan, who listed in the chair, her head resting on her fist.

"I'm okay," the little girl replied, rubbing her eyes.

"Come on," Fionn said, standing. "You brush your teeth and I'll check for fairies under the bed."

"Sharon told me that only you can see fairies," Rowan replied, following Fionn around the corner. Trace yawned and, rising to his feet, trotted after Rowan.

"Only when he's circlin' over Shannon," John whispered with a wink.

Rebecca looked at him questioningly.

"When he's had too much to drink," John rephrased, chuckling. "Here. You dry. I'll wash."

Nodding, Rebecca tossed a dish towel over her shoulder and began clearing the table.

"Sharon'll be asleep by now," John murmured to the sink.

"It is late," Rebecca said.

"Late, early. She sleeps all the time."

"She's really big, huh?"

"Aye." John laughed. "And she hurts when she stands, so she lies down. As soon as she's horizontal, she's asleep."

"The last month is hell—that's for sure."

"Two weeks, to be exact. We'll see. She's had breakthrough bleeding a couple of times.

"Scary." Rebecca nodded, remembering Sharon's call a month earlier. "Just a little longer."

"Aye," John replied.

As Rebecca dried the dishes, she rummaged around the kitchen, noting the full cupboards. There were cans of soup and vegetables, packages of gravy and sauces, a bag of sugar and shakers of salt and pepper. Two loaves of fresh bread wrapped in a cotton cloth sat on the counter next to a bowl filled with apples and pears, and to their left was a basket of yellow onions and potatoes. Opening the small refrigerator, she found it stocked with eggs, milk, butter, and cream.

"Who brought all this food?" she asked.

"Rose and Liz came by today to help Fionn's mum clean the place. They thought you'd need some things to eat."

It was all just too generous. Though Rebecca had offered to rent the cottage, Sharon had told her no one wanted her money. They were just excited to finally meet her after so many years and all of Sharon's tall tales. Glancing around at the food, Rebecca knew she had to find some way of paying them back.

"I think we have enough here to last till the end of summer."

John snickered.

"No fairies," Fionn reported as he poked his head into the kitchen. "Best be going, John."

"You're going?" Rebecca asked.

"Aye. You and Rowan are tired."

"I thought you were staying here."

Fionn stepped closer to Rebecca. She held the plate she was drying to her chest like a shield. His black eyes smiled at her.

"Thanks for the invite, Becky, but I really don't think the bed is big enough for the four of us and the dog." He grinned, turning to the door.

Rebecca looked at her feet, embarrassed.

"You know that's my parents' house up the road. Mum made supper and dropped it by before she and Dad left this afternoon to Doolin. Went to visit my brother, Danny, on the mainland or they'd be here to greet ya," Fionn said over his shoulder.

"Oh."

"Good night, John," Rowan called as she skipped to the open door of the bedroom in her nightgown.

"Thank you, John, for your help," Rebecca added.

"It's nothing. House key is on the table next to the fireplace, though there is really no need for it," he said, walking to the car.

Fionn lingered at the door.

"Good night, Fionn," Rowan said.

"Good night there, Rowan," he replied.

"Better get to bed, sweetie," Rebecca said.

Rowan turned back into the bedroom.

"I'm happy to have finally met Sharon's friend Becky," Fionn said with a smile.

"Mr. Fionn, whatever your last name is," she said, not returning his smile.

"O'Flahe—"

"You said you'd drive slow."

"Ah, I was just play—"

"I don't care if you're Sharon's friend or John's friend. I don't care if you're God's best friend. If you ever—*ever*—do anything to put my daughter in danger again, I'll make you the sorriest human being on this planet."

Rebecca slammed the door in his face. Stepping back, she stared at the bright blue paint of the door, her breath tight in her chest. Her blood surged in her ears as she strained to hear any sound besides silence beyond the door.

"Have you seen my face, John?" she heard Fionn ask.

"What?" John's voice was distant.

"My face. Miss Rebecca just ripped my face off, and I was wondering if she tossed it out here or if she took it inside with her sweet self."

She heard John's laugh. Fionn's feet crunched across the gravel drive as John started the car. The motorcycle's engine sputtered to a start. Rebecca heard the tires grind the gravel, and soon there was silence again.

"Bloody Irishmen," Rebecca whispered, leaning her head on the door.

"Mama?" Rowan called from the bedroom.

"Coming."

The heaviness of the day's travel landed squarely between Rebecca's shoulders. For a fluttering of an eyelash, she thought perhaps it wasn't the right thing to do—slamming the door in Fionn's face. But he had raced off with her daughter when he had said he would drive carefully. She had trusted him. He had broken that trust by saying one thing and then doing another. Flipping the living room light off, Rebecca clenched her teeth and stepped into the bedroom.

"It smells funny in here," Rowan said.

"Sometimes a new place takes a bit of getting used to."

"Fionn says the box on the dresser is from Sharon. He says she bought candles and embers so it would smell nicer."

On the dresser, Rebecca found a package the size of a shoe box, wrapped in paper with California poppies on it. She brought the box over to the bed and, with Rowan's help, opened it. Inside they found three candles and a plastic bag with hundreds of incense sticks. A box of wooden matches was tucked beneath the candles, along with a small incense burner.

"Want an ember?"

"Yeah!" Rowan declared, lying back in bed.

Pulling out a stick of incense, Rebecca struck a match and lit the brown ember. It burst to flame and began crackling.

"Shit!" she yelled, dropping the popping stick on the covers.

"Mama!" Rowan called, kicking the covers to keep the sparks from hitting her.

"Sorry, sorry. Shoot!" Rebecca corrected, grabbing the stick once more and racing to the bathroom. She dropped it into the sink and turned on the faucet. The stick sputtered in the water and sizzled out with a hiss and a puff of smoke. She hurried back into the bedroom.

"Are the covers okay?" Even as the words came from her mouth, she could see there was no charred spot on the blue bedspread.

"Sharon bought sparklers!" Rowan exclaimed as she laughed with surprise.

"Apparently. She thinks she's funny."

"She *is* funny!" Rowan laughed again. "She made pretend the sparklers were incense."

"Ha-ha," Rebecca replied, patting the covers. "Help me see if she put any real incense in the bag."

Shaking the contents of the bag onto the blankets, Rowan and Rebecca rummaged through the sparklers.

"I'll miss the fireworks this year," Rowan sighed, holding a sparkler to her nose and sniffing.

"I think Sharon realized that." Now that the danger was past, Rebecca smiled. "She's a good friend."

"I'll miss going to Redding, too. We always go there for July Fourth."

Rebecca's throat tightened. Redding was where she had grown up. Her father had loved the Fourth of July, and he always threw a big party for the whole neighborhood. Though her parents were gone now—they had died in a car accident ten years earlier—all the families that lived in their cul-de-sac still carried on Rebecca's father's Independence Day tradition. She always took Rowan to Redding for the Fourth of July to share that part of her parents with her little girl.

"I know. Well, we have sparklers. Okay?"

"Okay," Rowan whispered.

In all, there were only three sticks of incense among the sparklers. Rebecca lit one, placed it on the burner, and set it on the dresser. Sifting through the suitcases, she located her pajamas and toothbrush and headed back to the bathroom.

"He's nice, huh, Mama?" Rowan's voice reached her easily from the other room.

"Who?

"Fionn."

"He's"—Rebecca searched for a positive word as she scowled in the mirror—"considerate."

"And he has red hair."

"That he does," she agreed, squeezing out some toothpaste.

"I asked him if he played the fiddle."

"What?" Rebecca went back into the bedroom as she started to brush her teeth.

"Well, you said the man you marry will have red hair and play the Irish fiddle."

"You didn't tell him that, did you?" she exclaimed. Rebecca had made that comment to Rowan only once. It was last year and Rowan had kept asking if she was ever going to have a dad. In a moment of inspiration, Rebecca said she'd like to marry a man with red hair who played the Irish fiddle. Red-haired men are not common and finding one who played the Irish fiddle in Los Angeles or Virginia or whatever state they would live in was most improbable. The comment had the desired outcome: Rowan stopped asking. Rebecca had had no idea that her daughter had remembered the conversation.

"No," Rowan answered with a frown. She rolled over.

"Sorry, Rowan. I didn't mean to hurt your feelings."

"Okay, Mama."

Returning to the bathroom, Rebecca finished brushing her teeth and slipped into her pajamas. As she came back into the bedroom, she heard snoring. Rowan was in bed with her eyes wide-open.

"Who's snoring?" she inquired.

"Trace."

"What's he still doing here?"

"Fionn said he's good at catching fairies." Rowan giggled.

"He left the dog?" Rebecca growled.

"So we can feel safe in a new house. That's what he said."

Rebecca rubbed her face, a long sigh escaping her lips.

"You okay, Mama?"

"Yes," Rebecca replied, flipping off the light. "Can you see the ember?"

"Yeah."

Crawling into bed, Rebecca pulled Rowan next to her like a little spoon.

"Oh, you're toasty," she told her daughter.

The quiet of the house was broken only by the sound of the surf like the great boom of a giant drum against the walls of the cottage.

"I hear the ocean," Rowan whispered.

"Isn't it wonderful?"

"Can we go to the beach tomorrow?"

"We'll see. There may be no beach at all near this house. There're a lot of cliffs on Sharon's island, very few beaches. So she says."

"Can we look tomorrow?"

"You bet."

The ocean roared, and in the darkness Rebecca thought about how tiny this house was, how little this island. A shudder rolled down her spine, seizing her ribs. She was suffocating. Then, at the moment when she thought she was going to faint, she remembered Fionn's words, the words of the whole town: no safer place than here.

"You're squeezing me too tight," Rowan said, wiggling to loosen her mother's hold.

"Sorry." She took a deep breath and tried to think of something other than being alone with Rowan in the middle of the giant ocean. Her thoughts turned to Fionn's beautiful red curls.

"Rowan?"

"Yeah, Mama?"

"What did he say—about the fiddle?"

"He didn't answer me."

"He didn't say anything?"

"He laughed."

CHAPTER 6

Bobble

Bobble. 1. A stitch that looks like a ball. Bobbles vary in size based on the number of rows into which they are knitted. This stitch is very important, as it adds texture to the sweater or jumper, by either placing it singly within a pattern or grouping several bobbles together to form a pattern of their own. 2. Living things, like animals or trees. 3. People.

—R. Dirane, *A Binding Love*

Rebecca lay close to Rowan, listening to the crash of waves. The pink-red on her eyelids told her it was morning, but she had no reason to open them or get up from her warm covers, for her sweet dreams of the night before still lingered. They were filled with flying and houses and water softly rolling upon some far shore. At least she thought it was a far shore. Perhaps it was very close. Either way, there had been no Dennis dream—no falling, no white sweater or desperate voice calling for help, and because of that Rebecca smiled.

Lying still, she listened to Rowan's breathing and the ocean and rolled over to sleep again until she heard three taps on the bedroom window. Her eyes popped open and she quickly glanced over to the little window on the wall opposite the door. The white cotton curtains were drawn together with just a sliver of an opening between them, and through it Rebecca spied a beady black eye staring at her. She sat up. Next to the bed, Trace was standing at attention, his gaze fixed on the window with his ears pulled forward and his hackles raised between his shoulders.

"Easy, boy," Rebecca whispered as she slid out of bed. She brushed his head gently as she took two steps across the cold stone floor to the window. Slowly parting the curtains, she found a small bird standing on the windowsill. It had gray-feathered wings and a black-and-white-spotted breast.

It winked at her as it ruffled its feathers, looking as if it was smiling in the morning sun. Then it hopped off the ledge and landed on a limb of the bramble that grew outside the window. It cocked its head back toward Rebecca and carefully picked its way through the dusty, shadowed interior of the bush.

On her tiptoes, Rebecca could just make out a small brown nest with four little eggs tucked tightly together, warmed by one another and the dappled light of the sun.

"Ah, you have a family."

The bird bent its head and poked at a small twig that had dislodged from the nest.

"Awfully tight fit there. You sure that nest is going to hold all those babies?"

As the bird tucked the rogue twig back into place, another popped out on the opposite side. Skipping over the eggs, the bird grabbed the escaping twig and tore it from the nest.

Rebecca giggled. "Houses are frustrating, aren't they?"

Shivering, she suddenly realized how cold her room was.

"Well, thanks for showing me your nest. I have to go find the heater."

Quietly, Rebecca rummaged through the luggage, looking for her robe. As she lifted a pair of Rowan's overalls, she found her old scarf folded beneath, its edges frayed and ends tattered. Pulling it out, she touched the irregular stocking pattern, some stitches tight, some loose. It had been her first effort at knitting and her first lesson with Sharon.

"Ya need a little help there?"

Rebecca glanced up from her needles to find a girl with black hair and black eyes standing in the doorway of her dorm room. She sighed in exasperation.

"I can mathematically spin a circle around an axis and make a torus. I can tell you that when electrons are excited, they jump to higher orbitals. I can even tell you that the reason cars move forward at lights before the light turns green is an example of the anticipatory goal response. I can tell you all this, so why in the world can I not get these stitches to add up to thirty each time I knit a row?"

The girl laughed, slipping into the room and plopping onto the bed next to Rebecca.

"I'll help you with knitting if you help me with chemistry," she said, her Irish accent sparkling like the reflection of daylight in her black eyes.

"You in chem?"

"Aye. I'm in your class."

Rebecca smiled weakly. She hadn't noticed.

"Did ya not notice?" The girl giggled and gently took the needles from Rebecca's hands. Rebecca looked at her sideways, stunned that the girl seemed to have read her mind.

"I come from an island of knitters," she explained, holding the needles up to the light.

"Where are you from?"

"Ireland."

"I guessed that much," Rebecca said with a smile.

"Did ya now?" The girl stared into Rebecca's eyes, and slowly a crooked smile grew across her face.

"Aye," Rebecca replied, lifting her eyebrows as she stared back.

They grinned.

"I'm Sharon O'Connelly of the western islands."

"I'm Rebecca Moray of—of—from the land o' Redding."

They burst into laughter.

"Redding is north of here, isn't it?" Sharon asked, pulling the stitches off the needle.

"North of here. And east. My family comes from central California."

"Are they all chemists?" Gently, Sharon tugged at the yarn, pulling out one stitch at a time.

"My dad's a fireman and my mom is from a family of farmers. Almonds mostly. I suppose farmers are kinda like chemists. Your family are knitters?"

"Fishermen. Nothin' worth saving here. We'll have to rip back."

"That sounds terrible." Rebecca winced.

"Ah, just pulling it all out and starting over. I'll pull the yarn. You roll it back into the ball."

With wide eyes, Rebecca stared at the bumpy edges of the scarf. She could hardly claim that her knitting had improved since this first attempt. But it had been so long since she'd thought of that day, the first day she'd met Sharon. All of Rebecca's memories with Sharon had stopped on Thanksgiving Day six years before. That moment off Highway 1 on a cold, dark night with Sharon's arms wrapped around Rebecca's waist had burned all the memories of their earlier years together to ashes. It was her last night with Dennis.

Since that night, Sharon and she had stayed as close as ever, but Rebecca had rarely been able to speak to Sharon of anything but the weather and work. She always avoided discussing that Thanksgiving night—the memory she could not face and from which she constantly fled. Sharon, nevertheless, had remained there for her, ever patient. Now, as Rebecca ran her fingers across her irregular stitches, her mind filled with images of Sharon's black hair drifting over a pair of needles as she taught Rebecca how to knit. She smiled at the memory of their first tentative but warm moments of friendship, and tucking the scarf gently back beneath Rowan's overalls, she extricated a pair of socks and a bathrobe from the suitcase.

"I thought it was summer," she muttered through chattering teeth. She searched the walls of the cottage for the thermostat but found none. Then she heard a soft knock on the front door. She froze. What if it was Fionn? What would she say?

"Becky?" It was a woman's voice.

Crossing the living room, Rebecca turned the knob and cracked open the door. There, on the other side, was a middle-aged woman with a salt-and-pepper ponytail and sparkling hazel eyes.

"Good morning, Becky. I'm Sheila—Sheila O'Flaherty. Fionn's mum."

"Oh!" Rebecca replied, opening the door wider. "Thanks so much for supper last night."

"You're welcome. Fionn said he didn't get a chance to show you how to bank the fire."

"Bank the fire?"

"Aye. The cottage is heated only by the fireplace. You need to bank the fire at night so you have heat in the morning. Is it very cold in there?"

"Not so bad," Rebecca lied.

"May I come in to start the fire?"

"Oh. Sorry," Rebecca replied, stepping aside. "Please."

"We've waited so long to meet you," said Sheila, stepping through the doorway and heading to the fireplace.

"It seems everybody knows me."

"Sharon went the farthest from here of anyone. When she came back, we sat around and listened to her stories. You were always in them."

"We did everything together."

"She missed you when she came home."

"I've missed her, too."

After arranging several brown mud bricks in a tepee upon the gray ash and tucking a small wad of grass beneath, Sheila struck a match and held it to the grass. It began to smolder.

"Is that peat?" Rebecca asked.

"Aye. We've brought running water out here and heat for it, but my husband can't part with the peat fire. He says it smells like home. I made him put heat in our house up the road, though, so if he wants to smell home, as he calls it, he has to come out here by himself." Sheila laughed. The peat smoked as little flames lapped its edges.

"We'll keep it going today and I'll show you how to bank it tonight. Let me make breakfast. It'll give you time to settle in and I can watch the fire. I suppose you have unpacking to do."

Truth to say, Rebecca did have unpacking to do.

"Are you sure it's not too much trouble?" Rebecca asked, following Sheila into the kitchen.

"No trouble at all. Tea or coffee?"

"Tea, please."

Sheila smiled and nodded.

Quietly Rebecca opened the bedroom door. On the other side she found Trace wagging his tail desperately.

"Oh," Rebecca whispered. "Come on."

Trace followed Rebecca into the front room and stopped at the kitchen to study Sheila.

"There you are," Sheila announced, looking over her shoulder as Trace passed the kitchen. The dog halted in his tracks.

"H-he stayed here last night."

"He likes the smell of peat, too." Sheila chuckled again. "When we rent the place out to the tourists, it's quite an adventure. Can ya let him out the door?"

"Come on, Trace," Rebecca called. She opened the front door and the dog barreled out into the morning sun. The air was light, and a gentle, cold wind picked up the ends of Rebecca's brown hair and brushed them back over her shoulders. She smiled and shut the door.

"It smells green out there," she said. "I've never smelled a color before."

"Late-spring mornings are my favorite," Sheila commented as she cracked an egg in the white bowl before her.

Again Rebecca quietly opened the bedroom door to fetch her clothes, trying not to wake Rowan. The little girl giggled.

"Ah—you're awake. Funny dream?"

"Na-uh. That little bird."

Rebecca looked over at the window and saw the bird there, peeking through the curtains again.

"It said good morning to me, too. We'll eat breakfast and then we'll go outside. Fionn's mom's in the kitchen."

Rowan bolted from bed as Rebecca dug through her suitcase.

"Is Fionn coming for breakfast?" she heard her little girl ask of Sheila.

"No, he went home this morning," Sheila replied. "They probably won't be back till Christmas. You must be Rowan."

"I am," Rowan said.

Rebecca pulled on her jeans and a sweater from her suitcase and headed for the bathroom. She was quite relieved that Fionn was gone, and the fact that he wouldn't be back until after she left for the States at the end of the summer was even better. Though he had raced off with her daughter the night before, Rebecca had a heavy feeling in the pit of her stomach about the fact that she had slammed the door in his face.

As she stepped out of the bathroom, there was a banging knock at the front door. Sheila looked over her shoulder to Rebecca, who now stood in the kitchen doorway.

"That'll be my husband. His name's Fionn, too," Sheila said, poking at the frying pan. "He's smelled the bacon and eggs."

Rebecca opened the door and found on the other side of it a man with curly red-gray hair and black eyes grinning at her.

"You are pretty!"

"Thanks." Rebecca couldn't help smiling at that greeting. She opened the door wider.

"Tom said you were pretty."

"Did he?" Rebecca was oddly disappointed. She'd assumed Fionn must have said it.

"Mmmm. He also said you didn't like to flirt."

Rebecca shrugged with a half smile.

"Fionn, leave her be," Sheila called from the kitchen. "Tom's like his father here. If they meant anything by it, Maggie and I would have 'em living at the pub."

"Tom and I would never last. And who's this? Is this the legendary Rowan Moray of O'Flaherty's Pub?"

Rowan beamed.

"They're tellin' stories and singin' songs to your courage down there. May I shake your hand? That Sean'll not come near you now!"

Giggling, Rowan shook Fionn Sr.'s hand.

"Miss Rowan, if it's all right with your mum, would you like to go check on the cows with me after breakfast? You can ride the horse."

"Uh—" Rebecca shook her head.

"Can I, Mama?" Rowan pleaded, jumping out of her seat.

"Ah, let her go. She'll remind Fionn to come home. Sometimes I have to go out and fetch him in when he gets to talking with those cows."

Rebecca thought for a moment. She remembered John and Fionn talking the night before about riding the horse as a child. Rowan had never ridden a horse, but it was what children who lived on the island and called it home did. *No safer place than here*, she reminded herself. Rebecca nodded reluctantly.

"Thanks, Mama!" Rowan said, hugging her mother's legs. The little girl raced into the bedroom, Trace on her heels.

Glancing over at Fionn Sr., Rebecca found him studying her. He smiled broadly and slipped next to Sheila. "A peat fire, a breakfast cooking, and you. I am a happy man."

"Make yourself useful and pour Becky a cup of tea."

"A cup of tea for Becky, a peat fire, a breakfast cooking, and you. I am a happy man."

Sheila laughed. With a wink, Fionn Sr. handed Becky her cup of tea, and as Rebecca looked into his black eyes, she saw truly the older version of the younger man she had met last night. Her brow furrowed as she thought of slamming the door in Fionn's face the night before.

"You all right there, Becky?" Fionn Sr. asked, placing his hand on her shoulder.

"Sorry. Yes. Yes, I'm all right."

CHAPTER 7

Twisted Stitch

Twisted Stitch. 1. A twisted stitch is caused by placing the needle through the loop of a single stitch in the wrong direction. Though usually an error in the process of either knitting or purling, some patterns can be created by purposely twisting stitches (i.e., twisted-stitch ribbing). 2. Certain traits developed over a life that define the uniqueness of a soul. 3. A mother's touch.
—R. Dirane, *A Binding Love*

After breakfast, Fionn Sr. and Rowan headed out the door. Rebecca and Sheila watched them walk across the gravel drive with Trace following on their heels.

"Why's your dog called Trace?" Rowan asked, taking Fionn Sr.'s hand.

"He's my son Fionn's dog. Fionn gave him that name because the dog follows you around, tracing your steps."

Rowan giggled.

"You be careful, Rowan," Rebecca called.

"I'll look after her." Fionn Sr. waved over his shoulder.

Rebecca folded her arms in front of her, imagining Rowan falling off the horse.

"How big's the horse?" she asked.

"Not too big and very, very old," Sheila replied, placing a reassuring arm around Rebecca's waist. "Come on. I'll help you unpack."

Rebecca watched Rowan running up the lane as she stepped back into the house. Sheila shut the door.

"She liked his compliment on her courage," Rebecca said.

"It's all over town."

"Is it?"

"You meet Sean?"

Rebecca shook her head.

"In 1967 Sean lost his four sons—drowned in a storm while fishing. He's not been the same since. Not that he was too pleasant before, mind. He only speaks with Paddy and Eoman these days—usually just about the weather."

"Paddy and Eoman. I met them last night. Now, who are they?"

"They come from the oldest fisherman families on the island. Paddy Blake is from the Blakes and Eoman O'Connelly is from the Fitzpatricks, on Eoman's grandmother's side. Well, aside from the Morahans, but there's only Sean left there. Paddy and Eoman are partners."

"Paddy has one child," Rebecca muttered. Since she had slept well the night before, some of Sharon's tales had returned to her memory. "Siobhan."

"That's right."

"Rowan met her last night. And the farmer who has seven children?"

"Fitzgibbon."

"Right, right. Oh! He had a problem last night. John had to go there. That's how I ended up in the pub."

"What problem?" Sheila inquired, turning on the water in the kitchen sink.

"Uh—with bees and Trace?"

Sheila burst out laughing.

"What's so funny?"

"Ah, you'll see. You need to talk to his wife, Mairead, anyway. She has many knitting stitches from her family. She's from the island just north."

"Mairead," Rebecca repeated, filing the name with "Fitzgibbon" and "bees." "I need to write this stuff down."

She stepped into the bedroom, knelt down, unzipped the black duffel, and rummaged through its contents for a notepad and a pencil.

"Honestly, Sheila, you all on this island are so confusing! Fionn Jr. and Tom are brothers. Maggie, Sharon's sister, is married to Tom. Eoman O'Connelly is a Fitzpatrick on his grandmother's side. Sharon is an O'Connelly married to John Fitzpatrick, which means somehow Eoman and John are related."

"Cousins," Sheila said, grinning as she leaned against the bedroom doorframe, wiping her hands on a dish towel. "And it's not Fionn Jr. It's 'my Fionn'—the older one. And just Fionn—the younger one."

Rebecca fell back on her bottom.

Sheila laughed.

"It's hopeless. I'll never keep it straight. It's been years since Sharon and I talked about all this."

"Ah, Becky. Look how many of us there are. We've had stories of you from Sharon, but you—you have a lifetime of stories to remember about all of us. It'll come back."

Meeting Sheila's gaze, Rebecca found hazel certainty in her eyes. That was a comfort.

"You knit?" Rebecca asked.

"Aye."

"You working on something now?"

"Christmas gifts."

Rebecca stood up. "Can I see?"

"Don't you want to unpack?"

"That can wait," Rebecca said, sliding past Sheila toward the living room. "I want to get started." Grabbing her camera, DVD camera, and tripod, she opened the front door.

"Mine aren't like Rose's and Liz's," Sheila said as she followed Rebecca out the door.

"They're yours, though, and that's all that matters."

"So you're a doctor," Sheila said, trotting after Rebecca.

"Doctorate. Archaeology. I specialize in textiles."

"Textiles?"

"Clothing. Tapestries. My area of expertise is European fabrics. My dissertation actually dealt with the Viking tablet weaving of early Ireland. Anyway, I date, clean, preserve, and, mostly, study textiles. You can find out a lot about a people by their textile arts."

"So you're here to study our textile art?"

Rebecca looked back with a grin. "I want to record your stories from your own mouths so scholars don't have to try to figure out what you meant after you pass."

"I see."

The ocean breeze was at her back, and Rebecca listened to the waves crashing around her. Her purpose in life was to study, to research. In focus and silence, her mind sought stories and meaning from the past that were woven tightly in wool and cotton. Deciphering the intent in historical art was like solving a jigsaw puzzle for which the pieces were not all available. Some could be on the shelf of a library in New York. Others might be in a drawer in a museum in Paris. Rarely were all the pieces in one place. But with this project—the island sweaters—Rebecca had all the pieces. The islanders were famous for their unique sweaters. She was walking into the past with living people inextricably bound to it, and all she needed do was to sit and listen and record. Her heart soared.

When the women reached the two-story cottage, Sheila opened the front door and without a word they climbed a narrow staircase. Rebecca's tripod bumped the railing as she got to the top stair.

"Ah, sorry."

Following Sheila, Rebecca entered a tiny bedroom on the right. There, folded neatly upon a twin bed with an apricot-colored cotton bedspread, were two white sweaters. Sheila picked each one up and spread it flat on the bed.

"They're so beautiful, Sheila."

"Thank you. I'll take the compliment from the expert."

"I've come here as a student. To learn from the masters," Rebecca said with a wink.

"Well, that would be Rose and Liz, then. Not me," Sheila replied with a half smile.

"I don't know, Sheila. Look at these! They're wonderful. Tell me about them."

"What do you want to know?"

"Well, how long does it take you to make one?" Rebecca asked, unfolding her tripod.

"About forty hours—more or less. What do we do with the camera?"

"I need stills for the book, and film so I can get your voice. I want to record what you say, exactly how you say it. You just tell me who they're for, why you picked that stitch, anything you want to say."

"You gonna write that, then?"

Rebecca nodded as she clipped the DVD camera to the tripod. "They both have a chevron with bobbles," she noted.

"You'll find many families have patterns they tend to use in their ganseys," Sheila replied. "We don't call them sweaters."

"I see." Rebecca focused the camera on the sweater and hit RE-CORD. "Ganseys. Okay. These ganseys are so similar. One has a double zigzag—the other has a single one. The sweater—gansey—with the single zigzag seems more elaborate, though. Who are they for?"

"My husband and Fionn. He's like his father, but more complicated."

"The one with the single zigzag is your son's, then."

Sheila nodded.

"Your Fionn's has a braid. Tell me about that."

"Well, I made it for him and so, to me, that's our children—five of them. That's called a fivefold Aran braid."

"Braids are children?"

"Just to me."

"The zigzag traditionally means something, though."

"The double zigzag signifies married life—sometimes going up and sometimes down."

"What's the single one?"

"It usually means cliffs or something like that. For me, it means Fionn walks alone. He's not married and he's not getting any younger." Sheila chuckled. Rebecca grinned.

"Oops," Rebecca whispered.

"What?"

"Nothing."

"What is it?"

"There's a twisted stitch on your son's gansey. He'll never notice," Rebecca said, waving it off.

"He never does," Sheila replied.

Rebecca glanced up to meet Sheila's smiling eyes and then to the sweater for a closer inspection.

"There are twisted stitches all over this."

"Aye. He's a little twisted."

Rebecca stood over the sweaters as Sheila left the room. Pointing her camera at Fionn's twisted stitches, Rebecca clicked a picture and laughed.

CHAPTER 8

Diamond

Diamond. 1. A diamond stitch appears as its name and is knitted as a single column of diamonds, one ending where another begins. 2. Traditionally diamonds represent the stone walls that surround the small plots of land on the island. 3. The nature of a community of people who weather storms, celebrate sunshine, laugh, cry, live, die, and together rest eternally side by side.

—R. Dirane, *A Binding Love*

The next day Rebecca and Rowan stood on the small cement porch of Sharon's childhood home. Holding her little girl's hand, Rebecca wished Rowan would rub her finger. She needed comfort.

The last time Rebecca had seen Peg, Sharon's mother, was at the airport in San Francisco six years before. Tears had poured down Peg's cheeks as she made her way through security, waving good-bye as she and Sharon left for home.

Rebecca, with one-month-old Rowan in her arms, waved in return, but no tears had come to her eyes. She needed Peg and Sharon to leave. She needed to be alone—to forget what had happened to Dennis two weeks before on Thanksgiving night. They had been there, standing with her just off Highway 1. They were part of that memory and Rebecca couldn't forget with them in her house.

Now Rebecca stood on Peg's doorstep, having tried to forget for six years. With every thought of visiting Peg, the memory of Dennis returned. Her heart pounded, crawling up into her throat. Swallowing hard to keep it in her chest, she reached out and knocked.

"Mama? You're squeezing my hand too tight."

"Sorry, Rowan," Rebecca whispered.

Together, Rowan and Rebecca waited, listening to the shuffle of many feet and the cry of many names beyond the brown wooden door. Reaching over to her child, Rebecca tucked in the label of Rowan's overalls, which read MADE BY THE HANDS OF R. MORAY, back into place. Of all the clothes Rebecca made, overalls for Rowan were her favorite because she could use the same pattern over and over again as her little girl grew. All she needed to do was lengthen the legs and change the fabric. Today, Rowan wore the black pair with tigers lunging, stalking, and roaring across her chest and down her legs. It was her favorite outfit.

The door opened with Maggie and eight faces of varying ages peeping out from behind her.

"Ma, it's Becky!" Maggie announced.

"Good morning, Mags," Rebecca said.

"Mornin', Becks."

"All these yours?" Rebecca inquired.

Maggie chuckled. "I'm the house all the wee ones go to, Becks."

"Lucky you."

They laughed.

"Becky!" Peg declared as she crawled through the children blocking her way.

"Hi, Peg."

Touching Rebecca's face softly, tears fell from Peg's eyes.

"Oh, Peg, don't do that," Rebecca said, taking the older woman into her arms.

"It's been so long," Peg whispered.

"Now I'm here," Rebecca replied hoarsely, her throat tightening.

"Rowan, look at you! Last time I saw you, you were a tiny baby!"

Peg exclaimed, releasing Rebecca and grabbing Rowan. The little girl glanced at her mother over Peg's shoulder, unsure.

"Peg is Sharon's mother, Rowan. She came to California when you were born. You wouldn't remember."

"Heard you were having a—what's Sharon call it, Ma?" Maggie said.

"A moment."

"A moment with Fionn night before last," Maggie finished.

"News travels fast around here," Rebecca said, shrugging uncomfortably.

"I have all the news, married as I am to the pub owner," Maggie said with a laugh.

"Good reason to marry the pub owner, I suppose," Rebecca replied.

"Aye. Plus it's a small village. Steady income."

They laughed. Rebecca reached up and ran her fingers through her hair.

"Better be off with ya, Becky. Rose and Liz will be waiting. Supper'll be here when you've finished," Peg said.

"You okay?" Rebecca asked of Rowan.

"She'll be fine, Becks. Mum and I'll watch her. You know how to get to Rose Blake's house?"

"Past the church, around the corner, end of the road."

"That's right."

Rebecca bent down and kissed Rowan.

"She'll be fine, Becky," Peg assured her.

"Thanks. See you." Rebecca turned away, hoping to leave Thanksgiving night on Peg's doorstep. Unfortunately, it followed her down the steps and out the gate like a lost dog. The pale light in the ambulance, Rowan's diapered little body lying on the gurney, sirens blaring as Peg held her hand—all these memories flooded Rebecca's mind. She gasped, turning quickly to the left, trying to distance herself from the past.

"Watch out for tourists on bikes, Becky," Peg warned.

Waving over her shoulder, Rebecca turned down the sidewalk in front of Peg's house and walked toward the church's spire. Several cyclists whizzed by as she crossed the street.

"Good morning, Becky!"

Winded, Rebecca skidded to a halt. Turning around, she found Tom standing in front of his establishment with a broom. Eoman stood next to him, a twine of rope tossed over his shoulder. She couldn't tell which of them had called the greeting to her.

"Good morning, Tom. Eoman."

"Watch the bikes," Eoman warned.

"Peg already told me."

"All right then."

Shrugging her backpack farther up on her shoulders, Rebecca continued down the street. She passed the church, which stood cold and weathered on the opposite side of the road. Four young women who were talking and laughing loudly walked toward her, their accents clearly not Irish. Rebecca had to step off the sidewalk to make room for them, and when she looked up she saw three bicyclists racing toward her. Jumping farther into the street to avoid them, Rebecca felt the wind and heard the buzz of bicycle chains whipping by. Quickly she skittered back onto the sidewalk.

"Watch out for the bikes," she muttered, clutching her chest to still her racing heart. Peering up the street, she saw a lean man with brown hair shaved close to his head standing on the sidewalk in front of a line of bicycles. He smiled at her.

"Becky! I'm John Hernon."

"Hi," she replied.

"Tom says you'll be needing a bike."

"Oh, no, I don't think so. It's not that far to walk from the house to the town."

"No, but you'll be needing one to head out farther in the other direction to get to the Fitzgibbons'."

"How much?" Becky asked. She hadn't counted on renting a bike.

"Nothin', Becky. You'll need it. You havin' supper at Peg's?"

"Why, yes. I am."

"I'll drop it off there, then."

"Oh," Rebecca replied. "Well, thanks very much."

"No problem. If you need anything else, let me or Anne know. All right?"

"Annie Blake?"

"No," John replied. "My wife, Anne Hernon, Tom and Fionn's sister."

Rebecca nodded uncomfortably. She needed to write this down. "And so Sheila and Fionn Sr.'s daughter? I've not met her," she said.

"You will. Best be getting on there."

"Yeah—yeah. Thanks."

As Becky passed him, she glanced into the window. A sign on the glass read HERNON'S SHOP and the place was packed with people carrying backpacks, totes, and children.

"Busy in there."

"It's just the beginning. Wait till July." John chuckled, stepping back into his shop. "See you later, then."

Around the next corner Rebecca found Dooley's Bed and Breakfast with its tidy garden and quaint sign on her right, and at the far end of the street she spied two old women standing in the front yard of a house, hunched together with their backs to her. One was small and crooked and wore a red shawl, and the other had on a lavender dress with a white cardigan. Rebecca smiled broadly as she approached. The woman in the red shawl glanced over her shoulder.

"Becky?"

"Yes!"

"Good to finally see ya. I'm Rose Blake and this is Liz O'Connelly."

"I am so very happy to finally meet you two," Rebecca said, shaking Rose's fragile hand earnestly.

"Have you slept well?"

"Yes, thanks," she replied, taking Liz's hand.

"Sit, sit," Rose said, motioning Rebecca to one of three chairs in front of her little house. "Liz, can you check on the tea?"

Liz disappeared into the house.

"I see you have a spinning wheel," Rebecca said, noting the wheel that stood before one of the chairs.

"One must learn to spin."

"I see."

"We have a hand spindle for you."

"I beg your pardon?"

"A hand spindle. You'll start with that and then work your way into the spinning wheel."

"Oh, I don't need to learn to spin. I'm just here to talk to you about your ganseys."

"First learn to spin, then to knit, and then we'll show you our ganseys," Liz said, coming outside with tea on a tray. "Sugar?"

"Yes, please," Rebecca said. "I know how to knit."

"Who taught you?" Rose asked, casting a skeptical green eye upon Rebecca.

"Sharon."

"Excellent!" Liz declared as she placed the brown teapot on the small table next to the spinning wheel. "Then you'll spin and then we'll show you our ganseys."

"I really don't have a lot of time for—"

"Becky, to truly understand anything takes time. You have the summer here. Time enough to spin and knit and learn," Rose said, tottering to her seat.

"Father Michael!" Liz called.

A priest trotted down the street toward Rose's house, the dusting of gray in his hair and his white collar glistening in the sun.

"Good day to you, Liz. Rose."

"Have you met Sharon's friend, Father?"

"Our newest resident. How do you do, Becky?" the priest said, extending his hand as Rebecca stood.

"It's Rebecca, and I'm not really a resident, just a visitor," she replied, shaking his hand.

"We'll see you at Mass on Sunday."

"Oh, no. I'm not Catholic."

"You believe in God?"

"Uh—not really."

"Fine. We'll see you at church then. Good day, ladies."

Father Michael continued on past Rose's house and headed out of town.

"I won't be at church, Father," Rebecca called after him.

"See you Sunday," he replied without looking back at her.

Rebecca frowned, stood, and ran after him.

"Excuse me, Father."

Skidding to a halt, Father Michael turned around. "Yes, Rebecca?"

"I will not be coming to Mass on Sunday. I study religions as part of my work. They are nothing more than social constructs. No offense, but I don't really see them as necessary for personal development."

The priest met Rebecca's level gaze with his own, staring at her as if waiting for her to continue. Squinting at him, Rebecca shook her head. Father Michael smiled broadly.

"Good. See you on Sunday." He turned and continued on his way.

"You won't!" Rebecca yelled after him.

"Sunday!" he yelled back and disappeared around the corner.

CHAPTER 9

Ladder

Ladder (aka Ladder of Life or Jacob's Ladder). 1. A pattern running vertically on a garment, making the poles and rungs of a ladder. 2. Traditionally references Jacob's ladder, a way to heaven and eternal happiness, or more precisely a oneness with God. 3. In fishing terms, Jacob's ladders are the ropes that run from the deck of a vessel to the rigging above. 4. A connection that causes change.

—R. Dirane, *A Binding Love*

Sean was in a hurry. Although he had meant to tell Paddy of the impending weather yesterday, he had forgotten, for he had been preoccupied with Rowan, mahogany eyes, halos, sunny windows, and little feet walking. Now, even though it was early in the morning, the tourists were thick and thoughtless on the sidewalks, forcing the old man to step off into the street to make room for them, only to be nearly run down by bicycles.

"Gotta watch the bikes," he muttered as he turned the corner. Then he stopped.

There, crouched in a recessed doorway, was that little Yank, wearing a very strange pair of coveralls. As Sean watched, Siobhan skipped around the corner, halting but three meters away from where Rowan stood hidden.

"Come out, come out, wherever you are!" Siobhan called.

The little Yank sucked her stomach in as if to make herself thinner, not wishing to be found just yet. After surveying the area, Siobhan quickly trotted across the street. Scooting to the edge of the doorway, Rowan peered across the road, following Siobhan with her eyes. She giggled.

"I see your mother doesn't know how to dress you properly, either," Sean remarked as he walked up to the little girl, elated to get a chance to set things right.

Rowan spun around and stared up into Sean's eyes. But instead of looking frightened or hurt, she gazed up at him as if—as if he were not even there. Turning her back to him, the little girl walked calmly away.

"It's polite to reply to someone when they talk to you."

Rowan stopped with her back squarely to him. "I don't have to be nice to mean people."

"You were staring at me. That's rude."

"I was not staring."

"You were, too."

Rowan glanced over her shoulder. "I was watching your hands."

Sean cocked his head as something sounded in the distance. "My hands?"

"Yes. Your hands looked like they were knitting. I always watch my mama's hands when she knits. It makes me feel good when I'm sleepy."

Sean furrowed his brow. "You were sleepy in the pub?"

"We'd just got here."

"Where'd you come from?"

"California."

That was half a world away. Sean grimaced. "I didn't realize you were watching my hands."

"You should talk to people before you yell at them."

Sean's palms tingled as they began to sweat. Rubbing them on his thighs, he took a deep breath. It had been so long since he had apologized to anyone. Had he ever apologized to a child? To his children? He searched his memory to find just one instance, but none came to mind. Unsure what to say, Sean coughed a little. "I'm s-sorry, Rowan, for yelling at you."

Rowan faced him. "You said my name wasn't a good name for me. That hurt my feelings."

Peering into her mahogany eyes, Sean could see her pain. It was the pain he had put there. His heart skipped several beats, and he pressed his left hand on his chest to stop it.

"I'm sorry for hurting your feelings. It's—it's a good Irish name. It's a good name for you."

"Why don't you like my overalls?" Rowan asked, touching the roaring tiger on her chest.

"I—I didn't see they were tigers. I like them now," he replied quickly.

"My mama painted the tigers. That's my favorite animal. What's your favorite animal?"

Sean reached up with his right hand, straightening the cap upon his head. "I—I don't know. I've never really thought about it."

"Tigers are my favorite 'cause they purr really loud. You ever heard a tiger purr?"

"Can't say as I have."

"Their paws are as big as your head."

"Truly?"

"Yeah. And their stripes are magic."

"Magic?"

"Uh-huh. They crawl around in the jungle, which is green, but you can't see them even though they are black and yellow and orange. They blend in even though they're different. Magic."

Sean nodded. From the next street, the old man heard Siobhan calling Rowan's name. "You best be getting on there, Rowan. Siobhan's calling for you."

Without warning, Rowan smiled. Sean's breath caught in his

chest, for her mahogany eyes lit up like little wood fairies as they peered up at his face. How long had it been since a child smiled at him?

"Good-bye, Mr. Morahan," she said, her face beaming.

"Good day to you, Rowan," he choked, unable to loosen his chest.

Rowan skipped away, and as she did so a great pain welled up in Sean's heart.

"Rowan!" he called after her.

The little girl stopped, still smiling.

"You may call me Sean. Watch the bikes."

"Bye, Sean," she said and disappeared around the corner.

Sean grabbed his chest and leaned against the building, certain he was having a heart attack. But he did not pass out or fall over. He took shallow breaths, forcing his rib cage to release his lungs and heart. The sound rolled again in the distance. It was thunder.

"Paddy," he whispered, and pushing himself away from the building, he stumbled toward the docks, still holding his heart.

CHAPTER 10

Moss

Moss. 1. A pattern with a bumpy texture created by knitting a stitch, then purling the next, alternating between the two for two rows. The next two rows are created by purling a stitch, then knitting the next, alternating between these two. Can be used by itself or as the interior pattern of a diamond or square. 2. Traditionally represents earth (the island is mostly rock and it was from moss and seaweed that soil for crop cultivation was created). 3. The ground where a life grows.

—R. Dirane, *A Binding Love*

*R*ebecca sat on Peg's sofa that night after supper, watching her yarn twist from the tuft of wool she held in her left hand as her right spun the hand spindle, which then dropped to the floor, turning fast like a top. She could hear the clicking of Rose's spinning wheel nearby. The steady rhythm quieted her mind.

Throughout the day, as she had learned to spin, her thoughts spiraled with worry at the thought of returning to Peg's house for dinner. She hoped not to spend too much time alone with Peg so she could avoid any conversation about Dennis. She was relieved when Paddy came to Rose's house near suppertime and tucked his mother, her spinning wheel, Liz, and Rebecca all into the island's only car. Slowly, he wound through the pedestrians and bicyclists to Peg's house.

Rebecca's yarn broke. She sighed. Liz, seated in the chair across the room, stood up to help her mend it.

"You need to keep your right hand away from the triangle. If you don't, you're twisting the wool, not spinning it."

"Spinning our own wool is what makes our ganseys look the way they do," Rose remarked as her yarn spun easily from her tuft of wool. "The machine-made yarn is all one size and texture. Homespun has these little bumps in it. See?" Rose stopped spinning to show the slight irregularity of her yarn.

"That adds texture to the fabric," Liz said.

"Remember Claire's yarn?" Rose asked, setting her wheel in motion again.

"We used to sit behind Sean and the boys during Mass. They always wore ganseys to church and we would sit behind them to memorize Claire's stitches."

"Missed many a lesson doing that."

The old ladies laughed.

"Claire who?" Rebecca inquired.

"Morahan," Liz replied.

"Sean Morahan's wife?"

"Was. She passed on some years ago. Never told us how she came up with the patterns, though. She'd just smile and shrug."

"Sad about her sons," Rebecca said.

"Not long after that was when she left the island for Galway."

"Aye." Rose nodded. "My Padrig sailed her there. Never knew why she left. Sean was hard on her, mind you, even before the boys were lost."

"Hard on her?"

"Kept her close," Liz whispered confidentially. "Didn't like her spending time away from the house without him or the boys."

"He was controlling," Rebecca said.

"Controlling?" Rose inquired.

"He took away her freedom," Rebecca replied coldly, the memory of Dennis flashing across her mind. Dennis had always been waiting and watching—always there.

"How do you know that, Becky?" Rose asked, her eyes focused on her yarn.

Rebecca pulled the thin white fibers from her tuft of wool. Bending down, she lifted the hand spindle to her lap.

"Why else would he not like her to leave without him or the boys? He wanted to control who she talked to, where she went, what she did. She wouldn't be free, would she, if she couldn't make her own choices? If she had to concern herself with what he liked her to do or not to do."

Rose glanced up, her green eyes clear and piercing. "How could you guess such a thing?"

"Because, by how you talk about him, I once knew someone very much like him."

"Ought to be heading home, Becky. Storm's comin'," Paddy said as he stepped into the room.

Rebecca swallowed hard, grateful for the interruption.

Rose's spindle came to an abrupt stop. It was so sudden that it made Rebecca start. When she glanced up, she found Rose and Liz with matching frowns on their faces, staring at her. Rebecca shrugged, her breath caught somewhere between her breastbone and her throat.

"Not the worst we've seen," Paddy continued, winking at his mother.

"For now, best be getting home, Becky," Liz said. "The weather's not bad now, but it's good to be indoors when it grows."

"Well," Rebecca said, letting go her breath with relief as she set the wool and the hand spindle on the sofa. Quickly she stood. "Thanks for the spinning lesson today, ladies."

"Oh, no," Liz said, handing Rebecca the wool and the spindle. "You take this home with you to practice. There's a bag of wool by the door."

"A bag of wool?" Rebecca's eyes widened as she spied a large cotton bag full of unspun wool waiting for her. "Liz, that's really too much—"

"Take your time. Need to spin. Then we'll show you our ganseys," Liz said.

"Okay, okay," Rebecca said with a laugh. "Where's Rowan?"

"Here, Mama," Rowan replied, trotting into the living room with Siobhan in tow.

"Maybe you can sleep over one night, Rowan," Siobhan said. "We'll go fishin' on the rocks south of town."

"Can I, Mama?" Rowan asked excitedly.

"Whenever Paddy and Annie say it's okay, Rowan," Rebecca replied. The little girls giggled and hugged each other. Rebecca grinned.

As Rebecca lifted her backpack onto her shoulders, Liz grabbed the bag of wool and together with Rose, Paddy, Annie, Siobhan, and Eoman, they moved toward the door, pulling on their coats and sweaters. It appeared to Rebecca that the entire village was filing out of Peg's house. Why all these people ended up over for dinner, she couldn't imagine. Taking Rowan's hand, Rebecca slipped in among them.

"See you tomorrow, Mags," Rebecca said, stepping over to her bike, which John had dropped off earlier.

"All right then, Becks."

"You watch that wind, Becky," Peg warned. "It can catch you unawares on the north road."

With Rowan balancing on the handlebars, Rebecca pedaled into motion in the fading light.

The little girl waved as her mother headed toward the pub.

"Becks, your house is the other way!" Maggie shouted.

"I know. I just need to check something real quick," she yelled over her shoulder.

Turning into the growing wind, Rebecca rode toward the church's spire. As she passed the pub, she could hear laughter and bright singing within. Several tourists tottered down the street, arm in arm, heading for Dooley's Bed and Breakfast. When Rebecca reached the church, she stopped.

"What are we doing?" Rowan asked.

"Looking for what time the Masses are."

"Why?"

"To make sure we're not here," she replied with a wicked smile. There was no posted schedule, so Rebecca decided she'd ask Maggie or Peg nonchalantly the next day what time church started on Sunday. With a low, rumbling laugh, she stepped on the pedals and headed home.

The wind pummeled her little bike as she rode down the darkening road, but she decided it would have been much worse had the stone walls not lined the street. By the time they made it to their cottage, Rebecca was feeling quite proud of herself at having ridden a bike across the island in a growing gale without injury to herself or her daughter. When she bumped off the asphalt at the O'Flaherty house and pedaled down the drive, to her surprise Sheila opened the door. Trace stood next to her.

"Everything all right?" Rebecca called.

"Aye. You can put the bike in the shed over there," Sheila said, pointing to the left.

Rowan jumped off the handlebars and Rebecca took the bike around the corner of the cottage, where she found a small shed attached to the house. With the bike safely stowed for the night, she followed Rowan into the house.

"It's really going to blow tonight," Fionn Sr. said as Becky came through the door. "It's coming in from the south. We brought extra peat and some candles just in case the electricity goes."

"It gets to howling and you can hear the wind through the thatch," Sheila said. "But Danny, our youngest, came home from Doolin last summer and he and Tom replaced the roof then. It'll not be blowing off, so no need to worry."

"Aye, Danny's magic with thatchin'," Fionn Sr. said.

"You'll be fine here, but if you want you can stay with us," Sheila offered.

"No—no, I think we'll be okay."

"You'll get a lot of coals from that what's burning in there now. You'll want to scoop them together into a pile and toss two more bricks of peat on the sides of the pile about half of an hour before you go to bed. Just like I showed you yesterday."

"A small, steady fire is better for heating and cooking than a large one," Fionn Sr. told Rowan. "Takes less fuel and won't singe your whiskers."

"I don't have whiskers," Rowan replied.

"Trace does."

Rowan giggled.

"We'll keep an eye on you from our house," Sheila said as she walked to the door. "You sure you're all right? Sean says this'll be a strong one. He's not been wrong before."

"We're good," Rebecca replied. The wind burst into the room as Sheila opened the door.

"House has been here more than a hundred years," Fionn Sr. informed Rowan. "Hasn't blown away yet. If it starts to scarin' ya, Rowan, sing."

Fionn Sr. stepped out of the house, holding Sheila by the hand. Leaning on the door, Rebecca closed it with effort and then went to look out the window. She watched Fionn Sr. wrap his arm around his wife, presumably to keep her from blowing away. She turned around and gasped, startled. There stood Trace next to Rowan, wagging his tail.

"What's he doing here?"

"He wants to stay with me," Rowan replied, scratching Trace's right ear.

Rebecca rolled her eyes. "Come on, then. Let's get our jammies on."

"You scared, Mama?" Rowan asked, following her mother toward the bedroom.

To tell the truth, Rebecca was afraid, but she said to Rowan, "Nah. You heard what Mr. O'Flaherty said. This house has been here for over a hundred years. And they're watching out for us. Not scared at all."

Rowan nodded. After they'd changed their clothes, Rebecca pulled out several books and she and Rowan read with Trace lying on the floor at the foot of the bed. The wind rattled the roof, making a sound like the cry of a great gull careening across a sea-chiseled cliff. Rebecca couldn't tell if it was the nature of the gusts or the nature of the thatching that made it sound so. Whatever the cause, she lit several candles. As she blew out the match, the electricity failed.

"We can't read," Rowan whispered.

"Well, you go to bed," Rebecca remarked, "and I'll bank the fire."

She lit a stick of incense and set it upon its holder. As she tucked her daughter under the covers, she remembered the flashlight they'd brought. After spending the morning with Sheila that first day, Rebecca had unpacked and organized their things, and now she easily found the flashlight in the dresser drawer. She pulled it out and set it next to the bed.

"If you get scared, turn on the flashlight."

"No, Mama, I'll sing. That's what Mr. O'Flaherty said to do."

"Well, he must know."

Rebecca kissed Rowan's forehead. Without shutting the door, she stepped into the living room. The storm thundered outside and Rebecca's heart began to flutter. The screaming through the thatch came in waves, growing louder, then falling away.

"Sounds like a banshee," she muttered. Glancing around, she thought about how very small this cottage was and how close the sea; there was nothing but disintegrating cliffs between the house and the ocean.

"It's been here over a hundred years," she repeated, her palms and feet tingling with sweat. Perhaps they should have gone with Sheila and Fionn Sr. to stay at their house. Turning around in place, Rebecca couldn't decide what she should do next. As she pushed her hair away from her now sweating temples, she spied a small tuft of wool sticking out of her backpack.

"Need to learn to spin."

As she pulled out the hand spindle and wool, she gave a shudder, for a great screech echoed through the roof. Stiffly, she went over to the sofa and put the hand spindle and wool down on the cushions. Then she went to the fireplace and used the small shovel to gather all the glowing embers of the fire together. She set two bricks of peat on the sides of the little mound, as Sheila had instructed her. The peat smoldered, creating gray-blue smoke, which rose up and wound its way about the fireplace. Soon it would go up the chimney and be free like she was. Rebecca thought then about Rose and Liz and their discussions regarding Sean and his wife, Claire. Turning around, Rebecca spotted herself in the small mirror that hung on the living room wall near the front door. Her brown hair fell in tangles about her shoulders as her wide mahogany eyes gazed back at her from her thin, heart-shaped face.

"He was controlling," she whispered to her reflection.

Rebecca stood in front of her full-length mirror, admiring how the green woolen dress clung to her hips. Though Sharon had gone home four years before, shortly after graduating from college, she still must have had a clear enough picture of Rebecca in her mind to knit such a thing. It was by far the most beautiful birthday present Rebecca had ever received and she loved it. Smiling at herself, she felt as pretty as she had on the night of her senior prom.

At that moment Dennis came into the bedroom, stepping between Rebecca and the mirror as he made his way into the bathroom.

"I hate that dress," he said quietly, stopping to adjust his hair in the mirror. "Makes your hips look as wide as a whale."

"I—I love this dress," Rebecca replied, wincing at his stinging words.

"It's ugly."

"It is not," Rebecca whispered, straightening the hem.

Dennis turned around, eyeing her with his cold blue gaze. He stepped toward her. Rebecca backed up, her stomach churning.

"Wear something else."

"No. It's a dinner party and this is the nicest thing I have."

"I don't want to be seen with a whale," Dennis replied, taking another step toward her.

"It's a dress. It's on my body. If I want to look like a whale, I will."

"I'm the one who has to look at you all night. You can take it off or I will. Which do you choose?"

Rebecca stepped back, tears rising to her eyes.

"Why does it matter so much to you, Dennis?"

"Take it off or I will," he repeated, taking two more steps toward her.

Quickly, Rebecca slipped it over her head, shivering in her underwear.

"Give it to me," Dennis said softly, holding his hand out.

Rebecca shook her head, holding the dress to her chest.

"Give it to me, Becky," he repeated louder.

"It's my birthday present," Rebecca whispered.

Dennis ripped the dress away from her.

"It's mine," Rebecca said.

"You want to make me madder?" He was seething.

"No," Rebecca answered.

"Put something else on or you'll make us later than we already are," he said and with that, Dennis left the bedroom with the dress.

"It's my birthday present," Rebecca whispered as she wiped her eyes with her shaking hands, knowing she would never see the dress again.

Rebecca turned from the mirror and watched the smoke and the memory hang about the fireplace. She waited for both to rise up the chimney and be gone. Only the smoke drifted away. The memory did not. Still Rebecca could see Dennis walking away with her dress.

"He was controlling," she said, feeling a cold hollow in her heart. She picked up the spindle and sat down on the sofa.

Setting the spindle to spin upon the floor with her right hand, Rebecca pulled the tuft of wool straight up with her left. A long strand of white yarn twisted between the spindle and the wool. As it wound, Rebecca could just make out the little fibers of hair pulling off the tuft of wool, making what appeared to be an upside-down triangle. Its base was in the wool itself and its point entered the strand of yarn attached to the spindle. She spun the hand spindle again and with her right hand no more than two inches below the triangle, she rolled the white strand of yarn between her thumb and index finger.

"Not too tight," she whispered, watching the wool in her left hand disappear into the yarn she rolled between her fingers. She spun the spindle again as the storm raged outside. When the last strand of wool disappeared from her left hand, she peered down at the spindle on the floor. It was wrapped with beautiful white yarn. She smiled.

"Mama?" Rowan called from the bedroom. "I hear a bird singing."

"Birds don't sing in storms," Rebecca said, setting down the spinning and walking toward her daughter's voice.

"What's that, then?" Rowan asked.

Rebecca cocked her head, listening. From outside the bedroom window, she did hear the bird's song. "You have the flashlight?"

With a small shuffle and a grunt, Rowan flicked on the flashlight. Lifting her daughter into her arms, Rebecca walked over to the window and drew back the curtains. There, in the bramble, they spied the bird that had greeted them the morning of their arrival, now clinging to a branch, facing the wind, with rain pelting its feathers and face. Its little beak moved as it sang.

"Is it singing 'cause it's scared, Mama?"

"Does it look scared to you?"

"Uh-uh."

"Maybe it wants the wind to know that no matter how much it blows, it's not going to be scared. See the nest?"

Rebecca pointed the flashlight farther into the bramble, and the light fell upon another bird sitting on the nest.

"Is that the mama?" Rowan said.

"Maybe it's the dad. It doesn't look scared, either."

"Are there babies?"

"They're just eggs right now. Let's go to bed."

Rebecca put Rowan back on the bed, then took the flashlight into the front room and blew out all the candles. After checking the fire one last time, she went back into the bedroom, turned off the flashlight, and crawled into bed.

"I'm not afraid of the wind, either, Mama."

"Me neither," Rebecca whispered, and with her daughter in her arms, she fell asleep, listening to the little bird singing over the gale.

CHAPTER 11

Diagonal Ribbing

Diagonal Ribbing. 1. A pattern created by twisting stitches. It appears as the deep furrows of a field on a diagonal and is used as texturing. 2. The nature of learning.

—R. Dirane, *A Binding Love*

The gale blew through, and early the next day Rebecca stepped out into the fog that had risen with the sun and shuffled slowly around the side of the house to get the bike. When she returned, Rowan skipped out of the cottage with the dog at her heels and they made their way toward Sheila's house.

Rebecca and Rowan walked close together through the thick fog floating in the morning air. The storm had left the gravel lane as wet and gray as the fog itself. With her feet crunching loudly in the still of the morning, Rebecca reached through the mist, testing to see how dense it was. Fog wasn't just a type of weather to her; it was an entity—a living creature. Tule fog, the moisture that rose from the tule grass beds in the central valley of California, drifted thick in some places and thin in others, like it couldn't make up its mind where it wanted to be. Whether she was wandering through her grandfather's almond orchard in Turlock or walking to school in Redding, fog was one of Rebecca's favorite things—an old friend. Her hand disappeared at arm's length. She smiled, watching as Rowan trotted ahead and disappeared with the dog.

"Is that Rowan Moray?" Fionn Sr.'s voice drifted through the fog.

"Yeah!" Rowan exclaimed. She had become but a shadow to the right.

Rebecca moved toward the dark apparition in the mist, rolling the bike slowly over the gravel.

"Would you like to come with me to check on the cows?"

"We were going to town," Rebecca said. "She's going over to play with Siobhan."

"I'll take her. The cows are to the south anyway. The old mare should make it that much farther."

"Can I, Mama?"

Rebecca looked at Rowan and Fionn Sr. in the mist. For a moment she hesitated, thinking perhaps it would be safer for Rowan to stay with her. But then she remembered how much fun Rowan had had the last time she went with Fionn Sr. and the old mare. Rebecca grinned.

"No place safer than here," she said.

"Aye, girl," Fionn Sr. replied.

"Sure. Go ahead, Rowan."

"Come on, then," Fionn Sr. said, lifting Rowan over the wall. Trace hurdled the wall right behind her, his wagging tail rippling the fog as he cleared the stones. Rebecca watched her daughter and Fionn Sr. fade away in the mist until they were nothing but ghostly murmurs sifting through the thick air.

Inhaling deeply, Rebecca reached over to the wall and brushed the weathered stones with her hand. They were cold and rough, with moss sticking to them like barnacles. She thought she should go into town and try to talk to Rose and Liz, but as she stood there, she recalled that there was a small fort somewhere to the north of her cottage. She closed her eyes, hoping to hear its ancient walls calling to her. Instead she heard footsteps on the gravel coming at her from the direction of Sheila's house.

"Sheila?" she called.

"No," a man's voice answered, and slowly from out of the fog Fionn appeared. His saddlebags were flung over his right shoulder and in his left hand he held a pink cardboard box tied with string.

Rebecca's stomach dropped to her feet as she backed closer to the wall.

"Good day to you, Rebecca."

"Hi," she replied coldly.

"'Tis a morning for tea and hot pasties."

Rebecca offered no response. She felt as cold and stiff as the stone wall on which she leaned.

Fionn sighed. "Look. I apologize for racing off with your daughter."

"Really?" she answered.

"Aye. I told ya that I wouldn't and then I did. And, well, that's not a way to have you . . . trust me."

"Right! And—"

"I was just thinkin' that you knew me because I'm Sharon's friend. That I wouldn't do anything to put Rowan in danger. I'm supposing it's very important for the child to believe, without question, that her mum can protect her from anything when there's no dad. I understand, Becky. I am sorry."

His very black eyes were soft, gazing into hers so quietly that Rebecca felt her throat tighten. She coughed.

"Thank you," she replied hoarsely.

"Good. Now, I have a request."

"A request?"

"Aye. If I do something to piss you off, I would like it if you wouldn't wait to hit me with it when I'm leaving and then slam the door in my face."

"You're the one—"

"I'm the one who pissed you off. You're the one who slammed the door in my face."

"You drove off with my daugh—"

"I apologized. You accepted. You don't get to hang on to that just so you don't have to be wrong. You slammed the door in my face, Becky."

Fionn, of course, was right—right about the door, right about it being very wrong. She knew it was so when she did it. She hated being wrong.

"All right," she said, looking down. "I'll tell you what's pissing me off when it's pissing me off."

Fionn's eyes changed. They were still soft, but now they were as immobile and unfathomable as they had been the first night in the pub. He stood staring at her as if she hadn't said anything, completely undisturbed by the dewdrop that hung from the spiral of red hair above his left eye. Rebecca fidgeted from left foot to right, uncomfortable at being the object of his black gaze.

"Okay. I'm sorry for slamming the door in your face."

"Excellent!" He smiled a great smile and brushed past her, heading toward her house. "Let's have tea."

"I—I was going out," she stuttered.

Fionn stopped and turned around. He was but a blur in the fog. "Where?"

"Uh—to the fort."

"I'll go with you. Then we'll have tea." He spun around and continued toward her house.

"I— Rowan was going over to Siobhan's," Rebecca called after him. "I was going to be alone today."

"You know where the fort is?" His question was a bodiless voice in the mist.

"No."

"So you'll need to have someone show you. Especially in this fog. Come on, then."

With a scowl, Rebecca turned her bike around and grudgingly followed Fionn back to her house. She didn't want to be with Fionn. He wasn't supposed to come back to the island until Christmas. She wanted to be alone—to see and explore the fort by herself. All of her research since her time with Dennis had been solitary; it was the solitude she needed in order to balance her life. Finding the door to her cottage wide-open, Rebecca reluctantly leaned the bike against the house and stepped into the front room.

On the sofa she found a small musical pipe, a music pamphlet, and five hardcover books. Fionn came around the corner from the kitchen.

"I brought the pipe for Rowan. And a book on how to play it. Everyone on the island learns to play the whistle."

"That was thoughtful."

"I brought you something, too."

Rebecca stepped back, watching Fionn with trepidation as he nodded to the sofa.

"My mum said maybe you needed books on Irish knitting."

"Oh!" Rebecca exclaimed, offering a small smile.

"Come on, then," Fionn replied, coming closer to her.

Rebecca backed out the front door. He followed, closing the door behind him.

"Fort's this way," he said as he veered off to the left, away from the gravel drive. "I wasn't sure what you needed, so I asked the librarian at Trinity for help. There's patterns in those books. Sharon said you've been wanting to write about the ganseys for a while."

"Yeah. I was working on the grant for this project for a few years."

When Fionn came to a stone wall, he rested his left hand upon its surface and hurdled it as easily as Trace had done. Turning back to Rebecca, he offered her his hand over the wall.

Reluctantly she took it, sticking her right foot into a crevice between two rocks and lifting her left foot to the top of the wall, then leapt forward to the other side. Slowly, she removed her hand from Fionn's palm and ran her fingers through her hair with a quick smile.

Cocking his head, Fionn turned and struck out through the shin-deep brush. Rebecca followed him.

Her feet hit the uneven, grassy ground heavily, twisting her toes and ankles in opposite directions. Whenever she thought she had her foot on a level piece of ground, it would slide to the right or left as small bits of stone or smears of mud gave way beneath her weight.

"Sharon and John and I used to race to the fort after Mass. John always won," Fionn said over his shoulder.

"Was he faster than you guys?" she asked.

"No. Sharon and I would fight all the way, so we were too busy to compete." He chuckled.

"You fought?"

"Not hitting—with hands anyway. Just we'd argue about everything and were always in trouble because of it, so we'd run to the fort after Mass."

"Why?" Rebecca asked, steadying her left foot as she hopped over a puddle.

"'Cause Sunday supper was always at my house and Father Michael always would come. Sharon and I needed to have a break between homilies."

"Did Father Michael not have anywhere else to go?"

"Oh, he could have gone elsewhere, but Sharon and I were in need of special spiritual care, as he saw it. Poor John. He just got caught up in it with us."

The toe of Rebecca's left shoe was stuck in a crack in the ground. With a grunt, she freed it. They came to another wall and Fionn popped over it. He held out his hand.

"Let me try," Rebecca said, winded. With her left hand flat on the stones, she jumped up, achieving the top of the wall. She then stumbled over it.

"That was graceful," she breathed.

"Aye," Fionn replied with a grin and walked on.

Rebecca looked down at her knees, which brushed through the tall green and gold grass as she walked. Here and there grew equally tall maroon-colored weeds, the tiny seeds shaking loose as she passed, sticking to her damp pant legs. Gray rock outcroppings also rose from the brush. The rains had washed the soil off the barren stone of the island and collected it in deep crevices, making pockets of earth in which the grasses grew. Bending down, Rebecca touched the weathered rock.

"It must have been so hard to pull life from this stone," she muttered absently.

"Hard by yourself," Fionn replied.

Looking up, Rebecca found him stopped just ahead of her. "It had to be hard, period," she said.

"Aye. But hardships are easier to bear with others. That's what my dad says, anyway."

Rebecca rose to her feet, staring at Fionn and his red hair standing in the mist as if he, too, had just grown out of the rock. He was from this island, though he had left it. She could tell. She could easily imagine Fionn with his father, fighting the sea in those little fishing boats Sharon said they used to use on the island—nothing but oars and cowhide and tar and wood to keep them free of the waves.

"You ever hear that story?" Rebecca asked.

"What story's that?"

"The women of these islands knit such unique sweaters. Each one different—each one holding a picture of the soul of the person they knitted it for. They do this so if one of those boats—"

"A curragh."

"Cur-rah. Yes. If a curragh is lost and a body washes ashore, they'll know who it is. And his wife can bury him properly and let him go."

"I never heard it put that way," Fionn replied, smiling.

"You ever hear that story?"

"Aye. But it only happened once here that I remember. 'Twas the night Sean Morahan lost his sons. Only one body washed ashore and it was pretty banged up. It was his gansey that told 'em it was Matthew—Sean's eldest."

Fionn spun slowly on his heel and continued walking. Following his path, Rebecca watched how his feet hit the ground, never hesitating or slipping. She tried to walk where he walked, step where he stepped.

"You guys still make curraghs?"

"Aye. My dad has one." He skipped over a small stone hill. Rebecca did also.

"I'd like to see it sometime," she said, gaining speed as she followed in his wake.

By the time they reached the next wall, Rebecca was at Fionn's side. She grabbed the stones and hurled herself over the wall. She smiled triumphantly as Fionn jumped over behind her. He laughed.

"Can I ask you a question?" Rebecca said.

Fionn nodded, pointing east, and together they walked in that direction.

"Why'd you leave here?"

He tilted his head toward her, and a small smile grew across his face. "Many reasons. Sharon went to the States and John left to make music. I suppose I didn't feel I fit in here without them. And then, what I'm looking for wasn't on this island at the time."

"What were you looking for?"

"Home. Every O'Flaherty but me has it. Hard to be in a place where everybody has what you want but you."

A gull spiraled somewhere overhead, calling through the mist. Rebecca had no home either—she was like that gull, flying from place to place, never settling for long. But she had no parents, no family. Fionn did.

"Your parents' house isn't a home for you?" she asked, cresting a small hill. The land ended abruptly four hundred yards ahead, falling away into the sea. Beyond the end of the land, she could see where the deep gray waters rolled beneath the thinning fog, the surf causing ebbs and eddies in its mist.

"That's home, but not my home. Not a home I made."

Rebecca looked away from the sea, finding Fionn's eyes soft on her. She swallowed.

"Is that why you only come back at Christmas?" she whispered.

"Who says that?"

"Your mother."

"Talking to my mum about me, are you?" Fionn winked.

Rebecca shrugged with a little frown. "About your sweater—gansey, I mean." She started down the hill, leaving Fionn and his black eyes behind her.

"Ah, she's making me one! About time. I've had to wait a long time to get a new one."

"Why?" she called over her shoulder, stepping around a large square stone.

"She has five children and eleven grandchildren and makes two or three jumpers a year, unless someone's confirmed. Everyone gets a jumper when they're confirmed."

"Is it jumper or gansey?" The grass grew so short in this field that even tiny stones popped their heads out of the dirt. Rebecca skittered quickly down the incline, since it was finally easy to see clearly where she was going.

"Depends on where you are in the country. So what else my mum say?"

"She didn't say anything. Exactly."

"What's my jumper say, then?" he asked.

Rebecca smiled a small, wicked smile, skipping easily to the bottom of the hill.

"What's it say?" he called after her.

Rebecca giggled, trotting down the hill as the incline deepened. A gull shot by, crying as it sped toward the water.

"What's my mum up to?" he asked.

Rebecca laughed, thinking of the twisted stitches. "When's Mass?" she asked.

She had reached the bottom of the hill only to find she stood atop a four-foot-high retaining wall.

"I heard you don't go," Fionn replied, sliding up next to her, winded.

"I was just wondering."

"What are you up to?"

"Where's the fort?" she inquired, as she slipped off the retaining wall.

Gazing out to the ocean from the cliff, Rebecca watched four seagulls spiral in the mist, racing past the cliff wall so close she was sure their wings touched it. She realized Fionn had not answered and glanced over her shoulder at him.

He stood frozen on top of the retaining wall with a slight smile curling his lips.

"What?" she asked.

"You just walked through the fort, Becky."

Stunned, Rebecca spun around and looked up the slope. What she had taken for a hill was the fort itself—the retaining wall was its base.

"Oh," she said, startled at having missed it.

"Some archaeologist you are," said he, jumping off the wall.

They looked at each other and laughed.

CHAPTER 12

Blackberry

Blackberry (aka Trinity). 1. A stitch that creates one pattern by binding three stitches together. 2. Traditionally, this represents either blackberries or, more commonly, the Holy Trinity—Father, Son, and Holy Spirit. 3. The true Holy Trinity—child and parents.

—R. Dirane, *A Binding Love*

After their trip to the fort, Fionn and Rebecca went back to the cottage and sat down for tea, talking about pasties and curraghs and Mass. As Fionn left, he said he would return in a week to retrieve the library books. Rebecca watched him walk down the gravel drive toward his parents' home, the fog having lifted by midmorning. His red hair glimmered in the sunlight.

The rest of that day, her fourth on the island, Rebecca set about spinning the balance of the wool given to her by Liz and Rose. When Annie dropped Rowan off that night, the women planned a playdate for the girls after church. Then Rebecca would visit Rose and Liz. With her spinning done, she hoped to see their ganseys.

Sunday dawned fresh and clean, washed sparkling bright by rain and fog. With Rowan on the handlebars of her bike and the bag of spun wool in her basket, Rebecca headed out toward the O'Flahertys' house. Trace followed as far as the road and when Rebecca bumped off the gravel onto the asphalt, he halted. Rowan waved good-bye as Rebecca picked up speed.

The stone walls, fields, and surf were alive with sun and wind, and Rebecca's mood lifted. Perhaps it was the change in weather and being out of the house that made her feel light. Or perhaps it was the anticipation of facing Father Michael after Mass. She wasn't sure exactly why, but she felt as light as the Irish sky above her.

As Rebecca and Rowan came to a stop in front of the church, Father Michael was already outside shaking hands as his flock prepared to go back out into the world. When Siobhan trotted down the steps, Rowan ran from Rebecca's side and, with a brief wave to her mother, left with the Blakes.

"'Tis a fine morning, Rebecca," Father Michael called from the church steps. "Perhaps you'd like to come inside."

"Oh, I'm fine out here," Rebecca replied, grinning. "I tried to explain to you, Father, that I wasn't coming to church on Sunday."

"It is Sunday?" the priest asked, perplexed.

"Yes?"

Father Michael glanced up to the church's spire, then peered back at Rebecca. He raised his eyebrows. Rebecca frowned. Father Michael stepped back into the dark interior of the church, his smile as white as a Cheshire cat's as he disappeared.

"Good morning, Becky."

Startled, Rebecca spun around and found Liz standing behind her.

"Come, I've made my special cakes for you. We can look at your spinning till the father's ready."

"Ready for what?" Rebecca replied, her frown deepening as the old woman took her by the elbow and led her toward the priest's house.

Instead of answering, Liz said, "The wool we gave you is what we call *bainin*. Do you like that color or would you like to spin some oatmeal-colored wool?"

"Baw-neen," Rebecca repeated as she leaned her bike against the priest's gate and pulled her bags of wool from her basket. "Is it important what I like?"

"Just asking. Sharon teach you any Irish?" Liz asked, walking through the gate into the priest's rose garden.

The flowers were tight buds, not yet warm enough to open themselves to the late-spring sun. The garden itself had a checkerboard appearance, with flagstone walkways separating raised beds of flowers. To the left of the gate was a small wrought-iron table, its chairs dirty from a long winter of waiting for someone to sit.

"She tried, but I'm not very good at languages. The only thing I remember is *dubh* means 'black' and *falt* means 'hair' and if I was to say, 'Sharon has black hair,' it translates into 'the black hair is on Sharon.' I always found that funny because it's like the hair can decide to get up and go somewhere else."

"Well, it does with men, doesn't it? The hair leaves," Liz replied.

They snickered as they climbed the stair to the kitchen door. Liz opened it and Rebecca followed her in.

Father Michael's kitchen was small and sunny. To the right was a kitchen table sitting beneath a window. Rebecca placed the bag of spun wool on the table as Liz put water in the kettle and set it to boil. Coming back over to the table, Liz pulled Rebecca's spinning out of the bag.

"Ah, Becky, look at it! Like you've been doin' it your whole life."

"Maybe it's because I've spent so much time looking at old fabrics."

"Perhaps. You'll be ready for the wheel now."

"The wheel?" Rebecca inquired.

"Rose can help you better with the wheel."

"Liz, I really need to talk about your ganseys."

"You will. You will. First, the wheel. Sit. Please."

As Liz poured the water into the teapot, Father Michael came into the kitchen.

"Have you had one of Liz's cakes?" he asked.

"Not yet."

"They are the father's favorite," Liz said, setting the pot of tea and a plate of crumpets and cakes on the table.

"I'll tell Rose you'll be over shortly, Becky. Drink the tea while it's hot," Liz said, opening the door and stepping out of the priest's house. The door shut with a heavy click.

Rebecca shrugged uncomfortably as Father Michael seated himself. Glancing out the window, she watched Liz walk toward Rose's house. The tinkling of tea as it was poured into the cup echoed in the silence.

"I don't know why I'm here," Rebecca began.

"For tea and so I can get to know you."

"I have no desire to be a Catholic, Father."

"Well, I'm not here to convert you, Rebecca. Sugar?"

"Please."

"Every time I want to talk to somebody, they think I have some agenda."

"You're a priest."

"I'm a human being. If you're worried about agendas, I'd be minding Liz and Rose. They may look like nice little old ladies, but looks can be quite deceiving. They're the radical element of this town."

Rebecca chuckled.

"So your project is about ganseys, then?"

"It's more about the women who make them. Their feelings stitched into the rows—the memories in each pattern."

"The meaning of love as seen through a work of art," Father Michael replied.

"Yes! Poems written in wool and knots in the evening when the world slows down."

"When the world slows, it's easier to hear the heart."

"Much easier here, I think."

"How so?"

"It's just—slower here. No big rush."

"It's a big rush for you back in the States?"

"It seems there's hardly time for anything. Especially being a single mom."

Rebecca peered out the window, watching a group of cyclists race by.

"How long have you been raising her alone?"

"Why do you want to know?" Rebecca asked with a sideways glance.

"Just trying to know you."

"Not trying to get into my head?"

"Trying to hear your heart, that's all. Is it so hard to talk to me?"

Rebecca sipped her tea, eyeing Father Michael skeptically. She was a true believer in scientific inquiry. It wasn't that there was no God for Rebecca; it was that it didn't matter one way or the other. She was an archaeologist. She studied the ages. In her life, aside from being the objects moving culture, religion and God were personally irrelevant.

That being the case, Rebecca had never sat down with a priest before. All she knew about them she had learned from Sharon. By what Rebecca understood, priests had a way of getting into your private business before you knew it as you talked over tea or dinner. The last thing she had planned for the day was to get into any discussion with anyone regarding her personal business, especially any of her past as it related to Rowan. She shifted in her seat to rise, but the stillness in the kitchen held her to the chair. She took a deep breath, as if she was about to jump off a very high diving board.

"Since she was born."

"That would be?"

"Six years."

"Six years. A long time. Is it difficult for you?"

"Nah, it's easier alone. I see people arguing all the time about the kids. In grocery stores, in line at the gas station, at parks. No one to argue with when you're doing it alone."

"You argued a lot with Rowan's father?"

"Not really. He just didn't want what I wanted in life."

"What did you want?"

"A house, a yard, kids, a dog. You know. Barbecues on July Fourth. He wanted—I'm not sure."

"He never said?"

"Not really. Maybe to walk through a desert alone. Who knows?"

"Hard to raise children while walking alone in the desert, I suppose."

"Not if you're an Australian aborigine." Rebecca laughed. "But I'm over it."

"You'll never be an aborigine?" Father Michael said with a smile.

"No. That relationship. Can't blame him for being who he is."

Rebecca bit into the cake, looking out the window again. A rosebud the color of raspberry sherbet fluttered in a gentle breeze beyond the glass. Rebecca's heart fluttered, too.

⸺

Rebecca stood shivering in the summer breeze that blew up the high cliff walls. Her 1968 Volkswagen Beetle sat just off the asphalt as cars flew by, heading south on Highway 1 toward Half Moon Bay. She froze. If any of them merely nicked the edge of her bumper, she and the car would tumble off the cliff into the ocean far below.

So much had happened in the nine years since she'd started college. Sharon had left for home after they'd finished their bachelor's degrees five years ago. Straight out of Berkeley, Rebecca had headed south to Los Angeles to begin her master's, which she completed in two years. The day after her master's graduation ceremony, her parents had been killed in an accident on Highway 5, on their way home to Redding. Without a pause to grieve, Rebecca continued on to studies for her doctorate. It was slow going, as her mind and heart continually ached with loss, distracting her from her purpose. Now, with three years of research under her belt, she had begun to write the dissertation. But the heaviness of grief weighed on her. No one would be coming to her graduation. No one was left to celebrate with her. She had no home, no family, and as she stood looking out over the Pacific Ocean, she began to cry, for there was not even anyone to come and help her with her broken-down car.

"Hey," a voice called behind her.

Rebecca spun around and saw a young man about her age with sandy blond hair, blue eyes, and swimming shorts with Hawaiian flowers on them standing just behind her car.

"You okay?" he asked, licking an ice cream cone he held in his right hand.

"My—my car's broken," Rebecca replied, wiping her eyes.

"That's nothing to cry about," he said with a smile. "These things are easy to fix. Here, hold this."

He held out his ice cream for Rebecca to take. As she reached for it, he pulled it quickly back.

"Don't eat it," he said.

"I—I won't," Rebecca replied, taking the ice cream cone as he held it out again. It smelled of raspberries.

The young man skipped around to the back of the car and lifted the half-moon-shaped hood. Rebecca followed him, noting his blue Pontiac Firebird parked at an angle behind her car. His yellow surfboard was strapped to the top and his emergency flashers were on.

"You surf?" he asked, peering at the engine.

"I only boogie-board."

"I love the beach," he said as he tinkered with a lever.

"Me, too," Rebecca replied.

"You like raspberry sherbet?" he asked.

"Yes."

"Good. You can have the rest of that. This is going to take a while," he said, and as he stood up, he smiled a big white smile.

"I'm Dennis Mattos."

"I'm Rebecca Moray."

Rebecca started as a small bird with a black-and-white-spotted breast landed on the rose branch. It tilted its beady eye at her, blinking in the sun. It looked exactly like the little bird in the bramble outside her cottage's bedroom window. Her heart raced as she raised her cool hand to her hot face.

"Rebecca?"

She glanced warily over at the priest. She wasn't ready for this conversation. "I should go," she said hoarsely.

"You're upset."

"I'm sorry. I—uh—I sh—"

"You were saying you can't blame him for being who he is."

"No, I can't. He—he just wasn't for me."

"You ever going to marry again?" the father asked.

"Oh, I didn't marry him, Father," Rebecca replied absently, concentrating on slowing her heart. "I didn't make that mistake."

She offered a half smile, wondering how that piece of information was being processed in the priest's head. He just nodded.

"So, Rowan's father—you're over him."

"You can only move forward if you let go the past."

"That is true," Father Michael agreed.

"I really need to go," Rebecca repeated.

The bird fluttered away, and as Rebecca watched it go, she spied an old man tottering past the father's house. She wondered if it was Sean.

"I have a couple of ganseys my grandmother made. Perhaps you'd like to see them. They're very old."

Rebecca's eyes brightened.

"Maybe you can come back next Sunday and help me dig them out of the attic." The priest stood up.

"I'd like that."

"You introduced yourself as Rebecca. Are you Rebecca or Becky?"

"Rebecca," she answered. "My family calls me Becky."

"See you next Sunday, then, Rebecca," Father Michael said, opening the kitchen door.

With a nod, Rebecca stepped from his house and over to her bike. "Thanks for the tea."

"You're welcome. Be careful of the bi—"

"Bikes," Rebecca interrupted with a smile. "I know."

CHAPTER 13

Cable

Cable. 1. A very simple stitch that looks incredibly difficult, for it appears as two ropes entwining each other, creating a single cable. A cable needle is best used for this stitch. 2. Traditionally represents the cables that hold the fishing nets to the boat, ensuring the strength and safety of the net, the continuation of the food supply, and, therefore, life. 3. The making of one person from two people, which creates greater strength, and the continuation of life, is, of course, a child.

—R. Dirane, *A Binding Love*

$\mathcal{S}$ean opened his front door, taking in the scent of the sea and Sunday morning as he held his teacup to his lips. The wind was soft and from the east, blowing gently over the small hill that ran north to south down the center of the island. Though not cold, it wasn't a summer's breeze warmed by the island. Turning back to his house, Sean set his cup on the table beneath his front window, put on his old wool coat, and placed his cap upon his head.

Before shutting his door, he checked the seashell in its nook. It was still half full of holy water. The need to fill the shell was the only event that would bring Sean to the church's door, for he was not one to attend Mass. He hadn't gone since Claire left. As he still had water in the shell, there would be no need to go to the church today.

Stepping out into the world, Sean closed the door. A wavering to the left drew his attention from the group of bicycles that passed his house on their way south. It was a little leaf in the blackberry bramble waving at him in the morning breeze. He stared at it for a moment, memorizing the color. Then he stepped off his doorstep onto his gravel pathway, which led to the road.

As Sean approached town, he contemplated the certain shade of green on that singular leaf. It was almost a pine color, though it had a slightly bluer hue, with a silver undertone. The little leaf flittering in the morning breeze waved at him, as Claire had done when she saw him approaching from the sea.

Standing on the beach in the silvery fog, Claire waited for Sean to find a wave that would bring his curragh onto the sand. Her dress was blue, but the sea and the fog gave it a greenish tint. As he laid upon his oars, Sean wondered at the movement of the fabric in the wind and the beauty of his wife.

They had just been married and were making their home. But there were tales from the Continent. The Great War had ended nineteen years earlier, and whispers of conflict growing in the east drifted across Galway Bay onto the island like an earthy breeze before a great gale. Sean and Claire knew their time together could be short if that other storm built into a war.

Though he had been out but three hours, Claire's face was worn with worry. She smelled a gale upon the breeze, as had he, which was what brought him in early this day. This would be a small, watery tempest, but there would be a lasting bloody one soon on its heels, and so though the wave that could have brought Sean to shore rolled beneath his curragh, he let it pass. He wanted to watch Claire standing on the shore a little longer—to burn into his mind her beauty as she waited for him to come home.

A screeching flute startled Sean from his past. Looking ahead, he found Rowan sitting on a ledge near Paddy Blake's house. She was blowing on a tin whistle with a book on her lap.

"That's a nice pipe you've got there, Rowan. Where'd you get it?"

"Fionn gave it to me."

"Ah. Well, he should know that a person doesn't learn to play Irish music from a book. They learn from others. Has he helped you to play?"

"Does he know how to play?"

"All the O'Flahertys play one thing or another. Here." From the sleeve of his worn blue gansey, Sean extricated a flute.

"You play?"

"I play—mostly when I fish. It helps the fish come to the line. Look. The fingers are not as important as the lips when you're first learning."

Sean played a little tune.

"Cool!"

"To make high notes, you tighten your lips—lower notes, loosen them. Don't blow harder. Let's try this."

Sean played a four-note scale.

"Do it again," Rowan said.

Sean played the scale, and as he did so, Rowan touched his fingers as he moved them on and off the holes in the pipe. Her mahogany eyes were as soft as her little hand, and pain rose again in his chest. He stopped, holding his heart.

"You okay?"

"Aye. You try," he said hoarsely.

Rowan played the scale. Her pipe squeaked on the last note.

"Don't blow too hard," Sean whispered, slowly breathing in, trying to release the pain. "Tighten your lips at the edges like you're going to smile."

Rowan played again. Peering over her shoulder, Sean watched Siobhan step out of her house. The little girl halted when she spotted him.

Rowan stopped playing, following Sean's gaze. "Siobhan!" she called. "Sean plays the flute!"

Siobhan didn't move as she stared at the old man.

"You play?" he asked her.

"A little. My ma teaches me."

"Good. Good. Would you like to learn a little with Rowan here?"

With a reticent shrug, Siobhan tiptoed down the steps, skirted by Sean, and sat on Rowan's other side.

"Good," he breathed. "Now show Siobhan."

As Rowan showed Siobhan the scale, Sean watched the little Yankee girl. Her eyes flicked quickly and opened wide when she spoke. They looked at him brightly, peering past his aged face, lighting up his very dark soul. It hurt him, yet he could do nothing but smile. When the pipe hit her lips, her tone was as clear as Joe's—clean and smooth like a curragh floating in a calm summer sea with dazzling sparks of reflected sun tapping the body, warming the heart.

Sean could think on his wife and Matthew. He could remember Liam and his youngest, Brendan. But Joe was a void—a place he could not visit often. As he listened to Rowan's pipe playing a scale as easily as a seagull glides up and away from a cliff and slides down across the water, Sean could not stop the crushing pain in his chest.

"That's very good, Rowan. Siobhan, you too. You play well," he said, tottering to his feet.

"You leaving, Sean?" Rowan asked, grabbing his left hand to help steady him.

"Aye. Have fish to catch or there'll be no supper," he muttered. "You keep practicing."

Sean pulled his hat down to his eyes and shuffled down the street toward Hernon's Shop. The bikes and tourists were loud around him, yet he heard nothing but Rowan's pipe on the breeze. He crossed the street at O'Flaherty's Pub. Tilting his head in the direction of the church, he spotted a woman with straight brown hair peering out of Father Michael's kitchen window. He wondered if it was Rowan's ma. The old man lifted his foot and stepped into Hernon's Shop.

Standing frozen at the door, Sean growled under his breath at the tourists. They were talking and laughing. The line flowed from the counter, curved away from the door, and ended at the freezer in the back of the store.

"You need something there, Morahan?" John Hernon called.

"Has my wool come in?"

"Aye—aye. Come on back."

Sean slid through the crowd. Many of the tourists smiled at him as he passed. He did not return the kindness. When he reached the door to the back room, the old man found John up on a stool, pulling a large white cotton bag down from a shelf.

"You need help getting this home?"

"No, thank you."

"All right, then."

John handed the bag to the old man.

"Best go out the back door, there."

"Aye." As Sean tossed the bag over his left shoulder, his back crackled under the weight. Maneuvering around John and the shelving units, he carefully stepped down the back stairs and headed south behind Hernon's Shop.

The sun was bright above him as he walked. By the time he was at the edge of town, he was sweating under the weight of the bag. With a little jump, the old man adjusted it on his shoulder. How many bags of wool had he carried home this way? He tried to count, endeavoring to ignore his body, which was heating up under the sun and his gansey and his wool coat.

As soon as he could, Sean stepped off the asphalt onto the stone and dirt, which were soft under his shoes. He listened for the ocean, waiting for the wind to wipe his brow. As he listened, he could hear a pipe sliding up and down scales like a gannet flying in the island sky. He stopped abruptly, looking back over his shoulder. Surely he was too far away to hear her. But there was the scale, and very gently it came to him louder still on a little breeze that kissed his old cheek like a small child kisses a grandparent.

"Rowan," he whispered and as he clutched his heart, salty drops slid down his cheeks to his lips. Walking on, Sean convinced himself they were just sweat.

CHAPTER 14

Basket

Basket. 1. A stitch that looks like a tightly woven basket, with interlacing squares. 2. Traditionally represents the fisherman's basket, a large catch, and therefore bounty. 3. Honest intentions.

—R. Dirane, *A Binding Love*

The wind was cool on her hot cheeks as Rebecca stepped out of Father Michael's rose garden and headed for her bike. A mother and father were buckling two children into seats on the backs of two bicycles in front of Hernon's Shop. Flipping her kickstand up with her foot, Rebecca glanced at the blue sky above and found it dotted with three puffy white-gray clouds. They floated slowly to the north as she placed her feet on her pedals and rode south. As she came around the corner at Dooley's Bed and Breakfast, she skidded to a stop.

A group of about twenty bicyclists had stopped in the middle of the street, looking at a map and discussing which direction they should go. Climbing off her bike, Rebecca wove between them and when she was in the middle of the group, they all simultaneously straddled their bikes and pedaled off, like a school of fish darting away on an ocean tide. Their whizzing chains left a buzzing ring in her ears, so she decided not to climb back on her bike but rather to walk it to Rose's house.

When she reached the white cottage, no one awaited her outside the bright yellow door. Resting her bike against the house, Rebecca pulled her camera, DVD recorder, and tripod from her side baskets. As she reached up to knock on the door, it opened.

"Good mornin' to ya, Becky," Rose said in greeting, her red shawl slipping from her shoulder.

"Good morning, Rose." Rebecca stepped inside the cottage, her eyes very slowly adjusting to its dim interior from the glare of the bright yellow door.

"Did ya have a nice visit with the father?"

"Yes, thanks," Rebecca lied, setting her still-shot camera and DVD recorder on the table.

"That's fine. I have tea started."

"Rose, do you think I can see a gansey today? I've brought all my cameras and I need to—"

"I still say she needs to spin on the wheel," Liz muttered as she walked through the front door.

"She will," Rose replied. "But we have a great deal to show her. She can spin later."

Liz gently deposited a jumper on the table and made her way into the kitchen. Her eyes wide, Rebecca glanced from Liz to Rose to the sweater. Slowly, so as not to cause it to fly away, Rebecca stepped over to the table.

The gansey was very old; she could tell by the way the yarn had flattened out and the white color of the fabric had yellowed. The wrists and elbows were worn and thinning, but still maintained their integrity.

With a very calm exterior, Rebecca gleefully extended her tripod's legs, securing them tightly. The cups for tea pinged softly as Liz brought them to the table. Rebecca attached the DVD camera to the tripod and turned it on. Angling it down to the table, she focused on the gansey.

"Whenever you're ready, Liz," she said quietly, afraid her elation would burst from her mouth.

"When I was a young girl, I'd visit my grandmother's house on the mainland. I'd wake every morning and she'd hand me a basket to go pick blackberries. For my breakfast, she'd pour fresh cream over the berries and cut a big slice of warm bread. The smell of baked bread and blackberries always reminds me of my grandmother. You ever smell blackberry bushes on a warm summer's morning?"

"Yes. They grow everywhere in my hometown."

"Where's your hometown?" Rose asked as she sat down nearby and set her spinning wheel in motion.

"Redding. It's in north central California."

"Warm blackberry bushes," Liz repeated with her eyes closed. "Heaven must smell like warm blackberry bushes."

Liz placed a pot of tea on the table and sat down next to the sweater. Rebecca smiled, quickly glancing down at the camera, making sure Liz and her gansey were in the frame.

"One morning, I was collecting my breakfast when a boy ran up. He asked what I was doing and after I told him, he helped me finish gathering the berries. We talked so easily, like I had known him my whole life. When we were done, I thanked him and he went away. The next morning, he was standing there by the wall where the bramble was, waiting for me, and we talked as we gathered. I can't remember a time before when I had laughed so much, and to this day I couldn't tell you what was so funny. We had picked the bush clean near the bottom by the end of the morning.

"On the third day, I was walking to the bush and heard a muffled cry. The bramble was all in motion. I dropped my basket, ran around the wall, and found the boy stuck in the middle of the bush."

"Ouch!" Rebecca exclaimed.

"Aye—thorny. Through much fighting and fidgeting, we finally got him free. He was a mess, bleeding everywhere, with a particularly deep gash on his eyebrow, here." Liz pointed to the middle of her right eyebrow.

"I had to drag him inside so my grandmother could mend him.

She asked him what happened and he wouldn't say anything to her. She left to fetch something and I asked him what he was doing in the bush. He said he had climbed the wall to pick the best berries at the top for me and lost his balance." Liz sighed. "What beautiful eyes he had. I couldn't help myself. I just kissed him. Right on his hurt eyebrow. Then he left and I didn't see him anymore that summer."

"He was probably embarrassed," Rebecca said.

"I thought so, too. The next year, I visited my grandmother again and the first morning I went out to fetch my breakfast. There, sitting neatly on the wall, was the biggest basket of blackberries I'd ever seen. And every time I went to my grandmother's house, from that year until my seventeenth birthday, I'd find a big basket of berries on the wall on the first morning of my stay."

"What happened when you were seventeen?"

"I married him. The berry-picker." She giggled as she glanced over to the camera's lens. Rebecca smiled back to the woman through her camera's frame. This was exactly the kind of story she had hoped she'd find when she had thought about writing this book for all those years. Rebecca stepped over to the sweater while Liz poured tea. "Blackberries?" Rebecca asked as she touched a column of bumpy stitches.

"Hmm. It's called the Trinity stitch."

"And this is the basket?" Rebecca pointed to the pattern next to the blackberries.

"It is. Guess what was on my kitchen table every morning on the day of our anniversary."

"A basket of blackberries," Rebecca replied with a chuckle.

"And guess what I gave him?"

Rebecca shrugged.

"A kiss right here," Liz whispered, reaching up and touching Rebecca's right eyebrow. The old woman smiled and peered distantly at the sweater. Following her gaze, Rebecca noted a small column of stitches next to a section of diamonds. They were half an inch wide and reminded her of the propellers on the prop planes that flew across the fields in Redding. She touched the stitch, and at that moment a tear fell from Liz's eye onto Rebecca's finger.

"His scar?" Rebecca whispered.

Liz nodded.

The spinning wheel whirred softly behind Rebecca, who bent down and lifted her still-shot from the table.

Rose began to hum. Then she stopped and said, "There's an old song, Becky. I've forgotten the tune. Would you like to hear the lyric?"

"Please."

"How does it go, Liz? My memory, you know."

Liz wiped her eyes. "'They say a fairy has no heart, but sorrow now they feel. For mortal souls that grieve apart, they've sent a spinning wheel. Spin the warmth of wool, little wheel. Forget your fairy days. Spin for men so brave and leal, who guard the ocean ways.'"

"Aye. That's it. May I have a cup of tea, please, Liz?" Rose asked, setting her wheel in motion once again.

"We were married for fifty-seven years," Liz said as she poured the tea. "He passed into the Lord's arms five years ago."

"I'm sorry," Rebecca replied.

"We'll meet again," Liz said, patting Rebecca on the shoulder as she stood to give Rose her tea.

The rest of the day, Rebecca took still photos of Liz's gansey, talking with the women about their past. She also began a spinning lesson on the wheel. Near suppertime, Rebecca took her leave to collect Rowan from Siobhan's house. There she found not only Annie and the girls, but also Maggie, who mentioned that Mairead Fitzgibbon was still waiting to meet her. They agreed to make the trip the next day, after which Rebecca took Rowan home.

Darkness fell behind them as Rebecca pedaled Rowan up to their cottage. There, at the front door, lay Trace. He stood to attention as soon as he spotted them. Giggling, Rowan jumped off the handlebars and ran toward the dog, who wagged his tail so fast about the little girl's legs that Rebecca was certain she would have lost her kneecaps had she been wearing shorts.

Leaving her daughter and the dog at the door, Rebecca put the bike away in the shed. From her side baskets, she removed her cameras and a new bag of unspun wool. Upon her return, she found the front door open and no sign of Rowan and Trace.

It had been sunny and warm all day, but now dark clouds were building up to the north. Rebecca watched them slowly move southward, roiling and tumbling inexorably toward her house. She went inside and set the bag of wool and her cameras on the floor. As she turned to close the door, a huge gust of wind blew through the post and lintels, tearing the door from her hand. The wind barreled across the front room, knocking over candles and flipping the pages of the books that sat on the sofa. It blew Rowan's whistle book onto the floor, and when it reached the fireplace, it coughed, sending ash flying across the room.

"Ah!" Rebecca cried, grabbing the door and leaning her weight behind it. The wind whipped around and fought, pushing on the door to keep it open. With one great lunge, Rebecca slammed it shut, and the latch clicked into place with finality.

"Good Lord!" she exclaimed, brushing her hair out of her face and gazing through the ash that was now sifting to the floor.

"What happened?" Rowan asked from the kitchen door.

"Bloody wind." Rebecca turned around and found Trace standing next to her daughter.

"Rowan, Trace cannot stay here."

"He likes the peat fire."

"You've said. But maybe Mr. and Mrs. O'Flaherty would like him back."

"Mr. O'Flaherty says he usually stays here or at Mr. Fitzgibbon's house."

"Fitzgibbon. Bees?"

"Yeah! Mr. O'Flaherty says since no one else wanted to be mayor of the island, Mr. Fitzgibbon appointed Trace the mayor one night when he was playing darts with Father Michael at the pub."

"Appointed the dog mayor?" Rebecca repeated slowly.

"Yep. Mr. O'Flaherty says Trace goes where he wants on the island. The whole island is his house now that he's mayor."

Rowan said this with such a straight face that Rebecca could do nothing but stare at her. It was exactly how Sharon told stories—the sincere and honest delivery of an absolutely absurd tale. At times Rebecca had to actually think the story through before she could tell that Sharon was pulling her leg, just as she did now, staring at her daughter. Slowly, a smile crept up Rowan's chin and crawled onto her mouth. It was Sharon's smile. It was Irish.

"Right," Rebecca said, squinting at her daughter.

Rowan giggled.

"Let's find something for supper," Rebecca said, scratching Rowan's head as she slipped past her.

"Can I go with Siobhan and her dad fishing next week?" Rowan asked, following Rebecca into the kitchen.

"We'll see."

"Annie says she's gonna make me a pair of pampooties like Siobhan has. You know what pampooties are, Mama?"

"Go ahead and tell me," Rebecca answered as she washed her hands. Of course she knew what pampooties were. She was an archaeologist—old clothing was her specialty. But why ruin Rowan's pride in the newfound information?

"They're leather shoes that tie up around your ankles with a strap. Sean says when he was a boy, they used to put them in water at night so they wouldn't get stiff."

"Sean Morahan?" Rebecca asked, glancing sharply at Rowan, who was now washing her hands in the sink. "You've been talking with him?"

"Yes," Rowan replied quietly, not looking at her mother.

"I told you to tell me if he ever talked to you again."

"Sorry."

"I want you to stay away from him."

"Sean isn't bad, Mama."

"The people here stay away from him pretty much."

"I don't think they understand him."

"He yelled at you, Rowan. Kind people don't do that. You stay away from him."

"He said he was sorry."

Rebecca contemplated her daughter's face. Rowan's eyes were wide and watery.

"Rowan, look. There are people in this world that can seem really nice, but if you hang around them long enough, you find out they aren't nice all the time. And when they're mean, they can be very mean. I think Sean is like that. I think he is just pretending to be nice to you."

"He said he was sorry," Rowan repeated.

"He says sorry to you but is nasty to every other kid in town. Remember John and how afraid he was of Sean? That means he's not truly a kind person, Rowan, and it is only a matter of time before he hurts you. I don't want that to happen, so I want you to stay away from him."

"He's teaching me to play my flute," Rowan said, tears flowing from her eyes.

Rebecca brushed Rowan's cheek with her hand and sighed. Pulling her daughter into her arms, she sat down on a kitchen chair. The wind tapped triple-time on the window as Rebecca combed her fingers through Rowan's hair. Trace's claws clicked in rhythm with the wind as he circled around one spot, then finally flopped down on the stone floor.

"I know this is hard. I hear that you like him."

"He's not bad, Mama," Rowan mumbled into her chest.

"Look. A wise woman once told me a riddle. You are hot and hungry and as you pass this shop, a person inside asks you to come in and have—raspberry sherbet. Thinking the person kind for the invitation, you enter and sit. Then the person says, 'If you eat the sherbet, I'll slap you. If you don't eat it, I'll slap you.' Which would you choose?"

Rowan wiped her cheeks. "Do I get another choice?"

"What other choice would you have? The person said eat the sherbet or not. No matter what, you get slapped."

"I could leave."

"Yes! Exactly, Rowan! The person has something you'd like or want or even need, but they will hurt you if you stay. So it's better to just leave."

Rowan sniffled.

"I guess I can learn my flute from the book."

"You bet you can! You're very talented." Rebecca kissed her daughter on the top of her head. "Remember, Rowan, when you grow up, no one gives you your choices. Those you give yourself. You can always get up and leave. You're free. That's what I want you to learn from this."

Rowan nodded, drying her eyes on the dish towel. They sat together in the silence for a minute, and then Rowan said, "Mama! Listen!"

Rebecca's mind was so busy yelling at herself for letting Rowan go about the town so freely that she didn't respond at first.

"Hear it, Mama?"

Now she listened, but she heard nothing except her own anger. "Hear what?"

"The little bird."

Both of them were still again, and sure as the wind howled in the thatch, the little bird's song flowed from the bedroom.

"You think it has babies yet?"

"Let's check after dinner."

"Okay!"

As Rowan whistled scales on her pipe from the kitchen table, Rebecca peeled two potatoes and put them on to boil. From the small refrigerator, she pulled out four sausages and tossed them into a frying pan, which she had slid onto the cooker. The water boiled and the sausages popped and so did Rebecca's mind. So slow was the island—so small, so friendly, so safe. For the first time in six years, Rebecca had relaxed, and sure enough, as she had always told herself would happen, something came along and threatened Rowan. She could hear Dennis in her head as she mashed the potatoes in the pot, his voice repeating the words he had said to her over and over again from the moment he discovered she was pregnant.

You're too stupid to raise a kid by yourself. She'll probably die when you're not paying attention.

For five days she'd been on the island, and in five days, just as Dennis had said, she had stopped paying attention.

"So stupid," Rebecca whispered as she sliced up two apples.

The wind whined and thrashed the thatch as Rowan and Rebecca ate. Together they washed the dishes, Rowan talking about the old mare and how she would just follow a path to town and back. No one needed to lead her because she was just like everyone else on the island; she knew what needed to be done, and just did her part. So Mr. O'Flaherty had said, anyway.

After supper Rebecca and Rowan went to their bedroom window. Only one bird was in the bramble and it was sitting on the nest, so they couldn't tell if the eggs had hatched yet.

"What happened to the daddy?" Rowan asked as she brushed her teeth.

"We don't know if that isn't the daddy," Rebecca answered.

"That sounds like a mama bird to me," Rowan said. "Maybe something bad happened to the daddy bird."

"I don't know, Rowan," Rebecca replied, not wanting to go too far in this conversation. "He seemed like a very brave and strong bird. I bet you he's just getting the mama bird's dinner. Birds do that, you know."

Rowan nodded and rinsed her mouth out.

"Time for bed."

After tucking Rowan in, Rebecca sat before the fireplace, looking at the ashes as she listened to the rain and the little bird. Though nothing bad had happened to Rowan, a deep unsettled feeling weighed on her mind. She could hear Dennis telling her she was stupid.

"No. It's just Sean. The island's safe," she whispered to herself. "No safer place than here."

Rebecca rose to her feet to make a fire from the ashes left by the wind and as she turned, she spotted the bag of wool near the door. It was white—the color of Rowan's little gansey that Sharon had brought from the island when she and her mother had come for Rowan's birth. That gansey made of *bainin* wool had wrapped Rowan's little body on Thanksgiving Day six years ago. Shaking, Rebecca lowered herself back to the chair as that memory rolled across her mind.

Rebecca sat in her family room chair as Dennis stood by the front door, holding Rowan's tiny body swathed in her small white Irish sweater. Sharon had brought the sweater from Ireland, saying it was the kind given to all who were born on the island she was from. It had magical properties, and no harm could come to a child who wore it. As soon as Dennis had pulled up in the driveway for his first court-ordered visitation, Rebecca had slipped the sweater over Rowan's head. There was nothing else she could do to keep her daughter safe.

"You think you can just leave me?" he asked her.

"We don't belong together," Rebecca replied, measuring her tone in an effort to avoid making him angry.

"I will always be in your life. *We* have a child. You'll never be free."

His words and body were wound tightly, as they always were when he threatened. "Please, Dennis. Please don't hurt the baby."

"She's my baby. I can do as I please," he answered.

"She's her own self, Dennis." Rebecca started to weep, her throat tightening as she watched the tips of his fingers push Rowan's tiny body into his chest like the claws of a great predatory bird.

"Becky?" Sharon called from the upstairs. "You want me and Mum to come down yet?"

"It's all that bitch's fault," Dennis growled as he turned and walked out the front door. Rebecca jumped out of her seat and rushed to the door. She watched Dennis strap little Rowan into a car seat in the back of his Audi.

"Becky?" Sharon inquired as she stood just behind Rebecca at the front door.

"Happy Thanksgiving, bitch!" Dennis yelled and he slammed his car door.

"She'll be okay, Becky."

"She will?" Rebecca asked, not convinced at all.

A great clap of thunder sounded overhead. Rebecca jumped up from the sofa with a small scream. Trace barked.

"Mama?"

"It's okay, Rowan. That thunder just surprised me," Rebecca replied, her heart thudding against her stomach.

Turning off the living room lights and leaving the fireplace dark and cold, Rebecca headed for the bedroom. When she flipped on the light there, she found Trace on the bed with Rowan.

"What's he doing there?" Rebecca asked.

"The thunder boomed and he jumped up here. Can he stay? I think he's scared."

"I suppose," Rebecca said, as she slipped off her clothes and put on her nightshirt. Turning off the light, she climbed into bed, easing her body around Rowan and Trace. The dog crawled between Rebecca and Rowan, his smelly jaw nuzzled beneath their pillows.

"I guess Mr. O'Flaherty never taught Trace to sing when he's scared of a storm." Rowan giggled.

"I suppose not," Rebecca said. She rolled away from Rowan and the dog, listening to the storm, the mistle thrush beyond the window, and Dennis yelling in her head.

CHAPTER 15

Honeycomb

Honeycomb. 1. This stitch appears exactly as it is named. The cells of the comb can be larger or smaller, depending on the number of stitches used. 2. Traditionally represents hard work and its rewards. An entire jumper made in the honeycomb stitch is saying something worth thinking about.

—R. Dirane, *A Binding Love*

*R*ebecca had a rough night with very little sleep, and that, coupled with the fact that Rowan wasn't feeling well the next day, made her decide they would stay home. She called Maggie to tell her so, but she would have none of it. Within the hour Maggie, Annie, and Siobhan showed up at Rebecca's door with game boards, cards, and fresh bread from Rose's oven in hand. Their idea was to keep Rowan company at home so that Rebecca could go meet Mairead Fitzgibbon.

"I don't know, Annie. What if she's contagious?" Rebecca needed an excuse not to leave her daughter. She didn't want to be stupid again.

"Then Siobhan'll get it and Maggie's wee ones'll get it. They'll all get it. That's what it is to be on an island."

"Come on, Becks." Maggie pressed her to go. "It's a treat for me. Annie said she'd stay with the girls, so this is my day without work or the wee ones. I don't get out that often."

"You go with Maggie. We'll all be fine here," Annie said, pushing Rebecca out the door. "Besides, Mairead is very excited about meeting you. She doesn't get many visitors."

Frowning, Rebecca threw her backpack, which held her cameras, over her shoulders, placed the tripod in one of the side baskets, straddled her bike, and pedaled down the gravel lane behind Maggie, who was on her own bike. She glanced back as she bumped onto the asphalt. Her bright blue door was shut.

"It'll be all right," she whispered. "They'll stay home."

On the road there was not a breeze or any other sign of the storm from the night before. The only hint of rain was the little puddles that glistened in the sunlight as they sat undisturbed next to the stone walls. Pedaling through the town, Maggie and Rebecca waved to John Hernon and Father Michael, and then with a great burst of speed they raced past Maggie's house and the pub, lest someone spot them. Maggie was a woman with a mission—a day off.

Having successfully cleared the town, the two women rode directly into the back of a group of fifteen tourists who were heading to the large Stone Age fort that sat on the southernmost point of the island. As Maggie and Rebecca slowed down, becoming the back of the group, the puddles tapped Rebecca's memory with their dappling light.

She remembered Sharon telling her about sneaking out at night with John and Fionn to go to the fort. There they would sit and smoke and watch the Milky Way float across the midnight sky. Rebecca smiled. She loved that story, having a natural affinity for old places, and wondered if there ever was a time when the fort was without tourists. Was it possible to take Rowan at night—to sleep in a place where ancient people had slept in ages past?

"That's Sean's house," Maggie said, pointing to a white cottage that sat solitary near the sand to the west. "See. He has a beach. That's helpful if you fish with curraghs."

"No beach near my house," Rebecca replied.

"There's a stone walkway northwest of your house that leads down to a very small rocky cove. It's got a bit of sand. Fionn's grandfathers launched their curraghs from there. You should take Rowan."

Rebecca nodded. A mile or so later, Rebecca and Maggie veered east, leaving the tourists on their own. Up a slight slope and over a hill, they came to an old two-story house. Two golden-haired little girls watched with wide eyes as Rebecca and Maggie came to a stop.

"Good day to you, Ciara," Maggie said. "Meara. Where's your mum?"

"In the house with Tadhg."

"And your dad?"

"With the bees."

"Always," Maggie said, winking at Becky.

Resting their bikes against the stone wall near the house, Maggie and Rebecca watched the two little girls run inside.

"Twins," Maggie said. "First time havin' 'em and she pops out twins."

"What's 'tige'?"

"*Who's* Tadhg, actually. He's the little one. A year and a half if I remember right." As they reached the house, Maggie called in the door, "Mairead?"

"In the kitchen."

Rebecca walked into a small living room strewn with toys and papers and crayons and puzzles. The floor was also littered with three boys and a girl of various ages, staring once at Rebecca, then back to the television. Bowls of cereal sat drying up on the coffee table while on the staircase clothes were tossed haphazardly over the banister. The lampshades were tilted in such a way as to make the whole room look askew.

Stepping through a doorway, Rebecca found Mairead, her belly bloated with pregnancy and her eyes rimmed with dark circles. She sat in front of a high chair with a spoon in her hand.

"Mairead, Becky. Becky, Mairead."

"I'd go get the jumper, but if I don't stay with Tadhg here, he'll scream like a banshee," Mairead said. "The only gansey I could find is at the top of the staircase."

Maggie moved past Rebecca to fetch it. As she did so, the little boy glanced away from his tray, his eyes holding Rebecca in what seemed to her to be a look of disdain. He shoved a fistful of green beans into his mouth.

"How far along are you?" Rebecca inquired.

"Seven months. Twins again. Can you believe it?"

Rebecca smiled compassionately. One was hard enough, but nine? All she could think to say was, "Must be hard. I only have one."

"Not hard. Just a lot of work with no sleep. Can't sleep with a belly this big."

"Your husband must not be sleeping well now, too."

"Ah, he sleeps fine and then he goes to work."

"What's he do?"

"Organic farming. Well, I farm with the kids. He raises the bees."

"You farm?"

"Aye. Walking through the fields is getting rough—especially with Tadhg here. Thank the Lord for the girls." Mairead smiled at her daughters.

"They help in the fields?"

"Well, they watch Tadhg in the fields with the boys."

"And your husband raises bees."

"Aye."

"Here, Becky."

Turning around, Rebecca found Maggie holding a gansey. It was oatmeal in color and had only one pattern top to bottom—honeycomb. Rebecca glanced over at Mairead, who chuckled.

"If all I get out of him is honey, then all he gets out of me is that stitch."

Maggie burst out laughing.

"The bees bother you?" Rebecca asked.

"Look around. What do you think?"

"I think you need a break," Rebecca said.

"Aye!"

"Becky needs to know your stitches, Mairead, and in order for that to happen, I think you need time to yourself. Perhaps Becky should talk to your husband. He's one of her kind anyway."

Rebecca looked at Maggie quizzically.

"He's around back. Ciara, take Becky out to talk to your dad."

Skipping over, Ciara grabbed Rebecca's index finger and led her back through the living room.

"I'll make some tea," Maggie called after them.

Rebecca followed Ciara around the corner of the house to the back, and there, in a small field some twenty yards away, were two sheds. Or rather, there was one shed and next to it a disheveled lean-to, listing precariously to the north. Ciara stopped abruptly at the stone wall that separated the field from the house.

"Dad," Ciara called. "We have a visitor."

A very thin man who stood over six feet tall poked his head out the shed door. "Hello," he called, his accent clearly American. "You must be Sharon's friend."

"Yes," Rebecca said, letting go Ciara's hand. "You American?"

"No, Irish. Well, Irish now. Was from California."

"That's where I'm from."

"Really?" he said, smiling. "Where?"

"I was raised in Redding."

"I was born in Westminster," he said, walking over. "I'm Jim—Jim Fitzgibbon."

"Rebecca Moray."

"You moving here, too?"

"Nah, just staying for the summer."

"Ah, that's right. You're writing a book."

"How'd you end up here?"

"My grandmother was from here. A Dirane she was. When she

passed on, my cousin told me he was going to sell the place. My grandmother was the last of her siblings to go, and my cousin didn't see any purpose hanging on to the farm, he being the only Dirane left on the island and his wife's family being from Doolin, on the mainland. Couldn't really blame him for wanting to leave. So I finished my degree at Davis, packed it up, and bought the place from him. Been here ever since. Farming the land of my fathers."

"And beekeeping."

"Yes! You want some honey?"

"Sure."

"Come on, then."

Jim turned around and began walking to the shed without looking back. Searching around the wall, Rebecca found no gate, so she hurriedly climbed over the stones and trotted after him.

"You sure you have extra?" she panted.

"Oh, yeah. We're going to sell it, but Mairead hasn't made the labels yet."

"What labels?"

"The labels for the jars. There's money to be made in honey, you know."

"Mairead needs to make labels . . ." Rebecca repeated. "Doesn't she seem a bit—busy—already?"

"Aye. But she's the artist. She's very creative."

"Yeah. I saw your jumper."

"Great, huh?" Jim said, looking back at her with a broad smile as he opened the shed. "She knows I love the bees."

Rebecca nodded with a shrug. Peering into the shed, she caught her breath. Neatly stacked in crates rising to the ceiling were hundreds of jars of honey.

"That's a lot of labels," Rebecca murmured.

"Busy bees," Jim said. "These are not your typical honeybees. They're the brown bees of these islands. Suited for the weather and flora. You'll not taste honey like this anywhere else."

Rebecca nodded again with a small smile as Jim handed her a jar. "So, your kids help you out here?" she asked.

"Oh, no. Too dangerous for them. Maybe when they're older."

"Must take a lot of time. Bees, I mean."

"Keeping living things requires time and attention."

"Yes, it does."

Jim's eyes were filled with the reflection of the golden honey sparkling in the noonday sun. Rebecca squinted, trying to recall where she had seen that look before. Suddenly it came to her. It was the same vacant stare in the dusty pictures hanging on the walls of the Sutter's Mill museum. Men, struck by gold fever in the late 1840s, gazed out at the world with that same hollow look, frozen in sepia photos for all time. Jim was a man with the fever—a solitary forty-niner panning for little nuggets of riches while his life went by. At least Jim's nuggets were edible.

"Well, thanks for the honey," Rebecca muttered, stepping out of the shed.

"It's really good with Rose's bread."

"Ah! I got a loaf of that this morning."

"Best breakfast in the world."

Rebecca made her way back to the stone wall. Holding the jar of honey near her chest, she climbed out of the field and headed back to the house. She rounded the corner and found Maggie leaning against the front door, sipping tea.

"Sad, isn't it?" she said.

"What?"

"Jim."

"Sadder for Mairead and the kids, don't you think?"

"That's what we all say. We've tried to talk to him. Even Father Michael. Jim just doesn't hear."

"No, he really doesn't, does he? He actually likes Mairead's jumper."

"I know!" Maggie laughed.

Rebecca shook her head.

"It's a Dam Mad Situation, Becky."

"As opposed to a damn mad situation?" Rebecca asked.

"Aye."

Rebecca watched a sly smile grow on Maggie's face. "What are you up to, Mags?"

"Ah, we love that story of yours. Something has to be done, Becks."

"It's just a family story, Mags."

"We've all tried to help Jim. He needs a good American shake-up."

"You people aren't very good at confrontation, are you?"

"You people are."

"But he says he's Irish—not my people."

"Maybe his heart and soul are," Maggie replied with a snicker. "But his body and mind are still one of you."

Rebecca squinted into Maggie's eyes. "I reckon this'll take some planning."

"I reckon, Beckon. Want some tea?"

"Only if it's in a clean cup."

CHAPTER 16

Celtic Knots

Celtic Knot. 1. These vary in size and intricacies, but all are created with cross stitches and twisted stitches. Celtic knots are very complicated patterns and are best learned from more advanced knitters. 2. Music.

—R. Dirane, *A Binding Love*

The sun poured brightly through his sons' window, touching the yellow swatch Sean held in his hand. It had taken him six days to get the color correct, each swatch becoming cooler and cooler as he sprinkled tiny granules of blue dye into the yellow liquid. The twenty-two discarded scraps of cloth were scattered about the floor like so many dandelion flowers plucked by Sean's little boys on a spring morning some sixty years before, a few falling between small fingers as his sons handed them to their mother.

"Not that memory." Sean smiled. "Halos and the feet of a tiny man."

A shadow passed across his window, and following it, Sean found a mistle thrush flittering by his house, coming in from the sea. The bird tumbled in the periwinkle blue sky that was as clear as the sound of Joe's pipe. As that thought flicked across Sean's mind, the old man jumped up from his seat, staring at the periwinkle heaven. He had not seen a purplish blue sky since Matthew's fifteenth birthday.

I'm afraid, Da.

Sean grabbed the sides of his head, willing his brain to think of Brendan and halos.

"No!" he yelled to the floor. "Not that memory."

But the periwinkle sky didn't listen. It glared down on Sean, shoving its way into his darkened house and heart without a drop of mercy.

⌒

"I'm afraid, Da," Matthew said softly, gazing up into his father's face with pleading eyes.

"You asked for the bicycle."

"Sean, give the boy time," Claire said, holding two-year-old Brendan on her hip.

"The sky'll not be any clearer than that," Sean replied, pointing up into the periwinkle morning. "'Tis a dry day. The rest of your brothers gave up a lot so we could buy this bike for you. Now you'll be needing to get on it."

"I'm afraid."

"Get on the bike and I'll give you a push."

His eldest boy's shaking hands grasped the handlebars while he lifted his feet to the pedals.

"Wait, Da!" Matthew yelled as Sean gave his son a great push down the slope.

Claire gasped.

"Shut up," Sean said without looking at her.

Matthew raced down the hill, bumping over a rut in the dirt road where the bike skidded out from beneath him. The boy was airborne, flying into a ditch beside the road, headfirst.

"Matthew!" Liam screamed as he ran past his mother toward the ditch where his brother lay motionless.

Sean cuffed his four-year-old son on the chin, sending Liam stumbling back toward Joe.

"He's just a wee one, Da!" Joe yelled at his father, catching Liam before the little boy hit the ground. Joe was thirteen and as tall as

Matthew. Sean spun around to face Joe, who, upon meeting his father's eye, set his jaw as he pushed his chest out. Sean stepped toward him.

"Sean!" Claire said, grabbing her thirteen-year-old boy by the shoulder of his gansey and pulling him back.

"I said shut up, Claire!"

"Matthew's hurt," Liam whispered.

"He's not moving, Sean," Claire choked.

"Matthew!" Sean yelled angrily, baring his teeth at Joe as he turned back toward the ditch. He stormed down the sloping dirt road. "Matthew, get up from there!"

Sean stood over his son, whose limp body lay still. Climbing into the ditch next to Matthew, Sean shook him.

"Matthew!"

Matthew did not respond.

Sean slapped his son's face.

"Sean!" Claire yelled.

"Shut up! Matthew!"

Matthew's eyes fluttered open. "Da?"

"Get up!"

Slowly Matthew rolled over, but his right arm crumpled when he tried to support his weight with it.

"My arm."

"Get up and get on that bike." Sean reached down and grabbed Matthew by the collar of his blue gansey, which pulled the sleeve against the injured arm.

"My arm!"

"It's not that bad," Sean seethed into Matthew's ear in a menacing whisper. "You're worrying your mother something terrible. Now get on the bike and show her you're fine."

Matthew glanced back at his mother, leaving his right arm to hang limply at his side. He waved a little with his uninjured left hand.

"Good. Now get on the bike."

Matthew looked up into his father's face, his wide, frightened eyes reflecting the periwinkle sky above him. Tears glistened in the light as they rolled down his cheeks. Grabbing the handlebar with only his left hand, Matthew lifted his feet to the pedals with a whimper. Sean pushed the bike. Matthew was unable to keep his balance with the injured arm and fell over again. A small cry passed the boy's lips as he hit the dirt. He didn't roll over.

"You'll never be a man," Sean declared and walked away, leaving his son lying on the dirt road behind him.

"Sean!" Claire called.

He didn't look back. He didn't reply. He walked away.

Sean held his head, his knees buckling beneath him as the sound of his son crying in the dirt rolled across his mind. He hadn't taken Matthew into Galway until a week later to have his arm set.

Then the late spring wind blew, and Sean's memory shifted directions and he watched Matthew standing at the altar kissing his new wife, Mary, ten years after the bike accident. All Sean could remember of that day was the permanent bend in Matthew's lower right arm—a deformity Sean had put there. Matthew held Mary to him in front of the priest with that bent arm as Joe played his pipe.

Suddenly Sean pulled his hands from his head. He listened. There was a pipe playing beyond his workshop door.

"Joe?"

The whistle was clean, with no needless air rasping the notes. His feet scuffed the stone floor as he crossed it, sending the yellow swatches scattering in his wake. Opening the door, Sean trotted across the kitchen. The whistle climbed higher, its notes tickling Sean's aging ears. As he entered the living room, he found the music coming from outside.

"Rowan?"

He flung his front door open and leaned out into the clear morning air. The ocean roared behind his house to the west. The wind smelled of grass and dew, blowing in from the east. The music was from neither east nor west—nor north nor south. It just was, and Sean stood rock-still, his bare feet cool on his slate step, listening to it.

"Joe."

Sean tucked the swatch into his pant pocket and from within his tattered sleeve he pulled out his whistle. He raised it to his weathered lips and blew. His note was full of air like a cough. It was rough and grainy. He stopped, closing his eyes, listening for the scale. The surf pounded the shore. For a moment, Sean lost the whistle's sound.

"No," he whispered, stepping farther from his door. As the tide rolled away, the whistle poured down the scale like a tiny waterfall.

Quickly Sean grabbed his cap and coat from the hook inside his door and, leaving his house to the elements, ran around his cottage toward the ocean, his feet bare of shoes. Flying down a dune, he heard a scale no longer. It was a tune. It was bright and happy, skipping in waves around him but now and then silenced by the surf.

"Wait," Sean called, unbinding the ropes from his curragh and flinging them onto the sand. With a great grunt, he flipped his boat over, tossed the oars, his coat, and his cap into the bottom, and pushed the curragh toward the sea. Sand grew in mounds before his bow and crawled up between his toes, trying to keep the man on dry ground. But like all fishermen, Sean knew that as his boat hit the waves, the ocean would grab it and take it farther out to sea.

"I'm coming," Sean yelled, as a wave crashed over the bow. Cold, salty water splashed his face and stung his eyes as the bottom of the boat was lifted from the sand. Grabbing the side of the curragh, Sean pulled himself in, landing flat on his back in the bottom of the boat. Quickly he scooted his legs under him, seated himself, placed the oars on their pegs, and pulled. As he raised his oars, the bow climbed over the crest of an incoming wave, and water came crashing into the curragh. Sean dropped his oars in the water, pulling with his crackling back, pushing with his grinding knees. The next wave was smaller, and as he laid on the oars and crawled slowly away from the shore, he could hear the pipe more clearly.

He rowed in rhythm. The periwinkle sky touched his head, heating his scalp. Grabbing his cap, the old man popped it over his sparse hair and headed north, where he knew a kelp bed grew. It was there, on gentle spring mornings, that the sea was most quiet. He had found it sixty-eight years ago, the day after his father stopped talking to him—the day Sean became a man. He was fifteen years old and had left his father's house the night before, choosing that night to sleep with the cows in Claire's parents' barn. He had never returned to his father's house until the man passed on.

It was to that kelp bed Sean now rowed, his body popping and grinding. But he wasn't paying attention to his pain; he was hearing Joe's song. When he reached the kelp bed, he pulled his oars into the curragh. The boat slowed its forward motion and came to rest in the tops of the giant green forest below. Closing his eyes, Sean listened.

It was Joe, all right, playing the same tune he had played the first time out in the curragh with his father. Sean had lost the memory of Joe's pipe—so clean, with no wasted air. It was there, but blurred by time and pain, and the exact sound had been lost long ago. But now Sean heard it as if Joe sat before him in the curragh surrounded by the silent sea beneath a periwinkle sky.

From his sleeve, Sean pulled his pipe and put it to his lips. The music stopped. Startled, he stood up, straining his ears to catch one more sound—one more note. There was nothing but the ocean lapping the sides of his boat in the stillness of morning.

"Come back," he called, but no sound followed.

"Come back to me!" he yelled to the sky.

There was nothing. Falling back onto his seat, the old man rolled his pipe between his fingers. He brought the whistle to his lips and played. His sound was rough, the tune flat. He was like a person who had not sung for years trying to sing a song from long ago. The voice remembers how it is supposed to sound but can no longer hit the notes. Sean cringed at the miss.

"Come back," he whispered.

It was Joe. Only Joe sounded so.

Joe had a way with the pipe. It was Joe who taught his brothers the whistle. He helped with fingering and aperture. As Matthew played melody, Joe played harmony until the next son was old enough to play. Then, before the driftwood fire at night, Joe would give each boy his own harmony to all the songs he knew. Every night, for many years, Sean's house was filled with tin whistles playing over gales or through warm summer nights. But as his sons grew, there was less and less music, until there was but one pipe sounding around Sean's beach. It was Joe, playing somewhere else besides his father's hearth.

"Please, come back," he begged, but there was only the breeze blowing silently about the curragh.

From his pocket, Sean pulled out his yellow swatch, fingering the garter stitches as the sun heated his back. He hadn't thought of Joe for so long. He certainly hadn't thought of Joe's pipe. But when he had heard Rowan whistling away like she'd been doing it for years—like she was born to the island herself—then he thought again of his second son.

Tucking his pipe into his sleeve again, Sean turned the boat around and headed back to shore in silence. His oars were as heavy as his heart. Slowly, he pulled against the sea. Gazing out at the horizon, he let the memory of the music flow into him, burning the pristine sound into his mind. Perhaps it was Rowan, after all. Perhaps as she played, the island picked up her song and spread it through the air. But then, Rowan didn't know any tunes; she knew only scales.

Turning his boat east, Sean rolled ashore, hopping out of the curragh in his bare feet. Sand grew in mounds before his bow, seemingly angry with him for leaving the beach in the first place. With a great heave, he rolled the curragh over, leaving it resting on the sand, unbound to its mooring rocks. With the waves crashing behind him, he picked up his coat and climbed the dune to his house. The rosebushes were but dead sticks next to his cottage, and when he rounded the corner he found his front door open as he had left it. To the east, he spotted a small group of tourists watching him from the road.

"Go 'way," he muttered, and stepping into his house, he shut the door. He hung his cap and coat on the peg just inside and dipped his fingers in the small shell of water.

"God bless all here," he said. There was no answer.

In the kitchen Sean poured his cold tea into his empty cup. Lifting it from the table, he shuffled into his sons' room, grabbed the large bag of wool, and sat down on his chair, which sat lonely near the dark fireplace. He set his tea on the floor. After brushing the sand from his feet, he pulled his spinning wheel toward his chair.

"I have to make Brendan," he said to the spindle as he popped an empty bobbin onto it. Very carefully, he pulled a leader thread from within the bag of wool, tied it onto the bobbin, fed it through the hooks on the flyer, down into the orifice, and out the other side. There he made a knot and as he placed his right foot on the treadle, he reached down for his tea. Taking a sip, he peered sideways out the window at the periwinkle blue sky. He set the wheel in motion. It clicked loudly through the empty house, the spokes spinning in front of him like the wheel of Matthew's bike.

CHAPTER 17

Bobbles/Ribbing Between

Bobbles/Ribbing Between. 1. A bobble knitted and a single rib created between it and another bobble. The ribbing stitch appears as a string between the two bobbles and can be knitted as a straight line or curved like the letter *S*. 2. A new friend.

—R. Dirane, *A Binding Love*

The rest of the week, Rebecca endeavored to keep Rowan close to her without insulting anyone in town. Siobhan had come over again on Tuesday for the day. On Wednesday, Rebecca headed to Rose's house, inviting Siobhan to come along with Rowan while Rebecca learned to spin on the wheel.

Tom was ill on Thursday and Maggie asked Rebecca if she could help in the pub. It was a natural request, as Maggie put it, because Rebecca had been a superstar waitress through college, according to Sharon. Rebecca was glad to help out, especially since doing so allowed her to invite Siobhan over to play with Rowan and Maggie's two boys in the back of the pub for the day.

When Friday arrived, Tom was still ill, so Rebecca and Rowan pedaled toward the pub through heavy morning mist, the sun but a suggestion of light on the eastern horizon. They found Annie, Paddy, and Siobhan waiting for them in front of the Blakes' house. Paddy held fishing poles and Siobhan held flashlights.

"Time to go fishing," Paddy called.

"Oh—Rowan and I were going to help Maggie in the pub," Rebecca replied with a grimace. She wasn't ready to let Rowan run free quite yet. She hadn't even figured out how to keep Sean away.

"Let her go," Annie said. "I'll help you and Maggie in the pub."

"When will you be back?" Rebecca asked nervously.

"We're only going on the rocks south," Paddy replied. "If we're not back when you want Rowan, just come and get her. She might be a bit smelly, but she'll be fine."

Rebecca laughed and with a nod kissed Rowan's head. Her little girl skipped hand in hand with Siobhan south, following Paddy.

"Come on. Maggie'll have breakfast," Annie said.

With one final glance over her shoulder, Rebecca left Rowan to Paddy and the sea.

The town was quiet. There was no loud laughing, no people rushing down the streets speaking foreign languages, and no whizzing bicycles. Clearly tourists didn't rise before the sun while on holiday. By the thickness of the fog today, they would be in bed for some time longer. Rebecca supposed that mornings here were mostly silent like this, with the ocean wind whispering salty secrets to those who chose to rise before dawn.

Annie and Rebecca walked past the front of the pub and around to the back of it. With a little rap, Annie opened the back door, which led to the pub's kitchen.

"Good morning, Maggie."

"Mornin', Annie. Mornin', Becks," Maggie said without looking over her shoulder, concentrating instead on the sausages frying on the grill before her. "Have some coffee." She nodded to the steaming pot on the counter.

"Thanks," Annie replied, pulling two cups from the tray of twelve that sat next to the coffeemaker.

"Where's Rowan?"

"Ah—Paddy took her fishing with Siobhan. They'll have fun," Annie said, setting a full cup of coffee before Rebecca, who had taken a seat at the large butcher-block table in the center of the kitchen.

"Have you been thinkin' about the Mairead Dam Mad Situation, Becky?" Maggie asked.

"Yeah," she replied. "I think with seven kids, it's best if we just take Mairead for a day. My dad only had me to deal with, so the lesson took longer. It'll be a wonder if Jim can survive one day."

"Well, Mairead's mum's been asking her to visit. Mairead's from the island just north. That would be a one-day trip, with travel time and visiting time," Annie said, seating herself across from Rebecca.

"You know the Dam Mad Situation?" Rebecca asked, with raised eyebrows.

"Yeah, it's one of Sharon's stories about you."

"Ah, right."

"Maybe Paddy can take her," Maggie suggested, holding two eggs in her hand. "You like your eggs scrambled, right, Becks?"

"Yes, thanks. Can Paddy take her? He'd have to go back and get her that same day."

"Or Mairead's brother, Iollan, can bring her back. He's a fisherman, too, and has a boat," Maggie offered.

"When it works," Annie said with a snicker. "Let me talk with Paddy and I'll have Paddy talk with Iollan."

A gentle tap on the door brought Maggie, Annie, and Rebecca to attention. Fionn's head popped into the kitchen. He had left a week before, and, true to his word, he had returned.

"Good morning!" he greeted them, smiling broadly through his red beard. No one answered. "Did I interrupt something?"

"What are you doin' home?" Maggie asked with a frown.

"And good to see you, too, Maggie, my love," Fionn replied, shutting the door behind him.

"He's come to return the books he brought to me from the library," Rebecca replied with a little smile. He did have the most beautiful hair.

"That is one reason I've returned, yes. But there are two others.

The second—I come bearing a message from Sharon." Fionn helped himself to the coffee.

"What message from Sharon? She have her baby?" Annie asked excitedly.

"Nope, she hasn't. The third—I needed to talk with the father."

"The father," Maggie repeated.

"Aye. You're burnin' those eggs, Maggie," Fionn said.

"Ah!" she hissed, turning back to the grill. "Sorry, Becks."

"So what conspiracy were you three hatchin' when I walked in?"

Rebecca shifted anxiously in her seat.

"We were talkin' about the Mairead Dam Mad Situation," Annie replied.

"Excellent!" Fionn said.

"You know about the Dam Mad Situation?" Rebecca asked.

"It was one of Sha—"

"I know, I know," Rebecca interrupted.

"We're taking Mairead to see her mother and leaving Jim with the kids. Just trying to come up with a date now," Annie said, and as she finished her sentence the back door opened. It was Fionn Sr.

"Son! What are you doin' home?"

"He came for three reasons, the last of which was to see the father," Maggie replied, raising her eyebrows as she slid a plate of eggs, bacon, and tomatoes in front of Rebecca.

"You stay with Tom last night?" the older man asked, taking Fionn in his arms and giving him a hug.

"Nah, I stayed with Father Michael."

Annie whistled.

"Must be in some pain to stay with the father for an entire evening," Maggie said.

They laughed.

"You work it out?" Fionn Sr. asked.

"Workin' on it," Fionn replied. "Mairead needs to go home for the Dam Mad Situation."

"Really? When?"

"How 'bout tomorrow?" Fionn offered. "I'm here and we can take her over in the curragh. Becky wanted to ride in one."

"No," Rebecca began. "Not ride in one. See—"

"That'd be excellent!" Annie interrupted Rebecca. "Paddy'll have already missed a fishing day taking the girls out on the rocks today."

"Great! It's settled," Fionn Sr. said. "Maggie, I came by to let you know there's a line of hungry people at the door."

"Ah, buggers!" she said, wiping her hands on her apron. "Forgot to unlock the front."

"I'll get it," Annie said, standing up and heading out the kitchen door into the pub.

"I better be checking on the curragh," Fionn Sr. said, leaving by the back door.

"I'll come with ya." Fionn set his cup on the counter and followed his father.

"Wait!" Annie called after him. "What was Sharon's message?"

"Oh. Becky. I'm not allowed to bring you any more books. You have to come to Dublin to get them yourself. Not my message, mind," he said with a wide grin. "Sharon's."

Fionn shut the door with finality, and with a deep frown Rebecca stood up from the table. This was not what she had planned at all. She had responsibilities. She needed to write a book. She had a grant and only two months to do her research. Now she was mixed up in a Dam Mad Situation ten days after her arrival. She was a waitress at a pub and was going to cross a great ocean in a tiny little rowboat.

"Hey, Maggie," Annie said, coming through the kitchen door, "scrambled eggs, bacon, tomatoes, and a coffee."

"You eatin' your breakfast, Becks?"

Rebecca watched Maggie slide two eggs and a rasher of bacon onto a plate. She took a deep breath again and shook her head.

"Can you take yours out to whoever?" Maggie asked.

"The man by the window," Annie offered, filling three cups with coffee.

Rebecca took the plate and walked out into the pub. She made her way through the tables to a middle-aged man with salt-and-pepper hair who was sitting alone at one of the window tables.

"Eggs, bacon, and tomatoes?" Rebecca inquired.

"Yes, please, and can I have some coffee?" He was Scottish by his accent.

"Here ya go," Annie said, sliding a cup onto the table.

"Excuse me," called a young woman seated with two young men. Rebecca walked over to the table, which was near the fireplace.

"We'd like bangers and mash all around—and can you light the fire? It's cold in here."

Rebecca nodded and headed back into the kitchen.

"Three bangers and mash," she said. "Where's the matches?"

"Over by the coffeepots," Maggie replied. "You should go to Dublin, Becky. See Sharon."

"I don't have time, Mags. I've been here ten days and only have two ganseys."

Rebecca left the kitchen with the box of matches. Next to the fireplace she found a small stack of peat and a basket of dried grass. Pulling three bricks of peat from the pile, she created a tepee with them in the fireplace. Just as she had watched Sheila do her first morning on the island, she slid a small wad of dried grass beneath the peat, struck a match, and lit the grass. It glowed softly, quickly burning away. But before the flame went out, she added more dried grass until the peat smoldered gently at its edges.

"It'll take a minute, but the fire should get going shortly," Rebecca said to the young woman. She made her way back to the kitchen.

"Here's your bangers and mash," Maggie said.

"I have a doctorate in archaeology and somehow, in less than two weeks here, I've become a waitress again."

Maggie laughed as she handed Rebecca the plates.

"I can tell by the way you carry those plates that you're a good one. Sharon always said you were."

"Sure," Rebecca said under her breath as she took the plates into the pub, where the fire was now flickering happily.

"Three bangers and mash," she said, slipping the plates onto the table.

"Can I get more coffee?" the young woman asked.

"Just a sec," Rebecca replied. She walked back into the kitchen. Annie stood with the coffeepot, smiling. On the table was a thermos and a brown paper sack.

"We put some scones in the sack and poured you some tea, Becky," Annie said. "Go have breakfast somewhere. Take a day to yourself."

"Maggie needs help," Rebecca said.

"I'm here. Why don't you go see the big fort before the tourists get out of bed?" Annie said.

"You like old places, Becks," Maggie said.

"But there'll be more tourists. I should stay and help."

"It was only gonna be me and you today, Becks. Now, it's me and Annie. Maybe you'll find something helpful for your book."

"Are you sure?" Rebecca replied.

"Take the day, Becks. When's the last time you were alone without anyone or anything to take care of?"

Rebecca looked from Maggie to Annie.

"We'll be fine," Annie said, lifting the brown bag and thermos from the table and pushing them into Rebecca's hands.

"Paddy'll take care of Rowan. Go on," Maggie pressed her. "Take the road past Rose's house—like you're going to Mairead's."

"I remember," Rebecca replied, and with a small smile she took the thermos and sack from Annie and stepped out into the morning mist. It had lifted a bit and dawn sat gray on the horizon. After placing the thermos and the bag of scones into her side baskets, Rebecca pedaled off toward the church.

The wind was soft and gentle, brushing the mist before her, making small white ghosts for her to ride through. There were no people out on the road, and the gray solitude filled her mind with quiet. It had been so long since she was still; her life in the States was constantly filled with work and worry. This quiet was what she'd come here to find. Every now and then Rowan and Sean would pass through her mind and she'd slow down, thinking perhaps she should return to town. But then she reminded herself that Rowan was with Paddy. Paddy had a little girl. He knew how to keep little girls safe. So Rebecca pedaled on until she saw a great blackness far away in the mist.

Straight ahead, the island rolled off in the distance, rocky and flat. Huge waves crashed against sheer cliffs as hundreds of seabirds circled in their wake, their keening songs soaring to the Irish heaven. Slightly to her left, three concentric semicircles of black stones rose out of the rock and grass. The convex curvature of the semicircles' wall faced where Rebecca stood, the tips of its crescent-moon shape ending where the land fell steeply into the sea. She climbed down from her bike and walked it off the asphalt, leaning it against a stone wall, as there was no way to take it farther.

With her thermos and paper bag in hand, Rebecca approached the first wall. As she had learned from Fionn, she hurtled herself over it, walking with surety across the rocky land. Here, at island's end, the wind blew fiercely. The grass peeked warily from its tiny dirt crevices, shuddering as though afraid to grow too tall lest it be picked up and blown out to sea. The wind whipped her hair, flailing her cheeks and stinging her eyes as she climbed over another wall. The fort grew larger as she got closer to it. She estimated that its inner parapet was near twenty feet high, made of stones stacked one atop another. Jagged, irregular rocks like giant shards of black stone tumbled away at the base of the outer wall, and she carefully picked her way through them.

Walking toward the cliff's edge, she came around the end of the second wall and climbed up on the top of the inner parapet. Her heart beat against her chest like the waves crashing below. There was no sound but the pounding drumbeat of the tide. Its violent impact on the island sent little drops of salt water floating through the air.

Rebecca stood alone, watching the sea to the southwest, thinking of Sharon, John, and Fionn sitting here beneath the stars. How many times had Sharon told that story? It was the tale she repeated most. Rebecca's mind had made the scene a quiet one—soft murmurs and laughter of three teenagers lying head to head as they watched the Milky Way overhead. But that could not have been how it was. There was no silence here. There would have been no soft, sleepy conversation on tufts of green Irish grass. This place was hard and solid and eternal, tenaciously standing against the beating ocean—its roaring call daring all who heard it to stay and live. It would never give up nor would it allow any who lived upon its rocky shores to relent.

As Rebecca lowered herself to the ground in the wind, making herself small like the grass so as not to be blown away, she heard what Sharon had heard her whole life. She pulled a scone from her bag, a solitary person within an ancient black open fortress. She felt calm and still, and she poured herself a cup of tea and had breakfast with the great crashing voice of the island.

CHAPTER 18

Chevron

Chevron. 1. A pattern of stitches meeting at an angle, like the sleeve insignia worn in the military to designate rank. 2. A moment where there is an abrupt change in direction.

—R. Dirane, *A Binding Love*

$\mathcal{S}$ean tottered toward the church. The little shell by his door was empty; that was the only reason he ever bothered the priest. The fog was thinning, and Sean could tell the periwinkle sky would still haunt him another day. He knew it was above the mist, burning and beating and glaring, and with it the memory of Matthew's bike hung just out of sight but always threatening.

"Good day, Morahan!"

Sean looked about, wondering how he had ended up at the rocks south of town. He found Paddy holding a fishing rod, balancing on a rock with his daughter beside him.

"Getting the child ready to take after you, Blake?"

Paddy nodded with a grin.

Sean spied Rowan playing in Old Man Dirane's ancient dinghy— the white and blue paint chipped and peeling from decades of gales and children's play. It was the first boat the children of the island stepped into, pretending to be great fisherfolk catching giant shoals of fish out on Galway Bay.

"Would you do me a favor there, Morahan? I think the wee ones would like tea and something to eat. Could ya stay while I go back home and fetch breakfast?"

Sean smiled like the sun at the invitation. How long had it been since he'd been fishing with a child?

"That would be fine."

"Good, good," Paddy replied, handing the old man his fishing rod.

"Good day, Rowan," Sean said in greeting as Paddy walked away.

Rowan didn't reply. Instead she stared at him, stone-faced, and offered him but a little wave. Anger flashed through his mind, for this was not what he had expected from her. He was about to say—to say he was hurt. It wasn't anger; it was hurt. He swallowed.

"Everything all right, there?" he asked of her.

Rowan nodded and turned her back to him.

"I'll be back shortly, Siobhan. Listen to Mr. Morahan and do as he says," Paddy called over his shoulder.

"Aye, Da."

"You, too, there, Rowan."

"Okay," Rowan replied without turning around.

Sean stood still, listening to the waves gently kiss the rocks on which he stood. A buoy sounded in the distance to the south, its lonely bell tolling in the fog that lay upon the waves farther out. Sean did not usually come this way, partial as he was to the west. It was not a place to row to except in summer anyway, as the currents to the north and south of the island were, at any other time of year, strong. It was like rowing in mud; no matter how hard you pulled on the oars, you wouldn't move an inch. Only when Sean had had his own fishing boat with an engine did he venture on this side of the island, as the only docks were in town and the town was east. But forty years it had been since he'd had a boat with an engine. With no sons and no wife—no family to keep—and with no desire to partner with anyone else on the island, Sean went his solitary way, fishing from his curragh alone, and as that thought passed through his head, he reeled his line in a little bit.

He thought back on his last encounter with Rowan. He had not been mean or short. He thought he had left her in a happy mood, and as he ran all their conversations through his head from the moment he had seen her in O'Flaherty's Pub to the time he walked away from her followed by the sound of her whistle, a tug on his sleeve brought his attention to his left. There he found Rowan looking up at him with a frown.

"Did I do something to hurt your feelings again?" he asked softly, not sure if he had or hadn't.

"Are you pretending to be nice to me, Sean?" she whispered.

Sean peered down into her eyes and found—found—what was that look? "Did someone say I was pretending to be nice to you?"

Rowan didn't answer.

"If I don't like somebody, ya think they know?"

She nodded emphatically.

"Well, knowing that, ya think if I didn't like somebody, would it be like me to pretend to be nice to them?"

The little girl shook her head slowly.

"No, Rowan. I don't pretend to like anybody."

"So, you do like me?"

"Aye, Rowan. You're a good—friend."

She smiled with a little nod and when she did, a reflection of pink shined across her face. Sean turned to the horizon and found the sun rising in a fluorescent blaze as the fog cleared. Hundreds of puffy little clouds dotted the pink-apricot sky. Matthew's bicycle memory vanished. Replacing it was the thought of Liam and the little boy's first try at fishing.

"See those clouds there, Rowan?"

"Aye?"

"They look like hundreds of tiny sheep, don't they? My da used to say when the sky appears so, 'tis the Almighty gathering his flock."

So he had told Matthew and Joe and Liam and Brendan, and as he thought of his four sons he felt Rowan's tiny, soft hand slide into his rough palm. He squeezed it, holding on as gently as he could, and the great pain that welled up in his heart formed a single tear that rolled from his eye.

Sean looked down to his right and found Siobhan sliding closer to him. "Will we catch fish, Mr. Morahan?" she asked.

"I think it likely." He coughed, trying to control another tear that rested precariously in the corner of his right eye. Swallowing, he bent down and secured his fishing pole in a crevice between rocks. Then he removed Siobhan's rod from her hands and shimmied it between two rocks. The lines reached out, disappearing into the pink water that reflected the sunrise to the east.

"All right. When the lines are all laid and settled still in the water, now's the time to play a tune."

"Won't that scare the fish away?" Siobhan asked.

"Watch," he said, balancing his weight forward as he squatted down until his eyes were level with Siobhan's and Rowan's. He pulled his pipe from his sleeve and played a tune. He made it sound pink and gold, like sunrise; he called to the swimming creatures below to come and see the glittering light upon the surface. They heard him, of course. They always did, and suddenly both lines of the fishing rods began to shake. He stopped playing, winking at the girls with a crinkled smile.

"Rowan, you take this line," he said, handing Rowan the fishing rod Paddy had held. "Siobhan, you take the other. Careful now, as you pull it from the rocks."

Siobhan tugged the rod from its secure crevice. Sean held his hand to her back, steadying her on the rock.

"We don't pull the fish in too fast. We let the line out a little, then pull it back. Don't want it to snap and lose our supper, now, do we?"

"No," Rowan said, gritting her teeth as her rod bent down from the weight and fight of the fish.

"Reel yours in a bit, Siobhan," Sean said. "Slowly, slowly. Almost there. Watch it, Rowan!"

Rowan spun her reel sharply and from the little waves below the rock on which she stood, a mackerel popped out of the ocean, attached to her line.

"I got one! I got one!" she yelled triumphantly.

Sean lifted Paddy's net and quickly surrounded Rowan's fish. Siobhan leaned back, pulling a bigger mackerel from the water. It hit the rocks, flapping about the stones.

"I can't hold it!" Siobhan hollered. "It's too heavy!"

Quickly Sean skittered forward on the rocks and placed the net beneath Siobhan's fish.

"Your fish is bigger, Siobhan!" Rowan laughed.

Sean carefully picked his way across the rocks. He lifted each fish from the net, pulled the hook from its mouth, and dropped both into Paddy's fishing basket.

"Won't your da be surprised, Siobhan?" he asked with a grin. He took his cap off and wiped his brow.

"Aye." Siobhan smiled proudly. "Did your da teach you that song?"

"No," Sean replied, walking toward Old Man Dirane's dinghy. "'Twas my son Joe that knew such things. I was a good fisherman. He was a grea—" A lump formed in Sean's throat and he coughed instead of finishing the sentence.

Climbing into the tattered little boat, Sean sat down. The sky was bright and clear above him.

"You know whose boat this is?" he asked, changing the subject. Siobhan and Rowan crawled into it and sat down on the bench in front of him.

"Old Man Dirane's," Siobhan replied.

"Who was he?" Sean asked.

"The shanachie."

"What's 'shawnashee'?" Rowan asked.

"A storyteller. For the Irish, they keep the history, traveling from town to town, island to island, telling the wee ones the great deeds of the past so no one forgets."

"This was his boat?" Rowan asked, running her hand across the edge of the dinghy.

"Aye. The Diranes were great fisherfolk," Sean replied.

"My da says a gale blew through when his da was a boy," Siobhan said. "He told me Old Man Dirane was out in this very boat, coming back from telling tales on the big island. He had lost his way—couldn't see anything through the rain and the wind, and suddenly, he felt a bump. The boat just up and landed right here."

"That it did," Sean confirmed.

"Were you alive then, Sean?" Rowan asked.

"Aye. I was just back from war. No one has moved this boat since."

"My da says that all the children of the island play in it 'cause it calls to them. It's magic," Siobhan said.

"Magic?" Rowan asked, looking down at the splintered bottom of the dinghy.

"It's where we learn to go out in the water. The boat teaches us secrets," Siobhan said, leaning over to Rowan as if passing a secret herself.

"Some's as say it's Old Man Dirane himself whispering to ya," Sean added.

Rowan looked at Sean with wide eyes—mahogany surprise.

"Can ya teach me to play that tune that calls the fish, Mr. Morahan?" Siobhan asked.

"Aye, but it's not just the tune. 'Tis the Irish in your head with the song that gets the fish to come. That's what Joe taught me. You speak Irish?"

"Of course!" Rowan exclaimed. "Can't you hear her?"

"Hear what?"

"Her speaking Irish?"

Sean and Siobhan looked at each other and laughed. Rowan's brow furrowed.

"Sorry, darlin'. We're not speakin' Irish. We're speakin' English with an Irish accent—to you."

"There's an Irish language?"

"Tell ya what. Siobhan and I'll teach you Irish and I'll teach you two some fishing tunes for the whistle. And we'll all sit here and listen to what Old Man Dirane has ta say while we wait for your breakfast."

"Okay!"

"Where shall we start with the Irish, Siobhan?"

"How about the ocean?"

"All right, then. What's the word for water?"

"Uisce."

"ISH-kyuh," Rowan repeated.

"Fish?" Sean asked.

"Iasc," Siobhan replied.

"EE-uhsk."

Sean listened to Siobhan correct Rowan's pronunciation. As he sat there, he watched Rowan's eyes and began to focus on their color. Though he knew the sky was periwinkle blue above him, all he saw was mahogany.

CHAPTER 19

Dropped Stitch

Dropped Stitch. 1. Occurs when a stitch or a group of stitches fall from the needle without being knitted or purled into place. It is important to catch the loose stitch the moment this happens. If the rest of the row is finished without picking up the dropped stitch, it is possible to weave it into place after the fact using a crochet hook. If a dropped stitch is left unattended, it can, at best, cause a small flaw in the fabric or at worst, cause the unraveling of the garment altogether. 2. A lesson learned.

—R. Dirane, *A Binding Love*

Early Saturday morning, Sheila and her son, Fionn, knocked on Rebecca's door. She answered, her shoulders slumped and her body withered. She had not slept a wink, as she endeavored to figure out the conversation she would have with Jim about the Dam Mad Situation. When she was not concerning herself with that discussion, she was envisioning Rowan in a tiny boat crossing the giant sea to another island. Her mind filled with pictures of the boat turning over, Rowan trying to swim to a far shore, and the waves crashing over her as a storm stole her life. It happened out on these islands. Sharon said it did.

But when Rebecca stepped out of her door, the island was clean and shining. The sun, having broken free of the horizon, rose in a clear cornflower blue sky. She took a deep breath and the sea-salt breeze filled her lungs, dusting the night's worries away and inviting her to be as happy and awake as the island itself.

Sheila and Fionn came in and Rebecca made them breakfast. Their conversation was about anything but the Dam Mad Situation.

"We'll wait for you here," Fionn said after breakfast. He stood at the door and popped a bit of bacon into his mouth as Rebecca pedaled her bike down the gravel drive. When she hit the asphalt, she took a right, toward town. As she rode along, her memory floated back to her father and the first Dam Mad story. Her father had loved to tell it himself, and when Rebecca brought Sharon home every July Fourth, he inevitably would relate the story again. He always told it as if it was his first time sharing it.

When Rebecca was young, her father, a fireman, was gone quite often. He had several hobbies, not the least of which was golf, so when he wasn't at work, he spent a great deal of time working on his game. All this time away from his family left her mother to raise Rebecca alone. She was, by default, a single mother.

Rebecca's father came from a family of farmers, as did her mother. They grew great orchards of almonds in Turlock, a small town in California's central valley. Rebecca and her mother would drive down from Redding to spend time there. Racing through the orchards in the spring with the millions of white petals falling from the trees like velvety snow was one of Rebecca's favorite childhood memories.

But Rebecca and her mother would come to visit alone so often that her grandfather became very concerned. He was a farmer and was bound to land and family. Living things, like children, required time and attention to grow properly. He had taught his son this, yet his son was not acting like the man he was raised to be.

So one day Rebecca's grandfather and grandmother came to visit in Redding. That day they took Rebecca's mother on a trip to Calistoga, leaving Rebecca, not yet three, in her father's care. Alone, he would have to figure out how to fit fatherhood into his golf schedule. Though Rebecca's father greatly protested, his father and mother drove off with his wife, and instead of coming back at the end of the day they didn't return for three weeks. It was a difficult lesson, especially trying to figure out what to do with a three-year-old when you have to go to work. But Rebecca's father always said those three weeks were when he finally learned to celebrate life. It was when he slowed down enough to pay attention to the small things that children notice. It was those three weeks that made him a man.

Rebecca stopped just south of town. How could it be that she, her father's jewel, had fallen in love with someone who thought so little of her? This was a question she often asked herself, but as always, she had no answer. At first, Dennis was helpful and happy, sharing his sherbet, his surfboard, his life. But over time, very slowly, he changed. He would point out how he was from a great family of bankers, lawyers, and businessmen while Rebecca was from a family of farmers and firemen. In his mind Dennis believed himself to be better than Rebecca, and because he told her so, she began to think that as well. She started changing herself, adjusting who she was, how she dressed, what she thought, so that she would better fit who Dennis thought he was—to be good enough for him. She worked hard, hoping with each day that he would requite the love she felt for him—the man who had stopped to fix her car so long before. But with each change she made, Dennis would like her less, treat her worse, and the more she changed, the less Rebecca was her father's jewel until she forgot who she had been almost entirely.

A shadow passed above her. She looked up and spotted a little bird landing on the wall just to her right. It looked just like the bird in the bramble near her house. It cocked its head, winking a beady eye at her.

"Do you know how I ended up with him?" she asked.

The little bird puffed out its feathers, bent its head, and began to preen with its tiny beak. Gazing past the bird, Rebecca found that she had stopped right in front of the path that led to Sean Morahan's house.

"No? Me neither," she whispered. She stepped on her pedals and moved on, setting the bike in motion and the bird to flight.

Before too long, she bumped off the road, climbing the small hill toward Mairead's house. When she reached the top, she found Ciara standing next to the island's only car.

"Maggie!" the little girl called through the door. "She's here!"

After coming to a stop, Rebecca jumped off the bike into the floating dust, which had followed her up the drive like a wind following in the wake of a train. Maggie poked her head out the door.

"You ready?" Maggie asked.

"I think so. Where's Jim?" Rebecca inquired, setting her bike against the house.

"With the bees. Where else?"

"Great. You better be going."

"Aye. Mairead, time to go."

Mairead waddled out her front door, kissing Ciara on the head.

"You help your da, now, Ciara. And get your sister up to help, too."

"They'll be fine," Maggie said. "It's only a day."

Maggie helped Mairead into the car. As she came around the back, she smiled brightly at Rebecca, a low chuckle rolling up from her throat.

"I wish I could stay to see," she whispered, then giggled wickedly.

Rebecca smiled and shut the driver's-side door.

Maggie rolled down the window. "Don't be too long about it. Need to hit the water before the tide changes. It's hard to get the curragh in the water when the sea's farther out on O'Flahertys' beach."

"I'll be along."

Maggie smiled again as she started the car. Slowly, quietly, she backed down the drive. Ciara and her mother waved to each other until the car disappeared over the hill. Rebecca took a deep breath and let it quickly out. She glanced down at Ciara.

"Can I watch you help my da?" Ciara asked. A small whimper came from inside the house.

"We'll see," she replied, following the sound.

As Rebecca stepped through the door, Tadhg let out a scream. He stood by the television in his diaper and pajama top.

"I think you better stay and watch Tadhg until your dad gets in. Can't leave little guys alone, right?"

With a very disappointed look, Ciara nodded.

"No need to wake your sister, though. Your dad should be coming to fix breakfast very shortly," Rebecca said as she went back out the door.

Rebecca climbed the stone wall and headed toward the shed. She heard clinking of glass from the lean-to and as she approached, Jim came out of the shed's listing door with a honeycomb in his hand.

"Rebecca?" he inquired with a surprised start.

"Perfect timing!" she said with a smile as bright as Maggie's had been. "Tadhg is up and I think he wants breakfast."

"What do you mean?" Jim cocked his head, glancing toward the house. "Where's Mairead?"

"She left. Went to see her mother."

"What do you mean, left?" Jim asked. "She didn't tell me she was leaving."

"You sure about that?"

"Yes!"

"You sure she didn't say anything to you while you were busy with your bees?"

Jim stopped, staring with alarm at Rebecca. "Well—"

"Yes, Jim?" Rebecca smiled again.

"W-well, who's watching the kids?"

"I guess you are." Rebecca turned around and headed down the hill. She rolled her grandfather's explanation of fatherhood around in her head like a free ball in a pinball machine—waiting for the statement that would set off the lights and bells. She hoped Jim would say the right words.

"I'm not babysitting today! I have work to do!"

There they were! Perfect! Rebecca giggled softly. Straightening her expression she spun slowly around to face Jim.

"Is that what a father does, Jim? A father babysits his own children?"

Jim's eyes widened like full moons, meeting Rebecca's gaze.

"I think, Jim, you've got gold fever, shining at you through the jars of liquid in that shed."

"What are you talking about?"

"I'm talking about Ciara, Meara, Kieran, Luke, Jim Jr., Katy, and Tadhg—about leaving Mairead alone to take care of the house and the farm. With as much care as you've looked at those golden jars, have you looked at your wife? Mairead's become the mom and the dad while you've been busy, Jim. While you've been a busy bee. Mom—and—dad, Mad. She's Mad. And the last thing you ever want is for a Mad woman to take care of everything. She'll break down. I'm new here and I see it. Father Michael sees it. The entire island sees it."

Rebecca stopped for a moment to see if Jim had anything to say. He didn't; he just stood there, shaking his head, with his jaw moving up and down as if eating the words that wanted to come out. His reaction was normal, exactly what Rebecca had expected.

"Mairead's gone home to visit her mother for the day. Time for you to be the dad and the mom. Dad—and—mom, Jim. Dam, a Dam man. You'll need to work fatherhood into your busy bee schedule. If you need help, you can call for it. Most women do. Pick up the phone. Just about anyone in town can help."

With that, Rebecca headed back to the wall and easily hopped over it. Tadhg let out a scream as she straddled her bike, as if to punctuate the end of the conversation.

Chuckling, she pedaled down the drive, waving without looking back. As she rode back to the north, she found the road dotted with bikes coming the other way toward the big fort. The first ferry must have pulled into the dock. She passed through town, being careful not to hit the tourists who ambled around Hernon's Shop and the pub. Clearing town, she found far fewer people and in very short a time she turned left and bumped off the asphalt toward her home. Fionn and his mother stood outside her door.

"Rowan, time to go," Fionn called into the house.

Trace trotted out of the bedroom, tail wagging, followed by Rebecca's daughter.

"You eat breakfast, Rowan?" Rebecca asked, handing the bike to Sheila.

"Aye," she replied.

"Come on," Fionn said. "Dad's got Mairead climbing down the stairs to the beach where we have the curragh." Fionn took Rowan's hand in his own. "See ya later, Mum. You stay, Trace."

The dog slumped, tucking his tail beneath his haunches as he sat down. His sad, watery eyes gazed at Rebecca, pleading for her to contradict Fionn's command. Rebecca shrugged helplessly and followed Fionn and Rowan. She crawled over two walls and crossed three fields before reaching a rocky outcrop at the island's northwestern end.

"Your family fished from here?"

"Aye, and hauled the catch all the way to your house for generations. Watch your step going down the stairs. They're wet and slippery." Fionn picked Rowan up.

With her right hand on the rocky wall, Rebecca made her way down the steps. They were not so much stairs as slight indentations in the stone, hewn at irregular intervals down the rocky slope. She slipped twice, and after Fionn put Rowan down safely on the sand, he reached up to help her crawl off the last stair, which was three feet above the beach.

"They brought the fish up from here?" Rebecca looked up in awe.

"And the seaweed and sand to make the soil."

"Mornin', Rowan Moray of O'Flaherty's Pub!" the older O'Flaherty greeted.

Rowan laughed and ran across the small beach to where Fionn Sr. stood next to his curragh. The boat was black against the gray water. Mairead was already seated in it, hunched over in the cold.

"In you go." Fionn Sr. lifted Rowan into the boat.

Rebecca walked across the sand toward Fionn Sr.

"Put your life jacket on, Rowan," she called out.

"She doesn't have one," came Fionn's voice from behind her.

Rebecca stopped. "What do you mean she doesn't have one?"

"Doesn't need one. Weather's clear."

"We can't cross the open ocean without life jackets," Rebecca declared, her voice climbing an octave.

"Did you wear a life jacket on the ferry over here?"

"Well—no. But th—"

"This is just a smaller ferry."

"What's happening?" Fionn Sr. asked as he trotted across the sand.

"Becky thinks she needs a life jacket."

"Weather's clear, Becky," Fionn Sr. said.

"Well, what if a wave crashes in the side of the boat? What if we get hit by a—"

"Rowan's not afraid. Look," Fionn Sr. said quietly. He nodded toward Rebecca's daughter, who was standing in the curragh, staring in their direction.

"There are no 'what-ifs' on this island, Becky." Fionn Sr. spoke softly, holding Rebecca's elbow and bringing her closer to the boat. "If we lived by all that could happen, my father's father's father, all the way back, never would have survived here. It's a rock. How do you grow crops and families on a rock? But we did. We learned from the sea. We've rowed these waters for years. Fionn, me, my father, his father, his father before him. Today, we're just takin' Mairead home."

Rebecca's blood surged in her ears, drowning out the sound of the surf as all her worries from the night before rolled back through her mind.

"In you go," Fionn Sr. said, helping Rebecca over the side of the curragh.

"I left you the seat near the front, Becky," Mairead said, patting the little bench in front of her.

"I don't have a life jacket," Rowan said, sitting next to Rebecca.

"Don't need one," Mairead replied. "We'll be across in no time."

With a jerk and a splash, Fionn and his father pushed the curragh into the surf. Rebecca let out a little scream as she grabbed the side of the boat.

"We got wet!" Rowan laughed. "Just like on that log ride at the fun park at home, Mama."

This was no log ride, though, and Rebecca's heart pounded in her chest. She had to get out of this boat. She had to get Rowan back on land. She stood up as Fionn climbed out of the water and onto the bench before her, his pant legs wet to the knees.

"Sit, Becky," he said.

She looked over his shoulder and saw a wave rolling toward the bow of the boat.

"Sit, Becky," Mairead commanded.

Fionn pulled out two oars and landed them in the water as the wave splashed the bow. Mairead's hand had Rebecca's, pulling her to her seat.

"We okay, Mama?"

Rebecca dropped her chin to her chest, strands of her brown hair falling into her eyes. "Fine," she said tightly, squeezing Mairead's hand.

The ocean beat the sides of the boat. Rebecca couldn't breathe. She couldn't swallow. As she listened to the oars hitting the water, the sound of the surf on the sand lessened. Replacing it was Fionn. He was singing. As he sang, Rebecca gazed up through her hair and her terror and saw his steady black eyes coming now near to her and then moving away from her, as he laid on the oars.

Fionn stopped singing, peering with certainty at Rebecca through her disheveled hair. Holding his oars up together with his left hand, he reached forward with his right and brushed Rebecca's hair from her eyes.

"Sing more!" Rowan ordered, pulling her pipe from her sleeve.

So he did and Rebecca watched his eyes and listened to his voice, and slowly her heart and mind quieted until there was nothing but his oars in the water keeping rhythm with his song. Before long, Rowan was whistling along with him, and when they stopped she clapped.

"What's it called?"

"'My Lagan Love,'" Fionn replied, keeping his steady gaze on Rebecca.

Rowan pulled the pipe to her lips and began the song again.

Rebecca glanced left toward the west. The pull on the oars made the curragh jerk forward with each stroke, but the little black boat cut through the water cleanly and relatively smoothly. There were no sounds but Rowan's pipe, the oars, and the wind in Rebecca's ears. There were no cars, no planes, no smothering sounds—just five people floating in an endless sea. Over Fionn's shoulder, Rebecca could see an island, rising on the horizon like a green-brown sunrise.

"Almost there, Becky," Fionn said.

In no time they were nearing the island's shoreline. Fionn pulled on his right oar, slowing the boat as he and his father pointed the bow slightly east. A wave caught the curragh, sending Rebecca's heart beating. As a reflex, she grabbed Rowan's hand. The boat sped forward to the shore and just as the wave crested, Fionn jumped out of the curragh and pulled it toward the beach. Rebecca glanced back and saw that Fionn Sr. was out of the boat also, pushing it onto the sand.

As Fionn held the curragh, his father carried Mairead over the waves to the shore. Tugging against the sand, Fionn brought the boat onto the beach. Rowan hopped out and ran up the shore.

"Rowan! Wait!" Rebecca called, as she stepped out of the curragh.

Mairead and Rebecca followed Rowan up the beach. As they came to the crest of a dune, Rowan stopped. Coming up behind her daughter, Rebecca found a very small asphalt road and across it, a single-story white house sitting within a stone wall fence. It was longer than the cottage Rebecca was staying in and had a little herb garden at the door.

"We'll see ya a little later," Fionn Sr. said as he and his son stepped onto the road.

"You're not coming in?" Rebecca asked.

"We'll see how Iollan's getting on. That boy always has trouble with his boat," he replied.

Rebecca crossed the road, following Mairead and Rowan through the little red gate in the stone fence. Smoke rose from the chimney, which peeped out of the thatch of the house. The front door was red and wide-open.

"Mum!" Mairead called.

"Here I am," Mairead's mother replied from the kitchen.

"I've brought Becky, Sharon's friend from the States, and her daughter, Rowan."

Standing next to her cooker, Mairead's mother took her daughter into her arms. The woman was thin, with silver-gray hair pulled back into a bun. She wore jeans and a deep blue knit shirt, which was reflected in her eyes, making them appear as blue as lapis.

"Ah—you've come to see the ganseys."

"Yes!" Rebecca replied.

"Rebecca, this is my mother, Ina."

"Very nice to meet you."

"Come. Sit. I have tea."

Rebecca sat down at the table, which was pulled close to the fireplace. Rowan knelt by the fire, fingering a bag of loose wool and a hand spindle.

"Rowan, don't touch," Rebecca said.

Rowan stopped and looked up at her mother.

"She can help," Ina said, bringing the tea to the table. "You know how to spin?"

"Me and Siobhan are just learning from her mum."

"Go ahead and practice, then," Ina offered.

Rowan picked up the hand spindle and the wool that was attached to it.

"Mairead was the one who knitted the shanachie gansey for you," Ina said.

Rebecca smiled a little and shrugged. "It was beautiful," she said, her breath catching a little. She did not want to talk about that little sweater—the little magic sweater that Rowan wore on her first visit with Dennis.

"Every child born to the island gets one. My husband's mother taught me to knit them and I taught Mairead. Do you teach Rowan to knit?" Ina poured milk into three cups.

"Uh—no. I haven't gotten around to that yet."

"Good for her to learn while she's here, then," Ina replied, filling the cups with tea.

Mairead sat down at the table and slid the sugar bowl closer to Rebecca.

"If you have a gansey you're working on, Mum, maybe Becky would like to see it."

Ina nodded, putting her teacup to her lips and peering at Rebecca with her lapis-colored eyes.

"I do. Two little ones for the wee ones in there," Ina replied, reaching over and patting her daughter's stomach. Rebecca swallowed a large gulp of tea. It burned her throat as it went down.

"I suppose, since Becky has already seen the shanachie gansey, it wouldn't interest her," Ina said.

Rebecca didn't answer. Her heart was beating in her ears so loudly, she thought if she spoke, she'd yell over it.

"Did you know, Becky, that some say the ganseys were knitted by men?" Ina asked.

"Men?" Rebecca whispered, trying to control her voice.

"When the English were a power in the country, it's said the women spun the wool and the men knitted the ganseys. It was a code—information passed silently between them as they walked by each other or shook hands—met after Mass or had a pint in the pub."

"I didn't know that," Rebecca replied with great interest. "You know any men who knit?"

Ina shook her head, sipping her tea. She looked down at Rowan. "Some say that's how the patterns came to be. Messages passed from one person to another when a spoken word could not. We are a people of the spoken word. Imagine living in a world upside down—where you cannot speak your language, where you cannot tell your children what you value or your legends or your myths. That was our world for hundreds of years. A prison of silence. But we found a way, and that way, some say, is the patterns of the gansey. One man to another—planning freedom. One father to his sons—weaving the future."

"That's a beautiful legend, Ina," Rebecca said.

Mairead's mother smiled. "There are many legends about how the stitches came to be, Becky. You hear the one about the body washing ashore?"

"Yes, that's the one Sharon talked about when we were in college."

"Now you know the one about the men knitting their messages. There's another one. It concerns mistakes."

"Mistakes," Rebecca repeated, wishing she had brought a notepad or her DVD camera. She had been so worried about the trip in the curragh, it hadn't even crossed her mind that she might need to bring her recording equipment. Worry did that to her. It got in her way, and now she was frustrated with herself.

"Some say the patterns arose out of mistakes made while knitting. That's really all they are. Errors."

"That's not very—I mean, that isn't true, is it?"

Ina laughed. "No one really knows what's true about these stories. It isn't as romantic as the other stories. Now that's true."

Rebecca thought for a moment and then giggled. "Can you imagine if I got this grant and then wrote that? 'These sweaters are really great, but they're just a bunch of mistakes.'"

They laughed, Rebecca most of all.

"Aye. Not a very good book. But it is something to think on," Ina said.

The tone of Ina's voice caught Rebecca's attention. "What's to think on?" she asked.

"That something truly beautiful can arise from a mistake."

With wide eyes, Rebecca looked into Ina's lapis blue gaze, and the older woman smiled at her and then peered down at Rowan.

CHAPTER 20

Zigzag/Bobble Within/Ribbing Within

Zigzag/Bobble Within/Ribbing Within. 1. A single zigzag
with a single bobble in the "zig" and ribbing in the "zag." 2. A
memory of someone loved.

—R. Dirane, *A Binding Love*

As Rebecca picked up the rest of the lunch sandwiches and tea-
cups from Ina's table, Fionn, his father, and a man as old as
Eoman with brown hair and hazel eyes came through the door.

"Mum?"

"Have you met my son, Iollan, Becky?"

"OO-lan. Hi," Rebecca said with a smile.

"You ready to go catch some dinner, Rowan?" Fionn asked.

"Yeah!" Rowan said, dropping her hand spindle and wool by the
fireplace.

"What are you doing?" Rebecca asked.

"Since we're all here," Fionn Sr. said, "we thought it would be
fun for Rowan to come fishing in the curragh. No safer place to fish
than in a curragh with three fishermen on a clear day off the
islands."

"We do need supper," Ina agreed.

Rebecca peered over at Fionn as he crossed the room toward her.

"We'll be especially watchful," he said, brushing her shoulder with his warm hand. "My dad and I and Iollan. 'No what-ifs.'"

"No what-ifs," Rebecca repeated, though saying "No what-ifs" was easier for her than feeling no what-ifs.

"Excellent! Come on, Rowan," Fionn said.

Rebecca and Mairead followed the men and Rowan out to the beach. Rowan sat alone in the curragh as Iollan, Fionn, and his father pushed the boat out into the waves. In unison, they all flipped themselves into the curragh, with Fionn and Iollan on the oars and Fionn Sr. seated next to Rowan.

"She'll have fun," Mairead said. "Very mild in the water today."

"Sharon says the weather can turn, though," Rebecca replied, watching the boat bob in the sea.

"Aye. But someone as old as Sean can tell. He's not been wrong yet."

"Sean?" Rebecca turned her head to Mairead.

"Fionn's father confirmed the weather with Paddy this morning. Sean always reports changes to Paddy."

"I see. So, if he's always right about the weather, how is it he lost his sons?"

Mairead gazed at Rebecca, tilting her head as if listening to a far-off sound, her brow furrowing.

"I—I'm sorry, Mairead. I didn't mean to upset you—"

"It's not that, Becky. But thinking about that night always turns to Claire for my family. She was my great-aunt."

"Oh."

"You know Sharon's story—the one about bodies washing ashore, identifiable only by the gansey they wear?"

"Yes."

"That happened only once that I know of—and I would know, wouldn't I? My family's Dirane."

"Yes. The shawn-a—"

"Shanachies. Matthew washed ashore. It was morning and seemed clear the day they set out, just as it had been the day before and the day before that. Joe, Sean's second son—let's see, he would have been twenty-seven years old at the time—had been telling all the families a storm was coming. He'd been saying it for eight days because a mistle thrush had been singing when there was no wind."

"What's a mistle thrush?"

"A tiny bird that sings through gales."

"Ah. We have a nest of them next to our bedroom," Rebecca said, smiling.

"They're good luck. So Joe said the storm is coming. Sean's spine always hurts. A piece of shrapnel is lodged to this day in the middle of his back—a gift given him by the Nazis during the war. The week before he lost his sons, the shrapnel moves, so the doctor says, as Sean set the net upon its pulley. He's ordered to stay off his feet until he can get to the mainland to have an X-ray to see how close that piece of metal is to his spine. Then the engine goes out, and on the day of the storm the boat's still not workin', and so his sons don't go out before sunrise with the rest of the fleet. All the rest fish, go to market, and return by the time the boat is fixed. Sure as I am standing here, the sky looks clear, and the Morahan boys go out and doesn't it just turn—a great gale out of the south on a summer's day. Very queersome. It blows in like it was gonna wipe the islands away, and it was Sean's sons who were caught in it. The oldest boy, Matthew, his body was the only one that came ashore. On the sand near your house."

"Where we left this morning?"

"Aye. They couldn't tell who it was, so Padrig Blake—that's Paddy Blake's dad. You've heard of him?"

Rebecca nodded.

"Padrig Blake took the jumper from the body and brought it to Sean's house. When Mary, Matthew's wife, saw it, she became so caught up in grief that she went into labor."

"She was pregnant?"

"About six months along," Mairead replied. "She had the baby there, in Sean's house, but it had come early."

"It didn't die," Rebecca whispered.

"That it did. 'Twas a girl. Claire they named it. Mary started to bleed and they couldn't get her off the island because of the storm."

"Oh, she didn't die." Rebecca shook her head, not sure she wanted to know any more.

"She did." Mairead was quiet for a minute. "Terrible it was. Left a mark on all who lived through it. All the old people still go quiet when it's spoken of. Wasn't long after that, my great-aunt Claire left."

"Rose and Liz mentioned that. They said they didn't know why she left."

Mairead grew quiet, gazing out at the ocean. Rebecca followed her gaze. The curragh had disappeared.

"Where'd they go?" Rebecca asked as softly as if she stood in a church.

"To the west, if I know my brother. He said he saw salmon that way. You ever eaten planked salmon?"

Rebecca shook her head.

"Ah," Mairead replied, grinning. "Come. My father's mother was from the mainland and swore by oak. My brother always keeps us stocked with it. He has my father's fishing boat. It's old, but it makes a living."

"He catches oak?" Rebecca asked, confused, as she climbed the dune back to Ina's house.

Mairead laughed. "No, salmon. He brings the oak back from Galway. If he's seen salmon, he'll bring one home."

Rebecca was still confused, but she followed Mairead up to her mother's house anyway. They walked around the back, and in a shed they found a stack of wooden planks. Mairead pulled out four. Carrying the wood around the east side of the house, Rebecca found a pit with a stack of firewood next to it. A deep pail sat near the house, and

Mairead and Rebecca filled it with water from a spigot near the front door. Ina shuffled outside and pushed the planks into the pail of water as Rebecca set about lighting the fire.

The sun slid west as the fire matured. With a great cry of triumph, Rowan came flying over the dune, followed by Fionn, his father, and Iollan, each carrying a gutted salmon. Iollan wrapped one of the fish in paper from the house and handed it to his mother for storing. The other two he filleted, creating four separate pieces.

Iollan set the four soaked planks on the coals of the fire. Fionn and Rebecca watched the coals as Iollan, Fionn Sr., and Rowan went down to the curragh and pulled Iollan's net out of the boat. By the time they returned, the planks were smoking and crackling. Iollan turned the planks over so the charred side was up, placed one of the four salmon fillets skin side down on each plank, sprinkled each with salt, then covered the pit with a large aluminum pot.

Setting the kettle on to boil, Ina made tea as Iollan poured four pints—one for each fisherman and one for Rebecca. Ina and Mairead stayed inside to make potatoes and kale as everyone else headed out the door to watch the fire. Rowan played "My Lagan Love" several times, and Rebecca, warmed by the beer, the fire, and Rowan's music, watched Fionn, who laughed as his father tried to sing along with the little girl. Her pipe was far too high a pitch for his voice. Fionn's dark eyes reflected the floating embers of the fire and to Rebecca they appeared as a summer night's sky, soft and black. He gazed over at her and she quickly looked down, smiling at Rowan, who sat yawning by the fire.

It took forty-five minutes for the salmon to cook. Iollan finally pulled it from the fire as the oak planks continued to pop and smoke and took it into the house. They all followed and sat down at Ina's table for the meal. The fish was brown and smelled of smoke, and as Rebecca put a piece in her mouth, the smooth, salty flavor rolled around on her tongue. It was, as she stated to all there, the best salmon she had ever eaten.

The sky was purple when Fionn and his father pulled away from the shore. Rebecca looked over her shoulder and waved to Ina and Iollan. As the boat bobbed to the south, Rowan curled up beside her mother and fell asleep. Rebecca looked east and west, but not south, for Fionn was right in front of her, pulling on the oars.

"Remember we were talking about Sean," Mairead said quietly from behind.

"Yes," Rebecca replied.

"I've heard Sean has taken a liking to Rowan," she said.

"Has he?" Rebecca asked, glancing down at her daughter.

"Paddy says he's quite changed. Even Siobhan says he's nicer now."

"Well, I've told Rowan to stay away from him," Rebecca said. "He's got a nasty streak to him that she experienced the day she arrived here. It's only a matter of time before it comes out again."

Rebecca gazed through the purple light at Fionn. He was pulling on the oars, staring at the bottom of the boat. There was no sound but the water and the oars.

"To understand why Claire left, you should understand why she first stayed," Mairead said.

"I know why she stayed," Rebecca said coldly.

"Oh? And why is that, Becky?"

Rebecca looked west, clenching her jaw, thinking of raspberry sherbet and green knitted dresses. She said nothing.

"Matthew, Joe, Liam, and Brendan," Mairead continued. "There was eight years between Joe and Liam. Six of those years were the war. In those other two years, Claire had three stillbirths. Three, and all of them girls."

Rebecca rubbed her daughter's hair.

"My mother used to say Sean was a tyrant. That's what she and Claire would call him. It was funny at first because he wanted things to be just so when he married Claire. Perfect in every way for her because he was so in love with her. And Matthew came and then Joe. He became a little tougher with each birth. He was raising his boys and boys had to be men and men have to be tough. So his father had raised him, his mother passing when Sean was but a boy."

"They don't really, Mairead," Rebecca said.

"Well, Becky, that's true. Claire knew that. Sean—Sean knew different. He was raised by his father, and his father was tough on him—to make him a man. Claire said he struggled to not be like his father, but then sons came.

"So Sean was a tyrant and it just got worse with the birth of each son, as I've said. By the time Brendan was born, Claire couldn't come visit us anymore. Sean kept her close, just as he kept his sons. And he made it unbearable for us to visit her. He talked to her so terrible when we left that she just didn't invite us anymore. Just like his father had done when Sean was a boy, he kept his family apart from the rest of the island. Claire's only day to visit with others was Sunday after Mass. Finally, by God's grace, Matthew married. Mary was her name, and Claire seemed so much brighter after Mary came to live with them."

"They lived together in that house?"

"They did have plans to build another next door when the baby came."

Rebecca glanced over her shoulder at Mairead. "Why are you telling me this?" she asked, knowing there was some conversation happening in Mairead's story that had nothing to do with Claire.

"So you can know Sean." Mairead turned to gaze out at the sea. "After they found Matthew and knew it was him from his gansey, the father came."

"What father?"

"Father Michael. He came and read the last rites and baptized the babe. Claire is what Mary named her."

"But she died."

"That she did, and Mary not long after. They're buried next to Matthew in the cemetery in the center of the island. You should go.

Lots of designs on the old crosses there. You can tell the family by the carving on the crosses. They match the family's ganseys."

At this point Rebecca didn't care about the ganseys. She wanted to know what Mairead was doing by telling her about Sean. "Why do I need to know Sean?" she asked.

"It was after the funeral that Sean went mad," Mairead continued.

"Mairead," Rebecca whispered.

"And Claire left him. Not one night passed after her son, his wife, and her granddaughter were buried before Claire left. She came to shore in Sean's own curragh, washing up on O'Flahertys' beach. She didn't stop there. She showed up at the Blakes' and begged for Padrig to take her to Galway in his fishing trawler, which he did. When Sean found out, he followed her there."

"And he choked her," Fionn Sr. said.

"Aye. Almost killed her. But he's her husband and she left him without telling him and so they didn't put him in jail. That's how things were in this country back then. There was no divorce until 1996. So the family sent her secretly to Derry. No one knew where she was but us, and we paid for it from Sean for many a year. There she stayed. Over time, Sean just blew himself out, like a great fury rising in the ocean does. Nothing can keep going like that—yelling and cursing us for not telling him where his wife was."

Rebecca turned her head south, seeking the island. She wanted out of the boat.

"She died in Derry and is buried off island with her cousins. We didn't know how Sean would act if we buried her here. We didn't want to get him started again. Anyway, that's Claire's life."

Rebecca looked at Fionn, who was staring at her. His eyes were as steady as they had been in the morning.

"Becky?"

"Yes, Mairead."

"The storm was forty years ago. Forty years is a long time to hang on to something, but that's how long it's been for Sean. Forty years of not talking, of being alone in darkness. Of not even being able to see a hand held out to help him."

Rebecca held Rowan tighter, burying her face in the little girl's hair.

"But now he sees Rowan's hand. It's the first time in so long that he's seen anyone. And you have hold of her. And now we have you."

The surf sounded around Rebecca in the purple shadows. Fionn put up the oars and slipped over the side, the water rolling across his pant legs as he pulled the boat to shore. When the curragh was clear of the water, Fionn Sr. stepped up to Rebecca with his hands out.

"I'll carry Rowan up," he said quietly. Taking a deep breath and with great effort, Rebecca released Rowan. Fionn Sr. picked up the little girl as Rebecca crawled out of the curragh. She didn't look up at Mairead or Fionn as she followed them silently over the sand.

She knew Claire. She understood all too well what Claire was about. But for some reason, in this conversation, Rebecca felt as though she was Sean. All these six years, she had been in darkness, too. Had there been a hand held out to her? She hadn't had anything to hold on to; she had just been blowing in the wind—an angry, deafening wind blowing since that Thanksgiving night.

Fionn helped Mairead up the stairs. Rebecca crawled onto the first high step behind them, and as she set her foot on the second, leaning her weight into the rock, her shoe slipped.

She cried out as she listed over the edge, but at that moment Fionn reached back and grabbed her by her arm. She looked up into his face, which was dark in the fading light.

"I have you, Becky," he said, and his voice seemed to still the wind.

CHAPTER 21

Liam's Lesson

Liam's Lesson [Template 3 Pattern 3 Dye Lot 22] Center Panel—
1. Three braids, middle braid woven with Celtic knot triple spiral midway through. On each side of center panel, small bobbles knitted of angora, followed 24 repeat panel of single zigzag with ribbing. Moss stitch used as texture at edge. Color—apricot.
2. Creation.

—R. Dirane, *A Binding Love*

$\mathcal{S}$ ean stood on his beach Saturday evening, smiling as he thought of Rowan and Siobhan in Old Man Dirane's dinghy south of town. He had forgotten how to watch the small things that children notice. After sitting in the boat together, they had crawled about the boulders, poking their fingers into the sea anemones. The first time one spat, Rowan screamed and slipped backward. Sean laughed as he caught her. Crabs crawled sideways, peeping up through the little pools with their beady eyes, seeking a rock or shelter from the sun and the strange, giggling shadows above the water's surface. Seashells and sand and blackened, dried kelp made shapes of horses and birds as sure as any cloud could do in the sky. It had been so long since Sean had seen the world through a child's eyes.

The old man listened for the pipe, the pain of his missing sons raw in his heart this day. The waves rolled ashore, flowing over the sand and up to the tips of his shoes. They touched his toes, tickling and taunting him to come closer. But he knew better. Friendly as they were, pouring shallowly across the beach, in the catch of a breath the tide could pull the sand from beneath the feet.

Waves had a lesson to teach, and as Sean watched the sun slide behind the edge of the world, reflecting its purple-golden light upon the spattering of clouds in the heavens, he remembered Liam and the day his third boy learned the water's lesson.

"Da, look at the sun!" six-year-old Liam whispered, taking hold of his father's finger to share the awe of the sunrise.

"See those clouds there, boy?" Sean asked, pointing to the hundreds of tiny clouds scattered across the pink-apricot sky.

"Aye."

"My da used to say when the sky appears so, 'tis the Almighty gathering his flock."

The sun's light twinkled in his little boy's eyes at the wonder of God. Sean smiled, remembering the day his father had told him such.

"We're ready, Da," Matthew called from the curragh, his brother Joe standing next to him. Both tall and strong teenagers now, they had released the boat from its mooring stones and set the net without his help.

"Matthew and Joe and I are gonna turn the curragh and ready it for the day. You stay on the shore here. Don't go near the waves. And remember, Liam," Sean said, taking the little boy's chin in his hand. "Never turn your back on the sea. Your ma is not here to watch you, nor will she be anymore. Women are in the house. Men are on the sea. You're old enough to watch yourself. Watch yourself like the man you're learnin' to be."

His boy nodded courageously, turning his head again to the east to catch the rising sun with its flock of pink-golden sheep. Sean walked west toward his boys, the ocean, and his boat. With a great push, the three of them turned the curragh over, setting it gently on its keel.

"You mend those nets, Joe?" Sean asked as he grabbed the oars.

"Aye, Da. Me and Liam. There's still a snag in the middle, but it's not unravelin'."

"We need more rope for the cable," Matthew added with a grunt as he and his brother dragged the net to the curragh.

Sean needed new cable. He needed new nets. But the catch had been small again this season and was not likely to get better.

"Let me look," he said. The three of them grabbed the net in different places, pulling it wide upon the sand. Sure enough, there was a wad of string in its center.

"What's caused that?" Sean asked.

"Not sure, but it's a right snag," Joe replied.

"Da," Matthew said quietly.

"Aye?" Sean said, stepping lightly across the net.

"Where'd ya send Liam?"

"Nowhere." Sean squatted down to look more closely at the snag.

"He's not on the sand, Da."

Sean stood and looked up and down the shore.

"Liam!" he called.

"Liam!" Joe yelled, racing up the beach toward the house. "Liam! Where are ya?"

"Where is that boy?" Sean growled, walking carefully across the net.

"Da!" Matthew shouted, running toward the sea. "Da, he's in the water!"

Sean shot a glance out to the water and there, bumping on the pink-golden waves, was a spot of white. It was Liam in his gansey.

Sean spun around on his heel, twisting the net around his feet. He fell hard on the sand.

"What is it?" Claire's voice came down from the house. "Where's Liam?"

Sean rolled out of the net, tearing at it as he watched Joe and Matthew fly into the bitter-cold water.

"Wait!" Sean commanded. "Wait!"

Free of the net, he stood and raced after them, knowing that there would be only moments before the cold water would take its frozen fingers and still all three of his sons' hearts. It was early April and the water was as cold as stone walls in January—as cold as death itself.

"Liam!" Claire screamed from behind.

Sean was in the water, overtaking his boys, and pushing them back to shore.

"Get the curragh!" he yelled at them as the great rush of icy water crested his chest.

He was swimming now, his fingers crackling as if they'd turned to ice. He didn't care, for he could see his little boy lying lifeless in the water just ten yards away. Just ten, then nine, then eight. His heart pounded in his chest as his legs cramped underneath him.

"Liam!" he called breathlessly, only seven yards away. He heard the sound of oars behind him.

"Da!" Joe called.

"Get your brother!" Sean said hoarsely as he felt the wake of the curragh overtake him.

The boat passed by and Matthew dropped his oar, grabbing Liam by the back of his gansey, pulling him in. Joe's eyes were on his father, for Sean just floated there, his legs gone from beneath him.

"Matthew, pull the curragh around!" Joe yelled and with that, Matthew and Joe laid on the oars.

Sean watched them row, like they'd done it forever. He couldn't move his arms now, the water having seeped through his sweater. As he watched his boys come closer, Sean saw his father rowing toward him.

I've told you, Sean, watch the nets!

"Yes, Da," Sean whispered.

"*Da!*" Joe screamed and just when Sean watched his father's face look down upon him as he sank into the water, a hand grabbed his right shoulder. Another hand grabbed his left.

"Help us, Da!" Matthew cried. "Pull your legs in!"

Sean knew he had legs, though he couldn't feel them. He made his mind think about moving them.

"Da. We got you. We got you," Matthew groaned, heaving his father into the boat. Sean fell like deadweight in the bottom of the curragh.

"Da?" Joe called.

"Row!" Matthew ordered.

Sean's father was gone and only the memory of Liam being six yards away filled Sean's mind. "Liam?" he whispered.

"He's not breathin', Da." Joe wept.

"Shut up and row!" Matthew commanded.

The blood was rushing back into his extremities, causing a painful, prickly feeling throughout his legs and arms. The curragh bumped gently onto the sand. Looking up, Sean found Claire's face above him.

"Liam," he choked out.

Claire lifted Liam's still body from the bottom of the boat as Sean struggled to roll over.

"Squeeze his chest," he said hoarsely, now on his hands and knees.

Matthew and Joe pulled the boat ashore and then helped their father out of it. On shaky legs, Sean watched Claire pushing on Liam's small chest as the boy lay on his side upon the sand. He could see his son's jumper, its flat, tight stitches knitted together in a thatched pattern. It was what all the Morahan men wore, for it was the stitch that Sean and his father and his father before him believed would be best at keeping out the cold and damp while upon the sea, giving time to those who fell overboard. Cold water could kill faster than most anything.

Liam coughed.

"He's alive, Da," Joe whispered, his voice cracking with emotion.

Claire rolled Liam over as the boy gagged and spat up water. He started to cry as she rubbed his back.

"What happened?" Sean asked his little boy.

"Please, Sean," Claire said, taking Liam in her arms.

"What happened to you, boy?" Sean asked again, standing up.

"A wave caught me, Da," Liam blubbered. "It caught me and I was under it. I screamed and screamed but I was under the water."

"Did ya not see it comin'?"

Liam shook his head, spitting out words like they were salt water, making no sense at all.

"You had your back to the sea," Sean said.

Liam's mouth quivered as he nodded.

"Did I not tell you to keep your eyes to the sea?" said Sean.

Liam nodded again.

"Well, what were ya doin', then?"

"I was watching God's sheep," Liam whispered.

Sean ran both his hands through his hair and spun around. He gazed out upon the black water and for an instant, for a beat of a gull's wing, he was angry. Angry at Liam for turning his back to the ocean, angry at Claire for looking at him so, angry at Matthew and Joe for jumping into the water instead of taking the curragh. He glanced over at his net, which lay upon the sand in a chaotic knot and Sean— Sean was angry at God, furious that life was so hard, that he had to start his boys mending the net at four and gutting the fish at five and in the boat by six. In the curragh by six to get the sea under them so they wouldn't be afraid—so they could fish and survive.

But in a flash the anger passed. The dawn was apricot upon the sky and the tiny clouds hinted at a warm, sunny day.

Sean looked at the sky. He knew what he should do. He was wet and Joe's teeth were chattering. Matthew was shivering and Sean knew if he looked over at Liam, the boy's lips would be blue. Nevertheless, he should make Liam get up and help unknot the net and get in the curragh. It was what his father did to him whenever he fell into the sea, because a fisherman could not be afraid of the water. Food had to be put on the table. New rope and cables were necessary, and wool was needed to weave a man's suit. There was no time a fisherman could be too cold or sick or wet or frightened to fish.

But as Sean looked at the sky, he remembered the wonder of God's sheep—of watching the men fish and wanting to go with them, though the dream of fairy wings or a crab crawling on the rocks could draw him away from the boats and the nets as easily as his mother's call. He recalled being little, and though he was raising men, this day—this day, he remembered his sons were just boys after all.

"Claire?"

"Yes, Sean."

"Take Liam in and get him dry."

"I want to go with you!" Liam cried in earnest. "I want to fish!"

Sean turned around and looked at Liam's face. His lips were blue.

"We'll try again tomorrow, son. And tomorrow after that. It's late, and Matthew and Joe and I have to get supper on the table. To-morrow, you'll come. Today was—just practice."

"I want to go," Liam said with a whimper.

"I know. Tomorrow will be here and you'll be warm and dry and we'll try again."

Sean walked over and touched his son's head.

"Tomorrow I can go."

"Aye," Sean said and looked at Claire.

He saw the relief in her gaze. He nodded to her and Claire took Liam in her arms and made her way back to the house.

"We're cold now," Sean said to Matthew and Joe as he watched Claire carry Liam up the hill. "But if we get movin', we'll be sweatin' in less than half an hour. Remarkable things, these ganseys. When they're wet, they get hot."

"Aye, Da," Matthew replied.

Sean turned to his sons.

"You're seventeen now, Matthew. You need a proper suit of clothes and we need new nets and some supper. We've got to go out."

"Aye, Da," Joe said, teeth still chattering.

As Sean walked by them, he grabbed his sons in his arms and held them to his chest.

"You are good boys," he whispered and kissed each of them on the head.

Then, quickly, he released them and walked to the net. Tears flowed from his eyes and he thanked the Lord that his boys had done what he taught them to do. They looked out for each other and because of that he knew they'd survive.

⁓

Sheep and apricot-colored sky. Sean contemplated both, and as there was no pipe upon the wind he turned his back to the ocean, leaving the incoming tide to wash his memory away.

CHAPTER 22

Zigzag/Single Bobbles Within Each

Zigzag/Single Bobbles Within Each. 1. A zigzag with a single bobble within each "zig" and each "zag." 2. An unplanned journey with someone unexpected. 3. Dirane—family on the island that usually knits this stitch into their ganseys. The Diranes are the storytellers of the island. In Ireland, such storytellers are called shanachies.

—R. Dirane, *A Binding Love*

*O*n Sunday, Rebecca followed Liz into Father Michael's garden. There was no mist this morning and the blooms in the garden had started to open, turning their bright faces toward the sky and smiling gleefully to all who passed. Rebecca smiled back, bending over to a peach rose and breathing deeply. It smelled of peaches, which made Rebecca smile all the wider.

Climbing up the steps, Rebecca found the priest's bright kitchen warmer than outside. As she took off her coat, she spotted a very old sweater on the table. Moving closer, she studied the pattern of the sweater as Liz poured hot water into the teapot.

"I thought we were going through his attic."

"You can't even get the door to his attic open, Becky. He has work to do before he can take you up there."

"You know who this sweater belongs to, Liz?" Rebecca inquired.

"My grandfather," Father Michael replied as he stepped into the kitchen.

"This is very beautiful, Father."

Liz put the teapot on the table and said to Rebecca, "Rose and I have Rowan and Siobhan for the morning. Annie's already started them spinning and we'll continue that lesson. You come by when you're done. We have stories and then fresh fish at Annie's for supper. Do you suppose the girls will spin as well as they fish?" she finished by asking.

"I hope so," Rebecca replied.

"They caught ten fish altogether on Friday, Father. Rowan's first time," Liz said, shaking her head in disbelief.

"Aye. Siobhan mentioned that after Mass. She said it was because they sat in Old Man Dirane's boat," Father Michael replied.

Liz chuckled as she walked out of the kitchen.

"Who's Old Man Dirane?" Rebecca asked.

"Mairead's great-grandfather on her father's side. A grand story-teller. The boat tells stories, they say."

"Ah. A boat that tells stories," Rebecca repeated incredulously, feeling as though there was no end of the stories in Ireland. After the one last night about Sean Morahan, she wasn't sure she wanted to hear any more. But then, wasn't that why she'd come here? To hear stories about the sweaters to put in her book?

"Some say. I hear John Fitzgibbon survived his day as a—what's the phrase?"

"A Dam man," Rebecca replied, grinning.

"Aye. That's it. Had a little help from Liz and Rose, though. You know, he came to Mass all on his lonesome with his seven wee ones neat and tidy in the pews." Father Michael sat down as Rebecca poured milk into the two cups in front of her. She giggled.

"They weren't quiet, but then, they never are."

"I can't fix everything," Rebecca said, winking at the father.

"No, I suppose not. But Jim is a great accomplishment for you."

"It was my grandfather's idea actually," Rebecca said, pouring the tea.

"It's important to remember the things grandfathers teach. Like this gansey here on the table. 'Twas my grandfather's wedding gift. He wore it the day he was married."

"Do you know what the stitches mean?"

"Not sure exactly. Maybe 'dislikes water intensely'?" Father Michael laughed.

"Your grandfather didn't like water? He wasn't a fisherman?"

"He was later in life, but he was raised as a farmer. Would you like to hear his story?"

Rebecca had not brought her equipment. Again! She gritted her teeth with a hiss.

"Something wrong?"

"Yeah. I didn't bring my cameras."

"Well, how 'bout I tell you the story? It's been handed down, like the jumper there, so it may be worn and not of any value but sentiment. Maybe it won't be worth recording, but if you decide it is, you can come back and I'll tell you over again."

With a nod, Rebecca seated herself before the sweater and Father Michael poured the tea.

"My grandfather came from the mainland. Couldn't swim a stroke. From a family of sheep farmers, he was. That's how he met my grandmother."

"How did he meet your grandmother?" asked Rebecca, confused.

"His family had brought some sheep to Galway to sell, and my grandmother's family came in from the islands to buy new lambs. My grandparents met each other near the water. She began to talk of the ocean and my grandfather, never having set foot in water, talked about how afraid he was of it. 'The sound of the waves in the morning is my favorite part about waking up,' said she. 'The silence of the morning where there's nothing but a bird chirping is my favorite part of waking up,' said he. They talked about what it was to live near the ocean and to live on the land, each enveloped in the life of the other. So foreign to each other they were. There they sat on the dock as the day went away, their own fathers going about their business, and as dusk came on, my grandmother climbed in the curragh with her father and sailed away, returning to the island with two new lambs and the memory of endless fields of green swaying on a summer's breeze."

Father Michael stopped and took a bite from his tea cake. He brushed the escaping crumbs from the table and looked out the window.

"They met again another time," Rebecca prompted.

Father Michael shook his head.

"On his way back to the farm, my grandfather said he just stopped on the road. His feet wouldn't move an inch farther east. He looked down at his shoes and then at his father, who leaned against their cart and pulled his pipe and tobacco out of his pocket. Not a word whispered between them as his father lit his pipe. My grandfather remembered the flickering flame of the match in the waning light—the smoldering tobacco in the pipe bowl, the purple-gray smoke rising into the sky. He watched his father and his father watched him, and it was just as the sun reached the western horizon that my grandfather's feet turned him around. He found himself walking back to Galway, waving good-bye to his father, who just waved back, laughing and watching him go."

"He didn't try to stop him? That was his son!" Rebecca frowned.

"It was his son's choice, such as it was. My grandfather would have said it wasn't a choice at all. He'd found his home. So, after spending the night standing around the docks, he swallowed his terror of the water, climbed aboard a small curragh with a fisherman the next morning, and was at my grandmother's door by teatime that day."

"Shocking for your grandmother, I guess?"

"Not at all. She had laid a plate at breakfast for him and her mother had made extra cakes for tea. They weren't sure if he'd make it to their house by the morning or afternoon, so they prepared for either."

Rebecca held a crumpet before her mouth, staring at the priest as he sipped his tea. His face looked just like Rowan's had when she was telling the story of Mayor Trace. This was such an Irish thing to Rebecca. She could rarely be sure if the stories were true or just spun out of air. It made her feel gullible, and today she didn't like feeling gullible.

"Are you pulling my leg, Father?"

"Why would I?"

Rebecca put the crumpet back on the plate and shrugged. She turned her attention back to the sweater. "There's damage here. Moths."

"Time touches all things."

"Would you mind if I took it home? I'll see if I can clean it a bit and mend it. You'll need to store it differently to preserve it."

"Can you?" Father Michael asked, his eyes brightening.

"It's what I do."

"Brilliant! Come with me," the priest said, standing abruptly.

"Where are we going?" Rebecca inquired, following him reticently.

"To the attic."

"Liz says it's a mess up there."

"She cleans for me sometimes. She thinks I'm not organized," Father Michael whispered confidentially as he led Rebecca up a steep, narrow staircase. When they reached the top, the priest shoved the door open and together they entered a dim, dusty disarray of furniture, boxes, and bags.

"She has a point," Rebecca mumbled.

Father Michael grinned. "I think what I'm looking for is behind this wardrobe," he said, nodding toward a large étagère.

Rebecca raised her eyebrows.

"It's not as heavy as it looks," he added quickly.

"Sure," she replied and, grabbing the side of the wardrobe, she helped the priest scoot it to the left. Behind it, they found a window and just below it a large chest made of the same wood as the étagère.

"Ha!"

"I guess we've found what we're looking for?"

"Yep."

The priest flipped the latch and lifted the lid. Dust, disturbed by the sudden movement, burst from the top of the chest into the air like hundreds of tiny bees, buzzing around in the light of the window.

"Look!" he said as he pulled a vest out of the chest. It looked like tweed and had four brown buttons.

Rebecca held it up to the window. The weaving was fine, and she could see that the wool had irregular bumps. "This is homespun."

"Aye."

"Handwoven?"

"Always."

Rebecca cocked her head at the priest.

"My grandfather's last suit," Father Michael explained, reaching in and pulling out the coat. "All the fishermen of the island wore that kind of suit. Homespun and handmade. Better at keeping the water out."

"They wore suits fishing?"

"It was their everyday clothes back then."

"Really," Rebecca replied, noting the fraying fabric where the suit had been folded. "I think whoever packed it didn't get all the salt out."

"Look here!" The priest pulled out a very long piece of lace.

"Wow!"

"My mother's."

"Tablecloth?"

"Wedding dress."

Rebecca stopped. "Wedding dress?" she repeated, laying the vest back in the chest and reaching for the lace.

"She made it with her mother's help."

"How do you have it?"

"The Lord gave my parents one child only."

Rebecca peered up to the priest's face again. "I guess you won't be having any girls."

"No."

The lace had yellowed from being stored in the wooden chest, but it was as fine as any spun web.

"It must have been hard for them—you being a priest. Letting go of your future, I mean. I mean—"

"I know what you mean. But love called me elsewhere."

Rebecca nodded, a crease passing across her brow. "I wonder if I can do that," she murmured.

"What?"

"Let Rowan go to be—whatever."

"Love sets free and binds, all at once. For the parent, love is binding. Many freedoms are given up—choices are limited. Out of love and respect for the child's needs, no parent can do just what they want to at all times. A parent always is bound to the child, don't you think? But a child must be set free to choose her life. That is what it is to have a child. Sometimes parents think that they have children to teach the children something. Children are given by the Lord as lessons for the parents—the greatest lesson of love. And what do you suppose that lesson of love is?"

Rebecca glanced over at Father Michael skeptically. She worried that he was trying to teach her something religious, but she couldn't tell. His face was buried in the chest as he riffled through the clothing within.

"To be bound but to let go?" she replied.

"Yes, that's it. Look, I found the pants!"

"I don't think I can do that," Rebecca whispered, brushing the lace.

"And maybe watch Rowan make the same mistakes you made?"

Rebecca shot her eyes at the priest as he stood. He brushed the dust from his slacks.

"You're given some twenty years to work on it. You'll do it."

"I suppose." Rebecca stepped back from Father Michael as she folded the lace. Perhaps she should change the subject. "How do you know when love calls?" she asked.

"Has it not called you?"

Rebecca shook her head.

"You'll know. Your feet will show you."

"Like your grandfather." Rebecca smiled.

"Aye."

There was a loud knock downstairs.

"Now who can that be?" Father Michael asked, taking his grandfather's suit in his hands and walking toward the staircase.

After tripping over a box and making it down the steep staircase, Rebecca followed the priest into his kitchen, still holding the wedding dress.

When Father Michael opened the door, he found Fionn and his father on the doorstep. "Good morning, Fionn."

"Mornin', Father. Time to go, Becky," he said brightly.

"Beg pardon?"

"Sharon's in labor. Time to go to Dublin," Fionn's father said.

"I—I can't go to Dublin. What am I going to do with Ro—"

"Sharon has called for you. And don't worry—we'll take care of Rowan," Fionn Sr. said, taking Rebecca's elbow and leading her gently out of the house. "My wife's packed you. Backpack's in Fionn's saddlebags. You should hurry. Her labor has just started, but as you know these things are unpredictable."

The roses waved adieu as Rebecca left the priest's garden. Fionn started his motorcycle.

"I'm not going on that!"

Fionn revved the engine and winked at her.

"It's only around the corner to the pier," Fionn Sr. said, taking the wedding dress gently from her hands.

"And across Ireland to Dublin!"

"Sharon needs to see ya, Becky. It's been six years and she's poppin' out her first. Is it so much to ask?" Fionn inquired, meeting her eyes with his dark gaze and patting the seat behind him.

Rebecca cringed. She didn't like to be reminded of the time. "How else can I get there?" she growled as she fought with Fionn Sr. over the motorcycle helmet.

"No other way to get there in time," he replied, feinting right, then popping the helmet on her head from the left.

"My book," Rebecca protested. "When am I gonna write my book?"

"When you get back," Fionn Sr. replied, helping her onto the bike behind Fionn.

"When I get back," she repeated.

"Aye. We'll all still be here when you get back. We've been here for hun—"

"Dreds of years. I know. I didn't say good-bye to Rowan."

"She knows where you're going. She's excited. She'll be fine."

"You people don't listen very well!"

"Which people?" Fionn asked.

"Never mind."

"Bye, Rebecca." Father Michael waved from his door. "Everything's going to be fine."

Fionn lurched away from the curb, causing Rebecca to grab him around his waist so as not to fall off.

"That's what you people always say!" she yelled over her shoulder.

CHAPTER 23

Double Zigzag/
Moss Stitch Between

Double Zigzag/Moss Stitch Between. 1. A double zigzag with
the moss stitch pattern knitted between them. 2. Seeing someone as forever through the eyes of love.

—R. Dirane, *A Binding Love*

The motorcycle made its way very slowly toward the ferry. Tourists were out in force, and to avoid hitting them Fionn had to
drive carefully. Rebecca did not like motorcycles and never had—a
gift from her father. Never was she to ride on a motorcycle. So sitting
on one now and thinking of crossing all of Ireland to Dublin on it set
her stomach churning.

"Fionn, let me off at the ferry. I'll find another way."

"Only three ferry runs on Sunday, and then you'd have to catch a
bus from Doolin. It'll take a long time to get to Dublin and it'll cost
you. Your grant was small, remember? Couldn't stop over in Dublin
from the beginning."

"I hate motorcycles. They're dangerous."

"Like curraghs on the ocean?"

"Hey! Fionn!" a voice called from up ahead.

Rebecca peered over Fionn's shoulder and saw Iollan standing on
the deck of his boat at the far end of the docks. The motorcycle passed

the empty ferry pier and sped up. As they drew closer, Rebecca could see a metal plank lying between the dock and the fishing boat.

"Hold on," Fionn said, and with that he took a sharp left up the plank and onto the boat. He stopped the motorcycle at Iollan's feet.

"Becky! Good ta see ya!" Iollan said in greeting, grinning from ear to ear.

"Thanks," Rebecca muttered.

"Cast off!"

A young man who looked no older than seventeen untied the mooring line and tossed it up to Iollan. Then the boy jumped from the deck onto the thirty-foot trawler and with Fionn's help pulled the heavy metal plank onto the boat. Fionn and Iollan then secured the motorcycle to the side of the boat, where, to Rebecca's astonishment, there appeared to be a spot made just for it.

"You ride this boat often?" Rebecca asked Fionn.

"It's how I get to the island."

"You don't take the ferry?"

"Nah, I come through Galway, not Doolin."

"Why?"

"Because I dock at Galway," Iollan replied.

Rebecca shrugged and glanced over her shoulder. At least she didn't feel worried about Rowan. She was ready to trust that her daughter would be happy and safe sleeping overnight with her new best friend. She had her own worries now.

"I'll catch a bus in Galway," she said to Fionn as the trawler left its mooring. Sighing, she walked away from him and Iollan. On the port side of the boat she found a bench, and there she sat, wondering how it was that she had come to the island to be still, to figure out her life, and to write a book but ended up doing things she didn't want to do—things that had nothing to do with her goals. She liked the people she had met and she liked helping them—helping in the pub, helping with the Dam Mad Situation, and promising to help a priest preserve his old textiles. That at least was closer to one of her goals.

Now she was off to Dublin. None of it was what she'd come here to do. Twelve days in Ireland and she still didn't feel that she'd truly gotten started on her project. She sighed again.

Fionn sat down next to her midway through the trip, bringing two cups of tea and a tin of biscuits. They sipped their tea in silence. Rebecca was too frustrated to talk and Fionn was engrossed in a book he had brought along. A couple of times she thought she should say something, but he just sat on the bench, ignoring her completely.

When the ship arrived in Galway, the plank was put down off the boat, and Fionn drove the motorcycle onto the dock. Rebecca walked slowly down the plank.

"Thanks, Iollan, for the ride," she said and then turned to Fionn. "I'll find a bus. Can I have my backpack, please?"

"The bus will take forever, Becky."

"You are not listening to me, Fionn. I don't like motorcycles. I don't want to go on one."

"Look. We'll go a little way. We'll clear Galway and if you're still not happy by the time we reach Athlone, we'll find you a bus."

"Where's Athlone?"

"Halfway between here and Dublin. Come on, Becky. Meet me halfway." He held out her helmet.

"My dad hated bikes," Rebecca muttered, taking the helmet and putting it on her head.

"He never rode with me," Fionn replied, patting the saddle behind him.

With a wave, Rebecca and Fionn left Iollan, his single crewman, the trawler, and the city behind them, heading east to Dublin. Rebecca held on to the handle behind her. She knew the trip across Ireland to Dublin would take about three hours, and for the first time she thought of Sharon and what she was going to say to her.

It had been six years since they had seen each other, though they had talked on the phone every week or so. Six years since that horrible night. She and Sharon had never spoken about it, and now that she was heading east, heaviness enveloped her. The fields and stone walls and little towns of Ireland glittered in the early-summer sun, but Rebecca didn't see any of it. She was shrouded by the past.

As they approached Athlone, Fionn stopped the bike in a village just outside of the town and without so much as a dozen words, directed Rebecca to sit on a spot of grass while he went and bought something to eat. Rebecca had left Father Michael's house just before lunchtime. She hadn't eaten, having instead made the sudden trip into the priest's attic. Now she was hungry.

Before long, Fionn returned with two sandwiches, two apples, and a couple of bottles of water. Sitting down next to her, he unwrapped his sandwich, took a bite, and then opened his book again. Rebecca stared at him, looking at his red hair shining brightly in the sun. He had the most beautiful hair. As she gazed at him, she realized just how beautiful she thought him to be. Quickly, she looked down at her sandwich, still neatly wrapped. Suddenly she was uncomfortable sitting next to him in stillness. "Good book?" she asked, wanting some sound to break the silence.

"Huh? Oh. There's something waiting for me back at work and I wanted to figure it out before I got there."

Rebecca unwrapped her sandwich. "What do you do?"

Fionn looked up from his book, his mouth hanging open.

"What?" she asked.

"You don't know what I do?"

"No," she replied, leaning away from him.

"I work with John. You know what he does, don't you?"

"He owns a music studio."

"We—own a music studio. Sharon never mentioned that?"

"Well, I don't remember everything she says. We talk a lot." Rebecca bit into her sandwich. Now that he'd said it, she did remember, but she didn't want to tell him that.

"We produce Irish music."

"I like Irish music."

"Aye, you do. You have an affinity for the fiddle."

Rebecca nodded slowly, glancing at him sideways now. How did he know that?

"I know that about you because Sharon told me. I listen to her when she talks about you."

Rebecca frowned, remembering that Rowan had asked him whether he played the violin. She looked into Fionn's black eyes and her mouth went dry, making it difficult to swallow her sandwich. "I listen, too." Rebecca put her sandwich down and reached for her water.

"Really?" Fionn asked, his lip curling in a smile.

"Yes," she replied, mimicking his look.

Fionn shrugged and turned back to his book.

"So what are you researching for your work?"

"We're finishing up a recording session and the band asked me to come up with ideas for the jacket design. I really like this band. They remind me of—home."

"Your parents' or the one you haven't found yet?"

"You do listen to me when I talk," Fionn said, grinning.

"I pay attention, Fionn, whatever you might think," she replied, taking another bite of her sandwich.

"Excellent!" he said. "Then the one I haven't found yet. This band is very much like that island—alone with moody weather. Only it's warm, too, and—connected to everybody. It's together so there's no fear."

Rebecca glanced up at the sun. She felt its warmth above her.

"So I got this art book to help me. It has paintings."

Rebecca closed her eyes, feeling the sun on her back, smelling the grass around her, and thinking about what he was saying. To sing and be unafraid. She wanted that.

"There's a bird in the berry bramble outside our bedroom window. It sings in the storms."

"Mistle thrush."

"That's it!"

"What about it?"

"Only the Irish would have a bird like that."

"Really?"

"Maybe the jacket design could have a mistle thrush." Rebecca glanced over at Fionn and smiled into his black eyes.

He smiled back. Her stomach rolled. She looked away.

"Why would the Irish have a bird like that?" Fionn asked softly.

"That's what it is to be Irish."

"Really. You Irish?"

In her peripheral vision, Rebecca could see he was still watching her. She wished he would look away. "No. But I think I'm getting the flavor of it on the island."

"What flavor were you before?"

Rebecca peered at him cautiously. He was staring still. A wind brushed his red curls. She swallowed.

"Well?"

"Maybe just a mixed-up American."

"That's a good flavor."

"You think so?"

"Mmm. Potpourri."

He laughed. He had misunderstood her, but she had avoided saying anything she didn't want to, so she laughed with him. Then she took a bite of her sandwich, turning her head to the road. "Did you find any ideas for the jacket design in that book?" she asked.

"Only one."

"Can I see?"

Fionn flipped through the pages, stopping on one and handing her the book. She coughed. It was a picture of a woman lying in a bathtub, fully naked. Rebecca rolled her eyes.

"Figures," she muttered.

"What?"

"A naked woman."

"Why does that figure?"

"Never mind."

"What do you mean?"

Rebecca looked at Fionn. His black eyes were on her, but now they were as still as the day when she had apologized to him for slamming the door in his face.

"You're a man. It's a naked woman," she replied.

"Yeah?"

Rebecca shrugged.

"All men aren't the same, Becky." Fionn stood up.

"It's a painting of a naked woman, Fionn. What am I supposed to think?"

"You didn't ask me what I think. This was about it reminding me of home, remember?"

"Okay, why does it remind you of home?"

"Never mind." Fionn walked away.

Quickly Rebecca pulled herself up from the ground and gathered her lunch. She was mad. "You don't get to set me up like that, Fionn, and then just walk away!"

"How does it feel?" he replied, turning back to her.

Rebecca skidded to a halt.

"Makes you mad, huh? Doesn't feel very good. Welcome to conversations with you."

Rebecca's mouth flapped silently.

"Here, I'll be me, not you. That picture reminds me of home not because there is a woman naked in a bathtub, but because of the man painting her. As she aged, that woman spent more and more time in the tub. She was troubled in the mind. But he loved her and wanted to be with her, so he'd sit by the bath and paint her. You can't tell if this is her at nineteen years old or sixty, though her body is clearly portrayed. You know why we can't tell? Because the painter sees her as forever, the way she was when they met. To him, this is how she looks. All of her beauty seen with the eyes of love. Without this painter, all we'd see was an old woman with a troubled mind lying in a tub."

Fionn spun around and headed for the bike.

"I know a man like that, Becky. His wife isn't troubled. But I know that man who sees his wife as forever. I want that, and when I have it, then I'll have my home."

Rebecca stood on the grass, unable to move, unable to speak. If she hadn't known better, she'd have said his hair had turned brighter red. She wasn't sure if it was the sun or his anger. Slowly she pulled her feet forward, mired as they were in the fresh green grass, and made her way to the motorcycle. Nausea washed over her, so she dumped her lunch in a trash can. She wished she could leave. She wanted to run away from Fionn, but her only way to anywhere was with him.

"Fionn?" she asked quietly, stepping up to the bike.

He looked over at her.

"Who's the man you know like that?"

"My dad. He sees Mum as forever. Have ya not noticed?"

Rebecca nodded. She had noticed.

"I want that, Becky. And to get it, I have to see with clear eyes and hear with clear ears and speak with clear words. The dust of the past can be in my clothes, on my hair, covering my shoes, but it cannot be in my eyes or ears or mouth. I wonder, Becky, will you see the eyes of love when they look at you or will you see only the dust of your past?"

Fionn straddled the motorcycle and started it, handing Rebecca her helmet. She climbed on, grabbing the handle behind her. She wanted to be anywhere but riding behind Fionn.

They rode on in silence. Rebecca could feel her heart racing. It was three o'clock in the afternoon and she was on a motorcycle with a stranger in a foreign land. What if they had an accident? Had Sheila packed her passport? Would anybody know who she was if she died here on an Irish road? What would happen to Rowan? She let go of the handle and held on to the sides of Fionn's leather jacket. Within fifteen minutes of leaving their lunch in the garbage can, they reached the outskirts of Athlone and Fionn pulled over.

"You want to find a bus?" he asked through his helmet.

"No, thanks," Rebecca replied uncomfortably. "I'm fine."

"See, Becky, I do listen to you." With that, Fionn pulled away from the curb and they rode through the streets of the small city and out again into the Irish countryside.

There were more cars on the road the closer they came to Dublin, and with the increase of traffic Rebecca's anxiety increased. It had been so long since she'd seen Sharon, and she wasn't sure she could avoid talking with her about that Thanksgiving night if they were face-to-face. By the time they reached the city limits, she held Fionn around the chest, resting her cheek against his back. His red curls spiraled from his helmet and tickled her nose. She closed her eyes, hanging on tightly, taking in the scent of his hair. Her heart slowed a little as they made their way through the city streets and when the motorcycle stopped, she looked up.

"Where are we?"

"Sharon and John's house."

"Not the hospital?"

"We should find out what's happening," Fionn said.

As Rebecca climbed off the back of the motorcycle, the door to Sharon's house opened, with Sharon's mother right behind it.

"Peg?"

"Come in, come in. I'm so anxious, I've made enough tea for the island," she said, wringing her hands.

Rebecca laughed. Glancing at Fionn, she found he had a smile on his face, but his eyes were just as dark as they had been when she stood up from the grass two hours earlier. He opened his left saddlebag and pulled out Rebecca's backpack. He swung it over his shoulder.

"How far along is she?" Rebecca asked, quickly looking away from Fionn as she climbed the steps toward the door.

"She's been at it since yesterday afternoon. It's a hard one. I had to take the ferry yesterday and have Danny drive me here. But they want us to wait at the house."

"Danny?" Rebecca inquired.

"My little brother," Fionn replied, shutting the door behind him. "Is he still here?"

"He left this morning. Eat," Peg said, stepping into the kitchen. True to her word, there was a tea like no other Rebecca had seen. There were lemon tarts and scones, and salmon sandwiches with malt vinegar on a tray next to carrot-ginger sandwiches. Small pork pies and pasties and two pots of steaming tea rested on the table.

"Good Lord, Peg," Rebecca gasped.

"I know, I know. Eat."

Rebecca was hungry. She hadn't touched her lunch sandwich and with Peg as a distraction from Fionn's dark mood, she decided to sit, eat, and hope he'd brighten up.

As they ate, Peg talked of Maggie's births. They were both boys, and though Peg said she simply hoped for a healthy child, Rebecca knew she wanted a granddaughter. Sharon had said so right before Rebecca left the States for the island. Rebecca spotted a brown paper sack on the counter. Sharon had brought one just like it to California when Rowan was born. It contained the shanachie gansey. As that thought crossed her mind, a small gasp escaped her lips.

"You okay, Becky?" Peg asked.

"Huh? Oh—yeah. It's just the tea."

Peg peered over at the little brown package and, reaching for it, pulled a long box wrapped in California poppy paper from behind it.

"Here," she said, sliding it across the table. "Sharon got this for you. It's just a little something,"

Opening the box, Rebecca found a package of incense. "Are these sparklers?"

Peg burst out laughing. "No," she replied. "Incense."

"That wasn't funny, Peg. I could've burned down the house."

"Oh, come on, Becky. It was funny and you know it."

"Rowan thought it was funny," Fionn said.

"How do you know?" Rebecca asked.

"She told me. You think she only talks to you, Becky?"

Rebecca sighed. She should call the island to check on her daughter.

"You're gonna miss it this year," Peg said.

"Yeah." Rebecca shrugged.

"Miss what?" Fionn asked.

"Fourth of July. Party time for Rebecca."

"Really. I like parties," Fionn said.

"Well, this is a party of parties, huh, Becky?"

"How so?" Fionn asked.

"Oh, my dad was just crazy. Other people celebrated Thanksgiving or Christmas. We did, too, but nothing like we celebrated July Fourth. We closed off our cul-de-sac and everybody pulled out their barbecues. They still do. Rowan and I go back there every Fourth. Like keeping my mom and dad alive."

"I love barbecue!" Fionn declared. "What do they barbecue?"

"Chicken—my mom's chicken."

"What's in her chicken?"

"She had a rub and then she made a sauce."

"What's the rub?"

"Um—brown sugar, paprika—the smoky Spanish kind. Thyme, salt."

"What's in her sauce?"

"Fionn," Peg said, shaking her head. "Geez."

"I love barbecue," Fionn repeated.

"Ketchup, Worcestershire sauce, brown sugar, red pepper, a little soy sauce."

"What do you have with it?"

"Good Lord, Fionn," Peg declared.

"Potato salad," Rebecca replied, laughing. He was brighter now, and that made her happy.

"What's in it?"

"Potatoes, eggs, dill pickles, sour cream, green onion, bacon, and Louisiana Hot Sauce."

"What's Louisiana Hot Sauce?"

"Fionn, stop!" Peg shouted, holding her head.

Rebecca smiled at him. He smiled, too.

"American potpourri," he said with a chuckle.

"Yeah. Anyway, we swim over at the Hernandezes' pool and later at night have a big scavenger hunt. My dad was a firefighter, so we were only allowed sparklers. But we could line up the lawn chairs in the street and watch the city's big fireworks display from our cul-de-sac. After the fireworks, my dad pulled out the Constitution and everybody on the street took turns reading parts of it. Then we'd have a great toast to another year of freedom. Still do that part, too." Rebecca sipped her tea, feeling much warmer now that Fionn was more himself.

"July Fourth is the Thursday after next," Peg noted.

"And I've got sparklers," Rebecca said.

Peg grinned.

"Well, I best be getting home. You know, Becky," Fionn said as he stood, "I talked to my friend at Trinity, and he said you could come and use the library for your book. We'll see where Sharon is tomorrow, and maybe, since you're here, we could go."

"Yes, I'd love that."

"I'll drop by tomorrow," Fionn said, walking out of the kitchen. Rebecca and Peg followed. He opened the door and stepped out into the drizzle.

"See ya tomorrow," Peg said, kissing Fionn on the cheek.

Rebecca watched him straddle the seat of his bike. "Fionn?" she called, following him down the steps. As she stepped close to the bike, Rebecca stuck her hands in her pockets and looked down. "I'm sorry."

"For what?"

"For . . . saying what I said about men. It—it wasn't right and you didn't deserve that. I'm really sorry."

Fionn cocked his head with a half smile. Standing up from his seat, he leaned over and kissed Rebecca's cheek. "Better be going in, love. It's wet out here. See ya tomorrow." He put his helmet on his head, started his bike, and pulled away from the curb.

"Becky," Peg called from the door. "Rowan's on the phone."

Rebecca turned to take the call, but then she glanced back and watched as he rode off into the mist.

CHAPTER 24

Lattice/Bobble Within

Lattice/Bobble Within. 1. Lattice pattern with a bobble knitted into the center of each diamond. 2. A community suffering a loss together and together weathering the grief.

—R. Dirane, *A Binding Love*

Sean stood over his dead rosebushes, their skeletons bleached and crooked. So bare were they that the canes had no thorns, their prickly appendages scraped away by years of sand and wind. They were dead despite the fact that he had replanted the flowers over the last forty years, digging holes in the exact spot where he and Claire had planted their first bushes when they moved into his father's house, three months after the old man's death. She said the cottage needed roses. Claire loved roses.

The sun was straight overhead when Sean stepped out of his house on Sunday, the light diffuse and white in the gray drizzle. He had worked half the night on developing the color apricot. He had no luck casting the color warm enough to match Liam's sunrise, but he did happen upon an orangey gold that reminded him of Claire's favorite rose. That was what drew his mind away from his third boy and out to the side of his house to appraise the state of his rose bed.

"Well, Claire," he said. "You've left me with nothing."

As soon as the words passed his lips, he heard Joe's pipe on the wind. A mistle thrush flashed in front of his face. Startled, Sean spun around, watching the bird land upon the shallow keel of his curragh. He gasped, grabbing his heart as he watched a little black boat bob far out, heading north in the gray-blue water.

The entire island had come. The top of the hill where the cemetery stood was covered above the ground with more people than were buried beneath it. At least it seemed so to Sean, who stood to the south of the O'Flaherty family plot, watching Padrig Blake and Fionn O'Flaherty finish shoveling the rocky gray soil on top of Mary's grave. Claire wept softly next to him as the dust from the shovels fell in tiny clumps, wet from the gray drizzle that sifted through the air. Soon it would rain. Sean could taste it on the wind.

"Come on, Claire," Ina said. "The pub's closed and we've food laid out."

"We have enough at home," Sean replied, turning his gaze to the fresh soil covering his oldest son's grave.

"This burden is best shared, Sean," Father Michael said. The priest was in his mid-twenties, by Sean's reckoning. What did a young man know of burdens?

"We carry our own burdens," Sean replied. "We've no need for help. Come, Claire."

"Sean," Ina whispered.

"Claire belongs to me," Sean added, flicking his cold hazel eyes at Ina.

Turning from the graves and the people he had known all his life, Sean led Claire past the Dirane family plot and out the small gate in the cemetery's stone wall.

Morahan.

Sean turned around, freezing as he caught sight of Old Man Dirane. The shanachie stood next to his own grave, smoking his pipe as if the drizzle was not even falling from above.

"Sean?" Claire whispered.

"Do you see him?" Sean breathed, blinking in the gray mist, waiting for his mind to dissolve the ghostly vision.

"Who?" Claire asked.

That's quite a tale ya have to tell, Old Man Dirane said, smoke puffing from his mouth.

"What's wrong, Sean?" Claire asked.

"Shut up," he said, pushing Claire by her arm in front of him and down the hill. Her shawl slipped from her left shoulder. They walked halfway to the dirt road below, at which point Sean turned and looked hesitantly over his shoulder. There he saw Padrig Blake and the priest standing at the edge of the cemetery, watching him. Old Man Dirane was nowhere in sight.

Sean let go of Claire's arm, and in silence broken only by her quiet weeping and the sound of the surf, they walked home. The gravel crunched sharply under their feet, and when Claire opened the door she dipped her fingers into the little shell of water by the door and crossed herself. Sean followed, shutting the door behind him. He, too, touched the water in the shell.

"God bless all here," he said. There was no answer.

"Claire!"

His wife jumped.

"God bless all here," he repeated.

"Welcome home, love," she said quietly, pulling the fringe of her shawl through her fingers. "Would you like tea?"

"That would be fine," he said, squinting at her.

Claire went into the kitchen as Sean walked to the hearth. He tossed two bricks of peat onto the dead gray ash, tiny specks of dust bursting into the air as he did so.

"Bring me matches," he said.

The ash floated out of the fireplace, drifting to the floor and falling onto Sean's shoes. The soft tinkling of a teapot echoed in the kitchen. Sean spun on his heel and walked into the kitchen.

"Did ya not hear me?" he said.

Claire turned her head in his direction. She shook her head.

"I said I need matches," he repeated, seething.

The tears that had been softly falling from Claire's eyes for three days began to pour down her cheeks.

"You blame me," Sean hissed.

"No, Sean," Claire gasped, trying to catch her breath through her tears. Her blue-green eyes were wide. Sean grimaced.

"Yes, you do! You think I killed them."

He stepped closer to his wife. Claire backed up.

"It was an accident, Sean." She choked out the words, but he saw that her eyes said otherwise.

"When I ask for matches, I expect matches. When I ask for something, I expect it done. My sons understood that! Why can't you?"

Sean lunged at his wife, who tripped on the leg of the kitchen table, dropping the teapot with a sharp crash upon the stone floor.

"Jesus Christ, Claire," he yelled, reaching for her, but before he could grab her arm, his wife bolted for the kitchen door.

"Get back here!" he hollered, slipping on the shards of the teapot as he tried to follow her. Gaining his balance, he stormed into the living room. The front door was open and Claire was gone. Sean raced outside.

"Claire!" he called. He gazed up the gravel walkway and then to the left and right. She was nowhere to be seen. Stomping to the left, he came around the corner of his house and found her pushing the curragh into the surf.

"Claire! Get away from that boat!"

Sliding in, Claire lifted the oars as Sean flew down the beach. He could see her pulling on the oars, her face twisted in pain. His feet hit the water; he could just about grab the stern of the curragh. But the outgoing surf pulled the sand from beneath his shoes and he faltered, falling to one knee in the water.

"Get back here!" he screamed, lifting himself from the sand and marching farther into the surf. The waves pounded him like large, cold fists.

"Claire!"

He could not reach her. She struggled with the oars, rowing farther out, heading north and away from her home and her husband.

⁓

"Sean!"

The old man stopped. He looked at the bottom of his curragh and then at his oars. Sweat poured down his chest beneath his gansey as he glanced around in a daze. He was in his boat and had rowed far north of the kelp bed. There was a pipe on the wind.

"Sean!"

He heard Rowan's voice, and gazing over to the small spit of beach from which the O'Flahertys fished, he found Rowan and Siobhan jumping up and down and waving at him from the shore, flutes in hand.

"Come in, Sean!" Rowan yelled.

Fionn Sr. stood by his curragh, his red-gray hair shining like aged bronze in the sun. Turning his boat, Sean rowed in, his arms and back aching from the strain of all he'd put them through, though he couldn't even remember climbing into his curragh. The surf caught him, bringing the boat in, and when he hit the sand Fionn Sr., Rowan, and Siobhan pulled him ashore. Pushing his hat away from his eyes, he found Siobhan dressed in the same strange coveralls that were Rowan's uniform.

"Your mother make those for Siobhan?" Sean asked.

"I borrowed them from Rowan," Siobhan replied.

"Look! Look!" Rowan exclaimed, lifting her right foot and pointing to her shoe. There, on her tiny foot, was a proper pampootie, tied neatly around her ankle.

"Ah, the shoes of an island fisherman." Sean smiled.

"Annie made them for us," Rowan said, pointing to Siobhan's pampooties. "Were you racing us?"

"What's that?" Sean inquired, cocking his head.

"You were rowing hard behind us," Fionn Sr. replied.

"Ah—no. Just . . . looking for better fish," Sean said.

"We went fishing, too," Rowan said.

"Catch anything?" Sean asked of Fionn Sr.

"Just the sun. We're headin' in for some tea. You're welcome to come."

"Uh, I should be headin' back."

"Come on, Sean," Rowan said, pressing him to join them.

He looked down into her face, and though he knew there was a gray-white sky above him, there was no reflection of it in her eyes. There were only shades of earthy brown. His mind held no memory of earthy brown—no memory, that was, except Rowan herself. He nodded. His spine and knees cracked as he stood. It had been many years since he had set foot on O'Flahertys' beach, and as his left shoe hit the shore, a crushing pain seized his chest.

⁓

"Move or we'll miss the fish!" Emmet screamed as he shoved Sean hard, causing him to fall sideways out of the curragh. Very slowly, Sean saw his older brothers, Emmet and Ronan, turn and watch him go overboard. The net they held in their hands was around Sean's foot.

"No!" Ronan yelled.

As Sean hit the water, his knees hooked the boat's side and the curragh flipped over. Sean heard his brothers fall, but he could not see them through the black sea. Pushing himself up toward the light, he stuck his head above the water, gasping for air. At that moment, he felt a great tug on his left foot, which was still caught in the net. It dragged him under again. Spotting the overturned curragh as he went down, he swam in that direction and grabbed hold of it. He pulled his head from the water. The net flailed and tugged desperately at his foot.

"No!" Sean screamed, grasping the bottom of the boat, which was now turned to the sky above. He clawed at the sides, seeking a crack or a break in the curragh's seams, but this was one of his father's boats. It had none.

"Da!" he yelled, and under the water he went. Looking up at the light, he tried to keep himself near the surface. His lungs burned for air as he struggled. He couldn't let go his breath. He was surrounded by frigid water. His eyes knew it. His arms and legs knew it. His mind knew it. But his lungs knew only that they needed air. Sean stilled in the water, sinking lower and lower as he was dragged below by the weight of the net.

"Perhaps," said his lungs, "you should breathe." As he was about to do so, he could see his father above him. He reached out his hand, stretching as far as he could. His father grabbed him and pulled the boy up from the ocean.

"I told you to watch the net," his father said, seething.

Sean gasped as Peter Dooley grasped the back of his jumper.

"Emmet pushed me," Sean choked, clutching the interior of Dooley's boat. His leg was bent the wrong way. "Ah!" he screamed as pain shot through his knee.

"What's got you?" Dooley asked.

"The net!" Sean yelled, kicking his foot wildly to get free of it. His knee burned.

"Where's your brothers?" his father asked.

"They're in the water," Sean grunted, pushing his foot back and forth to get the net off his shoe.

"Where?"

"I didn't see them fall. Emmet pushed me! I went in first." The strap of Sean's leather shoe broke. Though he was just fourteen years old and small, the net's release caused forward momentum, and Dooley and Sean's father, with Sean in their arms, fell back in the curragh.

"Where are your brothers?" Sean's father yelled again.

"In the water," Sean whimpered, holding his knee.

"I don't see them."

Sean glanced up at his father and as their eyes met Sean's heart stopped.

"They're in the net!" Sean's father screamed.

"Who?" came a call from portside.

"Emmet and Ronan! They're in the net!"

Sean sat upright, looking toward the sound of the voice. There, in a curragh to the left, were Old Fionn O'Flaherty and his teenage sons, Tadhg, Nial, and Young Fionn. Tadhg and Nial stripped out of their jumpers and shoes and dove into the water. Had it been anyone else, Sean would have been worried for them, but not these two O'Flaherty boys. Tadhg and Nial were gifted swimmers, born to it like they were seals. Within a minute or two, the boys came up, struggling with the weight of the net.

"Emmet!" Sean's father yelled as he grabbed the net from Nial. "Emmet!"

The net rose above water with Emmet and Ronan white as sea foam within it.

"No," Sean whispered.

Emmet's dead gaze fell upon Sean. He shrank away.

"Row!" Sean's father screamed, and crawling from beneath his dead brother's eyes, Sean moved to lay on the oars.

As they rowed in, Sean's father desperately tore his sons from the net, pushing on their chests to clear the water, but it was no use. By the time the curragh hit the sand on O'Flahertys' beach, Sean's father sat as still and silent as his two sons laid out before him. Emmet, eighteen, and Ronan, just seventeen, were dead.

Tadhg, Nial, and Young Fionn slid their boat in and helped Sean's father lift Emmet and Ronan out of the curragh. Sean sat, his knee burning and his eyes stinging from the tears he dared not shed before his father.

"Sean," Old Fionn O'Flaherty said as he wrapped his arm around the boy's shoulder, "it's not your fault."

"Leave me be," Sean whispered, shrugging away from the comfort.

He crawled out of the boat and raced down the beach, his knee screaming in the pain that was tearing up his insides. He ran up the hewn stairs with his bare foot and kept running until all he could hear was the wind in the brush and the song of birds. He fell, burying his face in the dirt.

"I hate you, Emmet!" he shouted into the weeds. "I hate you! I hate you! I hate you!"

Being the youngest, Sean had always been pushed about by his brothers. They hit and kicked him and his father did nothing. *Make you tough*, was all the man said. Now Sean knew his father would blame him for their deaths.

A hand touched his shoulder.

"Leave me be," Sean growled.

"Sean, it's me. Claire."

"Please leave me."

She touched his hair, and beneath her fingers Sean could feel the pain rising in his chest, aching in his throat.

"It's all right," she said.

"They pushed me off the boat."

"They always do, Sean. Everyone knows that. It's not your fault."

"My da will think so."

Claire wrapped her arms around Sean's head, lifting it to her lap. The tears rolled painfully from his eyes. He didn't want to cry, but this was Claire. A Dooley she was, though in her arms Sean could feel her mother's grandmother. It was that part of Claire that could have compassion for the most wretched and kindness for the meanest. It was the part that saw Sean as he was inside. Only an O'Flaherty could do that.

"My brothers are dead," Sean whispered. "My father will never forgive me. I kicked them off my foot."

"You didn't know they were there."

"It won't matter, Claire. Don't you understand?"

"This is what I understand, Sean Morahan. Men die on the sea when they don't stick together. There is no greater truth than that, and everyone on this island knows that truth but your da. He raised his sons like he did, and now all but one are dead. Your father may blame you, but you need to know different. It was your da's own doing. And when we have sons, you'll remember this day and you'll make sure our sons know to watch out for each other and to stick together. That is the truth, Sean Morahan."

Sean knew Claire's truth and it was why he also knew he would have no other for his wife. That truth was how the O'Flahertys lived and loved and was why, over the years, Sean wanted more than anything to belong to that family. His father knew Sean's desire, and though the Morahans and O'Flahertys fished together, growing up Sean was never allowed to spend time with them. But that did not stop him. He wanted to love like they loved and he did. He loved Claire.

⌒

A small hand wrapped around Sean's left index finger. He shook his head, dispersing the past from his mind, and found Rowan holding on to him. A pipe played on the sea.

"Is something wrong there, Morahan?" Fionn Sr. asked, his brow furrowed deeply. Sean looked up at the bronze-haired man, who was not even a whisper in his father's mind when Sean's brothers died. This was Young Fionn's son, and now this Fionn had grandchildren of his own.

Sean turned around, facing the ocean. The music stopped.

"There's something on the wind," he said softly.

"I don't smell anything," Fionn Sr. replied, peering up into the white-gray sky.

"Come on, Sean. I'm hungry," Rowan said.

Stepping from his curragh, Sean willed the pain in his chest to stop. As he walked across the sand, he felt Rowan's tiny thumb rubbing the side of his finger gently. It was comforting, and when she released him to climb the rough stone stairs that led to O'Flahertys' house, he shook, as if without her hold on him he would fall back into the past. Quickly but very tenderly, Sean took Rowan's entire hand in his, and together they climbed away from the shore.

CHAPTER 25

Diamond/Tree of Life Within/ Ribbing Without

Diamond/Tree of Life Within/Ribbing Without. 1. A central panel with large diamonds and a single Tree of Life knitted within each one. On each side, within the angle where one diamond touches the next, ribbing is knitted. 2. A people's history.

—R. Dirane, *A Binding Love*

*J*ohn called the next morning, saying Sharon was no closer to having the baby. The doctors were debating a cesarean section the following morning if there was no progress today. That would be against Sharon's wishes, for she wanted to have the baby naturally.

Peg greeted Rebecca with all this news when she came downstairs for breakfast. Peg had indeed been busy that morning—breakfast consisted of eggs and sausage, black pudding, toast, tomatoes, and tea. Rebecca laughed and said that if Sharon didn't have the baby soon, Peg would need to open a restaurant.

Fionn was at the door by ten o'clock. He made Peg promise that she'd call if anything changed, and then he took Rebecca to the library, arriving at eleven. When Rebecca entered the building, she felt more at home than she had since arriving in Ireland. Libraries had a scent, an ancient perfume, and it was in libraries where she felt most comfortable. Trinity's library was older than any Rebecca had experienced, and the aroma of the building intermingled with the books' perfume to create the perfect setting for her. She was happy.

At the information counter Fionn handed the librarian a note from a friend of his who was a professor at the university and who had given Rebecca permission to use the library's resources. As soon as the woman nodded her acceptance, Rebecca asked her for the locations of textiles, art, and Irish history books. As she turned toward those sections, she found Fionn following her.

"Aren't you going to work?"

"I have to work tonight."

"Oh."

Rebecca had spent long hours of her life alone at tables in libraries, poring over manuscripts or bent over laptops, taking notes. Scholarship was a solitary endeavor, and no one had ever come along with her to share her work. But here Fionn was, following her into the depths of silence, going exploring. She was happy about that, too.

After locating the section dedicated to the west of Ireland, Fionn began to pull books from the shelves. He seemed to know better than Rebecca what was important, and as he placed the books on a table she sat down with her backpack and pulled out her laptop, a notepad, and her box of pencils. Fionn sat next to her. Without asking, he slid the notepad and the pencil box in front of him and opened a book.

They read together in the quiet of the library, Fionn scratching notes on his pad of paper, Rebecca watching him do so. She wasn't typing anything. She wanted to know what he was writing. After an hour, he stood and, taking his book, his notebook, and his pencil, he walked away, without so much as a wave or a good-bye. Rebecca shook her head, watching him go.

"He's not right," she muttered and sat back in her chair.

Since she had arrived in Ireland thirteen days ago, Rebecca had not succeeded in achieving any of the goals she had set for herself. She had very little in the way of film about the sweaters, very few stories from Rose and Liz about the patterns they used, and only a smattering of pictures. Most of her time had been spent with the townspeople. But somehow getting to know them kept turning her mind back to her past with Dennis. She hadn't come all the way to the island to remember the worst moment in her life. If anything, she'd come to free herself from those memories once and for all. And she had certainly come to set down on paper and film the history of a people's life. She had a grant. She had a responsibility.

"I have nothing," she whispered.

Sitting up straight, she opened the book to her left and found the history of Ireland—not the west but the whole of it. It was a shortened version, to be sure—only a thousand pages with pictures. Rebecca knew well that the Irish were old. Sharon had said so. The book fell open to a page with an ink drawing of the potato famine. A weeping woman knelt before a stone wall with her six small children and a babe in her arms. In the background were English soldiers, tossing out the contents of her small cottage.

"I have everything," Rebecca breathed, touching the page, and as she did so a memory from long ago passed through her mind.

Sharon sat on her bed in their dorm room, watching Rebecca knit her last row.

"How do you get the stitches off the needle?" Rebecca asked, holding her first knitted slipper out to her best friend for help.

"You cast off."

"What's that?"

"You bind the stitches into place, so they know where they belong. That's how it's done where I come from."

"Show me," Rebecca said, letting go of her needles into Sharon's hands.

"You have a place and it's just for you. You don't ever feel like you're blowin' in the wind, up against it by yourself. You know? Always, someone has hold of you, helping you stay in place, even if you travel, like me. I still have my place. It's there for me when I go home and in my soul when I'm away."

"I want that."

"You'll have it, Becky. One day. You'll see."

⟶

"I'm up against it, Sharon. Blowin' in the wind."

Rebecca closed the book and left the table. Heading into the art section, she searched for Fionn. She didn't find him. She looked in the textile section. He wasn't there either.

"I have to work," she reminded herself and grabbing her laptop and backpack from the history area, she settled into textiles for the rest of the day. She looked for knitting and wool but found instead a section on lace. She thought of Father Michael's mother's wedding dress and, distracted from her purpose, it was lace that she read about until she looked out the windows and realized the sun had fallen from its zenith. Fionn reappeared then, smiling a great smile through his beard.

"Where have you been?" Rebecca asked.

"Finding things for you. You done?"

"I'm done," she sighed, closing the book before her.

"Excellent! I'm famished. I've not eaten all day."

He led her out of the library to his bike. He didn't say one word—nothing about where he had been all day or what he'd found or why he was so happy. Watching his red hair catch the wind as he handed her a helmet, Rebecca glowered. He was so unreadable at times.

It was only a short drive to a pub and when they stepped in, several people called Fionn's name, waving to him from far tables and behind the bar. They slid into a booth by the window and Fionn dropped his notebook on the table.

"A pint of bitters and a pint of cider, love," he called to the woman behind the bar. Then he said to Rebecca, "I was reading a book this morning and it started discussing the jumpers of the islands. It said that some of the patterns can be found in the Book of Kells."

"Ah—I forgot the Book of Kells was at Trinity." Rebecca scowled. Her mind was not on her work.

"You knew that?"

"Yeah. There's a drawing in it that shows a man wearing what looks to be a gansey."

"Oh. Well, that's not what I found."

"What did you find?" Rebecca raised an eyebrow in inquiry.

"Guess."

"Knock it off."

"You don't like playing, do you?"

The woman from the bar set the drinks on the table.

"Can we get supper, please, Mary, my love?"

"Anything for you, Fionn."

He smiled and turned back to Rebecca. "Look."

He opened his notebook, and there Rebecca found a beautiful pencil drawing of an Irish knot. It was square and intertwined so as almost to create a trifold in the middle. She had seen this before.

"This is from the shawnash—"

"Aye—the shanachie gansey."

"You draw beautifully, Fionn."

Fionn's cell phone rang. He pulled it from his pocket to answer. "Peg!" he said. "Ah!" He was quiet for a minute, then said, "Then no baby yet?"

Rebecca frowned.

"Well, then she'll come with me."

"Come where? Is Sharon all right?" Rebecca inquired.

"All right, then, love. We'll see you later. Bye." He hung up.

"What's happening?"

"John's coming home to shower and Peg's going to stay with Sharon for a while."

"We should go help," Rebecca said.

"We're not invited. We're invited to wait. But now you can come with me," he said happily.

"To your work?"

"To hear a band."

"I thought you had to work."

"It is my work. That band is playing. The one I told you about. It has three fiddles," Fionn said, winking at her. "You think I draw beautifully?'

"Yes," she replied.

As Fionn flipped through several pages of his notebook, Rebecca saw more intricate Celtic designs drawn in pencil. Her eyes widened, for several of them looked to be from Father Michael's grandfather's gansey. Fionn stopped on a page that wasn't from the Book of Kells. Rebecca knew it wasn't, for the design was almost Japanese.

"A bird," she stated, touching the shadowy suggestion of wind blowing across the bird's open beak.

"A mistle thrush," he corrected.

"It's wonderful, Fionn."

"Thanks. You think the band will like it?"

"They'll love it." She beamed.

Fionn smiled, staring into her with his black eyes. To Rebecca's relief, supper arrived at their table.

Rebecca gazed at the mistle thrush and thought of holding Rowan in the storm as they watched the little bird in the bramble sing in the wind.

"Fionn? You know Annie's phone number?"

"You wanna talk to Rowan?"

She nodded. Fionn opened his cell phone and dialed. She was glad to hear her daughter's voice, and the news was all good. Rowan was happy with Siohban, and they'd spent a rainy day practicing their spinning. When they said good-bye for the night, Rowan sounded a little sad, but Rebecca knew she was happy and safe and the feeling would soon pass in the fun of her second sleepover night.

When they finished eating, Fionn and Rebecca climbed onto the motorcycle and rode through Dublin, the wet streets glistening in the fading sun and the glow of the streetlights. Fionn came to a stop in front of a row of houses, parked the bike, and tossed Rebecca's backpack over his shoulder. From there, the two of them walked five blocks to a club. Rebecca couldn't understand why Fionn had parked so far away; there was clearly room for his bike in front of the pub. She turned to ask him as they entered the place, but before she could get a word out of her mouth, she was standing in a pressing crowd. People reached over her to shake Fionn's hand, calling his name as they did so.

Sliding past men and women into the darkened interior, Rebecca felt her heart skipping and her chest tightening. As she was a single parent, she didn't go out much and when she did, she mostly went to quiet dinners with colleagues. It had been quite a long time since she had been in a club, and she found the crush of people a bit alarming. Turning around, she tried to move back to the pub door. Fionn grabbed her hand.

"I need to leave," she said quietly.

"What?" Fionn called over the noise.

Rebecca pulled his ear to her mouth. "I don't go out mu—"

"It'll be fine," he replied, his mouth so close to her ear that she could feel his breath. The bartender called Fionn's name and he shook the man's hand at the same time handing him Rebecca's backpack to mind.

"I can't breathe with all these people."

Fionn wrapped his arms around her waist and moved her farther into the club.

"Fionn, I'm serious."

"Almost there," Fionn replied.

Just as Rebecca was going to break free of his grasp and turn around, the crowd broke up. Holding her chest, she peered around. She was standing on a dance floor.

"Dance with me."

"Oh—I—haven't danc—"

"Play a little, Becky," he said. "Try to remember how. I know you used to. Sharon told me."

Fionn pulled her to his chest, swaying slowly back and forth. "I feel your heart pounding," he whispered, moving in time to a gentle fiddle singing in the background.

"It's the crowd."

"You sure?" he asked, pulling away from her a little, gazing down into her eyes.

She nodded.

"We're just dancin' and listenin' to the fiddles."

"We're not really dancing. We're just rocking back and forth," she replied, smiling a little as she looked over to the violins.

"Same thing."

And then they were silent, rocking softly together to the quiet song. When it was done, Fionn gave her a hug and said, "Come on, girl. Let's get you a pint."

At the far end of the bar, they found an empty stool. Rebecca sat down and in seven large gulps slammed down a pint of cider. Another appeared before her.

"Thirsty?" Fionn asked with a laugh, sipping a beer.

"Still a bit anxious, I'm afraid," she replied.

"About what?"

She met his gaze for a moment. "I—I'm not really sure. Maybe it's just that I haven't been out with—I haven't been out in a long time."

"Well, it's just me," Fionn replied. "The man who taught you how to hurdle stone walls like you were born to the island."

Rebecca laughed.

"It's good to hear you laugh."

She shrugged, looking down at her knees. She sat there with Fionn standing by her side, listening to the fiddles. Several people came up throughout the evening, each one introduced to her. But no one stayed to chat. Everyone was listening to the music. Fionn would now and then touch her hand gently or brush the back of her hair. A couple of times, she almost reached out to touch him, but stopped herself. It was then that her attention turned away from the music to focus inside. She wondered what was wrong. If it was Dennis and the past that was the problem, then surely she wouldn't want to be touched, period. Or so she thought. But she was glad when Fionn touched her. Rebecca just couldn't reach out to him.

When the band was finished, Fionn led Rebecca outside. The crowd was just as thick leaving as it had been coming in, but it didn't matter to her anymore. She was warmed by the cider and the music and she was behind Fionn this time. The bartender handed over Rebecca's backpack and they stepped out of the club into the night, holding hands.

"Did you like the band?" Fionn asked.

"I did," Rebecca said quietly, pulling her hand away.

"Are they like the mistle thrush?"

Rebecca thought for a moment, then said, "I don't know. There's no storm."

Fionn shrugged, putting his hands in his pockets as they walked back to the motorcycle. The drizzle fell heavily between them. "Well, here we are," he said finally. The bike's saddle glistened in the streetlight.

"Seat's wet."

"We're not getting on the bike."

"We're not?"

"No. I live here." He pointed to the door behind him.

"I'm not staying with you," Rebecca replied, squinting at him. "I have to get back to Sharon's."

"Come on, Becky," Fionn said, grabbing her around the waist and dancing her to the door.

"I'm not staying with you, Fionn."

"I've had drink. You've had more than me. The roads are wet. It's raining. Peg and John are both probably at the hospital. What's it matter?"

"I—I don't want anything to happen," Rebecca said.

"Like what?" Fionn asked, holding Rebecca in his arms.

Rebecca wouldn't meet his eye.

"Nothing's gonna happen."

"That's what they all say."

"You want something to happen?" Fionn let her go and slid his key into the lock.

"No."

"Then that's what will happen. Come on."

"I'm sleeping on the sofa."

"I don't think that'll be possible," Fionn replied, climbing the stairs as the door shut behind Rebecca.

"Why?"

Rebecca followed him to the second floor, where he unlocked the door to his flat. Stepping into his apartment, she found one room only. In front of her, a great window looked out on the spires of a church in the distance. His bed sat beneath the window. Directly to the right of the door she saw a small sink, a refrigerator, and a two-burner stove, and to the left, his dresser, stereo, and a thousand CDs in a bookcase pushed neatly against the wall.

"No sofa," she noted.

"You think it's small."

"Well . . . " She shrugged.

"No need for anything bigger," Fionn said, putting his keys on the dresser. "It's just me. It also prevents the accumulation of stuff. I move around a lot."

"You do?"

"Aye."

"So do I," Rebecca said.

"I've heard that. You looking for a home, too?"

Rebecca frowned, gazing around the floor. "I'll sleep on the floor."

"You'll sleep with me in the bed. Nothin's gonna happen."

Rebecca sighed. "I need some jammies."

"Jammies?"

"Pajamas. Nightshirt. You know."

Reaching into his top drawer, Fionn pulled out a T-shirt and handed it to her. "The loo is there." He pointed to the door on the far right wall.

Rebecca slipped into the small bathroom and changed into the T-shirt. When she opened the door and stepped back into the room, she caught her breath. There on the bed lay Fionn. He lounged on the pillows with his hands behind his head and his legs crossed, wearing nothing but his boxers and his grin. Rebecca swallowed hard as she stared at him, for his red hair was not only on the top of his head and beard but also upon his chest. He was so beautiful. She looked away to the lamp, which was tilted slightly, creating what appeared to her to be a purposeful effort on his part to place himself in a spotlight. She smiled wryly.

"Am I sleeping on the floor?"

"No. With me, please."

"Well, then, scoot over."

He obeyed. Rebecca walked swiftly to the bed, slipped under the covers, turned off the light, and curled into a tight ball. Her heart raced in her chest. Closing her eyes, she slowed her breath, trying to calm herself.

"Close your eyes," she said.

"How do you know they're open?" Fionn touched her back gently.

"Go to sleep."

"Guess what I'm spelling."

"Fionn, go to sleep."

"Come on, Becky. Play a little. Guess what I'm spelling."

"God," Rebecca breathed nervously. She opened her eyes and concentrated on her back.

"I-P-L-A?"

"Aye."

" 'I'?"

"No, 'A' is correct."

"Y-T-H-E-V-I-O-L-I."

Rebecca bolted up in the bed and flipped on the light. Fionn sat up with her, smiling a great smile.

"What do you mean?"

"I play the violin."

"What's that got to do with anything?"

"You said the man you marry will have red hair and play the Irish fiddle."

"Who said I said that?"

"Sharon."

"I never told Sharon that."

"No. But you told Rowan, who told Sharon—during a particular telephone conversation last year."

Rebecca frowned.

"No one's ever been that specific in asking for me before. And I know it's true, because Rowan asked me about it the very first day you arrived," Fionn said, chuckling.

"I never said that." Rebecca flipped off the light and flopped back down in bed. She had known Rowan had told him she liked the fiddle, but she hadn't realized her daughter had said more. The thought that the conversation had gone halfway around the world to a man with red hair who played the fiddle was embarrassing. She cowered, pulling the covers tighter under her chin.

There was a bounce behind her and Fionn was gone.

"Where are you going?" Rebecca asked.

"To get my fiddle." She could hear a drawer open and, shortly, metal clicking as Fionn opened his violin case. The overhead light popped on. "What do you want to hear?"

"Fionn . . ."

"Come on, Becks."

Rebecca rolled over, ready to deny that she'd ever said she would marry a redheaded, fiddle-playing Irishman, but the words stuck in her throat, for he truly was the most beautiful man she had seen in her entire life. She just stared at him, his fiddle tucked beneath his chin, his red hair gleaming in the light.

"What do you want to hear?" he asked softly.

Rebecca didn't answer. She couldn't. Gently Fionn laid the bow on the strings and from his fiddle poured a song. It was "My Lagan Love," the song he had sung to her as they crossed the ocean in a tiny boat—the tune Rowan played so well on her flute. It hurt so much to watch him, her throat tightening like she was going to cry and a pain crushing her chest like she was suffocating. But she didn't look away. She couldn't. As he finished the song, Fionn sat on the side of the bed and when he was done he laid the violin on the floor and crawled across the covers toward her.

"You play your fiddle for all the women you bring home?" she asked quietly.

"It's never been a prerequisite for lovemaking before," he replied, sliding on top of her.

"Are we lovemaking?"

"Oh, yes. You think I'm beautiful."

"You seem sure about that," Rebecca whispered, touching his beard.

"I have red hair from the top of my head to the tips of my toes and everywhere else in between. I'd be happy to show you."

Rebecca giggled.

CHAPTER 26

Zigzag with Ribbing

Zigzag with Ribbing. 1. A zigzag with ribbing inserted on either the "zig" side or the "zag" side so the pattern looks like waves coming ashore on cliffs. 2. Dreams.

—R. Dirane, *A Binding Love*

That night, the dream came again.

It was cold. The mist hung about the police car's flashing blue and red lights like a shroud. Rebecca spotted Rowan's tiny sweater clinging to the barrier railing off Highway 1 high above the ocean.

"Rebecca," Dennis called to her. "Rebecca, help me."

"Rowan?" Rebecca asked, stepping closer to the sweater. "Where's Rowan?"

"You think you can save her?" Dennis asked with a chuckle. His voice was close behind her. Rebecca spun around, her heart pounding in her chest, but instead of Dennis she saw Sharon standing just six feet away, holding her hand out.

"I've got you now, Becky," she said.

"Rowan?" Rebecca called louder as Sharon wrapped her arms around her waist.

"I won't let go. I've got you now."

Rebecca felt Dennis's hands grab her neck from behind, strangling her.

"Help!" she screamed, but when she turned around, she found nothing, just the night and Rowan's tiny sweater slipping off the railing.

"No!" Rebecca raced to the barrier, but she was too late. The sweater was gone. "Rowan!" she screamed into the black abyss of water below. "Rowan!"

"I've got you, Becky," Sharon called, her voice echoing through the mist.

⁓

"Becky. Becky."

Rebecca's eyes popped open and she found an arm holding her tightly around the waist as her heart pounded like an ocean tide against her ribs. Pale gray light whispered through the window above her head, suggesting that dawn was on its way.

"Let me go," she choked out quietly, shuddering under the weight of Dennis's hold.

"I'm here," Fionn replied softly into her ear.

"Dennis?" she whispered.

"No, Becky. It's me, Fionn."

"Where's Rowan?"

"She's safe. She's with Paddy and Annie—back on the island. Remember?"

"Rowan's safe?"

"Yes, Becky. Everything's fine."

Rebecca buried her face in the pillow. It smelled like Fionn.

"You're shaking. That was a bad dream."

Rebecca didn't answer. She could still feel Dennis's hands around her neck.

"You wanna talk about it?" Fionn whispered as he tucked her closer to him.

"He's here," Rebecca mumbled into the pillow.

"No, he's not. I'm here and I'm not him."

Rebecca closed her eyes tightly as Fionn kissed the back of her head.

"This is too hard. I can't do this," she said.

"Nothing happening, Becky. It's all fine. You can let it go."

"I don't know how."

"Turn over."

"I can't. I can't," she said, trying to pull away.

"Come here." Fionn pulled her back to the bed, gently wrapping his arms around her body as he laid her head upon his red-haired chest.

Rebecca had been pulled to the bed before and held down with harsh, demanding hands. She could still feel those hands about her throat. She was stiff and tight as she pressed her palms to her mouth. But as she lay there, she began to hear a hum in Fionn's chest. It was a low treble note, reverberating through his skin, tickling her cheek. He rubbed her back and her hair, humming "My Lagan Love."

"I'm broken, Fionn. Like that lady in the tub in your painting," she whispered.

"She wasn't broken, Becky. She was troubled."

"I'm troubled, then."

"No. You're a lot of trouble, but not troubled," he said with a chuckle.

Rebecca smiled, looking at his chest rise and fall as he sang, returning to his humming song, which buzzed through her ear. Fionn's hands were kind, brushing the hair from her face. She closed her eyes, feeling his touch—listening to his song.

"You sing well," she said.

"I'm better at the fiddle."

She looked up and found him smiling down at her. She smiled back, lifting her left hand and placing it on his chest, watching her fingers twirl his curly red chest hair.

"Don't you agree?" he asked.

"You play the fiddle beautifully."

"I know. And I have red hair—everywhere."

She chuckled. His laugh rumbled through his chest beneath her head. At that moment, his cell phone buzzed next to the bed. Rebecca closed her eyes, resting on him as he answered the line.

"Hallo? Oh—a C-section last night. Excellent! What is it?"

Rebecca rose up on an elbow.

"A girl! Einin Margaret Fitzpatrick. How's Sharon?"

"Ai-neen Margaret," Rebecca repeated, rolling over and grabbing her T-shirt.

"Sharon's fine. Huh? Why am I repeating everything you say out loud?"

Rebecca spun around and shook her head. Fionn nodded vigorously. Rebecca frowned, shaking her head adamantly.

"I like the sound of my own voice, Peg, my love. Look, I'll go pick up Beee-ckyyy and we'll come down to see wee Einen. Brilliant! Bye."

Rebecca stood, staring down at Fionn, who lay still, watching her.

"Can I take a shower?"

"Can I take one with you?"

"I—I'd like to take it alone," she said, picking up her clothes from the floor and backing into the bathroom.

"That's no fun." Fionn shrugged, climbing out of the bed. "I'll wash you and you wash me."

Rebecca shuffled backward into the bathroom, watching as Fionn walked toward her. The bathroom was so small, they had to scrunch together as he shut the door.

"I don't know how to do this," she said softly.

"There's nothing to do."

Turning the shower on, Fionn brushed Rebecca's clothes from her arms and backed her into the shower. They let the warm water wash over their bodies. Slowly, they began to wash each other. As Rebecca scrubbed Fionn, his red hair darkened in the water.

"I don't know why you put up with me," she said, rinsing his hair. "I'm a lot of trouble."

Fionn laughed. "Because, Becky, my love, from what I've heard for years, you are a tender soul. You're tender with your daughter. You're tender with Sharon, though truly, I don't know why."

Rebecca giggled.

"From what I've seen, you're tender with Maggie, with Rose, with Liz, with my parents. You've helped Jim Fitzgibbon. You like my dog."

Fionn turned the water off and grabbed two towels.

"You seem to be tender with everyone but yourself."

Rebecca looked up into his eyes as she took the towel from him. They were staring right into her and she wanted to look away, frightened of what he might see there, gazing back at him from Thanksgiving night. But if he saw that horrible thing within her, he made no move to look away.

"So, I'm tender with you, as you asked for me precisely, remember? Red hair? Fiddle?"

Rebecca smiled.

Fionn kissed her on the cheek and stepped out of the bathroom.

"I forgot my clothes in the rush to get in the shower with you," he said as he closed the door behind him.

Rebecca dried off and slipped into her clothes. On the other side of the bathroom door she found Fionn standing with a cup of tea in his hand. He gave her the tea and with another peck on her cheek stepped back into the bathroom.

She set her tea down and made the bed. On the nightstand she found the notebook that contained his drawings. She sat down on the pillows and flipped through the pages as she sipped her tea. The drawings Fionn had made from the Book of Kells were copies of the illuminations. Rebecca thought the spiraling, twisting patterns looked like the monks who drew them were celebrating life by dancing in ink. In her studies, she'd found only one reference to the island ganseys being derived from the Book of Kells. It was not so much a question of the origins of the patterns, but rather it was an actual drawing of a man who looked to be wearing an island gansey. She wondered if Fionn would have time to go back to Trinity, for all she had from a day in that library was his drawings. Turning the page, she found his mistle thrush. She touched it as he opened the bathroom door.

"You hungry?" he asked, shaking his curls and pulling a T-shirt over his head.

"A bit."

"We'll pick up somethin' on the way to the hospital."

"Can I keep this, Fionn?"

"It's your notebook, Becky."

"I mean, it has this mistle thrush."

"Ah. That one's for you. It's your Irish."

"My Irish," she repeated, setting the book on the bed and putting her shoes on.

Outside, Fionn and Rebecca found that dawn had brought a clear Dublin sky. Birds, bikes, and cars were all awake, filling Rebecca's ears with the the urban buzz that had gone from her mind on the island. She hadn't missed it. She hung on tightly to Fionn, anxious about riding on a motorcycle through city streets. After they stopped for coffee and croissants, they headed to the hospital, picking up a bouquet of flowers from a street vendor on the way. Together, they walked in, and as they got on the elevator Rebecca let go of Fionn's hand and stared down at her feet.

It had been six years since she had seen Sharon. Their telephone conversations were about work and life—knitting and their daily routines. Now, as the elevator rose, Rebecca felt the weight of that night six years ago pressing down on her shoulders, the entire mass of it heavy and unforgiving. Part of her very much wanted to see Sharon, but part of her very much wanted to get on the motorcycle and go back to the island.

The elevator bell chimed. The door opened and Rebecca didn't move.

"Come on," Fionn said.

"I can't," she whispered. "I haven't seen her since . . ."

"I'll help you," he said. She looked up and found his right hand stretched out to her as he held the flowers in his left. "Everything's fine."

Rebecca reached out and took Fionn's hand. The blood surged into her ears as she walked down the hall. Peg stood at the open door of Sharon's room, holding a small bundle of yellow blankets; Peg had held Rowan just like that six years before.

"Sharon, it's Becky," Peg called into the room.

Rebecca slowed down as she squeezed the pain that was crushing her heart into Fionn's hand. He pulled her forward through the door. Carefully, she gazed over at the bed, and there she saw Sharon. Her black hair was tangled about her shoulders and she looked tired and pale. But her black eyes were as steady and sparkling and sure as when Rebecca had seen them last. Rebecca put her hands over her mouth, muffling the cry that burst from her lips. Six years of tears poured from her eyes, the pain wrenching her heart.

"Come here, Becky," Sharon said, holding her arms out.

Rebecca came around the bed, leaning down and taking Sharon into her arms, crying on her shoulder. Sharon, however, did not shed a tear. Becky knew why. She remembered that Sharon had told her that for those born to the island, some feelings were so deep that weeping or laughing or talking could not express them. Rebecca knew Sharon had hold of those feelings now, and it was to those deep feelings that Rebecca clung as she wept, having been in free fall for six years and only now returning to someone that she knew had enough strength to grab hold of her.

"It's all right, Becky. I've got you. Here, lay down."

Rebecca shook her head, pulling away. "Doesn't your C-section hurt?" she mumbled through her tears.

"I'm fine," Sharon replied, moving over with a wince.

Rebecca didn't want to lie down, but she didn't want Sharon to spend energy pulling her to the bed. And now she remembered why she was here. Reluctantly, she climbed in as she said, "Where's your new baby?"

"Put Einin between us, Mum," Sharon said.

Rebecca stared in wonder as the tiny bundle of yellow blankets was tucked in the nook between her breast and Sharon's. A small tuft of black hair poked out of the swaddle.

"Remember the last time we laid like this?" Sharon asked.

"I don't want to," Rebecca whispered, tears rolling down her cheeks to hit the pillow.

"Remember, Becky."

Rebecca closed her stinging eyes, willing the memory away until Sharon brushed her cheek, as softly as she'd brushed Rowan's the day she was born.

⁓

"It'll have to be something strong and magical," Peg muttered, gazing out the hospital window to the gray-blue sky of a Los Angeles autumn morning.

"I don't have it yet," Rebecca whispered, brushing her baby's fine brown hair with her fingers.

"Okay, we'll come back to the baby's name," the nurse said. "What's the father's name?"

Rebecca looked up at Sharon, who stood next to the bed, looking as weary as Rebecca felt. It had been thirty-eight hours giving birth, but together, they had come through it.

"There is no father," Sharon replied, with a half smile.

"N-no father?" the nurse asked, glancing quickly in Peg's direction.

"Well, one man did apply for the job, but he didn't like Irish fiddles as much as he professed to have done in the beginning," Sharon added.

"I don't know who the father is," Rebecca affirmed. It wasn't really a lie. Technically, she knew Dennis was the man who was there the night her baby was conceived, but who he had become over the two years since they had met, Rebecca really had no idea.

"Fine," the nurse replied, her pen scratching loudly against the paper of the birth certificate in the silence of the room.

"Rowan!" Rebecca exclaimed.

"Rowan?" the nurse asked, looking up.

"Witchwood! Strong and magical, just like you said, Peg. Rowan is witchwood."

"'Tis a good Irish name, as my da would say," Sharon sang, her accent thick and lilting.

Rebecca chuckled, touching Rowan's perfectly round head. "Her name is Rowan Moray," Rebecca said.

"Can we have a moment?" Sharon turned to the nurse and smiled. Nodding, the woman stood, tucked the birth certificate under her arm, and left the room. As the door shut, Sharon sighed. "Everything's fine, Becky."

"Is it? My parents are gone—I have no home, no husband, and now look. No father for Rowan. I have nothing."

"You have your beautiful baby," Peg said.

"You have me," Sharon said.

"You'll go back to Ireland. Just like you did after college."

"You come with me."

"What am I gonna do on the island? I teach university."

"Study the sweaters. You've always wanted to do that."

Rebecca rolled her eyes.

"Find your home. Maybe—maybe your husband and Rowan's father is there."

"Her father is here."

"Where?" Sharon gazed around the room. "Not on that birth certificate. There's nothing holding you here."

"He's filed paternity. They'll test Rowan, and we know the answer to that."

"If we leave n—"

"He's already filed papers, Sharon. Court orders to stay put."

Sharon sighed again.

"I shouldn't have told him we would keep him off the birth certificate," Sharon mumbled, turning to her mother. "My temper. Sorry, Becky."

"It's not your fault," Rebecca said, pulling Rowan's tiny hand from the swaddle. The baby rested without a care in the world, not knowing the storm that raged around her. Rebecca looked up at Sharon and began to cry.

"Can you hold me?" she choked.

Sharon crawled onto the covers. Rowan lay safe and still between them. Sharon brushed the baby's cheek and then rested her arm on Rebecca's waist.

"You're not alone, Rebecca Moray. I have you and I'll not let go."

Rebecca wept, touching Sharon's freckled cheek.

"I'm still holdin' on," Sharon whispered.

Rebecca nodded, pulling the yellow blanket from Einin's face. The baby gazed up sleepily into Rebecca's eyes. "No freckles," she noted.

"Not yet, anyway."

"Green eyes," Fionn said.

Rebecca gazed over her shoulder and found him standing next to her near the bed.

"Just like all Dooleys. Right, John?" Fionn said.

"I'm not getting into this," John said from his quiet corner of the room.

"Her eyes are light, like all babies' eyes, Fionn," Rebecca explained.

"O'Flahertys have the green eyes," Sharon said.

"Don't get into it, Becky," John warned.

"O'Flahertys have the black eyes," Fionn replied.

"Dooleys have the black eyes and dark hair," Sharon said.

"Dooleys have green eyes," Fionn said.

Rebecca peered from Fionn to Sharon. They both had black eyes. She'd noticed but not really realized the connection before. Their eyes—the most trusted eyes in her life—were the same.

"O'Flahertys have hazel eyes and red hair. Everyone knows that. Dooleys have black hair and black eyes," Sharon said.

"You related?" Rebecca asked, gazing from Sharon to Fionn, astonished to find their eyes were exactly the same color and shape.

"It was your grandmother's grandmother who had the black eyes, love, and she was an O'Fla—" Fionn said.

"Your great-great-grandfather married a Dooley and that's where the O'Flahertys got the black eyes," Sharon corrected.

"Are they always like this?" Rebecca asked, rolling over to sit on the edge of the bed and turning to Peg.

"Always," Peg answered. "Fionn came out first. He was quiet until she was born and they've been arguing ever since. No peace on the island until they left."

Rebecca laughed. Einin yawned and gave a little squeak.

"Now look," John said. "You've woken up my daughter with all your bickerin'."

Rebecca lifted Einin, the baby wiggling around in her arms as she stood. Her hair was black and her eyes were light. Her lips were pursed just like a tiny bird beak, and slowly a wrinkle appeared on her brow. With that worried expression, her friend's daughter won Rebecca's heart. She knew this child would always be like a child of her own. "She's beautiful, Sharon."

"Aye."

A tear fell from Rebecca's cheek onto Einin, but it wasn't from pain. It was a tear of wonder. She watched it disappear into the yellow blanket.

"How long has it been since I cried? And now look—I can't stop," she said with a laugh.

Sharon smiled, her eyes shadowy and hollow underneath. The furrow on Einin's brow deepened as her baby-bird mouth formed a frown. Rebecca smiled wider, remembering that face on Rowan. Even as she missed her daughter, she knew she held a daughter of her heart in her arms. Looking up, she found Sharon with her eyes closed. "We should go. You look so tired, Sharon. We'll come back later."

"Aye," Sharon breathed. "I'm in here until tomorrow night. It'd be a great help to me if you'd stay until I got home."

"You bet," Rebecca said. She turned around and found Fionn right behind her.

"You want to hold Einin?" she asked.

Einin opened her mouth and cried.

"Look, Sharon! He has the exact same effect on our daughter as he has on you," John declared. They all laughed as Fionn took the baby.

"Ah, you're just like your mother, aren't ya now? There'll be no peace a'tall. Just temper and storm from now until the end of the end."

"I think she's hungry, Fionn," Rebecca said.

"Aye." Fionn bent over and slipped Einin onto the covers as he kissed Sharon's cheek. "She's a beauty, Sharon."

"Thanks," Sharon said.

"We'll come back later," he said.

Rebecca headed toward the door.

"I'd love you to do that," Sharon said. "Oh, and Becky?"

Rebecca turned around.

"You need the keys to the house?"

"Huh?" Rebecca cocked her head.

"How'd ya get in the house last night? Mum and John were here."

Rebecca's eyes widened, gazing from Sharon to Peg, who was smiling a devious smile. John chuckled as he stood up from his chair. He dug his hand in his pocket and extricated the keys, dangling them gingerly.

"You don't have to answer that one," Fionn said, taking the keys from John and leading Rebecca out the door.

"He has red hair," Sharon yelled through the door as they made their way down the hall.

"Did he play his fiddle?" John asked. Laughter roared out of Sharon's room through the hospital floor. By the grace of God, the elevator door was open.

Fionn and Rebecca spent the next day alternately between the library at Trinity and the hospital and helped Sharon home that night. For two days Rebecca stayed, talking with Sharon about babies, breast-feeding, sleeping, and C-sections.

The next Friday morning, Fionn pulled up to the house to take her back to the island. With tears in her eyes, she climbed onto the back of his motorcycle, sad to be leaving Sharon but at the same time happy to be returning to the island and Rowan. Burying her face in Fionn's back, she let out a sigh of relief, for even though she'd spent three days with Sharon, the subject of Dennis and Thanksgiving night had not been discussed. Her heart, though heavy with the memory it-self, was lighter now for knowing she need no longer be afraid to see Sharon.

CHAPTER 27

Joe's Magic

Joe's Magic [Template 5 Pattern 2 Dye Lot 1] Center Panel—A Celtic Knot/Tree of Life. Within, triple spiral at one-third and two-thirds of the way through the pattern. On each side of center panel, moss stitch to the column of lunettes (note small missed stitch at the top of each lunette, appearing like a whale's spout), followed 24 repeat panel by single braid. Basket stitch used as texture at edge. Color—traditional fisherman's blue. 2. Understanding what cannot be seen.

—R. Dirane, *A Binding Love*

The periwinkle blue sky did not bother Sean today as he made his way into town to shop for dye. His mind was filled with mahogany. It was not a color he knew how to make, nor did he have any dye that would create the particular brown in Rowan's eyes. He smiled, remembering how angry she had been when they had first met. He took great pleasure at having experienced firsthand her righteous eyes close to his nose. Chuckling, he entered the town with Friday's noonday sun just overhead.

The bikes raced by him as he crossed the street. He was very thirsty but had no desire to step into the dark interior of O'Flaherty's Pub. Rounding the corner to Hernon's Shop, he found a line of tourists. Weary from the heat and the walk, he sat down on the edge of the stone flower bed that ran the length of the church.

"Excuse me."

Glancing up, he found two young men on bikes stopped just to his right.

"Aye?" he replied, pulling his hat back from his eyes.

"Can you tell me where the fort is?"

"Down the street, then left at Dooley's, then right and straight south. You'll run into it."

"Thanks." The boys rode off.

"Good afternoon, Sean."

Peering to his left, Sean found Father Michael standing just inside his gate.

"Father."

"Would you like to come in and have some lemonade? Liz made it. It's the best on an early summer's day."

Sean was thirsty. "That would be fine," he replied, extricating himself from the flower bed and making his way to the gate. Inside it, he found rose cuttings and weeds lying about the garden paths. "Cleaning your flower beds?"

"I've a rose show Tuesday and I can't decide which buds to use. Every time I make up my mind which colors would go best with my pots, I go to those bushes. But I can't seem to cut the roses. Instead I just clip stray canes and pull weeds. Sit here." Father Michael pulled out a chair for Sean at the small wrought-iron table.

"What are your pots?"

"Brass," Father Michael replied, stepping up to his kitchen door. "I'll just be a minute."

Sean took off his hat. The table was situated under a tree, providing a bit of shade. Rubbing his head, Sean glanced around the garden. The roses were opening to the sun, smiling warmly in their rainbow of color. The scent came to Sean as whispers on the gentle breeze that blew through the gate. Closing his eyes, he slumped back in his chair, wondering when was the last time he had sat down and done nothing but smelled the roses. It was a long time ago, to be sure. His roses kept dying after Claire left.

"Father?"

Sean opened his eyes. Maggie O'Flaherty stood at the gate, her face drawn.

"Oh," she exclaimed when she spotted Sean in the shade of the tree. "Good afternoon, Sean."

"Good afternoon to you, Maggie," Sean said, standing up.

"What's happening, Maggie?" the priest asked from his kitchen step, holding two glasses of lemonade.

"Have ya seen Rowan and Siobhan?" Maggie asked.

"No," said the priest.

"Are they missing?" Sean asked, taking a step closer to Maggie.

"They told Annie that they were going to listen for fishing secrets. We looked arou—" Maggie began.

"Have ya checked Old Man Dirane's dinghy?" Sean asked with a smile.

"Anne Hernon went to the rocks, but she didn't see them. She had to get to the Fitzgibbons'—"

"What's happening there?" Father Michael asked.

"Mairead's in labor."

"Ah! A baptism! My favorite!"

"Me and Annie need to go help Liz and Rose with the birth. Anne's left Hernon's Shop to go get the Fitzgibbon children. Paddy and Eoman are in Galway and we called to have them bring the doctor. Liz says this will be a fast one for Mairead. I need to find the girls."

"You go," Sean said, touching Maggie on the shoulder. "I'll find the girls."

"Sean?" Maggie inquired, gazing down at the warm hand resting on her shoulder.

"There's only one place to listen for fishing secrets," he said with a smile. "No need to get yourselves all wound up."

Sean walked out of the gate, leaving Father Michael and Maggie behind. He smiled wider as he realized he knew more about what Siobhan and Rowan would do than the rest of the village did. Looking back just before he rounded the corner to the docks, he saw Maggie and the priest watching him, their mouths bobbing up and down like fishing hooks in the waves. He chuckled.

He came round the bend that led to the piers and was promptly engulfed in a stream of tourists flowing toward town from the ferry. Tucking his chin to his chest, the old man waded through the people, fighting like a salmon does when swimming upstream from the ocean. As he approached the corner, he heard a pipe, clear and smooth. It was Rowan. He had been right. As he came around the corner, he skidded to a halt.

In the distance he could see the outline of Old Man Dirane's dinghy on the rocks south of town, just where it was supposed to be. But right in front of him stood six-year-old Joe, playing on his little tin pipe.

"Joe?"

Sean's little boy pulled the pipe out of his mouth and looked up into Sean's face, his eyes wide and frightened.

Somethin's wrong, Da.

"It can't be," Sean whispered, grabbing his chest as his heart palpitated.

It was dark. Autumn had passed like a whisper of wind from the south, taking with it Old Man Dirane and the shanachie's bright laughter. Sean would miss him, to be sure, especially after a winter's day on the water. He looked toward the sea and there he saw Joe, who was but six and not half again as big as the lantern he held in his hand, standing still upon the shore behind their house.

"Da?" the little boy called over his shoulder.

"Aye, son."

"It's dark."

"That it is."

"How will we find our way?"

"When you're as old as me, Joe, you'll not be needing light. You'll know the sea like it was just more of your own soul."

At least, that was as true as Sean could manage. If he had been one to tell his boys all that a man feels at every moment of his life, he would have mentioned that for the last eight days he had been a bit confused out on the water. The shipping lanes of the freighters had changed since the war, and their oil smell was bitter and black upon the waves, masking the scent of sea and land. Residual chaos left over from that conflict, it was. People's lives were still settling, as the war had ended less than a year before. Stories of all the horrors still rolled across the news, creating a deep-seated, lasting fear, now that the world knew what one man could do to another.

Fear was a feeling a fisherman couldn't afford, particularly someone else's fear. Terror brought panic and panic brought chaos and the last thing a fisherman needed was unpredictability. Fish were skittish and simple. To find them, the sea and the weather needed to remain immutable. Sean was a fisherman. He needed no change, especially with winter coming on—especially because he had a family to feed.

"Something's wrong, Da," Joe insisted. "The waves aren't right comin' on the sand."

Sean looked at the surf. He couldn't see anything but darkness.

"It's just the lantern light, son."

"I'm afraid, Da."

"No need to be, boy."

A small breeze brushed Joe's hair and as it passed over to Sean, he could smell his little boy's scent upon it. He could also taste a certain earthy flavor. That did not bode well. Turning north, Sean closed his eyes but found the breeze clear.

"No need to be afraid, Joe," he repeated.

Matthew skipped up behind his father, chewing a bit of fish from breakfast.

"Let's get the curragh out," Sean said.

With his lantern in his small hand, Joe walked toward the boat, which sat upon the sand on its keel, ready to cast off to sea. Sean lifted Joe into the boat as Matthew pushed it into the surf. Taking up the oars, Sean and Matthew rowed out into the darkness.

"Something's wrong, Da."

"What ya talking about there, Joe?" Matthew asked, laying into his oars to keep up with his father. His eight-year-old legs and arms had to go at double speed to do so.

"Leave him, Matthew. It's dark. He's not been out in the dark."

"It's not that, Da."

"Be quiet, boy," Sean ordered.

Pulling on his oars, Sean maneuvered the curragh north and west. The last time the moon was new, mackerel ran from that direction and he had every intention of getting to them before the Dooleys or the Diranes or the O'Flahertys did. He had caught the fish by watching their run change slightly the month before. The rest of the island hadn't seen the shift, but Sean had, and he had returned with a full net when other nets came back empty. He knew they'd be watching him, and when they saw him they'd follow his bobbing light.

"Da!" Joe screamed, standing up in the boat, startling Sean from his thoughts.

"Sit down, Joe!" Matthew yelled.

"Be quiet, the both of you!"

"I hear them!"

"Sit down!"

"Can't you hear them? They're underneath us!"

"Who? What are you talking about?" Sean yelled.

"Wha—" Before his son could finish the word, a giant bump hit the bottom of the boat, raising the curragh clean out of the water and tossing Sean, his boys, and the lantern into the sea.

"Da!" Joe screamed.

"Da!" Matthew yelled.

Sean went under, a slick sensation brushing his fingertips in the blackness. He was up again.

"I've got the curragh!" Matthew shouted. "Where are you, Da?"

"Help!" Joe sputtered, not far from where Sean floated.

"Here, Matthew! I'm here! Hurry!" Sean yelled to his son.

"They're under me!" Joe's voice was shrill with terror.

"Hold on, boy!" Sean called, swimming in Joe's direction. "Where are you?"

Joe was silent.

"Joe!" Matthew called.

"Help!" Joe cried.

Sean swam, the frigid water seeping through his shirt. He felt splashing to his left. Reaching out, he grabbed Joe's hand.

"Da!" the little boy cried, clutching Sean's gansey.

"Matthew? Where are you?"

"Here, Da. Where are you?"

"Here." The wake of the curragh pushed Sean under slightly. He grabbed the side.

"It's right side up," Sean breathed, shoving Joe over the side.

"I have one oar only," Matthew said in the darkness, grabbing Sean's feet, helping pull his father back into his boat.

Sean lay on his back, looking up to the black heaven, silently thanking God. Joe crawled over and lay beside his father. He wept.

"It's all right, now. It's all right," Sean soothed, holding Joe to his chest.

"You hear 'em anymore, Joe?" Matthew asked in the silence of the sea.

"No."

Joe shivered in his father's arms. Sean had to get the boys moving, oars or no, because they were wet and it was cold. Small bodies don't hold on to heat like larger ones, causing sickness to take them, and Sean would never willingly allow the sea or sickness to take his boys from him.

"You're fine, Joe," Sean said, sitting up with his son in his arms.

"I'm afraid."

"You don't hear the whales anymore, do you?"

"No."

"So we're fine. We need to find the oars," Sean ordered, setting Joe on the bench next to him. If luck was with them, the Diranes or Dooleys or O'Flahertys saw the lantern before it hit the water, but Sean wasn't one to believe in luck. He had to make things happen.

"Which direction did you come from, Matthew?"

"I think north, there." Matthew's finger was a silhouette on the eastern sky, the horizon hinting of dawn. He was pointing south.

"That's south."

"South, then. That way."

"You didn't see the oars?"

"Just the one."

"Then we need to find the rest. Joe, you go up front and look at the water before us. Matthew, you look on the sides. No one stand."

Seated at the back of the boat, Sean rowed south with the one oar. If there was to be any fishing today, they'd need the oars. As he rowed, he looked at the back of Joe's head, nothing but a darker shadow in the early-morning darkness. Sean's feel for the sea had been taught to him by his father and his father and his father before him. If Joe could sense a whale in the water from shore, that was nothing Sean had taught him. Perhaps it was just coincidence. But Joe had also heard the whales below the boat. Sean had never known anyone who could do such a thing.

"Go that way, Da," Joe said, pointing east.

"You see the oars?"

"No, but they're that way."

Sean could just barely make out Matthew's eyes as he turned around to look at his father. He raised his own eyebrows and shrugged.

"All right, then." Sean turned the curragh east, and sure enough, the three other oars bobbed on the gentle waves just over the horizon.

"You're good to have around," Matthew noted, pulling an oar out of the sea. "Isn't he, Da?"

Sean nodded.

Joe beamed, shining in the darkness.

⁓

Joe was gone, as was his pipe on the wind. The old man's heart was heavy and hurting. He shuffled down to the rocks and when he came to Old Man Dirane's dinghy, he peered inside and found Siobhan and Rowan curled up together. They had fallen asleep in the warmth of the noonday sun.

Sean stepped into the boat. He sat down on the bench behind them and buried his face in his hands, hiding from his past.

CHAPTER 28

Entwined Zigzags

Entwined Zigzags. 1. Two zigzags knitted together, directly next to each other, in such a way that one is "zigging" down as the other crosses it and "zags" up. Sometimes one zigzag is on top as it crosses and on the next intersection it is on the bottom. 2. The struggle to understand.

—R. Dirane, *A Binding Love*

Fionn called Iollan. They could meet in Galway toward the afternoon. Grateful for his silence concerning Sharon and her red-hair comment days before, Rebecca held on to Fionn, letting his red curls, which peeped out from beneath his helmet, tickle her nose.

The feeling of Einin's little body in her arms was still fresh—a tiny, helpless person with her soft hair and her light eyes, wrapped securely in a blanket. Suddenly her thoughts about the baby were interrupted by a siren screaming to life ahead of the motorcycle. Rebecca closed her eyes, the flash of emergency lights beating against her eyelids.

Kneeling on the glistening asphalt, Rebecca heard small whimpers escaping Rowan's baby-bird lips as flashing red and blue lights pulsed in the fog.

"Becky," Peg's voice called in the distance. "Becky. Look at me."

Peering up through the mist, Rebecca found Peg squatting before her.

"Give Rowan to the paramedic."

Rebecca flicked her eyes in the direction of the young man in uniform, his arms wide to take her baby.

"He's going to take her with him," Rebecca whispered.

"He needs to look at her. We'll go too. Me and you. Give Rowan to the paramedic."

Slowly, Peg reached into Rebecca's arms and extricated the baby from her tight embrace. After putting Rowan into the paramedic's hands, Peg wrapped her arms around Rebecca's waist and pulled her up from the road. They walked together to the ambulance, and as Rebecca climbed inside, she glanced over and saw Sharon speaking to a police officer. Then Sharon turned toward Rebecca, her black eyes flickering in the flashing lights. She stopped talking, standing solid and immobile as a rock while the Pacific crashed far below. Sharon offered a small smile. Rebecca frowned.

In the ambulance Rebecca sat opposite her baby, the tiny body covered by nothing but a diaper. The paramedic ran his hands gently over Rowan's ribs.

"Her hip popped," Rebecca said quietly.

The young man looked up at Rebecca. "Which one?"

"Her right."

He put his stethoscope into his ears as he touched Rowan's hip. She whimpered, her eyes closed and her breathing shallow. The ambulance lurched forward.

"She's cold," Rebecca said. "The sweater saved her." She glanced over at Peg. "It's magic."

"Aye," Peg replied.

⁓

Dublin had been left in the distance when Rebecca finally pulled her face away from Fionn's back and her mind from the past. They rolled into the same small town where they had had lunch six days before. Pulling over, Fionn disengaged the engine.

"I'm hungry," he said.

"I—I want to get back to Rowan," Rebecca said.

"I know, but you need to eat," he said.

"I need to go," she said, tears threatening. As he reached for her, Rebecca stepped back, shaking her head.

Fionn let out a deep sigh. "What's wrong, Becky?"

"I—I just can't."

"Can't what?"

Rebecca looked away from his black gaze up to the clear Irish sky. She saw that it was beautiful, but she couldn't feel it. She felt only the hollow in her heart. "I'm broken, Fionn. I am," she whispered.

"No, you're not. You're hurtin' from somethin' that's past. Gone. You're just hangin' on to it."

"I can't let go."

"Come. You go fetch us lunch. I need to get something."

Rebecca followed him across the street and around the corner, wiping her cheeks as she walked. They stopped at a little shop with a red door. Fionn waved through the window to the woman behind the counter and she waved back, smiling.

"You go in here and get lunch. I'll be back in a few minutes. Pear and Stilton on a pita, please," he said, kissing Rebecca's cheek and trotting away.

A tiny bell rang as Rebecca entered the shop. She stood staring at the woman behind the counter.

"Everything all right there?"

"Yeah, yeah. Uh—two pear and Stiltons on pitas, please?"

"That's a good choice."

Rebecca turned around, gazing at all the Irish keepsakes displayed on the shelves next to the door. There were sweatshirts and four-leaf-clover key fobs. Claddagh picture frames with the Irish Blessing sat beside small statues of Saint Patrick. Next to a pair of praying hands, she found several crosses woven of grass, each six inches in diameter. She touched one to see if was plastic. It wasn't.

"Saint Bridget's cross," the woman behind the counter said.

"Saint Bridget?" Rebecca inquired.

"Aye. Also known as Brigid's cross."

"Breed's cross."

"That's how you say her name in Irish—Brigid."

"Breed. She's not a saint, then?"

"She's the mother of us all. Well, was before Saint Patrick." The woman glanced down as she sliced a pear.

"Before Catholicism," Rebecca said

"Aye. He was the first to try and make us something we're not. He tried to give us just 'the Father, the Son, and the Holy Spirit.' But we knew we had a Mother. Can't take the Mother away. So, we just made her something else so we could keep her and keep him off our backs about it. Did the same with the English. Pretended to be something we're not to get them off our backs till we could figure out how to get them out." She laughed. "We've always known who we are, though."

Rebecca nodded, turning away as a lump grew in her throat. She hadn't cried in so long, and now everything set her off. She took a deep breath of frustration. Glancing up, she found a Saint Bridget's cross over the shop's door.

"Crossroads are never comfortable," the woman said.

"Beg pardon?"

"Crossroads. Being in the center of things—exposed from all sides until you decide what road to take. Very uncomfortable. Good to have one of those with you for protection. Brigid crosses are the crossroads. We put them at our doors and nail them to the roof beams for protection."

"Why the roof beams?"

"Need somethin' up there when there's sparks comin' out your chimney and the roof's nothin' but thatch." She smiled and slid the sandwiches onto the counter.

"Ah! My money's in the bike. I'll be right ba—"

"You don't owe me anything."

"I don't?"

"You're with Fionn."

"He doesn't pay?"

"He usually brings me or my husband or our wee ones things from Dublin. Like bartering."

"I see." Rebecca smiled and picked up the bag from the counter.

"I put some blackberry tarts in there, too. It's not February 1, Brigid's Day, but since we were talking about her I thought I'd give you some of her tarts."

"Blackberry tarts are for Brigid's Day?"

"Blackberry anything is for Brigid. Oh, Saint Bridget. Since we were talkin' about her, good to celebrate her."

"Thanks."

"See ya."

Rebecca looked up and down the street but found no sign of Fionn. She stood there a moment, wondering what could take him so long in such a small town. She decided to try to think like him. It was difficult, but then she chuckled and headed toward the next street. She smiled broadly when she turned the corner and found him sitting on the same grassy spot where they'd eaten their lunch the last time they came this way.

"You were a long time about it," he said.

"I was learning about Brigid."

"Excellent! Have a seat." Fionn patted the grass next to him as Rebecca lowered herself to the ground. Opening the bag, she reached in for a sandwich.

"Here," he said, holding out a small jewelry box.

Rebecca's mouth dropped open.

"Go ahead."

Rebecca shook her head as Fionn took the lunch bag from her lap.

"I—I ca—"

"You need it," he said, eyes steady and sure.

"Need it," she whispered.

Fionn nodded. Slowly, Rebecca took the box. Fionn peered into the lunch bag and pulled out a sandwich. Opening the box, Rebecca found a small gold Saint Bridget's cross. She started to cry. Fionn chuckled.

"Does everything make you cry?" he asked, reaching for the box. He pulled the necklace out and undid the clasp.

"Apparently," she replied hoarsely.

"I thought maybe you could use this. You held on to me so tight I couldn't breathe comin' out of Dublin, I figured you needed something for protection." He placed the cross around her neck. She lifted her hair as he fastened the clasp.

"Now I see you're at the crossroads. So you need this double. You'll need to either let go or not. Can't find home if you're blowin' away." He kissed her neck.

She peered into his black eyes, tears pouring from her own. She didn't want to blow away anymore, but she didn't know how to stop.

"You gotta breathe to stop cryin'. Breathe down here," Fionn said, touching Rebecca's stomach. "Push your stomach out when you take in a breath. My dad says that's the best way to get air. When you row a curragh in a storm, you've got to get a lot of air. Fishermen breathe like that."

Rebecca pushed her stomach out as she breathed in. "That's hard."

"But you can do it."

Rebecca breathed as Fionn gazed back down in the bag. He grinned. "We have blackberry tarts. My favorite."

Fionn hummed as he ate. Rebecca ate a little, but breathed more. Every time she looked at him, she started to cry and she had no idea what the problem was. When she put her unfinished sandwich down, he picked it up and handed it back to her, nodding for her to have more of it. He didn't argue, though, when she said she didn't want her blackberry tart. He ate both of them, and when he stuck the last morsel into his mouth, he stood up, offering his hand, which Rebecca gratefully took, and together they climbed back on the motorcycle. Rebecca leaned into Fionn's back. Left to herself, she found her mind racing back to California and Thanksgiving night and sirens and babies. Now and then, Fionn would lift her palm from his chest and kiss her fingers, bringing her back to Ireland. Then he'd tuck her hand into his jacket pocket and hold it there a while, warming it.

By the time they entered Galway, it was late afternoon. Iollan's boat rested at the docks and when they pulled up to it Rebecca got off the bike. Fionn did not.

"You're not coming back to the island?" she asked.

"I need to get back to work."

She handed him her helmet.

"Almost time to go," Iollan said, grabbing Rebecca's backpack from the bike as he went by.

"Fionn?"

"Yes, Becky."

"Thanks for—the cross."

"You need it."

Rebecca nodded, heading to the boat. She stopped and turned around, swallowing hard.

"Breathe," he said.

She took a deep breath, and then, instead of her feet turning her around to the boat, they walked her back to the bike. She kissed Fionn and hugged him. He hugged her tightly.

"Thanks for holding on to me today," she whispered in his ear.

"I have you," he said in her ear.

Quickly, Rebecca let go and trotted onto the boat. Iollan and his partner pulled in the metal plank from the dock.

"See ya, Fionn."

"See ya, Iollan."

Fionn stared up at Rebecca. He wasn't smiling.

"Bye, Fionn."

"Bye, Becky."

The boat pulled away from the dock and Rebecca waved. Fionn waved back. She stepped over to the bench and sat down. The wind caught her hair and the cry of a gull overhead brought her attention to the sky. Something was wrong—very wrong. She felt a crushing pain in her chest, and clutching her heart, she was up, running to the back of the boat, looking to the shore, and there, still standing on the pier, was Fionn. She waved again. He waved back.

Rebecca watched Fionn grow smaller and smaller, waving now and then. He waved in return until he was nothing but a tiny red reflection in the distance. Rebecca didn't leave the stern, even when Fionn and the mainland disappeared. Her hand pressed the cross to her heart and as the boat headed west, she stared east and wept.

CHAPTER 29

Diamond/Basket Within

Diamond/Basket Within. 1. A diamond pattern with the basket stitch within. 2. A place where intentions are honest, though an injury occurs. 3. An apology. 4. Morahan—a family of the island that usually knits this pattern into their ganseys.

—R. Dirane, *A Binding Love*

The ocean surf rolled into the rocks, but only little rivers of salt water crested into the small tidal pools, flowing over the living creatures that found a home within their secure boundaries. Sean sat for a long while, watching the girls sleep. When he could take his thirst no longer, he reached down and shook Rowan. The little girl rolled over and looked up at him.

"I saw my dad," she said sleepily.

"Did ya now?"

"Aye. He was singing with the mistle thrush." She started to cry.

Sean watched the tears pour from her eyes, the color of her irises turning slightly redder. "I'm sure he's fine," Sean said quietly.

Rowan stood up and crawled onto Sean's lap. He jerked back a little as she wrapped her arms around his neck. He grasped the bench, steadying himself, less from her weight than from his own emotions. No one had held on to him in more than forty years. Carefully, he lifted his left hand and rubbed Rowan's back.

"Shh, there now, girl. Nothin' to worry about. Your da's probably buying you a doll, waiting for you to get back."

"I don't think so," Rowan mumbled in his neck.

"All das miss their wee ones when they're away."

Rowan lifted her head and looked into Sean's face. "You miss your sons?"

Sean swallowed and nodded his head. He changed the subject. "So, you hear from Old Man Dirane?"

"Siobhan did. He said that the south wind is magic. It was a south wind that brought him home to these rocks."

A south wind stole Sean's sons away from him. "Then the south wind is fickle."

"What's 'fickle'?"

"Sometimes your friend and sometimes not. I'm thirsty. You think Siobhan is ready to wake up? I think it's time to go."

Rowan crawled down from his lap. "Wake up, Siobhan," she whispered in her friend's ear.

The little girl yawned, sitting up and blinking in the early-afternoon sun. "I'm hungry," she announced.

"Come on, then."

Together Sean and the girls climbed out of the tattered old boat and headed into town. He wasn't sure where he should go, as the women were all at the Fitzgibbons' and Tom would have quite a menagerie in the back of his pub if Anne Hernon had returned to town with the seven Fitzgibbon children.

Bicycles whizzed down the street as Sean turned the corner. He grabbed Rowan and Siobhan's hands and led them to Father Michael's house. When they stepped through the priest's gate, the father was bent over his raspberry-colored rose.

"You found them," he noted as he stood up.

"Aye," Sean said. "We were wondering if you had something to drink and eat."

"Of course," Father Michael said, setting his pruning shears down in the dirt.

"Sit," Sean said to the girls, motioning to the small wrought-iron table.

The priest climbed his kitchen stairs.

"What are we doing here, Mr. Morahan?" Siobhan asked.

"Resting. Mairead's having her babies."

"Can I hold the baby?" Rowan asked, slumping into the chair opposite him. Her cheeks were pink from the sun.

Sean smiled, glancing around the debris in the garden. "I'm sure Mairead would appreciate any help," he said. "That's how it is on the island—everyone helping everyone else."

He stopped, listening to the words he had just spoken. That was what Claire had always told her boys. It was how she was raised. Sean's father, on the other hand, took care only of his own. Did he ever tell his sons such? He couldn't remember.

"Well, since the father is kind enough to feed us, we should help him clean up his garden," Sean said.

Father Michael returned with a tray of lemonade and sandwiches.

"I only had cheese for sandwiches."

"That'll be fine. The girls and I have decided to help you with your garden. After we eat, we'll clean and you can think about your pots."

"That would be brilliant," the priest said quietly, lifting a glass of lemonade. He held his glass to his open mouth, gaping at Sean.

"Anything wrong there, Father?" Sean asked, picking up his own glass. The lemonade went down his throat.

"No—no, not at all," Father Michael replied.

They ate in silence and when finished, they went to work. As Sean weeded the beds, Rowan and Siobhan swept and cleared the paths. They picked up leaves and canes, tossing them into Father Michael's garden bin as the priest poked around for his best roses.

All the while, Sean watched Rowan as she concentrated on a bug, as she laughed, as she talked, as she wandered around the garden exploring and cleaning. He focused on her eyes. The mahogany color changed as she moved from shade to sun—more brown when her lids slipped over her irises, more red when her eyes were wide-open. As the sun headed west, Sean stood, his back aching from the work.

"I better be headin' home," Sean said to Father Michael. "What shall we do with these wee ones?"

"I'll take them to the pub for supper. Tom should know when Paddy will return."

"Very well," Sean said, lifting his glass to his mouth and swallowing the last of his lemonade. He set the glass back on the table.

"You behave yourselves," Sean said as he walked out the gate.

"Bye, Sean," Rowan said.

"Bye, Mr. Morahan," Siobhan called.

Sean waved over his shoulder and walked south. A group of twenty or more tourists pedaled haphazardly down the road in the direction he was walking, heading straight into another crowd of bicycles coming north.

With a growl, Sean stepped off the road and decided to climb through the center of the island to get home. The sky turned a periwinkle blue as the sun sank in the west, taunting his memory, willing him to think on Matthew and his bike. But Sean had spent the day with Rowan, and her mahogany eyes occupied his mind as he tried to understand how to make the color. Achieving the top of the small hill, Sean headed due south. He came to an abrupt stop when he heard a pipe behind him.

"Joe?" Sean called, spinning around.

Joe wasn't there. Now the song came from the south, behind him again, so he turned back in that direction. It continued playing, and Sean, hoping to see his boy again, ran the crest of the island's center. As he crossed the only road that cut across the island east to west, he felt the wind of passing bicycles on his back and heard several expletives as the cyclists swerved to miss him. But he was not himself and so didn't take the time to answer the tourists in his true Sean Morahan manner. Instead, he simply trotted into the ditch beside the road and climbed the next rocky hill, clambering over a stone wall as if it wasn't even there. His head was filled with Joe's pipe. As he dropped down over the next wall, his foot caught the top and he went tumbling to the ground.

Blinking up into the sky, Sean lay on his back, wondering how long it had been since he had fallen. He rolled over and as he tucked his knees beneath him, he looked to his left. There, among the wildflowers and weeds, was a stone cross standing cold and stiff in the afternoon light.

Hastily, he pulled himself up from the ground. He was in the cemetery.

It had been forty years since he had come to see the dead. The cemetery was located in the middle of the island, and Sean was one who liked to stay close to the sea. Mostly he stayed close to the sea to avoid the cemetery, where memories reached out of the ground to grab his pant legs as he walked by.

When he noticed the Dooleys' plot to the left, he shuffled quickly to the right. He most certainly did not wish to hear from them. The Diranes lay about him, with Old Man Dirane chuckling as Sean skirted past the shanachie's bit of grass.

Been a long time since we've seen you, Sean Morahan, and long since we talked. Sit and I'll tell you a story.

"I don't want to talk to you," Sean whispered, his eyes wide.

Backing away through the cemetery, he tried to determine which direction was the shortest way out. He bumped into a headstone. Peering over his shoulder, he found that he stood on the grave of Old Fionn O'Flaherty. Each generation popped out a Fionn; this one was Sean's father's generation. He was the Fionn who'd been there the day his brothers died. Now he leaned against his cross, spiral and knots carved in the stone creating shadows and movement in the rock.

Sean. It's not your fault.

"Leave me be," Sean said, shrugging the O'Flaherty away, but it was no good. He was standing in the midst of the O'Flahertys, where the grass was kept free of weeds but not wildflowers and the headstones shone brightly in the failing sun.

Come, sit. Have a cup of tea.

They lounged about, some plucking fiddles, some whistling softly on their pipes as answers to the birds above, some singing old Irish tunes to the dipping, swaying wildflowers.

"Leave me alone," Sean growled, skipping quickly backward through the tidy grass. Bloody O'Flahertys.

"Leave me be!" he cried, but as he turned around in the direction he was going, he froze. The weeds here were knee-high and yellow. No wildflowers grew through their tangles. As Sean glanced down, he could make out Emmet's name on the headstone before him. He wanted to look away, but in his peripheral vision he saw the only small patch of green among the Morahans' weeds. He dared not look that way.

"Please," he whispered. "Please, leave me be."

Sean scowled at his brothers—Emmet's and Ronan's graves grew chill with his cold hate. Because of them, his father never forgave him and he was left with no family from his fourteenth year until he married Claire. In the corner of his eye, he caught a movement. He glanced over to Ronan's headstone and there he found a weed waving to him in the breeze. It was mahogany in color and through the dead golden grasses, it smiled up at him.

Sean thought then of Rowan, laughing as she tried to speak Irish. He remembered Matthew and Joe and the day he kissed their heads, telling them they were good boys for saving little Liam. He sighed at the memory of warmth and comfort as his head rested upon Claire's lap. His brothers had never had memories like Sean's, and Sean wondered if they ever would have experienced them even if they had lived,

The little weed waved at him again. He smiled back. Perhaps he didn't hate his brothers. Reticently, he looked to the right, where the only two Morahans with O'Flaherty blood lay resting—his son Matthew and his granddaughter, little Claire. Mary, though not O'Flaherty, rested beside her little girl. The three graves were as green and as nicely kept as all O'Flaherty graves were.

Sean looked back at his brothers. "I'm sorry for you," he murmured to Emmet and Ronan. Sliding past Emmet's headstone, he made his way out of the cemetery. His brothers were notably silent as he passed.

He headed down the hill, seeing only Rowan's eyes—her mahogany sunshine. That was how he experienced it. Walking home, the old man tried to clarify in his mind the color of Rowan's irises. He couldn't quite understand if the brown on the outside made the circle surrounding her pupil reddish in hue or if it was the reddish circle that made her eyes look just like mahogany wood. After he crossed the road, his feet hit the little ribbon of dirt that led to his house. Walking on, he continued to puzzle on the colors in Rowan's eyes, and then he had an epiphany.

"Ha!" he declared to the empty road and the lengthening shadow of the stone wall to the west upon it. "Berries!"

Rowan trees had berries, and they were red as red. He laughed, and as he went to take one more step toward home, a bird fluttered past his chest and landed upon the wall. It was a mistle thrush and it eyed him.

Sean backed away.

Da?

Peering ahead of him, Sean saw Joe standing upon the road, worry creasing the young man's brow.

"Aye, boy?"

Da, the mistle thrush's been singing for seven days now. I've seen gannets diving where there's no boat.

The mistle thrush fluttered its wings as it stood on the stone wall, and then it began to sing.

"I—I've not heard it."

Have you seen the gannets, Da?

"No."

There's a storm comin'.

"There's no scent of earth upon the waves, boy."

I'm afraid, Da.

Sean looked away from his son and the past and gazed out to sea. Silhouetted against the setting sun was a great cloud of birds. He squinted. Were they gull or gannet?

They're gannets, Da.

Sean bolted into motion, bursting through the memory of his dead son, flying down the road as fast as his creaking legs could carry him. As he turned onto the gravel that led to his cottage, his cap flew off his head. He didn't stop to retrieve it. Without taking his eyes off the cloud of birds in the sky, he raced past his house and onto the shore. He flipped his curragh over, pushed it into the surf, and jumped in.

Da, there's a storm coming.

Joe sat on the bench in the boat before the old man.

"I know, son," Sean replied as he laid on the oars.

I'm afraid.

"I know, son," Sean choked. He lost his breath in his push to get to the cloud of birds. He rowed and rowed, and finally he stopped and looked over his shoulder.

The birds were gone. Breathless, he stood, gazing around the purple ocean and the lavender sky for a fluttering of wings. There was none. He closed his eyes, smelling for earth. He smelled only the sea.

"Were they gannets?" he asked, turning back to the bench on which his son was seated.

It was empty.

CHAPTER 30

The Tree of Life

The Tree of Life. 1. This stitch looks like a sparse evergreen branch, with single pine needles emanating out and up. Patterns such as this have been found in even the most ancient of cave paintings throughout Europe. Historically, such paintings have been interpreted to mean arrows or lances for hunting, as the pattern usually appears in the midst of animals. In opposition, some archaeologists have revised their view, concluding instead that ancient humans drew life from both animals and plants. Therefore, each deserved depiction in a sacred space. Such an interpretation is consistent with the ancient memory of the people of the island through their oral history; hence the name of this stitch—the Tree of Life. 2. Traditionally, signifies long-lived parents, strong children, and the continuation of the tribe down through the generations. 3. The tenacity to hang on to life, with its joys, sorrows, celebrations, and trials, because every waking day brings the rapture of walking through Time and Creation.

—R. Dirane, *A Binding Love*

*R*ebecca was happy to be back on the island. She had picked up Rowan from the Blakes' and they all ate dinner together at the pub, talking about Mairead and her babies. As they talked, Annie mentioned that Ina had come to the island to help her daughter and had invited Becky to visit to talk about ganseys and see the babies the next day.

There was a soft wind blowing at their backs when Rebecca and Rowan pedaled to their cottage. Fionn Sr. and Sheila waved from their door as Rebecca bumped off the asphalt onto her gravel drive. Trace lay on the doorstep, waiting. He raced into the house after Rowan and plopped down on the floor at the foot of the bed, almost instantly falling into a sound sleep now that everyone was home.

Rowan talked about roses and Old Man Dirane's dinghy while she got ready for bed. Rebecca told her about Sharon's baby. They also spoke about seeing Mairead's new babies, although Rebecca warned Rowan that she might not be able to go the first day. She could only imagine the crowd that would be in that house tomorrow.

Finally, Rebecca lay with her daughter tucked safely into the crook of her body. She listened to the ocean, Rowan's breath, and Trace's snores, waiting to go to sleep. She was tired inside and out.

But as she lay there, burying her face in her pillow, she had a distinct feeling that something was missing—a foreboding feeling that something was not quite right. It rose as a great pain in her heart, and try as she might she couldn't shake it. Finally she fell into an uneasy sleep, her dreams filled with sweaters and blackberry tarts and mistle thrushes at her window singing "My Lagan Love."

She awoke on Saturday morning feeling as if she hadn't slept at all. She dropped Rowan off at the Blakes' and made her way toward the Fitzgibbon farm, followed closely by the discomfort from the night before. Something wasn't right.

The road rolled beneath her tires as worry rolled around her mind, and it was only when she heard a loud laugh that she looked up from the asphalt. There, up ahead, a large group of tourists had stopped their bicycles in the middle of the road. Rebecca squeezed her brakes hard and came to a breathless halt in the midst of them.

"Sorry," a young woman said, smiling weakly as she moved her bike out of the way.

Rebecca shrugged.

"You from around here?"

"Not exactly," Rebecca replied.

"You know where the fort is?"

"It's straight ahead, a mile or so on."

"Look, he's going out!" a young man declared, bringing his camera to his eye.

Rebecca glanced over and found that this group of tourists was parked in front of Sean's house. They were staring at it.

"What're those little boats called?" someone that Rebecca couldn't see asked.

"It's a funny word," someone else replied.

"Curragh," Rebecca offered as she watched Sean roll his boat over onto its keel. The camera clicked.

A sour taste hit Rebecca's tongue then, and she tried to find the word for it. Being an archaeologist, she had taken several classes in anthropology and often, as she sat in class, watching as images of tribal ceremonies or groups eating dinner before their fires flashed across the sterile white screen, she wondered how it felt to be the object of anthropological interest. What was it like to have strangers come and observe even the most intimate details of your life as a scientific study?

Sean rolled his curragh into the water and slipped into it. The camera clicked again.

Disgust. That was the word for the taste in her mouth. She was not of this island, but somehow she felt a part of it, and though she was sure she didn't like Sean, she was disgusted by some stranger taking a picture of him as a quaint Irishman working his curragh.

"Excuse me," she said to no one in particular. "I'm late."

The tourists moved their bikes off the road and Rebecca pedaled past them. She rode slower now, her mind filled with tourists and cameras and Sean pulling his boat onto the sand. Her wheels bumped off the pavement and onto the dirt and as she crested the hill, she found Jim outside, holding Tadhg, with his clan of children spread out in the front yard of his home, playing baseball.

"How are those bees?" Rebecca asked with a grin, riding past him.

"You're funny," he replied.

She laughed. The front door opened and Rose came out. "Rose? What are you doing here?"

"We came to spin with you. Liz has more wool."

"I'm here to talk to Ina about ganseys," Rebecca said, pulling her camera out of her basket.

"Yes, yes, that, too, and tea and spinning."

Rebecca sighed and slipped past Rose. The front room was clean and all the lampshades were straight. She smiled. Liz came out of the kitchen and reached for her hand. Rebecca tilted her head, a quizzical smile upon her face. As she followed Liz into the kitchen, she found the right side table spread with tea and cakes. Two spinning wheels sat near two chairs on the left, and on that side of the table lay a small sweater. As she stepped closer to the jumper, her throat tightened. She covered her mouth and tried to back away, but Rose wrapped her fragile arms around Rebecca's waist.

"It was Mairead who knitted Rowan's gansey," Rose whispered, repeating the statement Ina had made.

"I have to go," Rebecca said, her cracking voice muffled by her hands.

"Before you go, would you like to hold wee Sinead?" Ina inquired as she poured tea. "Or maybe baby Mark."

"Please, let me go," Rebecca whispered as she stared at the exact same sweater as the one that had fallen from the bridge. She swallowed, fighting back tears.

"I just thought you'd like to know what it means. My husband's mother and her mother and her mother before her knitted this pattern for every child born to these islands. Sharon's one of your best friends and Peg is one of mine. So—Peg and I thought a shanachie gansey should be knitted for Rowan."

Rebecca's body shuddered, the memory of Rowan's little jumper falling into the black waters of the Pacific Ocean pouring across her mind. Rose and Liz pushed her forward to sit next to one of the spinning wheels.

"It's time to spin, Becky," Rose said. "Have a sip of tea and then we'll spin."

"Is it time for tea?" Maggie's voice asked from behind Rebecca.

"Becky's just sitting down for hers," Rose noted as she seated herself in the chair opposite Rebecca.

"I've brought your DVD camera from your bike, Becks. I'll turn it on," Maggie offered.

"Don't," Rebecca begged.

"This isn't about what the gansey means to you, Becky," Liz said. "It's about what it means to all of us. Set the camera up, will you, please, Maggie?"

"The pattern isn't so much its stitches separately but rather what it means all together," Rose explained.

"My husband's family was the shanachies of these islands," Ina began. "The storytellers. The keepers of the old ways—historians. Some's as say these jumper patterns was started in the early 1900s. Some's as say it was the men who knitted. I don't know the truth of that, but what is fact is that this pattern has been around since before we were pushed from our lands to these small spots of bitter stone in the west."

"The Romans?" Liz asked.

"Some's as say it was so far back. When the Celts were pushed off onto the island of Eire itself."

"You getting this, Maggie?" Rose inquired.

"Aye. Camera's running."

"This pattern has only one recognizable stitch. The rest is not as three-dimensional as the modern ganseys we knit. Very flat and simple. See?" Ina pointed to the sweater. Rebecca didn't look.

"This jumper is given to the newborn of these islands. A memory from the past from generations who suffered at the hand of those who would push them off their lands and out of their lives. Romans, Normans, English, Scots. All the same. But we give this to our children and it means that we are here—now. To persist with a tenacious hope, to believe that tomorrow will come. We sing, Becky, like it's the brightest day ever and we live in rapture. Not that new idea of your American countrymen, who say the rapture is the end of the world and in a blink of the eye you'll be off this planet and into the Lord's arms. Young people are so simple. Americans are young. We're old.

"Our rapture is waking every day. To get in your boat and feed your family and see your grandchildren and live lightly so something is left for them. And when you die, there is still tomorrow—there is still the day you fall asleep from this world and awake in another. Rapture, Becky, even in death. Rapture in the bittersweet life of our islands—the rock bringing us hardship and life and love. That is this gansey and it is what my family gives as a memory to each who is born on these islands, from those who's come before."

When Rebecca gazed up at Ina, she couldn't hold back the tears any longer. They burned her cheeks. In her peripheral vision, she could see Maggie leaning closer to the sweater, camera in hand.

"It says all that, does it?" Maggie asked.

The women laughed. So did Rebecca. She wiped her cheeks.

"It's all right now, Becky," Rose whispered, taking Rebecca's hand. "Good to let it go."

"That is what it says. And it is why Mairead came to this island."

"I thought she came 'cause of Jim."

"Who in their right mind would marry Jim?" Mairead asked from behind. Everyone turned around and found her standing in the kitchen door, holding her babies. They all laughed again.

"Here, have some tea," Rose offered as she stood up to help Mairead with the babies. Shakily, Rebecca picked up her own cup.

"Truth to say, I do love him. He's a Dirane after all," Mairead said with a smile as she handed a baby to Rose.

"A deranged Dirane!" Maggie declared.

That brought a great peal of laughter from the older women.

"Maybe, but a Dirane he is. And when Aunt Claire left, there was no one here to knit the ganseys."

"Claire," Rebecca whispered over her tea.

"Here, hold a baby. These warm bundles offer great perspective," Rose said, gently depositing a small purple swaddling and baby in Rebecca's arms. The baby wiggled a bit, but didn't open its eyes.

"Sinead or Mark?" Rebecca asked quietly.

"Mark," Mairead replied.

"He's beautiful, Mairead." Mark had on his shanachie's gansey. Rebecca could see the ancient spirals and knots. They looked very much like Fionn's drawings. She knew only one stitch, though, by name. It was the Tree of Life.

"You know, Sean's quite changed," Maggie said, turning off the camera and setting it down before picking up her tea. "Well, didn't I just go to Father Michael's, looking for Rowan and Siobhan."

"Where was Rowan?" Rebecca asked quickly.

"Ah, safe, Becky. She and Siobhan are always about the town. Anyway, they didn't come when called and so we were out looking for them."

"Why didn't they come when called?" Rebecca asked, wondering why Rowan was running around the town with all the tourists about.

"Becky, let me finish."

"Sorry." Rebecca remembered to breathe and shifted Mark in her arms.

"Siobhan and Rowan and every child in town," Maggie continued, pointedly looking over at Rebecca, "were out and about. It was really warm. So, there I was, poking my head into Father Michael's garden, and who do you think is sitting in the shade there?"

"Sean?" Rose queried in disbelief.

"Aye. And I say I'm looking for Rowan and Siobhan and doesn't Sean just stand up and tell me where they are."

"How does he know?" Rebecca asked.

"He's been spending a lot of time with them at the Blakes', teaching them Irish and tin whistles," Mairead replied.

Rebecca looked up in surprise and met Mairead's steady eyes, but still she frowned.

"He goes to get them, and sure enough, he brings them back to the father's for lunch. He actually sits down with Father Michael and the girls and has lunch."

Awed silence met Maggie's last sentence. Rebecca looked up at the ceiling, wishing she had never gone to Dublin.

"And then, he stays and helps Father Michael clean his garden."

"No!" Liz exclaimed, her eyes wide. "He helped somebody?"

"That he did. With the girls. And then, about suppertime, he takes his leave and Father Michael returns the girls to Paddy at the pub, who told Tom, and Tom, not truly believing it, told me. I had to go ask the father myself."

Ina whistled.

"Aye," Liz said. "Wonder what's happened to move him so."

Rebecca gazed over at Mairead. They stared at each other and said nothing. Holding Mark while he slept, Rebecca silently stewed, angry at Rowan for disobeying her. But the longer she held the baby, the more she realized it was not Rowan's responsibility to keep herself from Sean. Nor was it Mairead's or anyone else's to care for her daughter. It was Rebecca's.

When Liz took Mark, Rebecca finished her tea and then Rose helped her to spin on the wheel. As the women talked of the past and children and the wonder of Sean Morahan, Rebecca quietly spun, watching the chaos of wool wind itself into useful yarn.

When lunchtime came, Rebecca excused herself, saying she had been away from Rowan and wanted to spend some time with her. She stepped onto her bike, waving at Jim and his seven children, still playing baseball, as she headed over the hill. As she hit the asphalt she turned right toward town. But she had no intention of going directly to get Rowan. With the wind blowing in her face, Rebecca pedaled north to Sean Morahan's house.

CHAPTER 31

Chevron with Bobble

Chevron with Bobble. 1. A chevron with a single bobble placed within its angle. 2. A person who brings abrupt change.

—R. Dirane, *A Binding Love*

On Saturday morning Sean opened his eyes. Something was wrong. He lay in his bed, listening to his breath, feeling his heart, slowly moving his arms and legs. Whatever was wrong, it wasn't inside of him, so he rolled over and felt the familiar crackling of his back as his feet hit the cold stone floor.

Sitting there, he listened for sounds of trouble, but there was only the gentle breeze in the thatch and the song of a mistle thrush. He stood up, slid into his pants and dark blue gansey, and headed for his front door. With no shoes on, he stepped outside, closed his eyes, and smelled the wind. Nothing was there but the scent of sea salt and blackberry bushes. Peering into the bushes, he found the mistle thrush, singing away as if it sat in a gale.

"You're daft," he muttered. The bird flew away.

The old man went back inside and put on his socks, shoes, and hat. In the kitchen, he shoved two pieces of bread and a thermos of water into a canvas sack, grabbed his fishing rod, and shuffled out his front door without a cup of tea. He went to his small curragh. He stood still and watched the tide roll in from the horizon, following the waves as they crashed upon the sand and then poured back into the sea.

Nothing. Everything was just as it had been the day before. But something was still not right.

He rolled the curragh over and pushed it into the waves. Slipping over the edge into the boat, the old fisherman grabbed the oars, laying on them, rowing as hard as he could away from shore. As soon as the curragh sat on the ocean, bumping gently on the waves, he stood and faced west. The sun was at his back as he watched the falling and rolling ocean for changes in color and rising mist.

There, far to the south, he found what he was seeking. The old man sat down and rowed in that direction, watching the water next to his curragh as he moved through it. It turned a certain greenish black, and there he stopped. He peered down into the depths of the sea, finding rainbows and, now and then, flickering silver as light pierced the dark water.

He removed his pipe from his sleeve and played. It was a tune beckoning that which lives below to come to that which lives above. Little high notes twittered as if a tiny, tinkling rain tapped the top of the great ocean, rapping gently at an unseen door, to make the occupants inside so curious they would rise to see who it was. They did. They came as a greater flashing of silver below the green-black water.

Sean pulled the pipe from his lips and watched them. For a few minutes, they were confused, for there was nothing new to see; it was just a large black shadow against the bright light above. The glitter of silver slowly dissipated, as it always did, becoming nothing more than rainbows and an occasional flicker of gray light.

Slumping back into the boat, Sean removed his hat and scratched his head. He felt his curragh rise and fall on the waves. The old fisherman had been upon the ocean for many years and had seen it change. The fish were far fewer now than they were forty, fifty years ago, and their patterns of schooling had changed. Sometimes Sean would pull rocks of oil from the sea, the black goo having congealed as it floated in the salt water—little gifts left behind by oil rigs or passing freighters. The sea was a far noisier place than it had been when he was a boy, especially when the shipping lanes moved. All these changes had happened over time—some of them slowly, some of them abruptly. But there was no new change upon the sea that Sean could find this day. He sighed and put his hat back on his head.

"Something is still not right," he whispered to his oars, and grabbing them, he rowed farther west.

He rowed all morning, circumnavigating the island. But he found everything as quiet as a summer's day. He stopped for an hour and ate his bread while he fished for his lunch. Finally, wearily, he rowed his boat home. The shore bumped gently beneath the curragh as he pulled the boat onto the sand. He grabbed the three fish he had caught, laid them on the beach, and rolled the boat over. He scaled and gutted the fish on the sand, leaving the entrails there for the keening seagulls circling above, and made his way into the house.

"Wrong," Sean grumbled, forgetting to cross himself as he shut the door. In the kitchen, he set the kettle on the stove, then pulled three new potatoes from the drawer, washed them, and put them on to boil. By the time the tea water was bubbling, he had his cast-iron pan heated for oil. He poured the water into the teapot, and just as he was about to lay the fish in the pan, there was a knock on the door.

Sean froze. He peered over his shoulder. Whatever was wrong was now knocking on his door, and he had an uneasy feeling that he himself was now the flickering of silver beneath the green-black water, being beckoned to the surface. The knock rolled through his house again. He turned off the stove.

Moving silently through his house, he reached for the curtain of the window. He stopped. Why was he afraid? He was no coward. He let go the curtain, grabbed the doorknob, and flung wide his door. There, standing just off his doorstep, was a young woman. Her hair was dark, her skin darker than an Irishman's, and her eyes were a certain shade of brown. It was her eyes that gave her away, for they were mahogany and Sean was very familiar with that color.

"Sean Morahan?" she inquired.

"Aye."

"My name is Rebecca Moray. I'm Rowan's mother."

"I know who you are."

"Good. Then you'll please tell me what your intentions are with my daughter?"

Sean opened his eyes wider. That was a funny question.

"She's a little young for me, don't you think, Mrs. Moray?" he asked with a friendly smile.

Rowan's mother did not smile back. In fact, a very chilly breeze blew across Sean's face from her direction. "I'm not Mrs. Moray and you know what I mean. I want to know what you want from her."

"I don't want anything from her."

"Then why are you hanging around her?"

"Perhaps—Rowan's mother—she's hanging around me."

"She doesn't need anything from you. It's you making this relationship necessary."

"She needs a father—Rowan's mother. Perhaps that is what she's looking for here." Sean placed his hand flat upon his heart.

"What?"

"She talks about her dad, you know. And a certain bird missing from a bush." Sean chuckled. "She wants to see him. Maybe if you'd take her back home to him, she'd not be wanting to spend so much time with me."

Rebecca stepped onto the doorstep. Sean moved back farther into his house. He peered into those mahogany eyes and felt that chilled breeze flow down his spine.

"I don't need you to tell me what my daughter needs, Mr. Morahan. And not that it is any of your business, but Rowan's father is dead."

Sean's eyes widened again. Rowan hadn't mentioned that. As he rolled his conversations with the little girl through his head, seeking any comment on the death of her father, Rebecca stepped through his door, bringing her face within five inches of his.

He was caught. He couldn't breathe. He couldn't move. And as he looked into the brown depths of this woman's eyes, he felt what he had felt as he sank into the bitter ocean when he had fallen out of the curragh while fishing with his brothers. It was cold and dead and gray, without a tattering of flesh or tiny bone whispering of a life before. It was the nothing at the bottom of the ocean pulling him down—a suffocating darkness.

"I know you," Rowan's mother whispered. "We've met before. Your hair is different, your accent is different and your face is older. But I am very familiar with you. I see that black hole inside of you, Sean Morahan. I know what it is. And I am now asking you respectfully to stay away from my daughter. If you don't, the next time I stand here won't be as pleasant."

Rowan's mother stepped back, holding Sean with her eyes. Then she turned and walked to a bicycle that lay on the dirt behind her.

"Good day to you, Mr. Morahan," she said without looking back. Straddling her bike, Rowan's mother pedaled away.

Sean stood there, immobile, watching her go. He couldn't tell if he was breathing, so he took a great gasp as Rowan's mother reached the road and headed north.

Slowly, purposefully, Sean shut his door. He looked around, sure he had been doing something before he had opened the door, but what it was, he couldn't remember. His legs shook, and stumbling over to the kitchen, he fell into a chair. Propping his elbows on the table, he held his head in his hands, breathing in and out, closing his mind to the dark memory of those mahogany eyes, the depths of the ocean, and the cold breeze on his spine.

"Wrong," said he.

CHAPTER 32

Diamond/Diamond Within

Diamond/Diamond Within. 1. A column of diamonds with another diamond pattern knitted within each one. 2. A secret.

—R. Dirane, *A Binding Love*

*R*ebecca rode home, furious at herself. Here was a man she knew nothing about and he somehow had been talking to Rowan about her little girl's worries. Rowan had mentioned nothing about missing her father to her—ever. Nor had she talked seriously about concerns regarding the mistle thrush. Her questions had just seemed like normal curiosity. Pedaling faster, Rebecca felt her daughter slipping away. Had she experienced much of their time on the island with her? She'd been so busy trying to research the book that she hadn't even taken the time to take Rowan to the fort. Her daughter was all around town, playing with Siobhan, making friends, while Rebecca was— She skidded to a halt.

Rebecca had come to the island to find out how to make a home. She was succeeding. Rowan had a very-best-friend. She had adults she could rely on. Freedom and play and security were here. Even when Sean was about, someone was watching. Rebecca rubbed her face, thinking of Father Michael and the attic.

"Having children is a lesson for the parent," she repeated.

She gazed out toward the water, knowing that at this moment Rowan was probably playing with Siobhan. If Rebecca went to fetch her, Rowan would not be happy.

"God, this is hard." She slid her hands down her face—and found Saint Bridget's cross dangling there.

"Crossroads are uncomfortable," she said, remembering Fionn and blackberry tarts. She smiled.

"Well, where to?" she asked herself. She needed ganseys and stories. She had also promised to clean various pieces of clothing for the father. So she stepped on her pedals and headed toward the church.

When she arrived, she found the priest busily working on flower arrangements, of all things. He stopped, looking at her in that way he had—trying to figure out what she was seeking. Seeing that he was busy, Rebecca simply asked for the wedding dress, the suit, and the gansey, which Father Michael retrieved from his front room and handed to her happily. On her way home, Rebecca did think of Rowan, but only in passing as she tried to determine when to pick her up. She also thought of Sean and when she did, she was very happy that she had gone to see him. Learning to let Rowan be free was one thing. Sean was another.

When Rebecca had returned to the island from Dublin, she'd found it just as Fionn Sr. had said it would be. Everybody was still there, exactly as they had been when she left—as they'd been for hundreds of years. But no one had time to talk to her about ganseys or island history or stories from their past. Mairead had had her babies. Most of the women were taking turns going out to the Fitzgibbon place to help. Everyone else was needed to handle the flood of tourists pouring onto the island, for the height of summer had arisen like a great green tsunami.

Over the next three days, Rebecca didn't think too much about the tourists or Mairead or summer. She was preoccupied with the fact that though everything was just as Fionn Sr. had said it would be, something was changing. Her heart would not stop hurting. But the island was abuzz and she had plenty of work to do, as there were constant requests from the pub for an extra pair of hands since Annie and Maggie had to help at the Fitzgibbons'. So Rebecca helped out at the pub at night, leaving Rowan with Paddy and Siobhan. During the day, she worked on Father Michael's clothing while Siobhan and Rowan played around their cottage. Through it all, she tried to ignore the crushing pain in her heart.

As she worked, she wrote down the story behind Father Michael's grandfather's gansey. Though she was certain he would have allowed her to come back to record him, she decided it was best to simply put down on paper the tale as she had first heard it. The gansey wasn't truly the father's anyway, nor had he made it. She wasn't convinced that she would use the gansey or its story in her book, but she did take still photos of it before cleaning the aging wool.

Days seemed to be easier. Rebecca felt she worked harder at night, for she could swear every human being in Europe was coming to the island for a drink at the pub. She worked to stop the pain, and as no one was about to help her on her project, she did what she could. Pulling her brushes, tweezers, cleaning solutions, and acid-free paper from one of her suitcases, she worked diligently on the wedding dress and the fisherman's suit. Sheila came to her door on Wednesday asking if she could take a turn helping out at Mairead's. Of course she agreed.

With Rowan on her handlebars, Rebecca rode into town. The day was sunny with puffy white clouds sending drifting shadows across the stone walls, passing like gray spirits flying from the light. Rebecca and Rowan laughed as they chased the clouds, screaming as they almost hit the walls when the shadows jumped over the stones.

Riding past the docks, Rebecca found Iollan's boat moored. Her heart rose to her throat as she stopped the bicycle.

"Iollan?" she called.

"Aye? Ah, Becky, good to see ya! Hey, Rowan!"

"Hi, Iollan!" Rowan called. "Is Fionn here?"

Rebecca was wondering the same thing.

"No. Just me. Came to see my sister and her wee ones."

The reflection of the sun on Iollan's cabin windows stung her eyes.

"And I have to make a special delivery. You goin' out to see my sister now?"

"Yeah. Our turn," Rebecca replied.

"Excellent!" Iollan looked at Becky and then he laughed.

"What?" Rebecca asked, not seeing what was so funny.

"Watch the bikes," Iollan said and stepped back into the cabin, chuckling to himself.

"What was so funny, Mama?"

"I don't know, Rowan, but I think he's up to something." Rebecca continued on toward the south, glancing back only once at Iollan's boat.

Arriving at breakfast time, Rowan and Rebecca found Jim in the kitchen with seven children, fifteen eggs, a pound of bacon, a gallon of milk, two loaves of Rose's bread, and honey. Tea was all that was missing, and Rebecca put the kettle on while Jim finished cooking. As she ate with the children Jim went upstairs to have breakfast with his wife.

"So what do you think about the new babies, Ciara?" Rebecca asked one of Mairead's nine-year-old twins.

"They're not like Tadhg," the little girl answered, stuffing a piece of bacon into her mouth.

"I take it that's a good thing?" Rebecca asked with a grin.

"Aye," replied Meara, the other twin, rolling her eyes.

Tadhg, who had been chewing contentedly on a pile of scrambled eggs his father had placed on his high chair tray, let out a shrill scream. At the end of it, he choked and then laughed. The rest of the children laughed with him, which made him scream again.

"None of that, Tadhg, my boy," Jim said as he entered the kitchen. "Use your words."

"Done," Tadhg replied, shaking his hands and spattering scrambled eggs about the kitchen.

"You can go upstairs now, Becky. I'll clean up. And then we're all heading out to the fields," Jim said.

"Rowan, take your plate to the sink," Rebecca said as she picked up her cup and walked to the counter. "We'll clear up, Jim, when we come back down. You go out now with the children."

"Thank you. That'll be fine."

Rebecca and Rowan went up to Mairead's room and knocked gently on the door.

"I'm nothing but a feeding machine," Mairead said by way of an answer. "Come in."

Rebecca stepped though the door. "Can Rowan see?"

"Sure."

Hesitantly, Rowan entered behind her mother. One baby was on the breast; the other lay next to its mother.

"A boy and a girl this time," Rebecca explained to Rowan.

"Aye. That's Sinead there. Would you like to hold her, Rowan?"

Nodding, Rowan sat down on the bed. Rebecca placed the baby in her daughter's cradled arms.

"Need to keep the head up. Sinead may wiggle, but it doesn't mean she wants you to let go. She's just moving. She'll cry if she needs something," Rebecca said.

"What's the other baby's name?" Rowan asked.

"Mark."

Rebecca smiled as she watched Rowan with the baby.

"Sinead has red hair, Mama," Rowan noted.

"Does she?" Rebecca replied. She had held Mark before, but not Sinead, and when she pulled Sinead's baby hat off her head, red hair popped out.

"Mama likes red hair," Rowan said, looking down at Sinead.

"Do ya now?"

Rebecca shrugged, putting Sinead's cap back on.

Mairead laughed.

"You laugh just like your brother," Rowan said.

"Do I?"

"He laughed like that when we rode by his boat this morning," Rebecca said.

"What's 'Sinead' in English?" Rowan asked.

"'Janet' is the best translation. I named her after Fionn's youngest sister, Sinead. She's one of my best friends."

"If you grew up on another island, how did Sinead become one of your best friends?" Rebecca asked. Maggie and Mairead must have met through their mothers, as Ina and Peg were best friends. Sinead was an O'Flaherty, not a Dooley like Peg.

"Sinead and I met at church when I was visiting with my da. I was six, she was four. So long ago, huh? When I left, I felt I had lost my sister. I cried and cried. Then one day, up on the beach rolled a curragh with Sinead inside. She had cried so much that her parents put her in the boat with Tom and Fionn and made them row her over to my home. When Fionn was bigger, it was just him and Sinead. I cried every time they left."

"I'll cry like that when I leave here," Rowan said.

"Will you?" Mairead asked.

"I love Siobhan. She's like *my* sister."

Rebecca thought she should say something, but she had no idea what. "We'll come back. Sharon's here," she offered.

"You promise?" Rowan asked quietly.

"Yes," Rebecca replied, glancing at Mairead, who just smiled.

"This baby smells bad," Rowan muttered.

"Oh, time for a diaper change," Rebecca said, happy to change the subject.

"So Iollan hasn't left yet?" Mairead inquired.

"He looked like he was about to," Rebecca answered, taking Sinead over to the changing table.

"He came by yesterday. I wonder what kept him moored at the dock overnight," Mairead said.

"He said he had a special delivery," Rowan said.

"Oh? He's up to something," Mairead replied.

"What?" Rowan asked.

"I don't know, but I'm sure we'll all find out soon enough," Mairead said.

The rest of the day was spent washing the babies and their clothes, and changing their diapers. Mairead slept when she could, which wasn't often enough, as far as Rebecca was concerned. Having twins meant someone was always hungry.

At three o'clock Rebecca put a roast in the oven. At four she put the kettle on, and at four thirty Annie Blake showed up with pasties, scones, and biscuits. She was followed closely by the entire Fitzgibbon clan.

Scattered about the house, the children had tea while Jim, Annie, and Rebecca discussed what still needed to be done by bedtime. After washing the tea dishes and helping to prepare the family's last meal of the day, Rebecca and Rowan took their leave. The sun was sinking in the west as they climbed on their bike.

"Thanks for your help," Jim said.

"It was nothing," Rebecca answered. "Hop on, Rowan." Rowan crawled up onto the handlebars and they pedaled down the drive.

"See ya tomorrow!" Annie Blake yelled.

Rebecca waved and slipped over the hill. The road north was empty and the shadows lengthened as Rowan and Rebecca rode past Sean's house. Rebecca noted the tiny wisp of smoke curling from the chimney like a thin purple spirit, flittering into nothing on the evening's breeze. She also saw that the beach was empty of Sean's curragh, which made her wonder who was in the house by the fire and where the old man could be as the sky darkened.

Rowan and Rebecca pulled into town, running directly into a traffic jam of bicycles. All were in line at Hernon's Shop, endeavoring to turn their bikes in before climbing onto the last ferry.

"Becky!" Liz called from Rose's doorstep. "See ya tomorrow! I'll bring my cakes!"

Rebecca smiled and shrugged.

"Looking forward to tomorrow!" John Hernon yelled as Rebecca squeezed through the tourists near his shop.

"What's tomorrow?" Rebecca asked under her breath, slowing down and pulling over opposite the shop, the scent of roses from Father Michael's garden heavy on the evening breeze.

"July Fourth?" Rowan answered.

"Rebecca! Can't wait till tomorrow. You want me to bring anything in particular?" Father Michael asked from his gate.

"What do you mean?" Rebecca asked, turning to the priest.

"What?" Father Michael inquired.

"Bring where?"

"To your barbecue."

"What barbecue?"

"The Fourth of July barbecue you're having tomorrow."

"I'm not having a barbecue!" Rebecca exclaimed.

"I have an invitation."

"What invitation?"

Father Michael skipped up the steps to his house and returned holding a small white card. He handed it to Rebecca. There, written in red and blue ink, was an invitation. Rebecca shook her head.

"What's it say, Mama?"

"'You are cordially invited to Rebecca and Rowan's First Ever Fourth of July Barbecue! Chicken, potato salad, and sparklers for everyone! Please bring a dish of your choice. Drinks provided by O'Flaherty's Pub. Party starts at 1 pm sharp and goes till the last sparkler sputters out! Don't miss it!'"

"We having a party, Mama?" Rowan asked excitedly.

"No! Who has these?" Rebecca inquired, holding out the invitation to Father Michael.

"Everyone in town, I think."

"Shit!"

"Mama!"

"Shoot, shoot. What am I going to do?"

"You didn't deliver this?" Father Michael asked.

Rebecca shook her head, and then she froze as she remembered Iollan and his laugh and his special delivery.

"It was Iollan!" she exclaimed.

"Iollan? Why would he——" Father Michael began.

"Fionn."

"Fionn?"

"This is Fionn's doing!" Rebecca snarled.

"Are you sure?" Father Michael asked.

"Rowan, hold on!" Rebecca growled, pulling away from the curb into the river of tourists.

"What should I bring, Rebecca?" Father Michael called after her.

"Your oils and vestments for the last rites, Father," Rebecca yelled over her shoulder. "I'm going to kill that son of a b——"

"Mama!"

"Sorry."

CHAPTER 33

Diamonds with Moss/Bobbles Within and Between

Diamonds with Moss/Bobbles Within and Between. 1. A column of diamonds, forming an "X" where one diamond meets another. Within the four corners of each "X," four bobbles are knitted. Moss stitch textures each diamond's interior. 2. A party.

—R. Dirane, *A Binding Love*

Rebecca heard Paddy Blake call out to her as she rode by, but she didn't stop to hear what he wanted to say. She didn't need to. Racing up the road, she thought of Fionn and his keen interest in her mother's chicken and potato salad. She had been gullible. She hated being gullible.

Skidding off the road, she flew down the gravel drive, sliding to a halt before her house. At her door were brown bags of potatoes and orange bags of onions. Boxes were stacked on top of one another, and in front of it all was a large barbecue grill tied neatly with a red, white, and blue ribbon.

Rebecca stood in the cloud of dust left in the air by her bike as Rowan jumped off the handlebars and raced to the nearest box. From it the little girl extricated a large bottle of Louisiana Hot Sauce.

"I'll kill him."

"Becky?"

Rebecca spun around and found Fionn Sr., Sheila, Maggie, and Peg standing at a safe distance from her. She glared at them.

"Now, Becky, let's not have one of your moments," Peg said.

"What the hell does he think he's doing?" Rebecca asked.

"Mama!"

"Heck, heck," Rebecca hastily corrected herself.

"He does this once in a while," Sheila said.

"Not to me he doesn't!"

"He's got too much time and money on his hands," Sheila explained, stepping past Rebecca and over to the bags of potatoes. "You should have been here when Maggie's oldest was confirmed. Every O'Flaherty in Ireland was invited."

"Aye, and we always have to bring the drink." Maggie sighed.

"We'll help," Peg offered.

"Help? Help? The whole damn town is coming!"

"Ma-*ma*!"

"Darn, darn," Rebecca corrected herself again.

"And our guests."

"The tourists?" Rebecca whispered.

"If he'd have got married and had kids sooner, he wouldn't have money for all this nonsense," Fionn Sr. said, shaking his head at Rebecca as if it was her fault.

Her mouth moved, but nothing came out as she stood in his black gaze. She coughed. "Why are you staring at me?" she asked of Fionn Sr.

"The chicken's at the pub," he replied. "You need to cut it up."

"Will he show up tomorrow?" Rebecca asked Fionn Sr., trying to keep her voice calm.

"Aye. He never misses his mischief."

"Excellent." She smiled for the first time.

"Come, Becky. Rowan can stay with Sheila. We've got chicken to cut up," Fionn Sr. said.

Rebecca climbed in the back of the island's only car, and they drove into town. She followed Fionn Sr. and Peg into the pub's kitchen, and when she opened the door to the large refrigerator, her stomach fell into her shoes. Whole chickens filled the shelves from top to bottom. Before she let out a word, Fionn Sr. plucked a chicken from the refrigerator.

"We'll cut. You make your mother's rub," he said.

"You have the stuff for the rub?" Rebecca asked.

Fionn Sr. pointed to a stack of boxes on the floor near the stove. She sighed heavily and without so much as a break for tea, Fionn Sr., Peg, and Rebecca worked into the early-morning hours preparing the chicken and simmering the barbecue sauce. When she finally arrived home, the sun hinted of a new day on the eastern horizon. She showered, and after drying her hair, she crawled into bed.

"Mama?"

Rebecca opened her eyes.

Rowan stood at the bedside with Trace. "Sheila's at the door."

"I just lay down."

"Mama, Sheila says it's time to get up. It's July Fourth."

Crawling out of bed, Rebecca looked at the white curtains. She heard singing.

"Rowan, is the other little bird back?" She thought she'd ask to see if Rowan would mention her worries.

"Can't see."

Lifting her daughter into her arms, Rebecca stepped to the window and pulled the curtains gently back. There, deep within the bramble, only one bird sat upon the nest.

"No daddy," Rowan said.

"Maybe he's getting food."

"That's what you said last time." Rowan frowned.

"Maybe we just keep catching them when he's gone."

Rowan sighed. "Maybe he's dead."

"Rowan, we don't know that."

"Sheila says it's time to get up," Rowan whispered, squirming out of her mother's arms.

Rebecca watched her daughter run out of the room. After pulling on a pair of pants and a shirt, Rebecca made her way into the kitchen. She found Sheila pouring water into the teakettle, but she did not find Rowan. "Where's Rowan?"

"She went with my Fionn to check the cows. Need me to start the bacon?"

"Nah. I'll do it."

As Rebecca diced and fried the bacon, Sheila washed the potatoes and set them to boil. Together, they chopped green peppers, onions, celery, and dill pickles. There was commotion beyond the front door, but there was no time for Rebecca to see what was happening. She had to make potato salad for hundreds, and she worked silently, with Sheila at her side.

People began to trickle down the gravel drive at noon just as Rebecca finished stirring sour cream and Louisiana Hot Sauce into the bacon, green peppers, onions, celery, and dill pickles. Sheila had peeled and cut into quarters one pot of potatoes and after folding in the sour-cream-and-bacon dressing, she left the kitchen with the first bowl of salad. Rebecca remained behind to fry more bacon. She was cursing Fionn as she sliced through another pickle and Father Michael walked in.

"Good afternoon, Rebecca."

"Yeah, right."

"Happy Fourth of July!" He passed her to fill the kettle with water.

Rebecca glared over her shoulder at the priest. "It was Fionn. Apparently he's done this before. His mother mentioned an incident with one of Maggie's boys."

"Ah, the confirmation. But Maggie's son is Sharon's nephew. How do you know it wasn't Sharon—through Fionn?"

Rebecca paused to rub her back. "I guess I don't really know. You bring your vestments and oils and such?"

Father Michael smiled. Rebecca did not.

"I suppose you'll not be missing your July Fourth in Redding this year so much," the priest said with a chuckle.

Rebecca looked up from the pickle. She hadn't thought of Redding once. "I guess not. I wonder if Rowan is missing it?" She hadn't seen her daughter since she crawled out of bed.

"She was playing with Siobhan as I walked in. They were pretending they were in a curragh, whistling to the fish. She doesn't seem to have any friends in Redding that she's missing too much this July Fourth."

Rebecca cocked her head as she watched Father Michael stir the bacon. "I reckon not."

"So, it's not such a bad thing—to have Fourth of July here, then, is it?"

"It's kind of been a lot of work," Rebecca replied.

"Better to start taking on the traditions of your parents if you're going to keep them, don't you think?"

"Look, Father," Rebecca said, standing up to wash her knife. "Maybe that's true, but I didn't plan for this and this isn't a good time to learn my family's traditions. I'm here on a grant to research a project. I have responsibilities. I have a book to finish. I have commitments and deadlines to meet."

"And this one party will stop you?"

"One party? One party! One party and one road trip and one Dam Mad Situation and three babies and two old women teaching me spinning instead of bellying up to the bar with information. I'm as far along on this project as I was when I stepped off the ferry. What have I got? Two sweaters, your family's clothing—"

"Ah! Have you finished those yet?"

"I just finished. They're on the sofa and you can take them with you. You've got those and I've got nothing." She plopped down in her chair and chopped an onion. She was tired and her back ached.

Father Michael turned the burner off. "You have everything, Rebecca," the priest said quietly over his shoulder. "Everything's right here. What do we do with the bacon?"

"It goes into this bowl with the vegetables after it's drained."

"Then what?"

"Then the sour cream and the Louisiana Hot Sauce."

Father Michael stirred the sour cream, Louisiana Hot Sauce, bacon, onions, peppers, celery, and pickles together while Rebecca peeled and quartered another pot of potatoes. As she folded the dressing into the potatoes, she saw someone enter the kitchen in her peripheral vision. Someone who had red hair and a leather jacket. She ignored him.

"Happy July Fourth, Becky," Fionn whispered into her ear. "Look."

In his left hand, he held half a dozen small American flags. He waved them gingerly. Rebecca picked up the bowl and shrugged past him without a word.

"You think you can handle the salad, Father?" she asked on her way out of the kitchen.

"Aye. If you see Liz, can you ask her if she's brought her tea cakes?" Father Michael asked.

"You bet," Rebecca replied.

She stepped out of the house, and as she rounded the corner she stopped. There, in her side yard, were tables and chairs and people and children running everywhere. There was laughing and music and dancing. She couldn't remember when the last Fourth of July party at home had so many people.

"You throw a wonderful party, Becky," Fionn said over her shoulder.

"Really?" she answered and skipped over to the barbecue, where Eoman stood on duty.

"Well, you see, love," he was saying to a beautiful blond woman, "you celebrate Saint Patrick's Day there, so we of the island thought it only fitting to celebrate your independence here." Eoman winked at Rebecca as she walked by.

Rebecca rolled her eyes at him, thinking perhaps she should warn the blonde about Irish charm. But maybe that was why the woman had come to Ireland in the first place. Why ruin someone's fantasy?

Fionn was at her heels as she set the bowl of potato salad on the nearest table and stuck a spoon into the bowl. He called out to the crowd, "Can I have everyone's attention, please?"

Rebecca spun around and glared at him.

"I would like to propose a toast!" He had to yell to be heard, for there were at least a hundred people gathered, by Rebecca's reckoning, and the ocean called from over the cliff.

Everyone grabbed a glass of what was in front of them. Fionn handed Rebecca a pint of cider freshly poured from the keg to her left.

"To Becky! For her family's barbecue recipes!"

"Yay!" everyone hollered.

"And her independence!"

"To Becky!" the crowd yelled.

Rebecca stared at Fionn, truly believing he must be mad.

"To you, Becky," he said, sipping his beer.

"Are you crazy?" she asked earnestly.

"Come, dance with me." He took her cider from her hand and set it on the table.

"No. You're nothing but trouble," she said, pulling away.

"Just a dance, Becky."

He pulled her into his arms and for the rest of the evening, through dinner, sparklers, and cleanup, there she stayed.

CHAPTER 34

Chevron/Ribbing Within

Chevron/Ribbing Within. 1. A chevron with ribbing knitted within the angle. 2. An abrupt change crashing onto your doorstep unexpectedly.

—R. Dirane, *A Binding Love*

bird was singing when Rebecca climbed out of the shower near noon the next day. Pulling on her shirt and pants, she listened to it and thought of Fionn and his constant humming. As she had danced with Fionn the night before, she'd rested her head on his chest and listened to him hum. And as she did so, a great stillness had come over her. It was more than peace. She'd felt as if she was anchored; she had a place.

Looking at herself now in the mirror, Rebecca felt that a heaviness as deep as the ocean weighed on her. In little more than six weeks, she would return to the States. As sure as Rowan would miss Siobhan, Rebecca would miss Fionn.

"The mistle thrush is singing again," Rowan called from the bedroom. "Maybe it's sad 'cause the daddy is still gone."

"We don't know if it isn't the daddy, Rowan," Rebecca said, turning on her hair dryer. The warm air blew over her face. She saw now that Rowan had made a connection between her father and that bird. Dennis was not a subject Rebecca had ever discussed with her daughter. She had simply said he had passed away. In her mind, Rowan was too young to take on the weight of her father's death, but apparently she was old enough now that not talking about it was creating its own problems.

"Mama, Sheila's here with your Fionn," Rowan yelled over the hair dryer. Rebecca turned it off.

"He's not my Fionn, Row—"

"Why not?" Fionn interrupted as he joined her in the bathroom. Rebecca looked at him in the mirror. She shrugged.

"Here," he said. Turning around, she found he held a gansey in his hand. It had twisted stitches all over it.

"Your mother made that for you," she said.

"How can you tell?" Fionn held the sweater closer to his face, inspecting it. Rebecca snickered.

"Well, it's yours for today," Fionn told her.

"Why?"

"Because you and I and Dad are takin' Ina home. Time to learn to row."

"Row?" Rebecca's eyes widened.

"Aye. Everyone learns to row. No need to worry yourself about Rowan. Mum's taking her and Siobhan to check on the cows. Put this on. Dad's already got Ina on the beach."

With that, Fionn slid the gansey into Rebecca's left hand and shut the door. She stood for a moment in stunned silence and then obediently pulled the gansey over her head. It was big and baggy. She held the ribbed collar to her nose and smiled. It smelled like Fionn. When she stepped out of the bathroom, she found the house empty. Quickly she put on her shoes and walked out the door, finding Sheila, Rowan, and Trace just off the doorstep.

"As clear as any Friday in summer," Sheila said to the sky. "Don't worry about Rowan. We have her."

Rebecca bent down and kissed her daughter's cheek.

"Don't forget to breathe in your tummy, Mama," Rowan instructed. "That's what Old Man Dirane says."

Rebecca gazed inquiringly at Sheila. The woman laughed softly and, taking Rowan by the hand, led the little girl down the gravel drive. Rebecca looked around and found Fionn far to the north, three stone walls ahead of her.

"Wait!" she yelled and hurled herself over the first. By the time she caught up and made her way to the stone steps, she was winded.

"You could have waited, you know," she said, carefully picking her way down to the beach.

"You needed to warm up. Hard work rowing."

When she hit the beach, Rebecca found Ina seated in the curragh with Fionn Sr. standing next to it. The morning sky was powder blue and clear.

"You take this side in the front, Becky," Fionn said, pointing to the left of the curragh. "I'll take the other side and back."

"Now, a wave'll come in and hit the front of the curragh," Fionn Sr. said as he stepped to the boat. "We need two waves close together to get off the beach. The first lifts the keel off the sand. Then you push hard. As it recedes, it helps carry the curragh farther out into the water. Then the first outgoing wave hits the next incoming one. It makes the second one high. When it crashes into the curragh, it lifts the bow. You slide in forward, belly first. You kinda have to roll as you're sliding in so your backside hits the seat there." Fionn Sr. pointed to the front seat of the boat.

"I'm in the front?" Rebecca asked, staring out at the crashing waves. Her heart skipped.

"Aye. Your eyes'll be on Fionn and you'll follow his motion. Okay. Now, see how the oars sit on these pegs?"

Rebecca looked where Fionn Sr. was pointing. She could see that the oars were built to mount onto the sides of the boat.

"When your backside's on the seat, you lift the oars high by pushing down on them. Then watch Fionn. As he drops his to the water, you do the same. Make sure your paddle is at a forty-five-degree angle to the surf when it hits the water."

"Forty-five degrees?"

"Yes. Forty-five degrees."

Rebecca gazed into Fionn Sr.'s face and then down at Ina.

"I think I'd just like to stay home," she said.

Ina laughed. Rebecca smiled.

"This is serious," Fionn said.

"Since when are you serious?" Rebecca guffawed.

"Since I'm the one rowin' with you. You need to row your weight."

"Push the boat, slide in the curragh, oars to forty-five degrees. I'm supposed to be remembering all that while the ocean's surging around me? I'm an archaeologist, not a sailor."

"Learn somethin' useful," Fionn Sr. said, taking Rebecca by the left elbow and facing her to the ocean. With a deep breath, she bent down to grab the boat.

"Look at me," Fionn Sr. said, gripping the sides of the curragh directly across from Rebecca. His right hand was in front of his left, resting on the side of the curragh. Rebecca mimicked his stance.

"No. You're on the other side of the curragh. Your left hand is in front."

Rebecca switched her hands.

"All right there, girl. Now we wait."

Rebecca's heart raced as she watched the surf, rolling the instructions through her head. The backs of her hamstrings pulled, and just when she was about to let go of the curragh to stand up straight and shake them out, Fionn gave a great push forward. Rebecca tripped over her own foot, her left knee hitting the sand, as she clung to the side of the boat. She was dragged forward.

"Get your feet under ya!" Fionn yelled from behind her.

"I a—" The first wave crashed into the boat, hitting her in the face, sending salt water pouring down her throat. She coughed, closing her eyes to keep the sea and sand out of them. The water was at her ankles as she held on to the boat. It slid forward easily.

"Open your eyes and push!" Fionn Sr. hollered.

Rebecca opened her eyes and saw a great wave coming directly at her. She screamed and jumped into the curragh, just where Fionn Sr. was landing. She hit his shoulder with her head.

"Ah!" he yelled over the waves. "No! You slide forward!"

He pushed her that way, her hip hitting the bench as she turned over. She was on her back on the bottom of the curragh, swinging her feet in the air, looking for something to catch them on so she could push herself up onto her bottom. She found something. It was Fionn Sr.'s left ear.

"Ahhh!" he yelled.

"Sorry," she said, pushing her feet against his chest.

"Get off!"

"Grab the oars!" Fionn yelled.

Rebecca turned over on her knees and crawled to her bench. She reached for an oar with each hand as a huge cold wave splashed over the front of the curragh.

"Lift your oars!" Fionn Sr. commanded, holding his left ear with his hand.

Rebecca pushed down. The oars were heavy and she flopped them in the water.

"Lift!" Fionn Sr. repeated.

Gritting her teeth, Rebecca pushed down.

"Lean forward!" Fionn Sr. said.

She obeyed.

"Drop the oars and pull back!"

She did as Fionn Sr. ordered, the oars catching the water. She pulled hard against the ocean.

"Watch Fionn," he said, pointing to his son over his shoulder with his right thumb. His left hand still cupped his ear tenderly.

Fionn lifted his oars. Rebecca followed. Fionn leaned forward, the oars moving backward. Rebecca did the same. As Fionn dropped his oars in the water, so did she, pulling hard against them. Rebecca watched Fionn, repeating his movements, and soon the beach rolled away south. The sound of the surf quieted and she could hear laughter—hysterical laughter. She gazed around Fionn Sr. and found Ina beet red, with tears pouring out of her eyes. Rebecca chuckled.

"Keep your oars even and at forty-five degrees and your eyes on Fionn." Fionn Sr. groaned, removing his hand from his ear.

"Oh, I'm sorry," Rebecca said, reaching forward.

"Keep your hands on the oars and watch Fionn!" he yelled.

"Sorry," she mumbled, shrinking away as she pulled on the oars. "I'm a lot of trouble."

"No more than him," Fionn Sr. said, pointing with his thumb over his shoulder at his son. Rebecca could hear Ina laughing still.

They made their way through the ocean, the breeze blowing on Rebecca's back from the north, cooling her neck in the heat of the gansey. Though the sweater was wet and for a while she was cold, the more she rowed, the warmer she became. Sweat trickled down her back and chest and dripped from her brow, stinging her eyes. Her arms ached, as did her legs, and her breath, shallow in her chest, tightened the muscles between her ribs, causing sharp pain on both sides. She gasped.

"Breathe in your stomach," Fionn Sr. said.

"I'm pulling with my stomach," Rebecca said, clenching her teeth as she pulled the oars.

"Pull with your arms; push with your legs."

"I'm doing that," she growled.

"Breathe here," Fionn Sr. said, poking her diaphragm with his right index finger. "Breathe out as you pull the oars—breathe in as you raise them."

Rebecca tried it, unsuccessfully. She had to keep taking an extra breath. "I need more air," she said.

"Then breathe out all your air as you pull the oars from the water, breathe in and out fast as the oars come around, and take a deep breath as they hit the ocean again. Breathe that all out and start again."

Concentrating, Rebecca did as instructed, pushing her stomach out as she inhaled. It did help the pain in her ribs, but her arms and legs burned.

"We're coming onto the island now. You're gonna let Fionn find the wave and then do what he does. When you can hear the surf about you, pull the oars in, slip out, and grab the sides of the curragh," Fionn Sr. said. "And watch out for my ears."

Rebecca heard Ina chuckle.

In front of her, Rebecca watched Fionn turn around. He offered her a half smile, then looked past her. He lifted his left oar out of the water, pulling shallowly and fast on his right. Rebecca did the same. The curragh turned and now they were heading east. Rebecca looked to the north. The beach where Ina's house was stood waiting, holding out its arms to grab the curragh.

"Why don't we just go in?" Rebecca asked. "The shore's right there."

"Have to find a wave," Fionn Sr. said. "The wrong wave can take you too far to one side or the other. There's rocks below. Tear the curragh up like it was a piece of paper."

"Here we go," Fionn called, lifting his right oar out of the sea and rowing quickly with his left. "Everybody say your prayers."

They all laughed as Rebecca followed Fionn's lead. The curragh turned again, and when it was pointed directly at the shore Fionn pulled on his oars. Rebecca did the same. The boat was picked up on a wave and nearly flew to the shore. Rebecca could see the white cresting of waves about her. Her heart sped up.

"Pull in the oars," Fionn Sr. commanded.

Rebecca lifted them with a grunt and laid them upon the hull. Ina helped set them into place as Fionn Sr. stood.

"Jump out!" he said as he did so. Rebecca rose from her seat and jumped. Her left foot caught the curragh's wooden frame and she hit the surf backward. The boat listed in her direction. Ina screamed.

"Get your foot out of the curragh!" Fionn Sr. yelled.

It was too late. The boat, in full forward motion, turned over and as Rebecca saw its dark shape falling down upon her, she could see Fionn grab Ina. Rebecca was under the water, her body still moving ashore with the curragh. In the confusion of bubbles and sound, she saw the bench she had been sitting on moments before above her head. She grabbed it and pulled her head up into the air pocket underneath the boat.

Her name was called out by alarmed and frightened voices from beyond the darkness of the curragh. She felt the sand beneath her bottom, and the water receded. Letting go of the bench, she lay there, breathing in the tar scent of the boat above her.

"Becky!" Fionn yelled.

The curragh was rolled off of her and she blinked in the bright Irish sun.

"Sweet Jesus, Becky, you all right?" He touched her arms and legs, feeling around her head. Ina and Fionn Sr. appeared in the sky above. Their eyes were wide and worried.

"You guys didn't pray hard enough, I reckon," she sputtered.

Fionn fell back on his bottom, pushing his wet hair out of his face.

"Guess not," Fionn Sr. said.

"I need a beer. A large, black, bitter, nasty pint. Maybe two." She smiled over at Fionn. Pulling herself up to sit, she gazed at the curragh.

"Michael row your boat ashore," she said.

"Alleluia," Fionn finished and they all laughed.

"Let's get you cleaned up," Ina said, helping Rebecca to her feet. "Then you can go to the pub. You'll need to take both Fionns with you. They need a beer, too."

Ina found an old pair of Mairead's jeans and a T-shirt for Rebecca to put on. They put her clothes in the dryer and hung the gansey by the fire. They sipped tea, laughing often as they re-ran the trip over to the island. When her clothes had dried, Rebecca slipped back into her pants, shirt, and Fionn's gansey, then followed Fionn Sr., Fionn, and Ina out the door. Ina shut it behind her as the sun sank in the west. They would have a quick supper and a pint before returning to Sharon's island. With very little discussion, Fionn Sr. and his son decided they would row back.

As she walked to town, Rebecca could feel nearly every muscle in her body hurting. What was a dull ache today would be throbbing pain tomorrow, for sure. Places hurt deep inside her where she hadn't known there were muscles. She concentrated on those places, wondering if it was truly her muscles or if it was the thought of leaving the island—and Fionn.

Five birds flew east overhead. Fionn Sr. stopped to watch them. Ina, Fionn, and Rebecca halted as well just outside of the small town that sat on the southeast corner of Ina's island.

"Now where are they goin'?" Fionn Sr. asked.

"Who?" Rebecca inquired, following his gaze.

"Ah, those birds have a little rock out there," Fionn Sr. said, pointing to the northwest. "They should be headin' the other way this time of day."

At that moment the wind picked up and turned itself around with a sudden gust, coming in from the south. It clapped as it did so, like a master calling a servant. At the same moment the horizon turned orange.

"Queersome," Ina breathed.

"You smell anything, Dad?" Fionn asked, taking Rebecca's hand.

"No. You?"

"No."

"Huh," Fionn Sr. said. "Come on. Let's eat."

They headed into town. Rebecca held on to Fionn's hand and when she looked over her shoulder to the west, the orange grew deeper, as if a fire burned over the horizon.

"Rowan?" Rebecca whispered, squeezing Fionn's hand.

CHAPTER 35

Zigzag Furrows

Zigzag Furrows. 1. A pattern created by twisting stitches. The deep furrows appear similar to diagonal ribbing, but are formed as multiple zigzags, looking like waves upon the sea. 2. A realization.

—R. Dirane, *A Binding Love*

Sean had received an invitation on Wednesday to a certain Fourth of July party at the old O'Flaherty place on Thursday. Though he thought it would be a very good thing to see Rowan again, he decided not to attend. Rowan's mother was the hostess, and if there was one person Sean did not wish to see, it was Rowan's mother. Ever since she had stood at his door like the cold, dead bottom of the ocean, something very deep had been wrong. To punctuate just how wrong something was, that little mistle thrush had been singing for seven days and Joe was hovering even now in the doorway. Sean hadn't crawled out of bed all day because of Joe. Rolling over in his covers, Sean peered up as the westward sun of Friday afternoon poured through the small window above his bed.

Eight days the mistle thrush has sung, Da.

"It's only been seven, boy."

Eight days and gannets are upon the waves.

"There's no gannets, I tell you."

There had been no gannets, though Sean had rowed for seven

days, encompassing the island with each outing. No gannets did he find, and the mistle thrush had been singing for only seven days. Sean looked up at his window. On the glass the sun reflected like a golden halo. Sean wondered at the color, smiling as he remembered Brendan's first step.

Suddenly, he bolted up in his bed. He looked to the door. Joe was gone. The bird had sung on the fence as Sean headed down from the cemetery last week Friday. On Saturday it sang in his blackberry bush, and he had heard it every day since. It had not been seven days the mistle thrush had sung. It was eight—eight days of the mistle thrush. Sean heard a whistle blowing in from the ocean.

Flying from his covers, Sean raced through his house and out the door in his boxers. As he rounded the corner of his cottage, he stopped short. A cloud of birds gathered close in, dipping and diving, this way and that. He could not see them clearly. His heart beat faster as he tumbled down the sandy hill and onto the beach. Not more than two hundred meters offshore, gannets gathered like a swarm of gnats, thickly flowing en masse.

"Paddy!" Sean yelled and without a backward glance, he sped back to his house. He jumped into his clothes, tripping into his shoes as he barreled out the door again, leaving his house wide-open to the wind.

The sky was as clear as any summer's late afternoon and the gentle breeze at his back smelled of nothing but seaweed and salt. But Sean knew. He remembered, and didn't Paddy tell him on Wednesday that he'd be taking an engine part to Iollan today after market in Galway? If Sean measured the time correctly, Paddy would be heading out to the little island north at this moment. The young man's boat was always having trouble.

"Bloody Iollan!" Sean screamed, but all that came out was a cough, winded as he was from running. His spine crackled in the effort and his knees burned, but he could see the sun lowering to the horizon. He had to get to Paddy.

From behind, Sean heard the distinct whizzing of bicycles speeding toward him. He jumped off the road, stumbling into the ditch as a group of cyclists flew past. They were late. The last ferry off the island would leave in—

"Oh God!" Sean called, his old body wanting desperately to stop, to breathe, to walk.

"No!" he yelled and pushed himself harder. If he were one to weep, he would be doing so now, but the sheer terror of a gnawing guilt drove him on. Grabbing his chest, he tripped into town and hobbled as fast as he could to the piers. Rounding the corner, he could see Paddy and Eoman just pulling out of their slip.

"Stop!" Sean shouted. "Paddy!"

Dodging a woman pushing her child in a stroller toward the ferry, he raced down the wooden pier, the waves gentle but already high on the pylons. He flung his arms about wildly. He couldn't breathe. "Paddy!" he choked.

Eoman called to Paddy.

"Stop!" the old man cried.

Paddy turned the engine off. "Morahan?" he called from his deck as Eoman slid past his partner to take the wheel.

"Don't go!" Sean yelled.

Paddy scratched his head, glancing up into the clear sky.

"Stay out of the water!" Sean called through his cupped hands. "She'll turn on you!" Sean stared into Paddy's eyes. His old body began to shiver it winter and all he had on was his little woolen coat. "Please, Paddy," Sean mouthed, shaking his head. "Please, get off the water."

"Eoman! Back up!" Paddy hollered over his shoulder. "We'll not be goin' out."

Sean covered his face in his hands. He stood still, waiting. The sputtering of Paddy's boat grew louder.

"Need a pint there, Morahan?" Paddy asked warmly once he was back on the dock.

Sean looked at the sky. "Aye. That I do."

"Why don't you head over to O'Flaherty's while Eoman and I set-tle the boat. We'll buy you one."

"You'll need to tell that captain not to take the ferry out," Sean said, pointing his shaking finger at the line of tourists waiting to climb aboard.

"You think he'll not make it to the mainland?"

"There's time yet, but not that much time."

"All right, then. I'll tell him."

Sean nodded and shuffled down the pier, his legs as heavy as if he'd just pulled himself from a winter's sea. He needed a drink to dull the searing pain in his back. His spine usually hurt, but the great race to the docks must have shaken the shrapnel near his spine, causing a burning sensation to slide from the center of his back up to his neck. Such pain didn't happen to him often, but when it did he couldn't ignore it. Holding his side with his left hand, Sean opened the door to O'Flaherty's. He looked about, startled to find his past staring back at him.

Dirane and Dooley and three of their boys sat at tables, drinking. Young Fionn stood at the bar, pouring a pint. Sean glanced around, looking for his sons.

"Evenin', Morahan," Fionn greeted him. "Comin' in for a pint?"

"Have ya seen my boys?" he asked, his back burning from bend-ing over the engine the last hour.

"They don't come in here often, Sean," Dirane replied. "You don't let them."

Dooley and his boys snickered.

"True enough," Sean said, shaking his head. "But I sent them here for supper."

"Ah. They'll be headin' out, then? Got the engine fixed?" Dooley inquired.

"Aye." Sean nodded.

"Is it true what Joe says?" the older Dirane boy asked.

"What's that?"

"A storm is comin'."

"I don't feel a storm," Dooley remarked.

"Neither do I," Sean replied. "Maybe he just doesn't want to go out tonight."

Dirane laughed. His oldest did not. Instead he said, "Joe says gannets is on the waves where there's no boat and the mistle thrush's been singing for eight days."

"Aye, so he's told me, too. But I haven't seen or heard."

"Neither have I," Dooley agreed.

"Mackerel to the north, Morahan," Dirane said. "That'd be a good direction to head out."

"I'll tell 'em," Sean replied, nodding as he turned around.

"Will ya have a pint, Sean?"

He turned to look at Young Fionn behind the bar.

⌒

"Will ya have a pint, Sean?"

The old man blinked. It wasn't Young Fionn behind the bar. It was his son Tom, and Sean was standing in the door, blocking the entrance.

"Oh," he replied, stepping through the door toward the fire. "Aye, a pint."

"Good, good," Tom said.

Sean creaked slowly into the chair nearest the hearth.

Tom set the glass of beer on the table next to the old man. "You all right there, Sean?"

"Aye," Sean murmured, wiping his brow with his hand.

He sipped his beer, staring into the flames. There was a certain orange color just above the yellow. It flickered like the sun coming through the window of his house—the sunset as orange as a fire's flame flickering through the window, casting a heated glow on Joe's face.

"We shouldn't go out, Da," Joe said. "Somethin's very wrong."

"I'll tell you what's wrong, boy. Not doin' as I say!"

"Da," Matthew said, "Joe knows things, Da. He says not to go."

"Sean," Claire pleaded.

"Shut up, Claire."

"You've got a wife and a wee one to feed," Sean reminded Matthew.

"I'm all right," Mary interrupted.

"Shut up," Sean replied, glaring at her. "What kind of man lets his wife who carries his child go hungry?"

"We've enough, Sean," Claire whispered.

Sean walked over to his wife, pulling his lips tightly across his teeth.

Liam slid between his mother and his father.

"No, Da," Brendan begged.

Sean backhanded Liam, sending the young man flying into the spinning wheel. It toppled beneath him.

"Sean!" Claire cried.

Sean grabbed her arm tightly, pulling her to face him. "Don't you cross me, Claire. This isn't your decision. Now get in there and make supper." He pushed his wife toward the kitchen.

"You too," he seethed at Mary, who was shaking, tears streaming from her eyes. She looked over at Matthew.

"Go, love," Matthew said quietly. She obeyed.

"You think you can read a sky better than me, boy?" Sean asked, fixing Joe with burning eyes.

"Da, I don't do anything better than you. I see things differently than you."

"Can you read a sky better than me or no?" Sean yelled.

"Sean?"

Glancing up from the flame, Sean found Eoman and Paddy pulling up chairs beside him.

"You're dry there. Eoman, go get three pints," Paddy said.

"Boat's secure?" Sean asked.

"Aye, and we called Iollan to tell his mates to stay out of the water, too."

"Good, good. And the ferry?"

"Told the captain, too. He's calling in to Doolin."

Sean nodded. Eoman came back with three beers. A gust of wind hit the window like it was a fast-moving bird, causing Sean to jump in his seat.

"Maybe I should go home," he muttered, looking out the window to a flaming orange sky.

"Have a pint, Sean, then come home with me for some supper," Paddy said, patting the old man on the shoulder.

"Never seen you so upset over the weather there, Morahan," Eoman said as he sipped his ale.

"I remember, Eoman O'Connelly," Sean whispered, his eyes fixed on the sky. "I remember." He lifted his beer.

The sky turned red.

CHAPTER 36

Chevron/Basket Within

Chevron/Basket Within. 1. A chevron with the basket stitch knitted within its angle. 2. A gale.

—R. Dirane, *A Binding Love*

The wind tossed Sean and Paddy down the street like they were nothing more than rose petals tumbling down Father Michael's garden path. Paddy had to grab Sean by the back of the old man's woolen coat to keep him from blowing past the house.

"The sky's clear!" Paddy yelled.

"Not for long!" Sean answered in kind, wishing he had gone home earlier.

"Come on," Paddy grunted as he pushed the old man through the front door of his house.

"Paddy!" Annie exclaimed, racing across the front room.

"What is it, love?" Paddy asked, pushing the door closed by laying his full weight upon it.

"I can't find Siobhan and Rowan. I've called and called. They're not at the pub. They're not on the rocks."

"Did ya check Old Man Dirane's dinghy?" Sean asked, his chest tightening.

"I called on the rocks. They would have heard," Annie said.

"Not if they fell asleep. They fell asleep in it a week ago," Sean said, heading to the door. As he turned the knob, the door blew out of his hand. The world was red-orange, as though a great conflagration seared heaven itself, and Joe stood beneath it on the path in front of Sean, his eyes wide with terror.

Something's wrong, Da.

"I know, Joe," Sean replied.

"What's that you say, Sean?" Paddy asked, coming behind him.

Sean blinked. Joe was gone. "Nothin'. We need to go."

Sean, Paddy, and Annie clung to one another as they cleared the gate. The sky opened up and a great wash of water hit the asphalt with a crash. Sean squinted through the gusting rain, watching several tourists rolling from the ocean pier toward the pub like sea foam.

"That sky was clear," Paddy yelled through the rain.

"It's not now," Sean replied. Sweat trickled down the old man's neck.

"Hope that ferry's all right," Annie called.

"Ferry didn't leave," Paddy told her.

Sean didn't care about the ferry. He didn't care about the tourists. He cared about Rowan—Rowan and her best friend, Siobhan. Pushing past the pub, he willed the little girls to come up from the rocks. Any moment, they'd tumble together hand in hand around the corner from the pier.

"Bloody south wind," Sean muttered.

Crossing the street at the church, Paddy and Annie held each other as Sean grabbed the cold brown stone. He crawled down the wall of the church to the corner. He wanted to see Rowan. He needed her to drag Siobhan to him. His heart raced as he got to the corner, the full force of the south wind slapping his face with rain as he came about.

"Can you see the rocks?" Annie called.

Sean couldn't see anything through the rain.

"Siobhan!" Paddy yelled, but his words flew backward.

Clutching the ferry building, Sean pulled himself south, toward the rocks. The rain pelted his face, stinging his eyes. Still he could see through to the rocks, and what he saw made him gasp. The water was over the stones, crashing up onto the road itself, forming little tidal pools in the ditches on either side. The boat was gone. The waves must have risen and swept it away.

"Jesus Christ!" Sean yelled.

"It's not there!" Annie gasped.

"Maybe they weren't in it," Paddy said. "We haven't searched everywhere."

Sean spun on his heel and grabbed Paddy by the collar. His body and soul were on fire like the Irish heaven above.

"Find Eoman!" he screamed, shaking the fisherman in fury. Suddenly he stopped. He heard a pipe on the wind. It came in from the north. He turned back to Paddy. "They're in the dinghy! Call Iollan! Get your bloody boats out on that water! North!"

Sean flung Paddy away and flew back up toward town. He needed his boat. An engine would cover up the whistle tune, and he needed to hear it—to find Rowan and Siobhan. The wind was at his back until he turned the corner, racing toward O'Flaherty's Pub. When he came to the corner of the church, he headed south, the wind shoving him north. Slowly, he passed Father Michael's gate. John Hernon was pulling in his bikes.

"Get out of the wind!" Hernon yelled at Sean.

"Sean!" Father Michael stood at his gate. "Get inside!"

"That son of a bitch stole my sons!" Sean's words spat in the priest's face. He spun away, fury and hatred pushing him forward. Joe's pipe played loudly in the screaming wind. "God'll not take my girls!"

⌒

"The storm's close, Da," Joe whispered. His boy had just turned fifteen and sat beside the fire across from Brendan, who was but four. He was teaching how to blow the tin whistle. Sean relaxed, his eyes closed, warming his feet near the hearth.

"Play your pipe, boy. Don't think on it," he said to Joe.

"I can't hear my pipe over the thunder."

"Your pipe sings whether you hear it or not."

"I want Ma."

Sean opened his eyes. There sat Joe, holding his pipe in his hands, shaking as the thunder boomed again.

"You a man or a baby?"

Joe's lip quivered.

"A man doesn't need his ma. He has himself."

A flash of lightning cracked the darkness of the dimly lit room. Matthew and Liam, whose little toes wiggled closest to the small fire, sat across from Sean, Joe, and Brendan. Their eyes were wide with fear. The thunder roared overhead.

"I want my ma," Joe repeated.

"You'll never be a man."

"I don't want to be a man!"

"No son of mine ever says that!" Sean yelled, grabbing Joe's pipe and breaking it over his leg.

"Play your pipe, Joe. I'm coming."

Sean struggled down the south road. If his body hurt from the run earlier, he didn't notice. The gale was all-encompassing—in his ears, his eyes, his soul. He had no idea how long it had taken him, but there was still light behind the burning red sky when he stepped onto his gravel walkway. Soon, though, it would be all blackness. As he pushed through the wind, he heard a mistle thrush. It sang sweetly in the banshee's wail. Sean went into his house, lit a lantern, and headed out to the beach. In the gale, the sand flew in the air and scoured the old man's face and hands. Sean shrank away from it as he untied the mooring ropes. The wind picked up the curragh and tossed it on its keel.

He looked out to the water, crashing upon his beach. The wind was helping him; he knew the sea would, too, for in his mind he knew that both the sea and the wind remembered forty years ago. They wanted him to come out. They'd waited forty years to settle with him.

"Not until I get my girls," Sean hissed. If the wind blew in fury, Sean had his own searing tempest. At this moment he could match anything nature could throw at him. With his entire body, Sean leaned into his curragh, pushing it into the boiling sea, which took him, as he'd suspected it would. Sliding onto his seat, he headed out. He didn't go west or south. The girls in that dinghy would be north, near the kelp beds, toward O'Flahertys' beach. He could hear Joe's pipe calling to him. Joe knew things. Joe could tell when something was wrong.

⁓

"Da, I don't do anything better than you. I see things differently than ya," Joe said.

"Can you read a sky better than me or no?" Sean yelled.

"Da, I'm not sayin' I can. I'm sayin' something's wrong."

"You're a coward, Joe!" Sean declared. "All of you are! I read the sky! I know best! If you'll not get in that boat, then I'll take her out."

"No, Da," Matthew said, stepping in front of his father. "The engine's not running right."

"How do you know? I fixed it while you ran home to your ma."

"You couldn't have. It needs a new—"

"First the weather, now the engine. Get out of my way, boy! Someone has to be a man for this family!"

Sean pushed Matthew to the side and reached for the door.

"We'll go, Da," Matthew whispered.

"What's that?" Sean asked with a sneer.

"We'll go," his son repeated.

"Matthew?" Mary called from the kitchen.

"Shut up, girl! Not afraid of the storm, are ya, Matthew? Need your ma?" Sean mocked.

"I said we'll go, Da," Matthew replied, and he opened the door and stepped out. The sky had turned orange.

Liam and Brendan grabbed their shoes and followed their oldest brother. Sean glanced over and found Joe staring angrily at him.

313

"Staying in with the women?" Sean asked.

Joe said nothing, brushing past his father. "I love you, Ma," he called as he reached the door.

"I can read a sky better than you, boy," Sean snarled, goading him.

Joe stopped at the door and slowly turned around. "Matthew knows engines, Da, and I know the water. Will you never let go of us to see that we have become the men you raised us to be?" He turned away and went out the door.

And then he was gone.

Sean pulled on the oars, the rain pouring from the red sky above him. Joe's whistle was clear, singing to the depths below. It was telling all those who lived there that there was a roiling and a spinning above. Best to stay below where it was cold and safe—still and peaceful. For years Sean had thought of the frozen darkness of the sea. He was a fisherman. It was never far from his mind. But it was something to struggle against; it was the great, grasping selfishness of God, created to tear a husband from his wife, a father from his sons.

Suddenly he stopped. The pipe had changed. It wasn't clear. It wasn't peaceful. The whistle blew "My Lagan Love." And it wasn't one pipe. It was two and they were shrill and terrified.

Sean laid on his oars, and as he did so the sea lifted his curragh up and dropped it heavily into the waves, angry at his defiance. He pulled and fought the raging water.

"You son of a bitch!" Sean screamed to God. "Not my girls!"

The sky writhed angrily above him.

"Keep playin', Rowan! I'm comin'!"

CHAPTER 37

Diamond/Zigzag Entwined

Diamond/Zigzag Entwined. 1. A diamond pattern with a zigzag entwined. The zigzag spirals around one side of the diamond, then follows the angle of the diamond so the two patterns
together appear to be double zigzags as they cross where the diamonds intersect one another. On the opposing side of the diamond, the zigzag spirals the edge of the diamond again and
follows the pattern as before, like a double zigzag. 2. Guilt.

—R. Dirane, *A Binding Love*

*R*ebecca had downed one pint, sending a whoop and a holler
across the small pub as she did so, for everyone there knew she
didn't like beer. Though another pint was slid before her, she didn't
drink it. Swallowing the first pint had merely confirmed for her that
she disliked beer. Instead of drinking more, she decided to eat, as the
rowing had exhausted her. She was famished, and so she ate not only
her own plate of fish and chips but half of Fionn's. He had stopped
eating, concentrating instead on the orange sky reflected against the
yellow-white of the pub's walls. Fionn and his father grew silent.

"Something wrong?" Rebecca asked.

Before they answered, Iollan came through the door. "There'll be
no goin' home for you three tonight," he said, turning to the bartender. "Pint, Grace."

"What's going on?" Fionn Sr. asked, rising from his seat.

"Paddy called over and said there's a gale comin' like a mad banshee from the south."

"Rowan," Rebecca said, moving to the edge of her seat.

"We didn't smell anything," Fionn said, resting his hand onto Rebecca's knee.

"No one did," Iollan replied. "'Twas Sean. The old man came racing up the dock like death itself was on his heels."

Grace slid the pint into Iollan's hand. He had only lifted it from the bar when his partner came flying in the door.

"We need to go out!"

"We were just told to stay in," Iollan said, setting his glass down heavily on the bar.

"There's a couple of little girls out on the water."

Rebecca spun around to look at Fionn, who slowly stood up.

"Which girls?" Fionn Sr. asked.

"Paddy's daughter and her friend from the States."

"No!" Rebecca cried, bolting for the door. "No!"

⁓

"You think you can raise this baby by yourself?" Dennis yelled at her. He sat on the edge of the bridge, the ocean pounding into the cliff far below.

"Please, Dennis," Rebecca said through her tears. "Please give me Rowan."

"That'd make you happy, wouldn't it? Taking the baby and moving to be rid of me! You can't move far enough away! You'll never be free!"

"Becky," Sharon called from behind.

"Dennis, just give her back to me."

"You think you can raise this baby without me?"

Highway 1 was dark and cold, and a deep fog rolled in from the Pacific far below onto the bridge.

It was Thanksgiving Day. Dennis had not returned with Rowan on time, and though Sharon wanted to call the police, Rebecca in-

sisted she shouldn't. Dennis had called. He was already mad, and so
Rebecca agreed to meet him on Highway 1 just north of Half Moon
Bay, where they had met two years before—where he fixed her car and
offered her raspberry sherbet.

Rebecca held her hands out in supplication before her, staring at
Rowan in her Irish sweater, cuddled next to her father's chest as he sat
on the edge of the bridge.

"You remember when we met?" he asked her.

Rebecca nodded, tears streaming down her cheeks.

"You were so afraid out here—so high up with your car stuck. I
helped you."

"Yes, you did." He had been so nice. He helped that day so selflessly.

"What happened to that girl, Becky? That pretty girl—that
smart girl that I loved?"

"You happened to me, Dennis," Rebecca whispered.

"No, Becky. That smart, pretty girl is still here," Sharon replied
from over Rebecca's shoulder.

"Shut up, Sharon! If it wasn't for you, she'd be with me still!"

The deep, burning hate Rebecca held in her heart for Dennis
turned to ice-cold terror. She wished he would die—just die and leave
her be forever so she wouldn't have to see him ever again. So she could
be free.

"Please, Dennis. She's a baby," Rebecca whispered.

"All you think about is this damn baby! You never think about
me! My wants! My needs! I should just throw her over!"

"Please."

"I'll just let her go." Dennis chuckled and turned toward the
black abyss behind him. He held Rowan away from his chest.

"No!" Rebecca cried, stepping closer.

"Becky, stay back," Sharon warned.

Glancing over her shoulder, Rebecca saw Sharon standing several
yards behind her, with Peg sitting in the car. They had come so she
wouldn't have to be alone with Dennis.

"Sharon, what do I do?" Rebecca asked.

"Shut up, Sharon! You caused all this by coming here! She'd be listening to me if you weren't here. She belongs to me."

"Stop blamin' everybody else for things that are your fault, Dennis. Becky wouldn't be with you even if I wasn't here because you're a bastard and you don't deserve her!"

"Give me Rowan," Rebecca begged.

"Give me your hand, Becky," Dennis commanded, offering his open palm.

Rebecca stepped forward.

"No, Becky. Stay away from him," Sharon called.

"If you give me your hand, I'll give you Rowan."

"You'll give her to me?"

"No, Becky!" Sharon yelled.

"I promise."

Her trembling hand reached out, her eyes never leaving the little bundle of wool in Dennis's right arm.

"I promise," Dennis repeated.

"Don't, Becky!"

As she reached for Dennis with her right hand, Rebecca grabbed Rowan with her left.

"Let her go!" Dennis screamed.

Rebecca shoved Dennis with her right elbow, pulling Rowan away from him. He backhanded her across the face, losing his balance on the railing.

"Shit!" he yelled as he slipped back, still clutching Rowan.

"Give her to me!" Rebecca hissed, wishing with all her heart he would just die.

"Help!" he screamed and as he fell backward, Rebecca caught Rowan's foot. Sliding off the bridge, Dennis pulled Rebecca to the edge, for she could not allow Rowan to take his weight.

"No!" Rebecca screamed, slipping over the railing with Rowan's foot in her left hand.

"Help!" Dennis yelled, terror in his voice. His right hand flailed for Rebecca.

For a split second, Rowan's little body in its sweater was all that kept him from falling, and as the jumper slipped, a pop sounded in the baby's hip. A shrill scream burst from Rowan's lips, piercing the night. Rebecca grabbed the sweater at Rowan's chest, her own hips cresting the railing. Hanging on to the tiny white sleeve, Dennis screamed again.

Suddenly arms wrapped around Rebecca's waist, anchoring her to the bridge and preventing her from grabbing Dennis's hand.

"I've got you now!" Sharon shouted.

"Rowan!" Rebecca cried, grabbing Rowan's other leg, holding both with one hand.

"Becky! Save me!"

The sweater slid over Rowan's head.

"Sharon, let go! I can reach him!" Rebecca yelled. All Dennis had hold of now was the left sleeve. Rebecca held all of his weight on nothing but the sweater. Her left hand held the sweater, which had nearly slipped off of Rowan's body completely, while her right hand held Rowan by both of her feet.

"You won't! You'll fall too! I'll not let go! I've got you now!"

"Becky! Help me!"

Still holding Rowan by the feet, in a flash of her eyelids, Rebecca let go of Rowan's sweater to grab Dennis's hand. But as she let go of the sweater, it immediately slipped off the baby and Dennis fell, his hand holding nothing but the empty little gansey.

"Dennis!" Rebecca screamed.

All she could see was his wide eyes as he fell through the mist onto the rocks below.

~⌇

"Becky!" Fionn yelled.

Rebecca turned her head as she struggled for freedom. She froze. It wasn't Dennis. It was Fionn.

"Becky, it's me."

"She can't be out in this storm. She has to be safe," Rebecca whispered, pulling him to the door. "I have to go."

"We're goin' with you. Iollan," Fionn said.

"Boat's acting up," Iollan said quietly.

"We have to go," Fionn said.

Iollan left his beer on the counter and led his partner, Fionn Sr., Fionn, and Rebecca out into the gale. The wind pummeled Rebecca as she clung to Fionn. All she could see was Rowan's little diapered body lying in the ambulance and Dennis falling away.

You think you can raise a baby by yourself? You're too stupid!

They crawled in the wind across the metal plank onto Iollan's ship. After Fionn pushed Rebecca into the cabin, he and his father released the mooring line and Iollan engaged the engine. Huge swells crested the boat's railing as Iollan pulled out beneath the red sky.

"They have any idea where to look?" Iollan asked his partner as Fionn Sr. and his son came into the cabin, soaking wet.

"Paddy said Sean indicated to the west, just north of their island."

As the boat sputtered, Iollan turned to the south. Rebecca wrapped her arms around herself, watching the bow point up into the red sky and then down into the black sea.

You were nothing before you met me! I should just throw her over!

"Come here, Becky," Fionn said, reaching for her.

Rebecca shrugged away from him. "Everything's not fine, Fionn," she whispered.

"No, it's not. You can carry this alone, Becky, like you've done for six years, or you can let someone help."

Rebecca looked over at him, finding his eyes steady and sure.

"You can let me help," he said.

"This wouldn't be happening if I hadn't—let go."

"All parents have to give their children their freedom."

"She's only six years old," Rebecca said, her voice breaking. In her mind, she saw her little girl out on the ocean, crying for her.

"It's not your fault," Fionn said.

"You're wrong," she replied. "It's all my fault."

Iollan turned the boat west and the hull heaved and creaked as the weather slammed it on both sides. The wind, wailing in from the south, pushed the boat north and sent the water crashing into Ina's island, only to be deflected back. There the wind tore across the sea, shoving the water at the boat, pounding it south. Time was measured by the slamming waves, and twenty minutes passed before anyone said another word.

"I see lights!" Iollan said. "It's another ship!"

"It's Paddy and Eoman," Fionn Sr. said, peering out the window as a great wave hit the wheelhouse.

Rebecca recoiled from the glass. After the water cleared, she leaned forward, watching the lights come and go as Paddy's ship rolled over the waves. Then she squinted harder, for there, turning on and turning off in the cresting sea, was a tiny little light out in the giant ocean.

"What's that?" she asked, pointing to the yellow light bobbing in the gale.

"It's a curragh," Iollan's partner replied quietly.

"It is not," Iollan scoffed.

"It is," Fionn Sr. insisted.

"Who'd go out in a curragh in this?" Fionn declared incredulously.

Rebecca looked over to Fionn Sr., whose eyes were glued to the madness beyond the calm, dry wheelhouse.

"Sean Morahan."

Ladder/Basket Within

Ladder/Basket Within. 1. Jacob's ladder with basket stitch knitted within the ladder's rungs. 2. A prayer.

—R. Dirane, *A Binding Love*

Sean could see Old Man Dirane's dinghy in the fading light. It was listing terribly, but even that brought a smile to his face. The old boat shouldn't even be afloat, ancient and tattered as it was, amid these swells that had grown as the gale raged. Sean could now hear his name on the wind. Rowan must have seen his light and was calling for him.

"I'm comin', girl!" he yelled, pulling hard. His other set of oars sat neatly upon the edge of his hull. He wished he had one of his sons—just one of them. Best would be his first, Matthew.

Sean found Padrig Blake standing wet on his doorstep, with Fionn O'Flaherty and the gale behind him. In his peripheral vision, Sean could see Mary clinging to Claire.

The sky had been clear, turning orange just two and a half hours before. The mistle thrush had been singing, but there was no earth smell upon the wave. There was no storm. Sean had sat before the fire, spinning yarn for Liam's suit, as his son had just turned eighteen. While he watched the wool in his right hand form a triangle as the bobbin spun, the sky turned red. Great walls of water hit the thatch above his head. Sean stood up from his chair. He had not been able to hear Mary or Claire breathing as the gale blew across his roof. Now he stood, the sea's fury blowing in his door.

"Wicked weather to be out," he murmured, his heart thumping so hard against his ribs that he could barely catch his breath.

"We found—we found—" Padrig Blake's eyes were wide and his face was ashen.

"A body's come up on shore near my house," Fionn O'Flaherty said. "We can't make it out, but—"

"It was wearing this." Blake finished the sentence, and from behind his back he pulled a drenched gansey.

It had the Trinity stitch knitted between two sets of double zigzags, bordering a huge Tree of Life as its main panel. Sean had made it for his oldest the week he found out Matthew was to be a father, for it had taken four years for Mary to conceive.

Mary was standing behind Sean. Holding on to Claire, she had been watching the whole exchange. Now she screamed, a cry pealing over the howl of the gale.

Sean himself stood mute.

"Are any of your sons here, Morahan?"

"No," Claire said. "They all went."

"Joe can swim," Sean said absently. "Joe's the strongest."

"Matthew!" Mary keened, holding her belly. "Please, Sweet Jesus! Not Matthew!"

Claire hugged her daughter-in-law, bringing her over to the fire where Sean had been sitting.

"We'll wait for the others," Sean said, staring absently at the gale beyond his door. "Joe will bring them back. Would you like to come in and have tea?"

"No, thank you. Best be headin' home. We'll keep Matthew in the shed where he is until the storm passes. We have him covered and well kept. My prayers are with you." Fionn nodded to Mary.

She didn't look up. She held her belly, rocking back and forth in pain.

"Thank you, Blake, O'Flaherty," Sean said.

They nodded and headed back out into the storm.

"Joe will bring them back," Sean muttered as he closed the door.

⌒

"Sean!" Rowan cried, hanging on to Siobhan. They were wet to their knees and the old dinghy was taking on water. The wind screamed from the south as Sean watched two fishing trawlers making their way toward him. It was Iollan and Paddy.

"I'm almost there!" Sean yelled.

The waves were rolling. Sometimes he could see Rowan over his shoulder, sometimes not. Light faded, and when his curragh slammed down into a furrow between waves, it was silent and black like the ocean depths.

"Not yet."

On the next crest, he could see the lights of the fishing trawlers aimed exactly where he was, and when he turned he found the dinghy right beside him. It sat now with its bow parallel to the next oncoming wave. Sean pointed his bow into the wave and gave one great pull on his oars. His curragh touched the dinghy's side.

"Give me your hands!" he yelled, pulling his oar in and holding out his hand to the girls. Siobhan grabbed his palm and as he pulled on the little girl, the oncoming wave slammed into the side of the dinghy and Sean pulled Siobhan into his curragh. When they crested the wave, he saw the dinghy recede in the furrow. Rowan fell out of it and into the sea.

"No!" Sean screamed.

The dinghy and Rowan disappeared.

"Hang on to the bench, Siobhan!" Sean cried, pulling the little girl off his body. The fishing trawlers were very close now. Sean could see Paddy on his bow.

"Wrap your arms around the bench and don't let go! Your da's right there!" The wave passed and Sean looked for the dinghy and Rowan.

"Rowan," Siobhan cried, clinging to the bench.

The tip of the dinghy rose up not ten yards from his curragh, and as it did Sean could see Rowan hanging on to its bow. Iollan must have spotted her, too, for his light spun around, reflecting on the tip of Old Man Dirane's boat, which floated upside down in the ocean. When Sean looked up at the light, he saw Fionn and, next to him, Rowan's mother. She stared at him, terror in her eyes. Sean jumped into the water.

He went under and it was cold. His body was weak. He had been cruel to it this day, first with his run to the docks to keep Paddy from the sea and then with his trip in the curragh out to find Rowan and Siobhan. But even in his weakness, all he could think of was Rowan in the rain and the sea with no gansey. Her life had to be fleeting. The fingers of the sea beckoned him below, but Sean pushed his head above the swell, swimming with all he had left to the dinghy. He was right there, his hand grasping for Rowan, who was still clinging to the overturned boat. Her eyes were closed, her face drawn and spent from her struggle to hang on, and he saw her fingers relax as she let go, without so much as a whimper.

"No! Rowan!" he yelled, diving under into the black. Iollan's light shone down in the darkness, reflecting on her little hand. Sean grabbed it and with a push, he lifted her to the surface. He came up behind her, his legs giving out. Holding Rowan with his right arm, her body still and unmoving, he fought the sea with his left hand, swimming to the curragh.

"Siobhan!" He coughed weakly, pulling Rowan to the side of his boat. Siobhan peeped over.

With his final effort, Sean pushed Rowan up. Siobhan grabbed her friend and pulled her in. Sean was now completely spent. He lay still in the water, receding into a furrow as a great swell rose, taking his curragh up on its crest toward heaven. He saw Iollan's boat veer into Paddy's with a great metal screech. As he gazed up, Sean could just make out Rowan's mother, her eyes glued to him.

Claire wept, wringing her hands as she paced her brother's kitchen floor.

It had taken Sean a month to find out where Padrig Blake had taken his wife. He had gone over to the Diranes' farm, demanding to know Claire's whereabouts, and wasn't it little Ina O'Connelly, who was over for a visit, who let it slip. Now he stood before his wife as the sun poured through the windows, lighting every corner of the house. But the warmth of early summer did not heat Sean's heart; it was as cold as any winter wave. He looked at Claire, who peered into his eyes, tears streaming down her cheeks.

"All gone," she whispered. "All gone."

"You think I killed them," Sean stated, his voice as cold as his heart.

"No, love," Claire replied, wiping her cheeks.

"Yes, you do. You think I killed them. Killed all of them," Sean repeated. "You think it's my fault because I sent them out."

"The storm took them, Sean," Claire whispered.

"If I hadn't have sent them out, they'd be standing here in the sun with Mary! You think that!" Sean was shouting now, moving closer to Claire.

"Sean, no," Claire said, her eyes widening as she backed away from him.

"Stop looking at me like that! It wasn't my fault!"

Claire looked away, sliding in front of the kitchen cabinets, toward the door.

"You're not getting away again!"

"I—I need—air," Claire said as she reached for the door.

Sean grabbed her arm, spinning her around.

"No! Sean!"

Sean had Claire by the throat, staring down into her eyes—her accusing, frightened, blue-green eyes. They had seen the truth, and they reflected it back at him now. He wanted them to close forever.

His heart was slow as the icy nothing at the bottom of the ocean curled its prickly fingers around his legs. He could no longer hear the wind or the water. Filling him with calm was Rowan's mother, gazing down on him from the deck of Iollan's boat. It had been so long since he had been looked upon so—as a man—a man who would save his children at the cost of his own life. He thought he smiled weakly up at her, but he was too cold to know if his face moved.

"Father, take care of my Rowan," he whispered. "And her mother."

Then, Sean Morahan let go and slipped below the surface of the water, into the blackness that embraced him.

CHAPTER 39

Lattice/Bobbles Between

Lattice/Bobbles Between. 1. A lattice pattern, and at each intersection a single bobble is knitted. 2. A community of people coming together to help others. 3. Holding on to one another so no one is blowing in the wind.

—R. Dirane, *A Binding Love*

*R*ebecca had watched Rowan fall out of the boat and disappear in the water and the wave's furrow. She almost screamed until she heard Sean yelling something to Siobhan. The little girl lay down, hiding from the turbulent sea and Rebecca's sight. But she saw Sean looking down into the water. Rebecca followed his gaze and as Fionn pointed the light, Rowan, in the water and the dinghy beside her, came up to the surface.

Rebecca stood on tiptoe, desperately trying to figure out how to get off the deck and into the water to reach her little girl. But Iollan's trawler was high in the waves one minute and then receding fast the next, causing the boat to slam into the furrow as another wave rolled toward it. As she was about to lift her leg to the railing, Sean met her eyes. He was calm and steady and he jumped into the sea.

Rebecca watched as he swam and fought the ocean, risking his life to save her daughter while she stood safe and helpless on the deck above. Dennis and the gale screamed in her ears, accusations of stupidity and weakness roiling around in her mind as sure as the sea boiled below. Her child's life now depended on the struggle of a cruel man. She had been in this place once before—hoping that a cruel person would spare her daughter's life. She had begged and pleaded back then as the burning hate within her wanted—willed—that man to die. At the time her conscious thought had been to save him, but when she reached her hand out to Dennis, had that burning hatred made her too slow and sent him to his death as she saved her child's life? Now Rebecca needed the help of a cruel man so Rowan would live, and even as she held that deeply in her heart, she hated herself for asking anything of cruelty.

Rowan went under for a split second, but Sean was on top of her, ducking beneath the wave. He rose with Rowan and crawled through the wild water, hoisting her into his own curragh.

At that moment, Iollan's engine whistled. Iollan screamed something indistinct out the wheelhouse door, and as the next wave crested the railing Rebecca felt Iollan's boat slam into Paddy's.

"Shit!" Fionn yelled. "Becky, get away from the railing!"

Paddy's boat was pulling away in a furrow as another swell threatened. Rebecca gazed at Sean. He smiled up at her, and went under. The screaming of her past and the ever-present gale went silent as Rebecca blinked in the stinging spray of the ocean's storm. His eyes weren't furious, turning to terror as Dennis's had been as he'd slipped into the black abyss. They were gentle—almost kind. Like a mistle thrush's wings fluttering as the bird darted by, Dennis's eyes falling away and Sean's gaze sinking into the depths passed through Rebecca's mind. Could cruelty have a different face?

A need as deep as her hate had been for Dennis six years before rose in her heart then, as red as the sky above her. It burst into flame, and Rebecca stood hot and sweating on the deck of Iollan's ship. She had no word for it. She pressed the Saint Bridget's cross to her burning heart and looked over to the curragh, so small in the great sea. Siobhan's face twisted in terror as she clung to Rowan's limp body. Without another thought, Rebecca climbed up on the railing. Taking a deep breath, she heard the air fill the depths of her lungs in the utter silence of the gale.

"Becky!" Fionn yelled. "Get down from there!"

Rebecca launched herself into the air and dove off of Iollan's boat. As she hit the water, everything went black. It was searingly cold—colder than any water she'd ever been in. She could feel the tug of the sea pulling her down as Iollan's boat rolled just behind her. Kicking her feet, she fought, beating the ocean with her fists until she came to the surface, breathing shallowly in the icy water.

Sean's boat was close and Rebecca started swimming. The water was frigid. She could feel her muscles tightening. Her gansey hung loose, getting in the way of her stroke, and as she crawled endlessly toward Sean's curragh, she peered down into the blackness.

Iollan's light passed over her head, and right below her feet Rebecca could make out something bright in the darkness. It was a gansey. It was Sean. There was no Dennis in the blackness below. There was simply a man who had put her daughter's life before his own and now was sinking away into oblivion. Taking a deep breath, Rebecca dove, pushing herself down in the freezing water. She found Sean's left hand. Struggling to lift him, she lurched toward the surface. Her lungs burned for air, but he was weighing her down. Suddenly a hand reached out and grabbed her, lifting her to the surface. She gulped for air.

"I have Sean!" she choked out, pulling him up.

"We're gonna freeze to death if we don't get out of the sea," Fionn yelled over the gale, reaching for the old man and pulling his head above the water. Rebecca and Fionn pulled Sean to the curragh.

"Siobhan!" Fionn called.

The little girl peeped over the edge of the boat, crying hysterically. "Rowan won't wake up!"

Fionn lifted himself over the side of the curragh as the sea receded. Another great swell was on its way. "Hurry! Give me your hand!" he said, reaching out for Rebecca.

"I'm still moving. Sean's not. Sean first," Rebecca grunted, pushing the old man forward.

Fionn tugged and pulled, turning his worried eyes to the south, and managed to get Sean into the bottom of the boat. Rebecca nearly flew out of the water as Fionn pulled her in. Quickly he sat down in the back of the boat and lifted the oars.

"Row, Becky!" he yelled, pulling on his left oar.

"Rowan." Rebecca leaned forward, ignoring Fionn's command as she reached for her little girl.

"We need to get the curragh perpendicular to that wave or we'll all be in the water and there won't be a curragh! Row, Becky!"

Fionn's eyes were imperative, staring over his shoulder at her. They widened as he looked past her. Following his gaze, Rebecca saw a huge wave coming toward them.

"Shit!" she yelled and quickly landed on the front bench. With Fionn at the back, Rebecca followed his moves as she had learned just hours before. The curragh was just barely straight on to the wave as it rolled beneath them, slapping their little boat with a great watery hand.

"Row!" Fionn yelled.

Rebecca laid on the oars. Siobhan lay next to Rowan, holding her tightly with her eyes closed. Rebecca wanted to reach down to her daughter, to touch her and see if she still lived, but if they didn't get to land, death would engulf them all. Rebecca knew that without being told. Struggling with her own mind and the sea, she willed herself to think only of rowing. There was no cold. There was no wind or worry. There was only breath and oars and the sea.

As they battled the ocean, rowing south, Rebecca looked to the east. Paddy was listing, as was Iollan, but together they were turning around, heading toward either Iollan's mooring or Paddy's, Rebecca supposed. She gazed at Fionn's back, pulling with him. She was warming beneath the gansey and when she glanced down, she saw Rowan's eyes open, shadowed by the lantern. She gasped.

"Rowan," she whispered, tears falling with the rain down her cheeks.

"I lost my pipe," she mumbled.

Siobhan started crying.

"We'll get you another," Sean said.

Rebecca saw Sean staring at her from the bottom of the boat. She had saved his life—cruel man though he was. But as she gazed at him, she felt that burning need in her chest again. She sought the word for it, but none came to her as she rowed. The heat of her heart tightened her chest.

"Need to breathe," Sean said. "Breathe to row and live."

"Aye," Rebecca replied.

"I'm cold," Rowan said, and she crawled over to Sean and lay down in the crook of his body. She pulled Siobhan over with her, and as Rebecca and Fionn fought the southern wind, the girls cuddled against Sean for warmth.

It felt as though they had rowed for hours, but finally Fionn lifted his left oar and navigated the curragh onto a flat, smooth shore. It was raining and black as Rebecca jumped from the boat, having no trouble this time pulling it ashore. She lifted Rowan and then Siobhan from the boat, holding both girls in her arms. Fionn helped Sean up.

"Where are we?" Rebecca asked Fionn.

But Sean answered, "My house. Can't get to anywhere else on the island in a gale."

When they came around the front of his house, Sean and Fionn opened the door. Rebecca followed them inside, out of the wind. Sean let go of Fionn, steadying himself by placing his hand on the wall. He flicked the switch.

"There's no electricity," he said.

"You make the fire, Becky, and get those girls out of their clothes. I need to tie down the curragh," Fionn said in the darkness as he headed back out into the storm, shutting the door behind him.

"Matches are on the mantel," Sean said. "Peat's on the hearth."

The old man shuffled through his house, holding on to his wall for support, and disappeared through a doorway on the right.

Carefully, Rebecca made her way to the sofa and set Rowan and Siobhan down upon it. She kissed her daughter on the head and breathed deeply of her child's scent. She had nearly lost her.

"I love you, Rowan," Rebecca choked.

"I love you, Mama," Rowan replied.

Pulling back, Rebecca held Rowan's face in her hands, but she could not see it in the darkness. Siobhan was weeping next to them.

"Everything's fine," Rebecca whispered, kissing Siobhan on the head. She felt the little girl shivering. "You're cold. I need to make a fire."

Picking her way through the darkness to the fireplace, Rebecca found the matches on the mantel just as Sean had said. She lit one and discovered a small pile of peat and a bag of dried grass on the hearth. Making a tepee of peat, she lit the tuft of grass beneath it. It smoldered as she fed the fire.

She turned around, looking at her daughter. How close had she been to losing her tonight?

"Mrs. Moray?" Sean said. She turned and found him dripping in the doorway to the right. He held a tiny shell in which a small wick was lit.

"If the fire's going, I have beds for them to climb into. I just need help moving a few things."

"We need to get them dry first. Do you have any clothing that they can put on?" Rebecca asked.

Sean nodded and turned to the kitchen.

"I'll be right back," she said to the girls. She stepped carefully onto the stone floor of the kitchen, which was made wet by Sean and now herself as the sea dripped from their soaking clothes.

Over the old man's shoulder and just off the kitchen, Rebecca could see light emanating from another room. Sean stepped into it. Rebecca followed, and when she entered she gasped.

The room was lit with old oil lanterns, some made from glass and metal, others from nothing more than a shell with a wick dancing in a small pool of oil. Wool lay upon the floor in great piles of fluffy white, and a spinning wheel stood in the corner, a spool of yarn upon its spindle. Hanging on the walls, driftwood rods held many skeins of colored yarn. A great wooden table directly to Rebecca's right had canisters and packets of dye sitting upon its scratched and stained surface. But mostly she gazed in wonder at the four huge mounds of knitted textiles that lined the far wall, piles tipping over like an avalanche and scattering about. A small chair stood next to a hearth, with many, many brown swatches tossed around its feet.

Sean turned, meeting Rebecca's wide eyes.

"These"—he motioned to the ganseys—"are my sons."

Slowly, silently, Rebecca surveyed the room, turning around in place.

"Rowan and Siobhan need something dry," she whispered.

"Aye," Sean replied. From a pile nearest him, he pulled out a yellow sweater. He handed it to Rebecca. It was as bright as any summer's day, with small circles like the halos on Byzantine saints and a pattern that looked like windowpanes. Knitted in neat rows beside the windows were tiny rounded stitches. Rebecca held the gansey closer to a candle.

"Those are toes. That was the day Brendan, my youngest, took his first step."

Rebecca's heart pounded as Sean went to the next pile. From it he lifted an apricot gansey and offered it to her. She took it and rubbed the fabric between her fingers. It was the color of a coming sunrise. In the main panel were fuzzy bobbles knitted into the interior of three large braids. A Tree of Life was stitched on either side of the main panel and next to those she found waves, large and curving, flowing down the length of the jumper.

"That is Liam's first lesson of the sea: Never turn your back to the ocean. You take those and change the girls from their wet things. I'll make tea," Sean said.

Rebecca backed out the door. Sean followed. Turning around, she walked through the kitchen and into the living room. There she found Rowan and Siobhan sitting close to the fire.

"I want my ma," Siobhan choked, looking up at Rebecca with terrified eyes as the storm howled beyond the walls of the cottage.

"It's all right now," Rebecca said, kneeling next to them. She took both of the girls in her arms, rocking back and forth to comfort them. The gale screamed outside and she could hear Dennis's voice again—she was stupid; she couldn't raise Rowan alone. His voice told Rebecca her daughter had nearly died. But even in his accusation, Rebecca held on to Rowan. Her daughter was here in her arms, alive, and she had saved her. In a gale on the ocean, Rebecca had protected her daughter, and she had also saved Sean—she had reached down and pulled the unredeemable from death. The girls shivered.

"It's still blowing outside, Siobhan, my love. We have to wait. Here, take off those wet things and you'll feel better," Rebecca said quietly.

"I want my da," Siobhan whispered. Paddy was out in the water, his boat injured and listing.

"I know," was all Rebecca could say as she helped the little girls out of their wet clothes. Sean came into the living room with two cups of hot tea just when Fionn blew in the front door.

"We need to clear the bed," Sean told him, handing the tea to Rebecca. "You'll help me. Rowan's ma should stay with the girls."

Rebecca passed the cups of tea to Siobhan and Rowan and, after taking off her soaking gansey, she slid between them, wrapping her arms around their shoulders. As she sat staring at the flames, she could hear the whistling wind through the thatch above and a mistle thrush upon the gale.

Sean came through the kitchen door, his hands full of brightly colored ganseys. He dumped them onto the chair next to the hearth. As he turned back, Fionn came in kind, and when she looked up into his face, his eyes were wide in surprise.

"He knits?" Fionn whispered.

Rebecca nodded.

"Who would've known?" Fionn said quietly.

"You think no one knew?" Rebecca asked.

"He doesn't talk to anybody—or didn't anyway, until Rowan here," Fionn replied, and as Sean showed up again with his arms laden, Fionn stepped away.

Looking down at the ganseys, which now tumbled off the chair, Rebecca spotted a dark gray jumper with large crisscrossing oars as the main panel. On either side of the oars were single zigzags, and next to those were semicircular shapes rising above diagonal lines made of stocking stitches. She reached forward and picked up the gansey. Holding the sweater before the peat fire, she could see a small hole at the top of each semicircle.

"Whales," said Sean, dumping another handful on the pile. "Took me a long time to figure out that stitch."

"And what's that one?" Rebecca asked, pointing to a gansey of the most amazing periwinkle blue.

"The day my eldest learned to ride his bike," Sean replied, staring at it distantly as Fionn came around and gently laid his armful of sweaters to the side. "He fell off."

Sean looked into Rebecca's eyes, his gaze black and deep and cold. In that icy abyss, Rebecca caught her breath, seeing Dennis in the darkness.

"I made him get up," Sean whispered. "His arm was broken and I made him get back on."

Dennis fell away, disappearing into the ocean.

Sean turned and with a heavy step walked back into his sons' room.

"How are the girls?" Fionn asked.

Rebecca didn't look at him. She gazed down at Liam's Lesson enveloping Rowan with warmth, seeing the black abyss of Dennis's death in her mind's eye.

"Everything's fine," she replied distantly.

"Let's get them to bed, then," Fionn said, reaching down and brushing her hair with his hand.

"Can you take Siobhan?" she asked.

Fionn lifted Siobhan into his arms as Rebecca stood. Picking Rowan up from the hearth, Rebecca hugged her daughter as she watched herself drop Dennis from the bridge. She followed Fionn through the kitchen and into Sean's sons' room. The old man was leaning over the fireplace, tossing another brick of peat onto what was the beginning of a fire.

"That should keep going for a while," he said, and with a reticent glance over at Rebecca, he smiled a small smile and shuffled out the door.

Two little beds had been cleared, each of them with three knitted afghans of various colors folded neatly at their ends. Fionn laid Siobhan on one of the beds and tucked an afghan around her. As Rebecca set Rowan onto the other bed, her little girl shook her head. She hopped off that bed and climbed in next to Siobhan.

Rebecca's chest tightened, a crushing vise squeezing her heart. She needed to hold her daughter—needed to feel something besides the guilt of Dennis's death. Crawling into bed with Rowan curled up safely next to her always dissipated that darkness.

You're too stupid to raise her by yourself.

Her little girl and Siobhan had almost become a story of these islands this night—a tale to be passed from one generation to the next over peat fires. Two little girls had fallen asleep in a shanachie's boat, which was picked up by the southern wind and floated over the sea into the land of the fairies, never to be seen again. An Irish tale with a tragically magical end. It could have happened, and as Rebecca rolled the story through her mind, she also realized she was losing her daughter altogether. Rowan didn't want to lie down with her. She wanted to lie down with Siobhan.

"Becky," Fionn said softly, "there's no need to cry now."

Rebecca looked over at him, touching her cheeks. There, surprisingly, she found tears.

"I'm losing her," Rebecca whispered.

"You're her mum, Becky. Mums never lose their children."

Gently he lifted Rebecca's soaked gansey over her head.

"They do if they die," Rebecca sobbed.

"She didn't die," Fionn said, lowering Rebecca to the bed. He helped her off with her shoes.

"She could have," she replied as she slipped out of her wet pants.

Lying down, she thought about how great the ocean's swells were and how little the boat was that had brought them safely ashore. Her tears wet the pillow on which she lay as she replayed in her mind the picture of Rowan's baby body on the gurney in the ambulance. She saw her daughter and Siobhan clinging to each other in Old Man Dirane's dinghy. How had Rowan not fallen off of Highway 1? How had she and Siobhan gotten so far out in that broken boat?

"Rowan didn't die, Becky. Why do you get stuck on that possibility instead of seeing the reality?"

Rebecca looked up into Fionn's face. His red hair danced like flames in the shadows of the peat fire.

"What reality?"

"That you—Becky—you jumped off a boat in a gale. I never met anyone who's ever done that. You swam through the ocean in a storm, saved Sean, climbed into a curragh, and rowed it to safety."

Rebecca stared at him. Pulling herself closer to him, she laid her head upon his chest. She had jumped into an ocean gale. How had she done that? If she could do such a thing, how was it, then, that Dennis had died? She buried her face in Fionn's chest—hiding from the truth of Thanksgiving Day. She hadn't wanted to save Dennis. She had wanted him dead. That must be the difference. Thinking back to the sea and the gale—she had jumped into the sea. She had felt differently about Sean, seeing him as he sank beneath the waves. She wondered at her own bravery as she lifted her head.

"I couldn't have done that on my own. I jumped off the boat by myself, but you followed. We did the rest of that together, Fionn."

"That we did."

Rebecca watched the light of the fire flicker across Fionn's red chest hair. Soon she closed her eyes, thinking about what she had done that night—what she and Fionn had done.

"We work good together," she whispered sleepily.

"Aye, that we do."

Rebecca finally fell asleep, wrapped in the warmth of his arms, listening to the beat of his heart—and for the first time she felt her darkness dissipating without Rowan.

CHAPTER 40

Ladder/Moss Within

Ladder/Moss Within. 1. Jacob's ladder with Moss stitch knitted
within the ladder's rungs. 2. Grace.

—R. Dirane, *A Binding Love*

Sean left Fionn and Rowan, her mother, and Siobhan in his boys'
room and walked through his kitchen to his living room, where
he lifted Rowan's untouched tea from the hearth and took a sip. He
was soaking wet and chilled. This used to be where he'd sit and warm
his feet as his boys played their pipes after a long day of fishing. It was
where Claire would bring them supper on cold winter nights so they
all could be warm as they ate. It had been a long time since Sean sat in
the warmth of his family's fire, and doing so now made his heart
ache.

Staring down into the cup of tea, Sean ran the night through his
head—his battle with the gale, his curragh over the swells, putting
his own life aside to save his children.

"If only I had known then," he whispered to the glowing embers.
But he'd had no idea forty years before that his sons were even in trouble that night. Not until Padrig Blake showed up with Matthew's
gansey did he know.

"I thought I had fixed the engine," he mumbled. For years he'd
been hearing Joe in his head, telling him that Matthew knew engines.
It was one of the last things Joe had said to him before he died, and all

this time Sean had believed it had been the engine that had failed that night. That was a truth to him, as sure as there were mackerel in the sea. But suddenly, sitting before this fire, remembering Rowan and Siobhan standing in the tattered dinghy so far north of the rocks from which their boat was lifted, he was not so sure. That dinghy should have gone down. In such a storm it should have sunk long before it even reached where Sean found it. But it hadn't. As he slipped his wet shoes off, he wondered at his sons, fishermen all, dying in a gale when two little girls in a broken boat survived.

His body ached. His spine cried out. It wanted to lie down—to have all the weight removed from it.

"Men carry the weight of the world," he whispered. So he had told his boys. *Have to be strong to do such a thing*, and as that thought passed through his mind, he heard Joe's voice.

Will you never let go of us to see that we have become the men you raised us to be?

Shakily setting his teacup down, Sean looked into his son's angry eyes sitting across from him even now. Sean had sent them out. Sean had made the decision and forced it on his boys, and not for the first time the old man buried his head in his hands, hiding from that truth. Engine or no, storm or no, his boys went out because he made them go.

Joe's the strongest. Joe will bring them back.

A tear fell into his teacup, making tiny concentric circles that rolled to the cup's edge. Sean breathed in, remembering Claire's eyes as he last looked at them—the eyes that saw the truth the night he tried to close them forever. The blue-green terror gazed back at him as another tear hit his tea. Then he saw Rowan's mother, staring at him from the deck of Iollan's boat. He was alive, but only because of her—pulled from the cold, dark death that had called to him like a siren from ages past. He had heard its call, heeded its beckoning song, and yielded to its embrace, only to find himself in pain and freezing in a curragh next to Rowan and Siobhan. He had another chance—to do what, he wasn't sure, but another chance nevertheless.

Watching Rowan's mother turn about his sons' room as she took in the full lives of his boys, Sean knew it was she who had pulled him from the sea. Her eyes had looked at him as he was going under the water just as Claire had once looked at him. It wasn't love. It was worth. He had saved her little girl because he could do nothing else, and for that act Rowan's mother felt him worthy. She pulled him from the cold, giving him life, just as Claire had done. Claire had married him, pulling him in from the bitter life of the Morahan family, giving him life in the warmth of the O'Flahertys and the Dooleys and every other family on the island whose blood surged through her veins.

"What do I do?" he asked of the fire. His heart and mind and body hurt. He was all alone. Usually when Sean felt this way he would go into his sons' room and knit—weave together one of their stories. But now there were others in the house and he couldn't get to his needles or his boys. He was exhausted, but he couldn't think of sleep. He had another chance. He yet lived. Suddenly the old man stopped thinking, looking sideways at his bedroom door. It had been many years since he had opened the wardrobe door and touched the top shelf. He knew what he needed to finish. It was the thing he had started and stopped over the years. It was almost done, knitted row by row, piece by piece, but he could never bring himself to complete it. Slowly, Sean stood and walked into his bedroom. Tiptoeing across the floor as if to keep sleeping ghosts at rest, he opened his wardrobe. He felt around the top shelf until his hands came to rest on a pair of knitting needles poking through a small wad of fisherman's net. Pulling the net down, he quietly closed the wardrobe door and crept back out into the front room. He sat down on the chair and unraveled the net.

From the net's stiff, thin cables, Sean pulled out the unfinished gansey, a ball of blue-green yarn, and his knitting needles. He laid the sweater pieces about his feet—the cool, deep blue-green warmed by the fire. He picked up the front panel, which was halfway complete. Cutting the yarn that had kept the whole thing from unraveling, Sean slid the loose stitches onto his needle. And as the storm raged on beyond his door like the guilt within his soul, Sean sat before his fire and did what he had not done for forty years. He sat quietly, spending time with his wife.

CHAPTER 41

Ripping Back

Ripping Back. 1. The act of pulling out stitches because a mistake has been made. This is a very drastic thing to do and should be reserved for times when there is a serious error in the pattern or the fabric is coming undone. Ripping back requires removing the stitches from the needles and pulling out the yarn, unraveling the work. It is best for a beginner to try to find a veteran knitter to help with ripping back because then it is more likely that the entire work will not be lost. A veteran knitter can spot the exact place where the error has occurred and can "unknit" the work to the point of the error. 2. Finding good counsel. 3. A priest.

—R. Dirane, *A Binding Love*

There was a knock on the door. Sean opened his eyes. He could see the morning light shining through the window. He lay stiff. As he moved slightly, every muscle in his body cried out in pain. Rolling over with a grunt, he tried to lift himself from the mattress, but decided against it, for there, next to the old man, was his wife— all that she had lovingly given him knitted in blue-green. The knock came louder.

"Morahan," Father Michael called from outside. Sean pulled himself up from the bed, his back screaming at him for having to carry weight again.

"Just a minute," he called, a cough from somewhere deep in his chest punctuating his sentence. He stood up, still dressed in his clothes from the night before.

"I'm comin'," he growled, and grabbing his wife from his bed, he opened his bedroom door. He froze. There, standing in his kitchen, was Rowan's mother. She was as dressed as he and looked back at him with the same expression that he was sure rested on his face—exhaustion.

The old man tried to smile, but he couldn't, as he was not sure if that look in Rowan's mother's eyes would stay as blank as it was at that moment or turn into something else. If she looked at him like he had worth, he'd be happy. If she gazed, instead, with those bottom-of-the-ocean eyes, he felt he would drop dead right where he was standing. So he nodded and quickly looked away lest she give some indication of what she thought of him at that moment.

"Siobhan?" Annie called from beyond the door.

"Ma!" Siobhan answered, racing from behind Rebecca to the door. She flung it open, and there on Sean's doorstep were the father and Annie Blake. Annie lifted her little girl, wearing Brendan's yellow gansey, into her arms, weeping as she stepped into the house. Paddy followed, grabbing his wife and daughter in his arms and burying his face in their hair.

"Da," Siobhan cried.

From behind Paddy, Sheila and Fionn Sr. entered. Fionn Sr. carried a large cardboard box.

"Son?" he called, setting the box on the floor.

"Dad!" Fionn replied, scratching his tangles of red hair as he moved past Rebecca. He grabbed his father, laughing as he held on.

Sean's chest tightened. And then Rowan skipped out, wearing Liam's bright apricot lesson. She grabbed her mother's hand.

"Rowan! I'm so happy ta see ya!" Fionn Sr. said, releasing his son and plucking the little girl from her mother's side. He swung her around in a circle, kissing her cheek as he did so. Sean watched Rowan giggle, and a smile cracked his old skin. When Fionn Sr. stopped spinning, his quiet black eyes rested on Sean. The old man stepped back a little.

"That was something else ya did there, Morahan."

"It was nothin'," Sean muttered.

"Rowin' a curragh through a gale isn't nothin'," Paddy Blake said.

"And you, Rebecca Moray! Jumpin' off the boat, makin' my son follow ya!" Fionn Sr. yelled.

Rowan's mother's eyes went wide and she shook her head. Fionn grabbed her around the waist and nuzzled her cheek.

"She rowed like she was born to it," he said. "You should have seen her, Paddy."

They all laughed as Annie Blake released her daughter and her husband. She crossed the room and pulled Rowan's mother into her arms tightly.

"Thank you," she said. "For savin' my daughter."

Then Annie let go of Rebecca and stepped over to Sean. She wrapped her arms around his stiff neck, kissing him on his old cheek. He was unsure what to do, so he patted her on her shoulders, his heart rising to his throat.

"Thanks for savin' Siobhan, Sean," Annie said, pulling away.

"And Rowan," Fionn Sr. added.

Sean nodded, looking at the gray ash in his hearth.

"I—I should make a fire," he said.

"We brought breakfast," Sheila announced, kissing Rowan on the cheek as she headed into the kitchen. "Would ya bring that box, son?"

"That's a beautiful gansey there, Sean," Annie Blake said, looking at Claire's sweater in Sean's arms. "You should let Becky look at it."

Paddy, Annie, Siobhan, and Rowan followed the O'Flahertys into the kitchen. Sean set the gansey on the back of his sofa without looking over to Rowan's mother. He bent down and grabbed two bricks of peat.

"So who's the gansey for, Sean?" Father Michael asked.

Sean bolted up straight, his back protesting as he did so. The old man had been completely oblivious to the priest standing there. The wind had calmed, brushing Father Michael's hair gently, playfully, through the open door, and Sean saw that the Irish sky was blue and smiling behind him. It was as if there had been no gale at all.

"It's my wife," Sean said quietly as the priest walked over and picked up the gansey.

"Your wife made it?" Father Michael asked.

"No," Rebecca and Sean replied together. Sean glanced at her. She looked into him with her mahogany eyes and then down at her feet.

"No?" the priest inquired.

"I made it," Sean said.

"You knit?" Father Michael asked.

"Ina says the men used to knit the ganseys," Rowan's mother said. "The women spun the wool."

"Is that so?" Father Michael declared, rubbing the woolen gansey between his hands. "I never knew that. So this is for your wife."

"Aye," Sean replied, turning to the fireplace.

"I have something to show you two," Father Michael said, looking at the gansey.

Sean turned back to the priest.

"You both have to see this. Would you mind coming with me? It's a short walk before breakfast. I'll wait outside while you put your shoes on."

The priest stepped out into the Irish world beyond Sean's door. The old man looked over to Rowan's mother, who gave him a questioning glance. Shrugging, Sean turned to his bedroom to get his shoes, then returned to the living room and walked out his front door. Rowan's mother followed shortly after.

"Come on, then," Father Michael said, tossing Claire's jumper over his shoulder and heading up the gravel walkway.

"Ya want to leave that gansey here?" Sean asked, walking after the priest.

"No. I'll take it with me."

Rowan's mother walked just in front of Sean. She looked back at him with that same quizzical gaze. The old man shrugged again. He followed the priest and Rowan's mother off his gravel drive and across the road. On the other side, the three of them stepped into the ditch and began climbing the hill.

"I was surprised to hear you saved Sean's life last night, Rebecca," Father Michael said.

"He was drowning," Rowan's mother replied.

"So you'd risk your life for a man like Sean after all?" Father Michael asked of her.

Rowan's mother stopped. So did Sean. He stopped walking. He stopped breathing. He held on, waiting for her to reply.

"He saved my daughter. I—I watched him go under. I just saw his sweater falling beneath me in the water."

"I see," the priest replied.

Sean let go his breath and continued following Father Michael. His mind raced with pictures of Siobhan and Rowan huddled together in Old Man Dirane's dinghy.

"I would always save a child if I had it in my power to do so," Sean said as he walked past Rowan's mother. She was still halted in her tracks.

"Is that so, Sean?" Father Michael asked. "I'm surprised to hear that."

Sean stopped again.

"The sea took my boys. It wasn't going to get my girls, too."

"Aye, that was an awful storm last night. A forty-year gale. As bad as the storm that took your sons."

"It was," Sean replied.

"I was wondering why you didn't take your curragh out after your boys all those years ago?"

Sean watched Father Michael continue up the hill without looking back, his eyes wide in wonder.

"I thought of it last night," Sean said. "I didn't know they were in trouble. I didn't know they needed rescuing."

"I see. After all, Eoman and Paddy got home last night all right. Iollan's engine had trouble and their boats were listing. Men, grown fishermen, would take care of each other."

"Aye," Sean said.

Rowan's mother passed him. The priest was quite a bit ahead now, so Sean had to pick up his pace to catch up.

"Where are we going?" Rebecca asked.

"You'll see."

Sean saw the stone peeping out over the edge of the hill. He slowed down as he caught up to Rowan's mother and Father Michael. Together, they crested the hill and entered the cemetery through a gap in the wall where the stones had tumbled from their place.

"Someone needs to fix that," Father Michael said quietly, as he picked his way through the rocks strewn about the golden grass next to Sean. The old man grabbed his heart as his ribs crushed his lungs. He didn't want to be here.

"Long time since we've been in this place together, Sean," the priest said.

Sean nodded his head, staring at Old Man Dirane, who leaned against his headstone, smoking his pipe.

"Here." The priest held out Claire's gansey. "Why don't you take this to your boy? Show him how you see his mother."

"I'm afraid," the old man whispered.

"Is a man afraid of his own son?" Father Michael asked.

Sean gazed over to the priest and then back to Old Man Dirane. Shakily, he reached out and took the offered gansey.

"You want me to go with you?"

"No," Sean said quietly.

As Sean passed the headstones, he saw all of them—the Diranes, the Dooleys, the O'Flahertys—standing silently in the blue morning sky. He didn't look over to the Morahan plot, for he had no desire to see his father or listen to his chiding and mockery. Instead, he looked back, finding Father Michael on this side of the cemetery wall and Rowan's mother, looking very pale, just beyond it. He met her eyes. She shook her head.

"Been a long while that you've been keeping your gaze behind—in the past," Father Michael said.

"Been a long while the storm's been comin' in from that direction," Sean replied.

"A fisherman must look ahead, even in a storm," the priest said.

"'Tis true." Sean nodded, and so he turned his head and stopped breathing, for not fifteen yards from him stood his son Matthew.

"Sean?" Father Michael called.

"I'm dying," Sean said.

"No. You're living," replied the priest.

Matthew's red hair shimmered in the morning light. Sean had not remembered it being so shiny.

Da.

Sean gazed into his son's black eyes. He took so much from the O'Flaherty side of Claire's family. Sean opened his mouth but nothing came out.

It's quite a burden you've been carryin' there, Da.

"What can I do?" Sean whispered.

Look around you, Da. The O'Flahertys. The Diranes. The Dooleys. How many sons died in the war you were in?

"That was different."

Asking the young to go out into a storm to care for the family. Doesn't matter if it's the sea or battle. It's been done in many ways for thousands of years.

"But you were my boys. Joe told me—" Sean's voice cracked. He wiped his watery eyes. "He said you were men. I didn't see it. You were my boys."

And each moment since, that mistake has clouded every joyful moment of your life. Do you really think Joe wanted you to live like that?

"I took his life!"

Would he take yours?

"No. Not Joe."

But you've been making him take your life for forty years.

Sean blinked as the periwinkle sky above poured over Matthew.

You've not thought about that, have you, Da?

Sean blinked again. Did that make sense?

You've been so busy reliving that one night, you've kept all of us—Matthew, Brendan, Liam, Joe, my wife, my daughter, my mother—all of us—here with you on this side of Eternity. Making us take your life every day instead of living it yourself. You need to let go so we can go home.

"That's too simple," Sean whispered.

We love you, Da. It is that simple.

A blue-green shadow passed to Sean's right, and when he turned to it, he stopped breathing. Claire stood next to Mary's headstone, holding the baby. She was exactly as Sean remembered her, as she had stood on that misty beach early in their marriage, waiting for him to come in from the storm. He gazed at her dress and then down at the jumper in his hand. He had tried so many dyes to achieve that color and had thought he had done so, but Claire's dress was slightly greener than was his memory of it and so his jumper was not perfectly matched.

"Claire?" Sean called softly.

She glanced up, tears rolling from her beautiful blue-green eyes. Sean fell to his knees.

"Claire, I'm sor—"

Claire shook her head and turned her back to him. Her shoulders shook as she wept.

"Claire, I need—"

She shook her head again.

He needed to talk to her—to tell her he was sorry. He needed her to listen and as he devised ways of making Claire listen, he glanced over his shoulder. There he found Rowan's mother staring at him, white as a ghost. Turning back to Claire, he laid the jumper on the grass of Mary's grave.

"I made you a gansey, Claire. Look, it has all your sons on it."

Reticently, Claire turned her head and looked down at the jumper.

"Here is Matthew on the front. See the wheels? Remember that day, Claire? The day Matthew tried to ride the bike. The sky was so blue that day."

Periwinkle.

"Aye. I made his jumper that color. Yours is the color of your eyes."

He was hurt.

Sean looked down.

"He was hurt, Claire. And I made him get back on. Made him. I've thought a lot about that day."

And what have you thought, Sean Morahan?

"That sometimes 'tis the more courageous man who can admit to himself that he cannot do a thing than the man who tries always to overcome. Matthew knew that."

Aye, Sean. He did.

Sean nodded and flipped the sweater over.

"Here is Brendan. See the halos? He learned to walk that day."

He came to you.

"That he did. I can still see his arms."

And what else do you see?

Sean glanced over to Matthew.

"Every day is a first step." The old man sighed. "Some are harder than others, Claire."

Who's on the left arm?

"That's Liam. Remember the first day we tried to take him out in the boat?"

He was looking at the Lord's sheep.

Claire chuckled.

What is Liam's lesson?

"Our children begin with words, Claire. Every word that comes out of our mouth when talking to the wee ones makes them who they think themselves to be. 'Tis from our words that their future takes shape."

Only good words need fill a child's ear—and gentle warnings.

"Aye," Sean whispered. He looked at Joe's sleeve and a lump formed in his throat. He glanced up to Claire. The tears streamed down her cheeks, glistening in the Irish sun.

And Joe?

Sean shook his head, weeping.

And Joe?

"I killed your sons, Claire," Sean cried hoarsely.

Joe.

"See the whales?" Sean choked.

The day you were tossed from the curragh.

Sean was unable to speak.

Something was wrong that day.

He nodded, covering his eyes.

He found the oars. He knew where they were.

"He knew things," Sean whispered. "I didn't listen."

What is Joe's lesson, Sean?

Sean looked up into Claire's blue-green eyes.

"Joe was a man—more of a man than I ever could hope to be—because he was your son. I needed to set him free to make his own way."

Set them all free, love.

"I miss my boys," Sean cried, picking up the jumper and burying his face in it.

Just tell them you love them.

"I do."

Now you are free.

"Am I?" Sean mumbled.

Bring me home, Sean. Lay me here, near Matthew and Mary and Claire. And when you pass on, lie next to me and hold me in eternity.

Sean wept and whispered, "I love you, Claire."

And I—you.

Sean reached out and as his hand touched the hem of Claire's dress, a cloud passed in front of the Irish morning sun and she was gone.

CHAPTER 42

Diamond Entwined Diamond

Diamond Entwined Diamond. 1. A diamond stitch with another set of diamonds knitted below. The pattern then looks like
a column of diamonds set on top of one another, out of sync. 2.
A shifting of memory that realigns the present.

—R. Dirane, *A Binding Love*

*R*ebecca hung back outside the wall, staring at the cemetery.
She had started this day feeling disoriented, and she felt that
way still.

In the morning, when the banging at the front door had startled
her awake, her mind was filled wih memories of Dennis coming for his
first visitation, and she'd been unclear about where she was or what
day it was. But in her confusion, a warm hand had laid itself on her
head, and when that happened, her world stopped spinning. She'd
found herself lying safely next to Fionn, and nearby, just as safe, were
her daughter, Rowan, and Siobhan.

The Blakes and the O'Flahertys had come into the house, bringing hugs and joy and breakfast. But it was only when Annie Blake
hugged her that Rebecca remembered what she had done the night
before. She gazed over to Sean, watching him as Annie hugged him as
well. How hard it seemed for him to be warm—to touch and be
touched. Now he knelt before a gravestone, crying. Rebecca had never
seen a man cry like Sean was doing.

"Now he's free," Father Michael said.

"It seems too easy," Rebecca remarked.

"Is forty years living like he has easy?"

"No."

"You saved him, Rebecca," Father Michael said.

This was the same comment the priest had made coming up the hill, and Rebecca had watched herself pull Sean and his white sweater up from the black abyss again in her mind as she walked with him. And each time she pulled Sean from the water, she watched Dennis fall, hanging on to nothing more than a little white gansey as he fell to his death. She had jumped to save Sean. She could save someone like Sean.

"How long are you going to live like you are, Rebecca? Six years is enough, don't you think? Why do you hold back from Sharon?"

"What are you talking about?" Rebecca asked.

"What is it that Sharon did that night that would make you treat her so?"

"I don't treat her badly," Rebecca replied, glancing into the priest's eyes.

"But you've pulled back from her. Not as close as you once were."

"How would you know?"

Father Michael pointed to his collar.

Rebecca looked away.

"Do you really think you killed Dennis?"

"Leave me be."

"You wanted him dead, so you pushed him over. That's what Sharon says you believe."

"Don't you listen?"

"And what did Sharon do?"

"She held me!" Rebecca blurted out. She saw Sean glance over his shoulder.

"She shouldn't have done?"

"I couldn't reach him," Rebecca hissed through her teeth. "He wouldn't be dead if she hadn't held me."

"You didn't want him dead, then."

"I—I—wouldn't carry his death if it wasn't for Sharon."

"Whose death?" Sean asked, rising from the ground.

Fury burned Rebecca's cheeks as she glared at Father Michael.

"Rowan's father, Dennis's," Father Michael replied. "You were going over, Rebecca. Over the railing."

"What stopped her?" Sean asked.

"Leave it be, both of you!"

"Sharon grabbed her. You would be dead, as would Rowan, if Sharon hadn't held you."

"I could have saved him!"

"If you wanted Rowan's da dead, why were you reaching over the railing of a bridge to save him?" Sean asked.

"I—I—was trying to save Rowan."

"And your best friend grabbed hold of you, not to stop you from saving your baby's father but because she wanted to keep you and Rowan from falling off the bridge. That doesn't seem so wrong, does it?" Father Michael asked.

"But I pushed him," Rebecca whispered, wiping her burning cheeks.

"You grabbed your baby. He slapped you and he slipped."

"I wanted him dead."

"Maybe before," Sean said.

"What?"

"You wanted him dead before you were savin' him."

"The moment before, w-when he was sitting on the bridge," Rebecca stuttered.

"But not in that moment—the moment when Rowan's da fell. You were savin' him. You're hangin' on to the wrong moment," Sean said.

Rebecca stepped back, startled.

"Haven't thought about it like that, have ya?" Sean added.

She shook her head, running the scene through her head again.

Becky! Save me!

"I can't," Rebecca whispered, backing farther away from the priest and the old man.

"What do you want, Becky?" Father Michael asked quietly.

"What do you mean?" She couldn't breathe.

Dennis slapped her, slipping as he did so.

"Your life. What do you want?"

"I don't know."

Dennis fell away, terror in his eyes. And he fell away again. But Sean came up and came up again.

Her chest burst into flames just like it had the night before as she stood on the deck of Iollan's boat and watched Sean go under.

"Yes, you do. The first time we talked. Over tea. Remember?"

Becky! Save me!

"Rebecca?" Father Michael called softly.

"I'm broken," Rebecca choked out. "I'm in that tub."

"What tub?" Sean asked.

"I want," she said hoarsely, "baskets of blackberries and kisses on scars."

"In my kitchen, Rebecca. You want a house—and?"

"A yard and kids and a dog and—" Rebecca shot her eyes at the priest.

"And what?"

"And barbecues on July Fourth."

"Yes." Father Michael smiled.

"Fionn."

"Yes, you want that, too. He's been trying to bring you what you want. Not noticed, have ya?"

Rebecca looked down at her feet. She gasped, for her heart burned so hot, her Saint Bridget's cross was glowing, she was sure.

"You'll have to let go of Rowan's da to grab hold of what Fionn's tryin' to give ya," Sean said. "Can't hold on to two men."

Rebecca turned to Sean, tears of surprise flowing from her eyes. She knew the word for her burning now, and as Sean Morahan stood before her, her heart poured out in his direction. Grabbing the old man, she held him tightly, weeping onto his shoulder. His arms embraced her firmly around the waist, holding her heat to his frail old body.

"Thanks for saving my daughter," she whispered.

"Thanks for savin' my life," Sean replied softly. Pulling away, Rebecca held his old face in her hands.

"I can't hang on to two men."

"My son says ya have to let go of the dead."

Rebecca stared into his hazel eyes, feeling the word roll around her mouth. "Love binds, Sean Morahan, and I have hold of you now."

"And I you," Sean whispered.

Rebecca nodded as she pulled away from the old man. Then she stared into Father Michael's eyes and then down at her feet and the next thing she knew, she was flying down the hill. Her mind filled with moments—Fionn riding his motorcycle and eating his sandwich and waving his silly American flags. Fionn dripping in the fog and playing his fiddle. Fionn's red hair.

"I have to go home," Rebecca called, racing down the hill.

She flew like a seabird down the hill. She jumped across the ditch and headed up Sean's drive, bursting through the door. She ran through the front room and skidded to a halt at the kitchen door. There sat Paddy, Annie, Fionn Sr., Sheila, Siobhan, and Rowan, eating breakfast.

"Fionn?" Rebecca panted.

"Aye?" Fionn Sr. replied.

"Not you! My Fionn!"

"He went back to your house. Said he forgot somethin' there."

Rebecca launched herself out Sean's door, down his gravel pathway, onto the little dirt path at the side of the street, speeding north back into town. By the time she reached the village, her lungs were burning. She stopped, breathing hard as she rested against Father Michael's gate.

"Becky?" John Hernon stood up from between his bikes.

"John. I need a bike," Rebecca said, coughing.

"You all right?"

"Fine," she replied. "I'm just kind of in a hurry."

"Take the red one," John said. "You need help?"

"Nope. Nope." Straddling the seat, Rebecca took off. "Can't hold on to two men."

She pedaled faster, the wind whipping the strands of her hair about her face. She bumped off the road and raced up her gravel drive. Jumping off the bike, she ran to the door and opened it. She pulled up short in the living room. Fionn peered over at her as he slowly dropped another brick of peat on the fire.

"Becky?"

Rebecca shook her head, doubling over, trying to catch her breath. Fionn stepped toward her. She held up her hand to stop him.

"I've been in that tub, Fionn," she groaned, holding her ribs.

"What tub?"

"I'm like that woman in the painting in the tub."

"Ah, the painting," Fionn replied, nodding.

"I haven't seen you," Rebecca said. "I—I—"

"I'll get my paints," he said quietly.

Rebecca stared in disbelief, and though Fionn's eyes were as black as that night on Highway 1, she found no memory of Dennis in them. Instead she found the Irish night sky. Reflected in them, the peat fire sparkled like stars in the Irish heaven. She wanted always to be in those eyes.

"I can only hang on to one man," she said, weeping.

"Aye," Fionn replied, slowly stepping closer.

"I love you, Fionn," she said.

"That you do. You think I'm beautiful."

He chuckled as Rebecca placed her fingers on his lips. He was the most beautiful man she'd ever seen.

"Will you marry me?" she asked.

"Look down," Fionn mumbled through her fingers. She peered down and there, on Fionn's open palm, was a simple gold ring.

"I see you as forever, Becky."

Fionn lifted her chin and kissed her, and as he did so Rebecca wrapped her arms around his neck. Entwining her fingers in his red curls, she knew that she would hold on to him until the day she died.

CHAPTER 43

Cluster Rib

Cluster Rib. 1. Rib stitches clustered together every so many rows. A common pattern would be to create a rib by knitting two and purling two, making ten stitches total for ten rows. On the tenth row, the ten stitches that make the rib are slipped onto a cable needle, wrapped with the yarn three times; then all ten stitches are slipped back on the knitting needle. This pattern appears as a column of ribbing bound horizontally every ten rows. 2. Tall, dry grass cut and bound together at the center to make easy-to-carry bales for thatching the roof. 3. Making a home.

—R. Dirane, *A Binding Love*

The next day, Rebecca slowly rode the red bike into town. She didn't feel quite in a rush anymore, for she wasn't leaving and there was much on her mind. How should she tell Rowan about Fionn and getting married to him? How would she help Rowan feel better about moving to Dublin, away from Siobhan? How would she finish her book living away from the island? She thought about it all, but none of it worried her. Her only concern, as the sun warmed her back, was the memory of a steaming pot of tea on the table and no Fionn in the bed beside her when she awoke.

Turning the corner to Hernon's Shop, Rebecca found Father Michael at his garden gate.

"Good morning, Rebecca! You missed Mass."

"I don't attend, Father," Rebecca replied with a warm smile. "Have you seen Fionn?"

"Perhaps," the priest replied. "I have heard you're getting married."

"He's been by, then."

"Aye. Very early. For confession and then Mass."

"Confession?"

"He was not right with what you two were doin' last night."

"What?" Rebecca exclaimed.

"You have something to confess?"

"I'm not Catholic. What's he telling you our—private—"

"It wasn't sitting right with him. So you'll be getting married Saturday next, then?"

"No. W-we haven't set a date," Rebecca stammered.

"The invite says Saturday next."

"What invite?" Rebecca whispered, shaking her head.

Father Michael trotted up the steps into his kitchen and returned with a small card. He held it out for Rebecca. She didn't take it.

"You want to look?" he asked.

"No." Rebecca sighed. "I've been through this before."

"He said he'd leave you to tell Rowan."

"Thanks," Rebecca said and stepped onto the pedals.

"So Saturday next, then," Father Michael called after her. "Here in the church."

Rebecca stopped the bike. She peered over her shoulder.

"I'm not getting married in the church, Father," she stated clearly, staring into the priest's eyes.

He met her steady gaze. "We'll have the Mass on the steps, then, Rebecca. Good day to you." The priest turned on his heel and bounded up his kitchen steps.

"Father!" Rebecca called.

Father Michael paused at his door.

"It's Becky, Father. My family calls me Becky."

"Ah!" Father Michael grinned. "Saturday next, then, Becky."

"On the steps."

The priest laughed as he disappeared through his door. Rebecca stared at the empty doorstep and then up to the crystalline sky above her. Not a cloud tainted the blue of the Irish heaven. A low chuckle rose in Rebecca's throat and she pedaled over to Hernon's Shop. Maggie opened the door.

"You're getting married."

"Yes, Maggie, I am."

"To an O'Flaherty."

"Small town. Not much to choose from." They laughed. Rebecca glanced up to the sky again.

"Becky?"

"Aye?" Rebecca replied, returning her gaze to Maggie.

"What are you lookin' at?"

"Maggie, I feel that I need to take some control of this situation."

"So what's new?"

"What are you doing today?"

"The usual."

"Come to Galway with me. I need stuff for wedding favors."

"What are wedding favors?"

"Gifts given at weddings. I have a feeling that these will be a necessity."

"What are you talkin' about?"

"Come with me to Galway."

"All right. I'll have Mum watch the wee ones."

"You can bring them. I'm taking Rowan. I'll meet you at the ferry."

Rebecca handed the bike to Maggie and trotted toward the Blakes' house. As she rounded the corner, she found Siobhan and Rowan racing toward her hand in hand, with Annie and Paddy bringing up the rear.

"We're staying! We're staying!" Rowan yelled, smiling like the sun.

"Yes, we are!"

Rowan and Siobhan flew into Rebecca's arms. Rebecca looked over their heads to Annie and Paddy.

"Sorry, Becky. Siobhan got to the invite before Paddy and I realized it had been slipped under the door."

Rebecca shrugged and turned to Annie. "I need to go to Galway. Can you and Siobhan come?"

"Aye. Need to get a dress?"

Rebecca let go the girls and stood. "No. Stuff for wedding favors."

"What are wedding favors?"

"Gifts we give out at weddings. I was hoping Paddy could take me."

Annie looked at Paddy.

"I've got things I can pick up there. Sure."

"All right, then," Annie said. "What kind of gifts?"

"These will be useful ones, to be sure," Rebecca said, gazing up once again to the sky. "Because you know that can't be trusted."

"What?" Annie asked, following Rebecca's gaze.

"That!" Rebecca pointed to the blue Irish heaven.

Once in Galway, Rebecca searched several shops until she found acrylic paints in the exact colors she needed. She bought brushes, too, and then they had to stop by four different stores to find enough of the actual favors that she was going to paint. Before heading back, they stopped for lunch. On the return trip, Rebecca looked out at the water. Over her shoulder, she watched Annie and Maggie talk as the children ran up and down the deck. For the first time in her life, she could truly say she felt like she was going home.

"Becky, you'll be needing this!" Rose called, as she, Annie, and Maggie with their children climbed off Paddy's boat. Rebecca turned and found Rose and Liz walking quickly down the street carrying large paper bags.

"Don't hurry yourself, there, Rose," Rebecca said, walking toward the two women. Maggie followed.

"We hear you're getting married," Liz said with a grin.

"I am." Rebecca laughed as she reached them.

"Here." The women held out the paper bags. Inside, Rebecca found spun wool.

"What's that for?"

"It's all the wool you spun for Fionn's gansey." The old ladies smiled mischievously.

"Father Michael said you two weren't to be trusted."

They laughed.

"What patterns are you goin' to use?" Rose asked.

"I—I hadn't thought about it."

"Well, you better decide and then we'll help you knit it. You've not much time till your wedding day. Good evening to you, Becky," Liz said, and arm in arm, the old ladies walked toward Rose's house.

The small car was parked in front of Peg's house. As Maggie went inside to retrieve the keys, Annie helped Rebecca stow the wool and the wedding favors in the backseat. Rowan and Rebecca climbed into the car and slowly made their way toward their cottage.

"Mama?"

"Yes, Rowan."

"Do I have to call Fionn Daddy?"

"I think you can call him what you want."

"I've never had a daddy."

"No, you haven't."

Rowan rolled down her window. "I think I'll ask Fionn if he wants to be called Daddy."

"If you'd like." Rebecca watched Rowan's brown hair dance in the wind.

"Mama?"

"Yes, Rowan."

"I don't want to be a flower girl."

"You don't?"

"No. I want to play my pipe."

"Oh."

"Like when you walk down the aisle."

"I'm not getting married in the church, Rowan."

"Oh."

Rebecca flicked the blinker on and pulled onto the gravel drive.

"Where are you getting married?"

"On the church steps." Rebecca chuckled.

"Why?"

"That's complicated."

"Can I play my pipe as you walk up the steps?"

Rebecca stopped the car and stared at her doorstep. Two small brown paper packages rested against her door. She turned the engine off.

"I need a pipe."

"Okay, Rowan," Rebecca replied absentmindedly as she opened her car door.

"Can Sean and Siobhan play with me?"

"I suppose," Rebecca muttered as she climbed out of the car and crossed the drive. Bending down, she picked up one of the packages. It was square, as big as a small sofa pillow. Rowan picked up the other one, which was long and thin, like a jewelry box.

"This one has my name on it!" Rowan declared excitedly.

On Rebecca's was written: *For you, Becky, and Rowan and beyond!*

"Can I open it?"

"Sure."

Rowan ripped the paper from her package and opened the box. Inside was a silver musical pipe.

"A pipe!" she cried, pulling a little card from underneath it. "What's it say?"

"'For you, Rowan. This was Joe's. His mother gave it to him when his was lost in a fury. Can't break a silver whistle. I've held on to it and now I know who it belongs to. Joe would agree,'" Rebecca read.

Rowan dropped the box and played a scale.

Rebecca gently pulled at the tape that sealed the other package and as the brown paper fell away she found white lace wrapped in acid-free paper, exactly as she had left it with Father Michael.

"What is it?" Rowan repeated.

"My wedding dress," Rebecca whispered.

CHAPTER 44

Double Zigzag/Basket Between

Double Zigzag/Basket Between. 1. Double zigzag with a basket stitch knitted between. 2. A wedding.

—R. Dirane, *A Binding Love*

he day was shining as Rebecca stood in Father Michael's kitchen, looking at herself in the mirror. Father Michael's mother's lace dress was just a bit too big around the waist and an inch too short, but Rebecca didn't care. The apricot silk shell she wore beneath it warmed the lace's whiteness and with Rebecca's dark hair flowing about her shoulders, she could honestly say she had never felt so beautiful in her life.

"You know you don't have to go through with this," Paddy said.

Rebecca grinned.

"Well, good thing someone knows he's alive. I haven't seen him since the day I asked him to marry me. I'd think he'd run off if there wasn't invites on everybody's doorstep."

"Oh, he's not going anywhere," Maggie replied. "He just didn't want to have to confess again. He hates that part."

Rebecca laughed.

"Sky's so blue," Paddy noted as he stared out Father Michael's window.

"Sure it is." Rebecca smirked.

"Well," Paddy said, "are you ready?"

"Never been readier," Rebecca replied.

Maggie opened the door and as Rebecca made her way down the steps, she saw Annie coming through the gate.

"You've got quite an audience," she said. Stepping out of Father Michael's garden, Rebecca found a large group of tourists standing on the other side of the street near Hernon's Shop. She chuckled. Just as they passed the gate, Rebecca heard Sean, Rowan, and Siobhan begin to play "My Lagan Love."

Rounding the corner, she found everyone in town in their Sunday best, holding a wedding favor and smiling broadly. Rebecca looked up the steps. Sharon stood on the right with Maggie, grinning from ear to ear, and on the left was Fionn, his beautiful red curls sparkling in the sun. Next to him stood his brother Tom and his best friend, John. A large gust of wind blew Fionn's hair into his eyes, but he never took his gaze off of Rebecca. A shadow drifted overhead. Rebecca smiled at him and then down at Rowan, who played her pipe at the bottom of the steps with Sean and Siobhan.

"Becky?" Liz whispered from behind Rowan. "What do we do with these favors?"

"Keep them closed until you need to open them."

Liz nodded with a shrug and then passed the information to Mairead, who stood next to her. She then told Jim, and so a whisper flowed through the townspeople.

"Who gives this woman to be wed?" Father Michael asked.

Rebecca looked up and smiled wickedly.

"Well," Paddy replied, "I believe she gives herself, but the rest of us are not sure why she'd pick Fionn."

The townspeople laughed. Fionn slowly came down the steps and before he took Rebecca's hand, she touched his sweater. Columns of cluster ribbing ran side by side with diamonds/moss within. Double zigzags were knitted next to diagonal furrows as texture stitching where front met back. The sleeves were nothing but diagonal furrows, and in the central pattern Rebecca had stitched a row of Celtic knots.

Between the knots were spirals, and sitting within each spiral was a small bird. Rebecca touched one of the mistle thrushes.

"Nice gansey," she said. "Your wife knitted that."

The wind gusted.

"You think I'm beautiful," Fionn whispered, bringing her up the stairs.

"*You* think *I'm* beautiful," Rebecca corrected.

"Oh, I do," he replied.

"We're not to that point in the Mass, Fionn," Father Michael stated and pulled Fionn's hand away from Rebecca. Rebecca looked up at the priest.

"Almost there, Becky," he noted, looking back to the church door. He returned his eyes to Rebecca, lifting his eyebrows.

"Better make this fast, Father. Sharon seems a bit peaked. She just had a baby and traveled all of Ireland to get here," Rebecca said with a smile.

"All right, then."

The sky went dark. Father Michael looked up to heaven and back down to his book. Rebecca watched a raindrop hit his page.

"I think, Rebecca," Father Michael said carefully, "the Lord is inviting you personally into His house."

A raindrop hit Rebecca's head.

"It'll be fine, Father. Did you get a wedding favor?" Reaching over to John, Rebecca took the wedding favor from him, opened the umbrella, and handed it to the priest.

CHAPTER 45

Casting Off

Casting Off. 1. A fishing term used to describe the net or line being tossed into the water. 2. A boating phrase used to command the release of the ship from its mooring. 3. A phrase used to define the release of something that is no longer of any use. 4. The act of tying one stitch to another at the end of a knitted work, which releases the work from the needle. 5. An ending of one thing and the beginning of another.

—R. Dirane, *A Binding Love*

Sean peered up at Rebecca, standing like an apricot sunrise on the church's steps. He studied the color of her dress and the brown shadow the lace made on the silken fabric beneath. He had seen that before.

"Sean, look," Claire whispered. Rolling over, he found Matthew suckling his mother's breast, the apricot sunrise warming his wife's skin, casting a brown shadow on his newborn son's cheek.

"Is he eating, Claire?"

"Aye."

Sean began to weep, his tears falling on the pillow, and he touched his little boy's head.

"Matthew'll be fine, Sean," Claire said softly, touching her husband's cheek. "He didn't know what to do and I had trouble showing him. That's all."

"I love you so much, Claire. You're the beat of my own heart," Sean whispered.

"And you, mine."

⁓

"Sean." The old man looked down and found Rowan gazing up at him.

"Liz needs you."

Sean found Liz holding out a camera.

"Can you take a picture of this, please, Sean? You're standing farthest out."

A raindrop hit the lens. Sean frowned and looked around. He caught his breath. Taking the camera quickly, he trotted across the street to the large group of tourists who had gathered in the rain.

"Can you believe it?" one man gasped as he clicked his own camera.

Sean turned and held the camera to his eye. "I didn't smell the rain," the old man murmured.

He centered the picture. There on the steps stood everyone in town, and in every hand was an open umbrella. Shades of green and yellow and red and apricot and periwinkle blue were brushed lovingly onto the nylon canvas—the painted patterns of Sean's own ganseys.

"I love the Irish," a woman sighed.

Sean rolled his eyes and chuckled.

Author's Note

$\mathcal{R}$ ebecca did finish a book in completion of her grant and her life's dream, but not the one she intended to write when she arrived on the island. Instead, she wrote *Casting Off: The Fiber Arts and Fishing Tunes of Sean Morahan,* recording all of his knitted work. Having achieved that dream, Rebecca settled into her next one and raised a family with Fionn.

The epigraphs at the beginning of each chapter are from *A Binding Love,* a book Rebecca's daughter, Rowan, wrote and published herself as an adult. In its entirety, the book explores the knitting patterns of the island and the history of the island's people. Rowan came to know both so well for she is, after all, a woman of the western islands. But that's another story. . . .

About the Author

Nicole Dickson resides in North Carolina, where she tends to her daughter, two dogs, and an unforgiving yard of acorns. For updates on Nicole Dickson, please visit her Web site at www.nicolerdickson.com.

Casting Off

NICOLE R. DICKSON

This Conversation Guide is intended to enrich the
individual reading experience, as well as encourage us
to explore these topics together—because books,
and life, are meant for sharing.

A CONVERSATION WITH NICOLE R. DICKSON

Q. Is the island in the story a real place?

A. I write "place" as if it is another character. So there are three main characters in *Casting Off*—Rebecca, Sean, and "Island." The Aran Islands consist of three islands and it would be difficult for me to write about a specific one. So, in building the character "Island," I took pieces from two of them—the big fort from the large one, Inis Mór, and the size, both in land and population, from the middle island, Inis Meáin. Then I imagined what it would be like to be on a tiny stone speck of land facing the tempest of the Atlantic Ocean. That is how I built not the Aran Islands, but "Island."

Q. Casting Off *deals with domestic violence. Why did you choose to put that subject into the novel?*

A. My intention in writing the novel was more as an exploration of love—what love is and what love is not. Love is binding but does not bind. It is freeing but is not free. And the first tenet of love? Love never, ever intentionally injures with thought, word, or act. Which doesn't mean love doesn't hurt. People are imperfect. But the *intention* is not to harm. As I look at domestic violence, it is this basic nature of love that is confused and then misused. In both Sean and Rebecca, we see domestic violence as the forced binding of another and freedoms taken away, not freely given up. It is in the learning of love that Rebecca and Sean, as two sides of the same coin, have found no resolution in the past, but resolve each other in the present.

Q. How did you come up with Rowan as the name for the little girl in the novel?

A. When I first started the story, I took my daughter's middle name, Rowan, as a placeholder as I wrote. Rowan is an Irish surname and suited the character for the discussion with Sean about it not truly being a given name. While researching this novel, I happened upon a book on the Irish pagan traditions. In that religion, the rowan tree, or witchwood, has certain magical powers, and from it, wands are made to manifest those magical qualities into the real world. I thought long about the rowan tree and witchwood and the character Rowan. She is a conduit for change in the novel—like a little wand. The name was perfect for the character, so I left it. Serendipity.

Q. Do you knit?

A. Yes, my mother taught me. She was a great seamstress and home artist, though she wouldn't have put it that way, I'm sure. She would say she just made things.

Q. Do you spin?

A. No, but I spent many an hour at the Puyallup Fair in Washington State watching women spin. There are groups of spinners who have demonstrations there and I would stand and watch them, listening to their conversation. Then I'd leave and get a corn dog and walk around a bit and return to watch them more, hanging around in the back of the crowd. I didn't want them to think me odd because I watched and listened but never spoke with them. I'm not sure it worked.

Q. Why does Fionn have red hair?

A. I had Rebecca tell her daughter she would only marry a red-haired fiddle player. I think it funny to this day. It is sometimes so hard to discontinue a conversation with a child, and in this case Rebecca tries to do it by describing a person completely improbable (redheaded, fiddle-playing Irishmen are not common in the current 6.7 billion world population). She thinks that's the end of it. The last thing she expects is for that person to actually show up! So when he does, and in fact knows she made the comment, it seemed to be a good setup for a relationship. I'll admit, though, that I got myself into several pickles with this particular point of the book. Every redheaded man I'd run across, I'd stare at, trying to get Fionn's color. Several times, I unexpectedly found a man staring back—oops. Once, I found a man's wife staring back—bigger oops.

Q. So what's your next novel?

A. I've been working on several. Please feel free to visit my Web site at www.nicolerdickson.com for news.

QUESTIONS
FOR DISCUSSION

1. Discuss how the gansey, in representing the person for whom it is knitted, also reflects the vision of the maker. How is this true in the case of Liz? And in Sean's case?

2. In the beginning of the novel, Rebecca is almost run down by bicycles and says, "Gotta watch the bikes." Sean does the same as a parallel. They are so different in so many ways. But in what ways are they similar?

3. What is Rebecca teaching Rowan when she has the raspberry ice cream conversation? What is the moment in her own past where she learned that lesson?

4. Both Dennis and Fionn offer to help Rebecca upon first meeting her. What behavior in those scenes portends the relationships that form afterward? How is her reaction to their offers of help different, and what does that tell us about how she's changed? By the end of the novel, she's changed again. How do you think she'd react to offers of help in the future?

5. What is the symbolism of the mistle thrush?

6. Sean and Rebecca have lived in the past for years. As new relationships form, they are held in the present, which begins to change

how they see their past. Both of them feel this change as if "something's wrong." Why?

7. Sean and Rebecca both reach a crossroads during the storm, choosing to put their lives on the line to save others. What drives them to the choices they make at this point in the novel?

8. Does it seem Rebecca chose Dennis? Does she choose Fionn?

9. Why is Rebecca scared to see Sharon? Are her fears realized when she actually does see her friend? How do her fears change after they are reunited?

10. Why is it so hard for Rebecca to let go of her past with Dennis? Is it because of the guilt she feels from her role in his death? Or is it because of the guilt she feels for getting involved with him in the first place?

11. Sean is also tormented by guilt about his past actions. Do you think he has become mentally unsound because of it?

12. What is the most important turning point in the story for you personally? Is it the storm? When Becky sees Sean's sweaters? Or the scene at the cemetery?

Whitewater Handbook
3d edition

Also Available from
the Appalachian Mountain Club

AMC River Guides
Maine
Massachusetts/Connecticut/Rhode Island
New Hampshire/Vermont

AMC Quiet Water Canoe Guides
New Hampshire/Vermont
Massachusetts/Connecticut/Rhode Island
Alex Wilson
Pennsylvania
Scott and Linda Shalaway

Sea Kayaking along the New England Coast
Tamsin Venn

AMC Trail Guides
Guide to Mt. Desert Island and Acadia National Park
Guide to Mt. Washington and the Presidential Range
Hiking the Mountain State (West Virginia)
Maine Mountain Guide
Massachusetts and Rhode Island Trail Guide
North Carolina Hiking Trails
Short Hikes and Ski Trips Around Pinkham Notch
White Mountain Guide

Nature Walks in Eastern Massachusetts
Michael Tougias

AMC Guide to Winter Camping
Stephen Gorman

Trail Building and Maintenance
Robert D. Proudman and Reuben Rajala

Organizing Outdoor Volunteers
Roger L. Moore, Vicki LaFarge, Charles L. Tracy